When I
Think
of You

When I Think of You

MYAH ARIEL

BERKLEY ROMANCE
New York

BERKLEY ROMANCE
Published by Berkley
An imprint of Penguin Random House LLC
penguinrandomhouse.com

Library of Congress Cataloging-in-Publication Data

Names: Ariel, Myah, author.
Title: When I think of you / Myah Ariel.
Description: First edition. | New York: Berkley Romance, 2024.
Identifiers: LCCN 2023031116 (print) | LCCN 2023031117 (ebook) |
ISBN 9780593640593 (trade paperback) | ISBN 9780593640609 (ebook)
Subjects: LCGFT: Romance fiction. | Novels.
Classification: LCC PS3601.R536 W47 2024 (print) |
LCC PS3601.R536 (ebook) | DDC 813/.6—dc23/eng/20231024
LC record available at https://lccn.loc.gov/2023031116
LC ebook record available at https://lccn.loc.gov/2023031117

First Edition: April 2024

Printed in the United States of America
1st Printing

Book design by Daniel Brount

For ambitious Black girls who dare to live out their dreams in spite of those who said we couldn't.

For dreamers and grievers . . . and people who've been made strong by leading heavy lives.

For my mother.

Author's Note

Shortly after I began drafting this novel, I lost my mother. While contending with the loss, I thought a lot about grief and how it affects us. Naturally, potent reflections on parental and partner loss became a tertiary but still important part of this love story. While I can promise a truly incandescent happily ever after for our main characters, I caution you to proceed knowing that there will be moments of painful reflection that may be difficult for some.

When I Think of You

chapter

1

*P*ING!

My head pops up at the sound of the elevator. Like Pavlov's dog, I'm conditioned to snap to attention at the sound of a call, a text, even a microwave. It's an occupational hazard.

Some people call me "The Face" of Wide Angle Pictures, a specialty production company on the Galaxy Films back lot. Never mind the fact that those "people" are mostly Tommy—everybody's *favorite* mail courier whose daily greeting almost always borders on harassment.

On paper, I'm the receptionist. To the execs that call the shots, I'm "the front desk girl." And to the directors, writers, and producers who churn through each day to pitch ideas and hawk scripts—I'm a greeting committee of one. And it gets old.

What felt prestigious about this job to a once bright-eyed film school grad has slowly faded over the years. Yet here I sit with a forced smile on my face. Eyes forward. Shoulders back. Soul empty.

The elevator deposits a clique of my colleagues onto the

glistening marble floor of the reception area. Like gum, they always come in a pack. And because I'm of no use to them at the moment, they dodge me like a speed bump in an empty parking lot. Still, I manage to catch snippets of their conversation.

"You won't believe the clusterfuck I had to sort out last night with Allison and Keith's travel. Apparently booking flights in coach is always the wrong choice. Even when first and business class are full. Even when it's the last flight out of New York and their kid's spelling bee is the next day."

"Well, at least you didn't have to bail on a hot date after an SOS text from Louis. I had to pull out midthrust and drive the Outlaws *digital print all the way to the Palisades for a last-minute request from the Bel Air Circuit."*

Believe it or not, I envy them.

Their work/life balance might look like a lone panda on a seesaw but at least they've managed to ace *Industry Gatekeeping 101*: Get a job supporting the daily functions and navigating the erratic idiosyncrasies of a Hollywood executive for one to two years. In your nonexistent spare time, make sure to ear-hustle every call said executive takes. Never enter that executive's office without a notepad or tablet for documenting their demands. Before bed each night, speed-read every book, script, or article that's come across their desk. Write up coverage that's whip-smart and spot-on. Do it all well—and *voilà!* You're promoted and on the executive fast track.

Or at least a track fast*er* than the one I'm currently on, which seems to have taken the off-ramp toward *Admins 4 Lyfe R-Us.*

Ping!

I flinch again. This time, it's my desktop. I click out of Outlook and scan my cluttered screen for the culprit, grimacing when I find a little snarky gray bubble of a message from Nick-in-Publicity.

NickatNite: Hey Kaliya. I'm not sure if you've made your rounds yet. But tracking says my Vitamix should have arrived in the mail room an hour ago. Just wanted to put this on your radar!

Unfortunately for me, at WAP, being receptionist means both business *and* personal deliveries fall under my purview. While I'm never one to say a task is beneath me, I won't pretend that tending to the emotional wounds from this dead-end job hasn't taken its toll. I'll probably never crawl out from under all the debt I've racked up from the top film school in the country by sorting other people's mail, either. But when duty calls, I answer. So with a huff, I'm up and on my way to the dusty dungeon of the mail room.

Posters of the top films WAP has made over the last two decades line my path down the hall, and for a moment, my soul stirs. Corny as it may seem, this corridor of hits is why I'm still here. Right now, I may be on the hunt for someone else's juicer. But some day, the name *Kaliya Wilson* will be on one of these posters with the hallowed words *Produced by* in front of it.

But as I've come to expect from this place, any flicker of hope is quickly doused by reality—this time in the frazzled form of Sharon-in-Accounting as she barrels toward me looking stern and impatient. I am briefly distracted by the lack of movement in her blunt, red bob. And after a few failed attempts to blink myself invisible, I'm swiftly cornered with a USB thrust beneath my chin.

"Kaliya, the Xerox is on the fritz again." Sharon's tone drips with accusation, like the printer and I have conspired against her. I fight the urge to roll my eyes because her version of "on the fritz" usually means it's either unplugged or experiencing a paper jam.

Her French-tipped fingers wave the USB beneath my nose like smelling salts. "I need you to get twenty copies of these budgets printed, stapled, and collated," she demands. "And I need them on my desk in fifteen minutes."

"I'm on it!" I announce. Then begrudgingly, I accept the memory stick and pop it into my pocket. Training a false smile at her, I note that she's still blocking my path. We're essentially in a standoff until she squints at me for a beat then spins on her heel to stalk back down the hall.

Upon entering the mail room I head straight for the sorting bins, which have been filled to the brim with Amazon boxes and AmEx bills. I am elbow deep in the slush when a call comes in from the main line. My boss, Gary, whom I've un-affectionately titled the VP of Paper Clips, upgraded me to a headset with a long range—heaven forbid the reception line ring more than once because I stepped away.

I fumble to click on my earpiece without dropping a package, but it's already on the second ring, *dammit*, when I catch the call.

"Kaliya . . ." Speak of the devil. My name out of Gary's mouth might be my least favorite sound.

"Yes, Gary," I reply, biting back my irritation.

"I just got an email from Tom-in-Business-Affairs, and it appears the ants are back in the twelfth-floor conference room," he says in a clipped tone. "I thought you'd gotten to the bottom of that last week."

I grimace. "So did I," I say. "But don't you worry, Gary, I am on it."

"I certainly hope so," he shoots back coolly before clicking off the line. I take a few calming breaths, open my eyes, and spot the juicer.

LUNCH TIME ARRIVES LIKE A COLD GLASS OF WATER ON A HOT day. Even though I'm stuck downing a smoothie at my desk because there aren't any interns around to cover the phones, I seize the opportunity to dive back into my current audiobook obsession.

Normally, I wouldn't dare listen to this type of material on my work-issued computer. But in this case, WAP has optioned the novel and given the green light to go into preproduction on a feature adaptation soon. Since employees are encouraged to become familiar with the studio's newest projects, *technically*, I'm just doing my job.

I pick up where I last left the young billionaire and his impressionable new girlfriend. Moments into my listening, he's just yanked out her tampon so they can *do the deed* and I've crossed my legs in shock. I hear a gasp, realize the sound came from me, and shut my mouth so quickly I almost chip a tooth. *No way this scene gets past the MPA.*

Ping!

I'm still clutching my proverbial pearls when the sound of the elevator provides a sobering jolt. Quickly, I reach up and press the button on my earpiece to power off my headset. Then, the unthinkable happens.

"Tell me how bad you want this rock-hard cock," Caleb groaned through gritted teeth, hands firmly gripping the globes of her ass.

"Yes! Yes! Give it to me, Caleb. Please don't make me wait," Ashley cried in wanton ecstasy at the same time he thrust into her swollen cleft.

I am a deer in headlights, immobilized at the sound of smut blasting from my desktop at my place of work. The voices coming from the elevator are growing louder, too. Their footsteps are drawing nearer. Panicking, I fumble with the mouse in search of the X that will put an end to the rapidly escalating scene.

"Come for me, Ashley!"

"I'm close, Caleb! So close!"

And *I'm* close to being caught red-handed—like Shaggy with the girl next door.

But not today, Satan.

I am frantically scanning my desktop in search of the elusive culprit window that's hidden somewhere among the fifty tabs cluttering my screen. With time running out, as a final Hail Mary, I grab the plug to my speakers and yank it like a lasso. In the name of all things holy, everything goes silent. Heart racing and chest heaving, I'm still gripping the speaker plug when two figures enter my periphery. Stiffly, I turn to offer my customary welcome. But the words seize up in my throat when my eyes land on him.

Danny Prescott.

I am a slab of granite. For seven years I have on equal fronts feared and anticipated our reunion—even rehearsed it in my mind. I'd run into him on a hot afternoon in the South of France at the Cannes Film Festival. I'd have a flute of champagne in one hand and Idris Elba's bicep in the other. I certainly wouldn't be attempting to hide the fact I'd been listening to erotica on my treasonous computer at a reception desk on a Friday afternoon.

I decide my best shot at salvaging the dregs of my dignity is to get through this cursed encounter without being recognized. So, against all odds, and past the lump in my throat, I force out a greeting as they both close in. "Welcome to Wide Angle Pictures. H-how can I help you?"

At the sound of my voice, Danny's sage-green eyes scan upward and lock with mine. He freezes, causing his glamorous companion to collide with his shoulder, which in turn knocks him slightly off-balance.

"Um. Hello," he says, cocking his head to the side like a confused puppy. "I'm . . . Danny—" He stops short and that voice—it's a shallow fragment of the one I remember. He falters for a moment or two, fidgeting with his collar, before abruptly burying his hands in the pockets of his jeans and carrying on. "—Prescott. Um, I'm here to meet with Jim Evans?"

To my utter dismay, it seems as though he knows who I am. Still, I desperately cling to my act, practically chirping, "Sure, I'll let Jim know you're here!"

I will my hands steady and dial up Jim's office to notify his assistant their one o'clock appointment has arrived. Hanging up, I clear my throat and gesture toward the plush sofas to my right.

"If you'd like," I say to Danny and his companion as I channel the poise of a flight attendant, "you can have a seat while you wait. But do let me know if I can bring you coffee, tea, or water."

He's saved from responding to me when the phone rings—my constant companion. With my headset now charging on its base, I pick up the handheld and avoid Danny's stare of astonishment.

"Hi, Gary, what can I do for you?" I try to project calm, as if everything is business as usual and my college ex isn't standing before me watching my every move. Gary honks into the phone at a volume loud enough for Danny to hear a few feet away. I turn slightly, cupping a hand over the receiver to create an auditory shield.

"Kaliya, Rose-in-Marketing is complaining of a foul odor coming from the love seat in her office. I'm concerned we have a rodent problem again—" Gary drones on about checking mouse traps and procuring rat poison and I'm grimacing, eyes shut tight, hoping that when I open them, by some miracle, Danny will no longer be standing here witnessing my humiliation.

Damn it all to hell, Gary.

I inhale sharply and breathe out a plan: "I'll call Peter in pest control ASAP and then I'll set Rose up in the conference room with a temporary workspace."

If nothing else can be said for this utterly desolate moment, it's that I'm damn good at my job. People throw their problems my way and I fix them. I return the phone to its receiver and stare at it in surrender—trying to ignore the sustained bafflement on Danny's face.

Then, his friend looks up from her magazine. "Umm . . . hellooo," she coos, waving to get my attention. "I'll take a green tea, no sugar, bag out."

I recognize her now as Celine Michèle, the lead actress from a nighttime soap I'm ashamed to admit I watch. She's pushing thirty but plays a high schooler at the apex of a love triangle with two vampire brothers. She's tall and willowy with pale skin and a mane of silky brown hair. She's stunning. Worst of all, she's Danny's creative partner and girlfriend—the things I once wanted to be.

Snapping out of it, I rise to go prepare the tea. But remembering my front desk etiquette, I stop and turn to Danny. "Anything for you, sir?" The *sir* rolls off my tongue like a hairball and by the look of it, he's not too fond of it, either.

Danny does a micro grimace before clearing his throat. "No thanks, Kaliya—um, I mean I'm fine." The corners of his lips turn up in a small, contrite smile and his eyes soften just slightly.

When Danny Prescott says my name, it does strange things to my executive function. No longer capable of processing it all, I bolt away on wobbly legs toward the kitchen. Once tucked away in its tight quarters, I finally feel like I can breathe again. But that just conjures all the *feelings.*

Kaliya, you will not cry on the Keurig.

No, I'll save that for later when I'm in my car, as I do often. LA traffic tends to have that effect on me.

With trembling hands, I head back to the reception area cupping a piping hot mug for Celine, only to see the backs of her and Danny as they glide down the hall toward the elevators with Jim's assistant.

I zero in on Danny's retreating form. His tight russet curls gradually disappear into a close fade that brushes the collar of a crisp white shirt that's fitted to perfection across broad shoulders and strong arms. Dark-wash jeans cling to his slim hips and taper down two very long legs. His signature, impeccably clean and uncreased Jordans finish off the look. What can I say? The man still has swag.

When he steps onto the elevator, somewhere in my chest there's a wave of relief running beneath a strange sense of loss. Defeated, I slump back into my seat and take a long sip of Celine's tea. As if on cue, the ominous theme from *Jaws* rings out from my purse. Swiping open my screen, I find a text from Gary, who must be away from his desk.

> VP, Paperclips: Kaliya, Sharon has emailed to say she feels you have no sense of urgency. Let's have a chat on Monday about how you might better show up in this role.

And for the briefest moment, I envision sending a company-wide email. Two words. All caps. I QUIT.

One day. Just not today.

chapter

2

I'VE SPENT AN HOUR contending with the "foul odor" incident, yet somehow Danny's return is more upsetting. To compound things, news of his visit has the office aflutter with colleague after colleague sailing by my desk blabbing about Celine and Danny's It Couple status.

"Oh my god, aren't they just the sexiest couple you've ever laid eyes on?"

"What I wouldn't give to be a mirror on the ceiling of that bedroom!"

". . . like Bennifer but better. They're . . . Danneline."

I stifle the urge to challenge them to repeat that mash-up five times fast and the twin urge to bang my head against my desk. I'm starting to wonder if this has been a setup. If perhaps I'm the unwitting subject of some sadistic social experiment—or a rebooted reality show where Ashton Kutcher jumps out of the bushes laughing maniacally after convincing me I've just run over a stroller.

Hollywood is a small town, and I had wanted—no, *needed*—to be further along in making a name for myself whenever an inevitable run-in with my ex occurred. Because everybody knows exactly who Danny is: the son of Nathan Prescott—prolific auteur director and four-time Oscar winner, who, according to our film school textbooks, *perpetually succeeded in striking the elusive balance between art and commerce.*

Danny hasn't been a slouch, either. His debut feature-length film was what one calls a *festival darling*—having racked up rave reviews and lead to him being subsequently labeled *one to watch* by *Variety*'s measure and "the Next Scorsese," according to *THR.* A year ago at just twenty-eight, he was nominated for the Best Director Oscar for his third studio-backed film, *Optical Illusion.* He didn't win. But it's only a matter of time because everything the man touches turns to gold. At least, that's how it felt when we first met seven years ago.

It was a Sunday, the week before my first year studying film at New York University. I was fresh off the plane from Arkansas and had just been deposited by a dusty cab onto the corner of 10th and Broadway. As the bells in the clock tower of Grace Church rang nearby, I struggled to maneuver my grandfather's massive hand-me-down suitcase. With one corner wheel jammed and the other hanging on for dear life, it was essentially a fool's errand.

Having survived the harrowing trek from LaGuardia Airport to Lower Manhattan, I was intent on soaking up every detail, sight, and sound of the city that would be my new home. After coaxing my luggage onto the sidewalk, I stopped to scan my surroundings and was briefly stunned by the Gothic Revival arches and ornate stained glass of the church. Then my eyes drifted downward, focusing in on a man crossing Broadway by foot. With his head down, he still stood a few inches above the crowd around him. I couldn't yet make out every detail of his face, but in an instant, the frenetic pace of the city from moments prior stilled into slow

motion. I'd seen Brad Pitt in *Meet Joe Black* and Denzel Washington in *Mo' Better Blues*. But I hadn't seen a man more striking
than this one.

He was tall, with skin the color of aged parchment and ma-
hogany hair that framed his face in a soft curl pattern. Long legs,
broad shoulders, angular jaw—the works.

Transfixed by his approach and oblivious to the dangers of my
surroundings, I did not see the cyclist before they whizzed past,
clipping my arm and sending me toward the pavement. Next
thing I knew, all my clothes, including the unmentionables, were
flung across the sidewalk like dandelions, tossed about by wind
and pedestrians. Then out of the blue, two DaVincian hands
appeared, grasping at my aforementioned unmentionables. Mortified, I looked up to inspect their owner and was met by two
glimmering pools of green and a smile that made me forget my
name.

The owner of the piercing eyes was the same man with the
legs, the jaw, the shoulders, and if he hadn't been staring directly
at me, he'd have realized he was clutching a pair of my panties.
And not the cute ones. In a flash of panic, I moved to snatch them
from his hand.

"Um, thanks but I think I can manage from here," I offered
with a feeble smile. He looked down, realizing what he'd been
holding and gingerly placed the undergarments in my palm.

"Welcome to New York," he said. "Always keep an eye out for
the cyclists." His voice was so deep it startled me.

He began to scramble, gracefully somehow, and made one big
heap of the clothes still strewn on the sidewalk. Together we stuffed
them into my broken suitcase.

"Going far?" he asked.

"No!" The shout escaped me and my face flamed. "I mean, no

thanks, I'm just here," I said with a more measured tone as I gestured toward my dorm, Brittany Hall.

"That's right. Welcome Week," he remembered aloud. Then, he tilted his tall frame down to lift my suitcase before turning toward the entrance. I could do nothing but follow and gawk.

Once inside the lobby, he set down the suitcase, pulled out an NYU student ID and waved it at the security guard.

"I'll just get you to the elevator," he said.

"You really didn't have to do this," I muttered. "I'm grateful, don't get me wrong. I'm Kaliya by the way." Five minutes. It took me five minutes to remember my name in his presence.

The elevator opened like a long-awaited blessing, and I stepped inside. He set my suitcase at my feet, and before walking off, he stopped short, turning back to me. "You're welcome, Kaliya." The sound of my name on his lips sent a chill down my spine. "I'm Danny. Maybe I'll see you around."

When the doors closed, I exhaled for what felt like the first time.

That was our meet-cute. A near cinematic introduction to the *then* man of my dreams that even today leaves me a little bit misty. But just when I resolve to stop sulking and get some work done, the Golden Boy himself pops around the corner from the elevator bank while I'm midbite on a substantial muffin. Danny's large and expressive eyes are as I remember them, clear and piercing and swoony. They lock with mine, then go wide as he heads toward me with intention.

Okay, so we're really doing this.

I wonder what he thinks of what he sees, aside from a woman having a private moment with a decadent pastry. Some things have changed since Danny and I last saw each other. For one, I'd done the "big chop" right before college. So the short dark chocolate–

colored spirals he once leisurely ran his fingers through have since become a mane of wild coils that falls to my shoulders. But more than my appearance, I wonder what he thinks seeing me *here*, answering the phones.

With Danny still approaching, I try and fail to discreetly chew a large chunk of my muffin. I've still not managed to swallow it when he reaches my desk and promptly exhibits a case of verbal incontinence.

"Kaliya. I want you to work with me on my next film. As my director's assistant. I mean, not *my* director's assistant. But rather, assistant *to* me. Because I'm the director. In case that wasn't clear. I direct movies now. But you probably knew that already. Or maybe you don't. Shit. I don't mean to imply that you've followed my career or anything . . ." He trails off, eyes dancing haphazardly as if they might land on something to help ground him. They settle on mine.

Still chewing, I nearly choke, which he takes for an opportunity to proceed. "I don't know if you're happy with"—he makes a loose gesture with his hand—"whatever it is you're doing here. I mean, *I think* you aren't. I mean—" Again he stops short, perhaps thinking better of how he'd planned to finish that sentence.

For a second, my brain short-circuits in response to how blunt he's just been. And after composing myself enough to safely swallow, I bristle at the indignity of having my profession questioned by my ex. "And how would *you* know if I'm happy here, Danny?" I ask, sharply. "You don't know me anymore. And the last thing I need is a handout from you."

Danny eyes the muffin just as I realize I've been aggressively wielding the pastry in his direction—for punctuation purposes of course—and shakes his head. "I'm not offering you a handout, Kaliya. I'm offering you a job," he says. "I know it's been ages since we've worked together, but you can't be so different from the girl who wanted to do big things. My next project is unlike anything I've ever done, and it's a chance for you to get back in the game."

That sounds exactly like a handout to me. I look at him now in total disbelief because it's been more than a while since we worked together on *The Last Song*, his senior thesis film. And that's way too long for him to assume he knows anything about what might have changed for me. For starters, I've never really been *in* the game enough to warrant his help with plotting a comeback. Not since film school at least. Still, something that feels a little bit like hope has begun to encroach on my resolve. I push it down though, beneath the knowledge that Danny Prescott is not to be trusted. Not again.

"Is your number the same?" he asks with an urgency that reminds me he didn't come here alone. That Celine is likely waiting downstairs.

I nod on instinct. Then, struck by the fact that he still has my number, I blurt, "You still have it?"

Without bothering to mask any lingering resentment he replies, "I do. Maybe you'll consider unblocking me now?"

For the briefest moment, a flash of remorse penetrates before I swat at it, deciding to unpack it later when I'm safely out of his orbit. Who knows? Maybe I deserve some of his anger. We had been *something* to each other all those years ago. He messed up. *Big-time.* Then he faded away faster than I could grasp on to him. And when he finally resurfaced, I gave him no chance to grovel or explain. At the time, icing him out completely felt like the path of least resistance toward moving on.

The phone rings again, saving me from having to answer him.

I pick up and quickly transfer the call. Once I've set it down, Danny startles at the chime of a text ringing out from the pocket at his hip. He checks it and I don't miss the way his face tightens.

"I'm being summoned," he says flatly. "But you don't need to give me an answer now. I'm doing a Q and A after a screening of one of my dad's films at the School of Cinematic Arts tonight. If you can make it, I'll have a seat reserved for you and then maybe we can talk about this over coffee after?"

He pauses for a beat, probably waiting for a sign of agreement that I'm not ready to give. His shoulders sink almost imperceptibly. But he's not deterred. "I'll text you the info."

I cross my arms and look away, ignoring the sexy way his eyes wrinkle just a bit more at the corners now.

He turns to leave before I can tell him not to bother. As he nears the elevator, I look down at the muffin in my hand, for the briefest moment wondering what he'd do if I pelted it at the back of his head.

But then I wave off the thought. After all, blueberry is my favorite.

chapter

3

IT WAS A RAT. Shortly after Danny's drive-by proposition, Peter from pest control called to report the results of his recon: a dead rat found burrowed beneath the upholstery of Rose-in-Marketing's love seat. Understandably, she was put off being productive for the day and took her leave. I, on the other hand, spent a good thirty minutes burning candles and Febreezing the shit out of her office.

At five o'clock, I punch out and flee to the *relative* safety of Coby, my Chevy Cobalt. A gift from my grandparents during my senior year of high school, some might call her a lemon. I prefer to think of her as well used and well loved. But I'm a fan of all things *old*. I may have entered the scene toward the latter half of the nineties, but I've always considered it to be the Last Great Decade, primarily because of the music. So as me and Coby head south on the Hollywood Freeway with her windows down and Mariah Carey's "Dreamlover" as our soundtrack, I shout the lyrics into the billowing wind, ignoring, if only for a moment, the decision I have to make.

By the time I cross the threshold of my Los Feliz apartment, it's early evening. Neha, my best friend and roommate, is stationed in the center of the living room sitting cross-legged on her yoga mat. She's surrounded by medical books and plunging a ladle-sized spoon into a carton of Ben & Jerry's.

I plop down on the couch. "Share. Please?" I ask, putting on my most convincing sad-sack face.

She quickly obliges, climbing up to join me. "I take it you had another harrowing day at the office?"

"Sumfingliihkthaht," I mumble, swallowing a mouthful of delicious cookies 'n' cream before launching into my recap. "A rat entombed itself in a piece of office furniture, and naturally, I had to manage the aftermath." A shudder rolls up my spine as I recall the stench. "The next time I'm asked if I've ever smelled a dead body, I can no longer legitimately say no—which feels significant somehow, but also totally mundane given the context."

I look over at Neha, who's got her head cocked to the side and her brow furrowed at hearing what isn't even the most absurd event of my day. "Oh, also, Danny Prescott came by the office with his TV vampire girlfriend and offered me a job assisting him on his next movie." I look down into the ice cream bracing for Neha's reacti—

"WAIT! STOP! Say that again!" She's up on her knees, eyes wide and mouth stretched to an exaggerated O.

"A rat died in a piece of office furniture and—"

"I can't believe this!" She's standing now, her voice an octave higher.

"I'm sure if you leaned close you might catch a whiff of the decaying animal carcass—" I deserve the pillow she pelts at me.

"You have somehow managed to avoid a run-in with Danny Prescott for the better part of a decade. And you're telling me that out of the blue, he walked into your office today and just . . . offered you a job?"

Fully cognizant of how preposterous this all sounds, I merely shrug in response. Neha is deeply acquainted with my and Danny's college *entanglement*. I suppose that's what you'd call a romance that was fast and furious, yet impossible to forget even years after it ended. But Neha was a front-row spectator to our very unlikely union—me, the bright-eyed country bumpkin, and Danny, the world-weary metropolitan nepo-baby. She cheered us on in our speedy ascent toward love, then became my shoulder to cry on when we crashed and burned just as fast. So fast and surreal that if it were not for Neha as my witness, I'd still wonder if me and Danny were just a figment of my own imagination.

"It's not like I said yes to the job," I offer up in my own defense. Although, I'm not sure if it's me or Danny she disapproves of at the moment.

I get my answer with the second pillow she pelts at me. "I'm sorry, come again? You *didn't* say yes?" She's shouting at me now. I clutch the ice cream to my chest, a sort of dessert shield from her impending lecture.

"For four years, you've been at the beck and call of an office that treats you like you're invisible one second and an indentured servant the next. Every morning, you head to work like you're off to a funeral, and every night, you walk through that door under a cloud of despair. I'm *this close* to sage-ing after you!"

"But I can't work for *him*!" I'm shouting now, too. Neha is the one person I should not have to explain this to, which makes it all the more upsetting that I do.

I've abandoned the ice cream now in favor of wide gesticulation. "He made me fall in love with him, with his creative genius and charm and his sexy vulnerability—and those ridiculous eyes. Then he took my v-card and practically vanished, only to pop up with another girl."

"Technically, you guys didn't have *sex* sex though," she offers matter-of-factly.

"Who are you? Bill Clinton?" I'm shrieking at this point. The ice cream's melting in its carton, nestled between the couch cushions, and I am on the brink of hyperventilating.

Sensing my distress, Neha takes a deep breath, gesturing for me to do the same. Pressing pause on her inquisition, she sits gingerly on the sofa, speaking softly. "No, I'm not Bill Clinton. I'm your best friend who is about to give you some tough love." She stalls for dramatic effect. But I'm not having it. I flap my hands, urging her to get to the point.

"Remember when you threw your hat in the ring for the executive assistant position under that bigwig production guy at your job?" she asks.

I nod, unsure of where she's going with this.

"And HR-Stephen-something-or-other didn't even pass along your resume because he said you were"—she makes air quotes—"'too green'?"

Ah. Yes. That was a dark time. I'd wanted to tell him, *I'm sorry sir, you're mistaken. I'm not green, I'm Black.* But I just tucked my tail and went back to the front desk.

"And instead of standing up for yourself and your credentials—your cinema studies degree and producing minor, the numerous student films produced *by* you, that summer you spent working *at* the Producers Guild of America for heaven's sake!—you just let him dismiss it all. You know this industry inside and out. But he called you a novice, and somehow, you believed him."

I could cry. Because it's true. Somewhere along the way, after all the close calls and closed doors, I started to believe every person who fed me the same excuse—that I hadn't yet paid my dues. That assisting a powerful film executive so that I could finally have a seat in the room where moviemaking happens (even if in the corner of that room) was an opportunity I simply wasn't ready for. I let them convince me of it to the point that I eventually stopped throwing my hat in the ring.

"You, Kaliya Wilson," she declares, "have been waiting a long time for an opportunity like this. And here you sit, mulling it over instead of jumping at the chance to finally show everyone you can do more than grunt work. And yeah, it's coming from the guy who broke your heart in college. I can admit that part sucks. But guess what? In life, we don't get to choreograph the play-by-play. You've finally got your opening. Now take the shot."

There are times in life when the hardest thing to hear is what most needs to be said. This is one of those times. I *want* to protest, to poke holes in Neha's argument, but she's pinned me down like a butterfly to a board. It is *very* unlikely another chance like this will come along. Unlike the execs at this company, Danny at least *wants* to give me a shot. And even though I'm highly suspicious of his motives, at least he's seen what I'm capable of. After all, I did produce his thesis film. And yes, working closely with him again is a major risk for me emotionally, given how badly things ended last time. But it could also be a major breakthrough for my career.

After a pregnant pause, I lay down my defenses. "You've been watching *Coach Carter* again, haven't you?"

Neha laughs and the tension between us melts with the ice cream. My phone buzzes on the coffee table and SALLIE MAE flashes across the screen. I'd given in and unblocked Danny after the rat fiasco. Then, I panicked and changed his contact name to deter myself from picking up if he made good on his promise to get in touch.

The buzzing continues.

Neha looks quizzically between me and the phone. Then,

reading me like a novel, she grabs it before I can get to the DE-CLINE button. "Hi, Danny, this is Neha. You'll probably remember me. Kaliya couldn't be trusted to answer your call so I'm running interference." She switches to speaker in time for me to hear Danny chuckle in response. My stomach flips over at the deep rumble of his laughter.

"Neha. Of course I remember you," Danny says. "Thank you for overriding your friend there."

I take stock of how confident he sounds when speaking with Neha, much more so than when he was propositioning me at the office. He'd stumbled over his words like he was nervous, like I *made* him nervous. "I was honestly calling to see if Kaliya still had me blocked," he explains. "And if she got my text invite to a screening I'm hosting tonight at USC."

Neha's eyes flash with excitement. With a quick swipe and a tap, she locates my messages, scrolling down to the one in question. "It would appear you're no longer blocked, Mr. Prescott," she needlessly confirms. "Kaliya also did receive your text. I assume she's allowed a plus one?"

Another deep laugh from Danny and this time, something much lower inside me flutters. "I'm sure I can arrange that, Neha," he answers.

There's an awkward pause where Neha's shimmying on the sofa and I'm chewing the side of my cheek. Danny clears his throat. "Well, I guess I'll see you ladies in about an hour or so."

"We'll be there," Neha hums into the speaker before ending the call.

It's settled. I'm attending a screening and having coffee with Danny Prescott tonight. I sit frozen, teetering on the edge of timid excitement and raging anxiety as Neha bounds off the couch to go pick an outfit.

RUSH HOUR MAKES THE drive down to USC long and tedious. Neha's behind the wheel mumbling profanities at inattentive drivers, and I'm busying myself googling Danny's father.

"Did you know," I ask no one in particular, "that on top of writing and producing over *twenty* feature films, Nathan Prescott periodically taught history of cinema classes as an expert in residence at USC's School of Cinematic Arts?"

"Well, that would explain why we're on our way to schmooze with his former students and colleagues now wouldn't it?" Neha mumbles, craning her neck to see around a G-Wagon.

I scroll down the page for more distracting facts. "*And*, according to Wikipedia, in the years after his 'tragic death,' the school dedicated an entire wing in his honor."

I glance over to see that Neha's now mean-mugging a minivan. "Are you expecting to be quizzed on all this later?" she asks.

"No," I say. "Just calming my nerves with intimidating facts about my wealthy and famous ex's wealthy and legendary father." I click on a photo of Nathan Prescott in one of those oversized nineties tuxes. He's on a red carpet with one arm wrapped tightly around the waist of his dazzling wife, Minnie Prescott. Both would have been in their early forties in the picture, with a toddler-aged Danny nestled between them. For the nineties, they were on the older end of the new-parent spectrum. Danny told me once that they'd struggled for years to conceive. Their sheer elation at finally being a trio is written all over their beautiful faces. I suppress a whimper.

We've come to a full stop now and Neha turns to me directly. "And how's that research working for you?" she asks.

"It's not," I blurt, eyes still glued to my phone screen as we begin to slowly creep forward.

Out of nowhere, Neha slams on the brakes and my phone flops out of my hands, smacking me in between the eyes. Her right arm juts out protectively across my chest, as if the twiglike appendage could outdo an airbag. "Sorry about that," she pants. "That biker has a death wish, I swear!"

Rubbing my forehead, I drop my phone into my tote bag. If I needed a sign to stop obsessing over the Prescotts, it just came and smacked me in the face.

By the time we arrive, park, and speed walk across campus, we've got just minutes to spare. Neha and I bound through the double doors of USC's Norris Theater to find Danny anxiously pacing in the lobby. The sight of him does funny, wobbly things to my legs as we approach. He's in a cashmere sweater, slacks, and shoes that probably cost a month of our rent. When Danny notices us, I'm glad I let Neha talk me into wearing a short black wrap dress instead of the wrinkled linen number I had on earlier. His head-to-toe perusal lasts maybe two seconds, but leaves me feeling warm and tingly everywhere his eyes touch.

Without warning, Neha bounds forward, pulling Danny into

an overly familiar embrace. He dips down, circling her in his arms. They beam at each other like dear old friends, and I'm left standing awkwardly off to the side, like a bathroom attendant waiting to offer them a hand towel and mints.

"Hello, handsome!" Neha practically sings. "Never thought I'd be seeing *you* again live and in the flesh!"

"I can't say I expected it, either, but it's a nice surprise," Danny replies, full of enthusiasm. "How have you been?" His deep voice penetrates the space around us, making my skin tight and the little hairs on the back of my neck stand at attention.

"Kicking ass. Taking names," Neha muses. "Dissecting cadavers in my final year of med school at UCLA. Damn you, by the way, for dragging me to the University of Spoiled Children." She's milking the attention, and it's all I can do to keep my eyes from rolling out of my skull.

"Let the record reflect that you invited yourself," I cut in, attempting to ground this weirdly perky reunion between Judas and Brutus. Neha may have swiftly reestablished a playful rapport with Danny, but I'm not so sure how to navigate the tension between us. My heart races and my palms sweat as my body takes note of being close to him for the first time in years. There's also still the offer to work for him hanging in the air between us, along with a whole lot else.

Danny's cautious but hopeful eyes meet mine. "You made it," he states the obvious.

"Against my better judgment" shoots out of my mouth before I can stop it. Still, I'm fighting a smile. It's like we are two teenagers making stilted small talk in front of our giddy, scheming moms.

"I'm glad you did." His eyes crinkle at the edges, their own version of a smile.

Words escape me and Neha's well of overly zealous banter is apparently tapped out, too. So we simply linger in a moment or two of awkward silence before it occurs to Danny that he's about to miss his cue for the film's introduction. So he beckons for Neha and me to follow him into the theater where he's reserved us all front-row seats.

AFTER DANNY DELIVERS THE INTRODUCTION TO HIS FATHER'S final film, *The Irreverent Prophet*, he finds his place in the audience—next to me. The house lights dim, and the familiar film score surrounds us. I am keenly aware of how close our hands are, mine resting on the purse in my lap and his draped over a rapidly bouncing knee. The rhythmic movement is a jolt from the past, and instantly, it's like the first day of freshman year all over again.

I sat near the back of a screening room at the King Juan Carlos Center on the south side of Washington Square Park. Anxious and excited, I waited for my first college class, Language of Film, to begin. Just as Professor Kohl stepped up to the lectern and began shuffling her notes, he walked in. The same boy who'd saved me from an erupted suitcase and public undergarment crisis on move-in day exactly one week prior.

Danny, he'd said his name was. He looked tired, scruffy even. But as he made his way toward the back of the theater where I sat, I was certain the air grew thin. And when he sat directly behind me, the temperature ratcheted up a dozen degrees. But I had little time to fully catalog my visceral response to his reappearance, because within seconds, Professor Kohl began to talk.

"Good morning, everyone, I'm Professor Kohl. Welcome to Language of Film. For some of you, this course will be an intro-duction and for others, it will be a review. But the goal of the syllabus is to give you a solid foundation for appreciating cinema as art." She spoke with the measured cadence of a pendulum, and I rushed to jot down as many words as I could catch.

"We will tackle every aspect of film form," she continued. "From camera movement, positioning, and angles, we'll move on to sound devices and the fundamentals of editing. We will then examine the aesthetic properties of color and light before digging deep into the conventions of film genre and artistic movements. I can promise you that upon completing this course, you'll never watch a movie the same way again."

At this, the tiny hairs on my forearms stood on end. And not because the man of my dreams was a mere two feet behind me, but because I had finally gone and done the damn thing. Here I was, a girl who'd been obsessed with yet simultaneously starved of culture in her stifling hometown, who'd beat the odds and made it to New York City to study the movies.

"But, before we get started," Professor Kohl continued, "I want to go around the room and ask you each to introduce yourselves, your name, and your major. Then for fun, tell me your *favorite* movie, the *best* movie you've seen, and the best movie you *haven't* seen yet."

I wasn't expecting the prompt, and I was not prepared. No doubt, all sixty or so of us would analyze one another's responses to see how our own taste and movie knowledge stacked up.

But before I could dwell too much, Professor Kohl pointed to the first row of the theater and one after another, each of my class-mates began introducing themselves and naming their three movie picks. There were a few *Casablanca*s and *Vertigo*s from the fans of the classics. A *Gladiator* here, a *Braveheart* there for those inclined toward sweeping epics. A *Godfather Part I* or *Part II* thrown in a half dozen times because, of course. But by far, the most popular choice for a favorite movie from the bunch was *Citizen Kane*.

When it finally came time for me to introduce myself, I was a nervous wreck. Far too frazzled to contrive a sophisticated response, I went for bare honesty. "I'm Kaliya Wilson and I'm a first-year cinema studies major," I said. But something stirred behind me and for a moment I was distracted. "*Favorite movie* changes for me just about every day," I went on, "but today I'd say it's *Funny Face*. The *best* movie I've seen is *Bamboozled* and the best movie I *haven't* seen is, well, apparently it's *Citizen Kane*."

Laughter fanned out around the room, and I fought a surge of embarrassment. I was either a total philistine compared to everyone else in the room, or just the only one brave enough to cop to having never seen "the great" *Citizen Kane* by Orson Welles. It wasn't lost on me either that, so far, I'd been the first in the class to name a film made by a Black director.

Even now I am liable to talk a stranger's ear off about Spike Lee's *Bamboozled*. It's pure brilliance. A film that blends shock and humor to expose the entertainment industry's dark history with blackface and minstrelsy—while showing how little Hollywood has changed. The first time I saw it I laughed to the point of tears and at times shrieked in horror. It's the kind of movie I could never forget.

"Excuse me, Mr. Prescott. You're up," Professor Kohl called out, and I sat up straighter. I felt Danny shift behind me, heard him clear his throat. At the time, I'd found it odd that Professor Kohl knew him already. But it all made sense later after I'd googled him and uncovered his Hollywood lineage.

"Hi, everybody," he'd said. "I'm Danny Prescott and I'm a production major in my last year here at Tisch. My favorite movie these days is *Breathless*." I noted his callout to French New Wave, an artsy cinematic movement that always felt inaccessible to me somehow—kind of like he did. But then, he surprised me.

"The best movie I've seen is . . . also *Bamboozled*," he declared. I could hear the smile on his lips. Reflexively, I turned to face him as he told everyone the best movie he hadn't seen was nothing other than *Funny Face*. I nearly dropped my notes.

The rest of Professor Kohl's lecture was also lost on me on account of my acute awareness of Danny's closeness. When it was time for our fifteen-minute break before the second half of the class, there was a light tap on my shoulder. I turned and was struck, once again, by jade in the form of irises.

"I hope I wasn't too much of a distraction for you." Danny's voice was like butter on bread. It made every word out of his mouth delicious.

Well, aren't you perceptive, and a little cocky at that? I thought.

At what must have been a look of confusion on my face, he elaborated: "It's just . . . most people who sit in front of me in class end up shooting glares back at me."

I still wasn't following.

"You know," he went on, looking a bit sheepish, "because I'm always bobbing my leg. It's involuntary, by the way. Just helps me focus somehow."

My attention fell to his lap where I saw his knee rhythmically bouncing up and down at a rapid pace. Suddenly, it made sense. I'd felt a subtle vibration from time to time during the lecture but figured it was turbulence from a train passing underground.

"I barely noticed," I said brightly, warmed by the glow of relief in his smile. It was the kind that started with the eyes, then worked its way down to the cheeks, lips, and chin. His was a full-faced smile, and it was practically immobilizing. "Thanks again, by the way," I blurted in a rush. "You know, for your help with my luggage catastrophe the other day."

He shrugged his shoulders, kindly suppressing a laugh on my behalf. "I'm glad I was there when it happened."

I remember sitting frozen, unsure of where to go from there until he threw me what felt like a lifeline. "So you're a fan of Spike Lee, too?" he asked.

And that worked for me because I could talk about movies until the cows came home. "I saw *Bamboozled* a few summers ago and haven't stopped thinking about it since. Spike Lee's range is incredible. *Malcolm X* and *School Daze* are some of my other favorites but—"

I stopped speaking when he held up one finger as if pressing pause. He hastily scooped up his things and made his way down to my aisle. My heart raced as he got closer. When he folded his long, lean frame into the seat right next to mine I breathed in his scent. It was nothing fancy. Just something clean and citrus with the faintest hint of spice. But it was perfect.

"So you were saying, *Malcolm X* and *School Daze*?" he asked.

That fifteen-minute break felt like an eternity and an instant all in one.

Now, the better part of a decade later, I'm fighting the same electric pull that sitting next to Danny Prescott entails. Movie watching is already an inherently intimate experience. Even more so when you're helplessly attracted to the person whose shoulder is pressed against yours. With the knuckles of his right hand, Danny lightly taps my left knee, which I now notice is bouncing in concert with his own.

"Don't tell me my habit's rubbed off on you now." He doesn't turn to face me, but grins slyly up at the screen. Seconds later, we're immersed in the world of the film.

chapter

5

MY FAVORITE PART OF a movie screening is at the end when the audience stays in their seats to watch the credits roll. When there's no jarring burst of diffuse chatter or rushing toward the exits—just a quiet audience paying respect to hundreds of mostly faceless names who made the movie-magic they all just witnessed. The experience becomes surreal when you've been in The Industry for a while and can connect faces with those names—the hair and makeup artists, the key grip, best boy, and *Shop Girl Number Twelve.*

But when the final credit fades on Nathan Prescott's *The Irreverent Prophet,* it's a free-for-all with dozens of audience members closing in around us, angling to get to Danny, the arbiter of his father's legacy. I bob and weave, peering through handshakes and shoulder pats to find him doing the same, seeking me out. When our eyes lock, I'm with Neha at the end of the aisle, swept away by the riptide of the crowd.

"Welp, I've got two missed calls from Sam, so I gotta go see what's up with him. You don't mind, right?" Neha shouts over the clamor, referencing her boyfriend of ten years. We're close enough that if I turned, we'd be pressed flat against each other face-to-face.

A slight panic settles in at the thought of being left alone to lurk while Danny works a room full of strangers. But I'm a big girl, so I crane my neck and call out in reply, "No, go—I'm good. Sam okay?"

"It's probably nothing," she chirps. "He's out with work friends. I'll be back in a jiffy!" Seconds later, she's disappeared into the crowd.

Ten minutes pass and I'm still holding up the wall at the back of the theater people watching. Or, more accurately, *person* watching. Danny's too busy schmoozing to notice me shamelessly ogling him, taking stock of all the ways time has been good to the man—like a leather jacket that gets better with each wear. Danny's perfect posture elongates a tall frame that hints at strength more than boasts it. Faint contours of lean muscle create movement under the soft cashmere of his clothes. He turns his back to me, and my eyes drop lower, pausing on his perfect ass.

I could use a fan.

My tote buzzes and I fish out my phone to find a text from Neha.

NAYNAY: You okay getting home? Sam's stranded at a bar on the Westside. Bouncer took his keys.

I text her back that I'm fine flying solo before it sinks in that I'm about to privately interact with Danny Prescott for the first time in seven years and without the buffer of my chatty best friend.

Tamping down the panic, I zero in on a girl with pale pink hair who's standing next to a middle-aged man. The latter of the two has just commandeered Danny's attention. I might be a few dozen feet away, but I'd recognize Danny's strained posture and nervous gestures a mile off—he's always hated schmoozing.

The older man stands unnaturally close, directing his enthusiasm directly into Danny's ear. Danny holds up a hand to excuse himself while the man is midsentence. He fishes his phone out of his pocket before tapping rapidly across the screen. A few seconds later my bag vibrates.

SALLIE MAE: Option A come be my wing woman

SALLIE MAE: Option B meet me for coffee in 20

Before I can reply, a third text comes through. Danny's dropped a pin for a coffee shop on campus. Since we both know I, too, would rather submit to corporate sponsored diversity training than attempt small talk in a room full of Industry People, the decision is an easy one.

ME: I'll see you in 20 ;)

POWER WALKING TO THE OTHER END OF USC'S CAMPUS FEELS like traipsing through the set of an *Animal House* reboot. It's dark out but the grounds are scattered with high energy clusters of carefree students, likely en route from pregaming in the dorms to parties on Greek row.

Passing through McCarthy Quad, I'm cut off by a quartet of girls who appear to share a wardrobe. With arms intertwined and a neon flask being passed from one to the next, their laughter crackles against the brisk night air. Theirs is the youthful energy of an age that both attracts and repels me. Back then, I was chasing myself—so obsessed with who I wanted to be that I missed the chance to get to know who I was in the moment. I still miss that girl. But I wouldn't want to be her again.

It's a quarter after nine when I arrive at Ground Zero café where Danny dropped his pin. "Name" by the Goo Goo Dolls wafts out from the sound system as I breeze through the frosted glass doors, heading straight to the coffee bar. After placing our order, I find a booth at the far side of the café where it's cozy and quiet and I'm left to sit with only a table number and all my feelings.

With its multicolor mood lights, threadbare lounge seating, and a small stage that's set up for what looks like a poetry slam—this place is an invitation to settle back into the younger version of me that I took for granted. The version of me who, at eighteen, left her Southern hometown for the wide-open possibilities of New York City. The me that had never been kissed or asked out on a date but was determined to unleash the Black Carrie Bradshaw that was surely latent inside. The same me that got swept off her feet less than three hours into the whole adventure by an enchanting boy who was unaware of the power of his appeal.

That boy is now the man who's just walked through the same frosted-door time warp like he just stepped onto a movie set. I scan the café for a gaffer's rig because seemingly every light in the room is aimed his way. With my chest thumping wildly at the sight of him, it's painfully obvious how ill-prepared I am to sit across from Danny Prescott in this booth.

But there's no escaping it now. He flashes me a megawatt smile and despite my reservations, a returned grin creeps across my lips.

When he arrives at the booth, his smile hasn't wavered but his eyes look utterly exhausted. "Have to admit I'm a little disappointed you turned down Option A back there," he says, sliding in the booth like a ball of ice dropped into a whiskey glass.

"Oh really?" I ask, suppressing a full body shudder. "Because from where I stood it looked like you were having the time of your life. I didn't want to encroach."

He regards me for a moment, the corner of his mouth tipping up just a fraction as his eyes sweep from my face to my hands and back up again. Flames lick across my exposed skin under the magnifying glass of his undivided attention.

All his nervous energy from before is nowhere in sight. Now his vibe is relief mixed with a hefty dose of people fatigue. "You ever wish you could blink and just be . . . anywhere else?" he asks, gently resting his eyes on mine.

"Only every Monday through Friday between eight and six," I confess.

He laughs, adjusting his position. Our knees brush under the table in a fleeting connection that sparks electricity. On instinct, I move my legs aside and try not to mentally archive his look of disappointment.

Attempting to gain some composure, I straighten my spine and square my shoulders, rebuilding the wall I'd so far let come down. I plan to change the subject, ask him about the job offer when the barista delivers our drinks.

"This for me?" Danny cuts into my thoughts, gesturing to the tiny cup of espresso next to a larger cup of coffee the barista sets on the table.

My face heats. "I wasn't sure if you still went for a Red Eye," I murmur, more than a little embarrassed. Remembering Danny's coffee order after all these years feels like I've just hired a plane to etch *I'M NOT OVER YOU* in the sky.

I expect him to call me on it, but he doesn't. "You know what they say about things changing, but always staying the same," he says, before gracefully lifting and pouring the espresso shot into his coffee cup. "Thank you." He lifts the cup to his mouth.

I'm not proud about the way my eyes track his Adam's apple as it bobs up and down the contours of his neck. Or how I can't look away when his mouth meets the brim and his lips pucker for a long drag of the coffee. I uncross my legs, squeezing my knees together hoping it will relieve the pressure coiling where my thighs meet. Twenty-two-year-old Danny was a boyish heartthrob. But Danny pushing thirty oozes S-E-X. Apparently though, I'm the only one coming apart at the seams here, because he seems at ease—like he's barefoot at home after a long day.

"Speaking of, where did Neha run off to?" he asks, casually placing his cup back on the table and pulling me out of my heat spiral.

I take a prim sip of my coffee, thankful for a somewhat neutral topic to latch on to. "She's off to collect her boyfriend, Sam, from some bar on the Westside. Said he had his keys taken by a bouncer."

A sour expression darkens Danny's features, like a random smell just triggered a bad memory for him. "This the same Sam she was off and on with back in New York?" he asks.

Surprised at this level of recall, I tilt my head. "You remember that?"

He sets down his cup, hands falling back to his lap. "I remember everything about you and me in New York, Kaliya."

The admission lands like a cinder block of *feelings* dropped on the table between us—a signal that the time for small talk is over, and now, we're off toward more precarious terrain. Silence stretches between us like a rubber band that could snap under the weight of what we haven't said.

Danny's brow furrows. "Can I ask you a question?"

Instead of muttering *You just did,* I steel myself by taking another sip from my mocha latte. "Be my guest."

"What's got you answering phones and calling pest control at a movie studio instead of running the damn place?" His tone is one part curiosity, one part bewilderment, and all parts direct enough to throw me off balance.

I wait a beat, as if time will conjure an answer good enough to satisfy us both. Seconds pass and I've come up empty. "If only you realized how loaded and unfair that question is," I huff.

Danny leans forward as I pull back. "I'm sorry. I didn't mean that to sound—"

"Elitist? Arrogant? Privileged?" I'm fuming, but without fire. We've reunited for less than a day and, more than once, Danny's already called out the quiet part of my shame.

"You're right. And again, I'm sorry," he says. "But along with all those things, I'm just . . . confused?" Danny's fidgeting with his collar now—a tell that his nonchalance from a minute ago has all but evaporated.

"You're confused?" I ask, flatly.

"Yes!" he exclaims. "It's been nagging at me all day." Danny pauses for a deep breath. "Earlier when you were on the phone with that Gary guy talking about rat poison of all things, all I could think about was the girl I knew back in New York. She was unstoppable. Determined to be the fir—"

"The first Black woman Best Picture Oscar winner." We say it in unison.

"Yes!" Danny's eyes light up. He leans forward. "The Kaliya Wilson who edited countless drafts of my script, created the pitch, and used it to crowdsource our funding online. Who secured an eleventh-hour backup theater for the final scene after the insurance fell through for the first location. Who coached my lead actress through a nervous breakdown when I couldn't get her to answer my calls." He pauses, practically vibrating.

"That Kaliya was destined to be a movie producer, not a receptionist. Don't get me wrong, it's a good job if it's what you want. But I can't believe that's true. So what is it? Did you stop wanting those things? Because the Kaliya I knew wanted nothing else."

He's wrong about that last part. I wanted him. I wanted us—just as much as I wanted to be the Black girl version of David O. Selznick, minus the racism, sexism, and general megalomania. I didn't get any of it, and not for the lack of trying, which seems like what he's implying. Something I can't let stand.

"The Kaliya you knew," I force out, "was naïve and hadn't had as many doors slammed in her face as the Kaliya you're sitting across from now. Do you know how many times I've tried to break free of that reception desk? How many studio lots in this town I've schlepped across in a blazer and flats carrying a portfolio that barely gets a once-over? How many mixers and lunches and screenings I've tried to 'network' at? No one cares about my passion or my potential—they just want to know if I've already done the job that I can't find anyone to give me a shot at."

Breathing a little heavier than before, I release a humorless laugh and take a look at my latte before wishing it was something stronger. "They tell you *don't meet your heroes*," I say. "Well, the same should be said for all the dreams we dream up when we're kids. Because even when you're almost there, reality reminds you *almost* doesn't count."

Danny is hard to read. He adjusts in his seat, leaning back in the booth and casually crossing his arms. "So you're saying the thrill is gone?" he finally asks.

That's when my exasperation takes over. "No, the thrill of filmmaking is alive and well. It's just being had by people who are not me—present company included." I flick a dismissive hand his way.

"And you've just resigned yourself to that? You're not even gonna *try* to find it again?" he volleys back, with an edge that spins it into a challenge.

A cocktail of embarrassment, anger, and exhaustion crashes down on me like a wave. The stirrer I had been idly fiddling with stills in my cup. I glance up at Danny with his forest-green eyes expectantly peering into mine. Suddenly, it occurs to me that I don't have to do this. I don't owe him my indulgence of his morbid curiosity over my professional failures.

"Trying to *find it again* is why I came here to meet you tonight." I break our eye contact and push away my cup. "But clearly this was a mistake. I came here to learn about your movie and the job you offered me," I grind out. "I didn't come here to be interrogated about my failure to break through Hollywood's glass ceiling by twenty-six. Because unlike you, Danny, I don't have the privilege of automatic doors. I have to find a way to kick them down." I shake my head, resigned to the fact that this was a complete waste of my time. "But kicking is exhausting," I say before grabbing my purse.

After scooting to the edge of the booth, I stand. I've got tunnel vision for the exit when a warm sheath that's soft and rough, like fine sandpaper, encircles me. I look down and Danny has gently wrapped his hand around my wrist.

"You're right. I'm being an ass," he admits. In his eyes is a silent plea: *Stay.* His grip on me loosens as his fingers splay farther up my forearm, scattering chills up to my shoulder. His touch is like a spell, willing me back into the booth. When he withdraws it, suddenly I'm cold.

Danny lifts his palms in surrender, and I eye him cautiously. "What is it exactly that you want from me anyway?" I ask.

He exhales sharply, a thin whistle carrying his cool breath across the space between us. "I really just want to know you again, Kaliya," he admits. "We aren't the kids we used to be. I can't really explain it other than . . . the movie we made together in college is the last time I felt like I was really doing this right. Before my agent and the attention from the festivals and then the praise and critics. We wrote *The Last Song* with nothing but pens and prayers and it was still perfect. Mostly *because* of you. I want to feel that again. Especially for *this* movie."

Those last words land with heaviness, almost reverence, and they send a jolt of recognition through me. I know exactly what it means. "You're finally telling your parents' story," I say.

It's not a question because even after seven years of trying to forget him, I've failed at that, too. I remember it all—the curves of his face, the hollow-shaped sounds that escape him when he's turned on, the way he slams his eyes shut before he's going to cry as if he'll somehow trap the tears. And I remember the story of how his parents, one Black and the other white, met as children in the sixties—how eventually their forbidden love ran them out of Tennessee, and how they made a life together in New York City before the world even knew the name *Prescott*.

I also know it's the story Danny's always dreamed of turning into a film. Now he's finally doing it, and at the studio where I happen to work. It could be a scheme or pure coincidence. Either way, it feels a lot like serendipity.

With a smile on his lips, Danny confirms, "The working title is *What Love Made*."

Deep understanding of the reference almost takes my breath away. "Your dad's Oscar speech," I say.

Danny looks down at the table, drawing abstract lines across the surface to busy his hands. "You know this already about me—

that growing up, there was no wanting to be the next Michael Jordan or Tiger Woods. For me, there was only my dad."

Danny and I had opposite upbringings. My mom had left me with my grandparents when I was ten, which started a cycle of mutual overcompensation—theirs, to show me the kind of parental love I'd long missed out on, and mine, to prove myself worthy of it. So I was the ever-studious teacher's pet who never gave them trouble with grades or boys or drugs. Danny, on the other hand, was raised on his dad's movie sets—a refuge for a restless kid who was deemed too unruly and unfocused for a classroom.

Danny used to tell me how his dad would scoop him up from school in his vintage Mustang and whisk him off to wherever they were shooting that day. On set, he'd sit right next to the director's chair, with script in hand and a headset on so he wouldn't miss a thing.

He was seventeen the night his dad accepted an Honorary Oscar for a lifetime of achievement from the Academy. Danny and I wouldn't meet until years later, but ever since I could read and write, I'd never missed an Oscars telecast. I didn't know him yet, but I saw him that night. I remember sitting on the rug of my grandparents' living room, probably far too close to the TV screen, beaming up at a teenaged Danny with floppy curls and an oversized tux as he helped his megastar dad down the aisle of the Shrine Auditorium. Nathan Prescott's diagnosis wasn't public knowledge back then, but his posture sloped forward and his footsteps were slow and tenuous.

"I nearly carried him up the steps that night," Danny recalls aloud, a glossy film covering his eyes. "Helped steady his hands as he gripped the statue."

Every detail has remained vivid for me—cameras scanning an audience of dazzling faces. Every one colored in a mixture of concern and admiration. Nathan Prescott spoke in stilted phrases as he delivered his acceptance speech, the words of which I could never forget:

After spending my life telling stories that so many of you seem to like—unless you're handing these out to any old man over sixty—you might think the awards and credits are my life's greatest accomplishment. But you would be wrong. My life's greatest accomplishment is winning the love of my wife, Minnie, and sustaining it all these years. I love you, sweetheart, fiercely, and with all of my heart. Without you, we wouldn't have our son, Danny. One day, his films are going to blow mine out of the water.

"He turned to me, and then back to my mom before finishing off," Danny recalls. *"Look what love made.*

"I stood up on that stage at the Shrine looking out into the audience at my mom. Everyone was watching him, but I was watching her. I saw an alchemy of emotions—pride, sadness, joy, and fear each taking turns dancing across the planes of her face," Danny speaks in almost a whisper, as if only for me.

"She loved him." My voice is quiet, too, smothered by a blanket of sadness.

"It was more than loving him," he says almost forcefully. "She *knew* him. Every part of him. And she loved him because of, and in spite of, all of it."

"That's *it*, right?" I wonder aloud. "The thing everyone wants? Your parents had it."

Danny had been staring blankly at the table, but now, his eyes latch on to mine. "For a long while there, yeah."

Suddenly uncomfortable, as if we're both showing too many cards, I clear my throat. "So your idea for this movie, it has a happy ending?"

He gulps before answering, willing back the unshed tears coating his eyes. "I'm not planning on telling the story of how severely multiple sclerosis limited him or how he died, if that's what you're asking," he says. "I want to make a film that honors their love, how they lived, what they overcame together."

I'm smiling now, ignoring the butterflies of excitement I have about this project. "Good," I say. "They deserve that."

At this, he smiles broadly, too. Next I'm fighting the urge to touch him. Holding myself back from leaning across the distance and wrapping my arms around him so I can feel him breathe against my chest. But that's not what we're doing here. All too soon, I've forgotten that he's hurt me before and that I don't trust him, that he's in a relationship with Celine Michèle, the triple-threat actress, executive producer, and girlfriend. That this is only business.

But that twinkle in his eyes is back, inviting me to take the plunge with him. Safety net be damned. "What do you say?" he asks. "Will you be my director's assistant? I'd offer you more if I could but without union membersh—"

"No," I cut in. "I understand." I extend my hand for him to shake before I change my mind. "I'm in."

He gifts me with the kind of smile that, if only for a moment, feels entirely free of every piece of baggage flung between us.

chapter

6

IT'S MONDAY, LESS THAN two hours before I can gleefully put in my two weeks' notice with the VP of Paper Clips, and I can hardly contain myself. My alarm sounds and I pop out of bed, patting myself on the back for having the forethought to make today's wake-up anthem Diana Ross's "I'm Coming Out."

Phone in hand, I strut down the hall to the bathroom where I plan to shower away seven years of false starts and disappointments. It feels like forever that I've been signaling for an exit from this cycle of discontent, and now, I finally have a green light for the off-ramp . . . even if it's thanks to Danny Prescott.

———

TRAFFIC ON THE CAHUENGA PASS IS FLOWING LIKE A STACKED parking lot and even that can't dampen my mood. The sun is shining. Breezy palm trees sway over Spanish-style condos and midcentury bungalows that speckle the hills on either side of the Hollywood Freeway.

Finally, my lane starts to crawl forward, allowing me to press a little on the gas. The sign for my exit is up ahead, and as I inch closer, my grip tightens on the wheel. A spool of anxiety forms in my chest when the reality that I'll be working with my college ex on a near-daily basis sinks in. Seven years ago, I quit the man cold turkey, and now, I'm officially off the wagon.

I should be immune to him. Heaven knows enough time has passed. But years spent willing my mind to forget have done nothing to help the fact that my body still remembers. With Friday as a test case, there's no longer a question of whether Danny Prescott still has the power to affect me. He waltzes into a room, and as if on cue, I find myself repeating the same dance of gastric butterflies and bated breaths that my heart choreographed when I was eighteen and in love with him.

But when I veer toward my exit for WAP's offices on the Galaxy Films lot, despite the circumstances, one question echoes in my mind—*Am I ready for this?*

Am I ready to stretch creative muscles that have been dormant for years? To finally have a seat at the production table? To gain a legitimate movie credit to my name? To say goodbye to being the front desk girl? The answer is simple.

I've been *ready.*

THE STUDIO DOORS ARE PROPPED OPEN. THE MORNING MAIL has been sorted and delivered. Coffee, both decaf and regular, is brewing in all three kitchens. Oat, almond, and standard creamers have been certified fresh. And now the internal countdown for my days left in servitude can begin. *One-thousand, four-hundred, and seventy-three down—thirteen more to go.*

Now that I'm perched at the front desk where I am avoiding erotic audiobooks like the plague, I'm ready to draft my resignation letter. Opening Outlook has never sparked more joy. With each letter I type, I am one step closer to living out the dream I came here four years ago to pursue.

Date: Monday, April 4, 2022
From: Kaliya.Wilson@wideangle.com
To: Gary.Anders@wideangle.com
Subject: Two weeks' notice

Dear Gary,

I have so much gratitude for the opportunity you've given me to serve Wide Angle Pictures as a receptionist and office coordinator. However, I am now writing you in order to give my two weeks' notice. I have accepted a position as "assistant to the director" on Danny Prescott's latest production, *Working Title: What Love Made,* which was recently greenlit by Jim Evans. I look forward to working closely with our development and production teams in this new capacity as we shepherd such an important project forward. My final day as receptionist will be April 15, 2022. Please let me know if I can assist with the transition as you look for my replacement.

Sincerely,
Kaliya Wilson

I take in a deep breath, hold it, close one eye, and hit send. Magically, the familiar *whoosh* of my outbound email carries my anxiety about ruffling feathers away with it. Without a doubt,

Gary will consider this a betrayal of epic proportions. Never mind the fact that I've stated openly in every annual evaluation meeting that my intentions are to move up the ladder toward becoming a creative executive, and eventually, a producer. Each time he smiles and nods, merely tolerating my aspirations with no intentions of aiding me in getting there. But knowing that my days as his minion are numbered feels like wind at my back.

The phone rings. It's Gary. I pick up the receiver as if handling a grenade, bracing for the very likely explosion.

"Good morning, Gary. How are you?" I ask, my voice hardly above a whisper.

"Fine, thanks. Listen, Kaliya, Bella Carmichael will be coming in shortly," he says, his words springy and clipped. Oddly, he seems entirely unfazed, just like his typical uptight and patronizing self.

"Bella's a new hire," Gary continues. "Jim Evans, the head of production's, niece. I need you to get her set up in the cubicle outside of Danny Prescott's temporary office on the eleventh floor."

In an instant, my skin feels three sizes too small for my body and the easy breaths I took a minute ago come in like shallow puffs at thinning air. "Okay. Sure," I say. "Can I ask what the new position is? For onboarding purposes of course."

I'm aiming for casual, unbothered, but my understanding of how this town thrives on nepotism has me already spiraling from the implications. Jim Evans's niece requires a desk outside Danny's new office, and this can't be good news for me.

Gary heaves an impatient sigh, as if humoring my request for details will derail his entire morning. "Bella's going to assist Danny Prescott on the new film he's brought to us. Jim set it all up. And while you're at it, I need you to create an email for her. It'll be dannyprescottassistant at wideangle dot com."

On the verge of hyperventilating, I push myself to pry one more time. "Oh-kayyyy. So she's his *personal* assistant, right? Like ordering lunches and picking up the dry cleaning?"

I privately cringe, knowing I've got no business asking these questions. But my need to know that what I *think* is happening is not *actually* happening steamrolls any remaining rationality. It simply cannot be the case that I've been supplanted in my new position on the very morning I've given my notice for the old one.

"What's with you this morning? So many questions," Gary mumbles mostly to himself, "—and you need to get these phones checked because I can barely hear you." The *clickity clack* of his typing fills a beat of silence. "If you must know, Kaliya, Bella is taking on the role of assistant to the director on our latest project from Mr. Prescott. She's on leave from her junior year studying film at Chapman and Jim felt this would be a prime opportunity for on-the-job training."

With every word he utters, a component of my nervous system shuts down. Searing numbness takes over each limb and it's a miracle that I've remained upright. I might not be able to *feel* my face, but that hot sting behind my eyes is unmistakable. I'm about to cry.

"What the hell am I looking at, Kaliya?" Gary shouts, more than likely having just discovered my ill-timed resignation email.

Screwing my eyes shut, I brace for a verbal attack.

"Tell me my eyes are playing tricks on me." His voice slithers through the receiver, scattering chills across my neck. "Because I've just read a resignation email from you foolishly claiming *you've* been offered the role of Mr. Prescott's new assistant. Tell me you're kidding because I can assure you this is absolutely *not* the case."

I open my mouth to speak but cognitive function has ceased. I emit a sound that's nothing short of a mewl.

Gary ignores it to continue his verbal assault. "You know what, I don't have time for this. Just get Bella set up ahead of her arrival at ten a.m. We'll discuss the rest of this later."

The line goes dead—much like my soul.

Springing into action, I reach for my phone to contact the one person who should have the answers. Regardless of our tangled history, I know Danny wouldn't intentionally blindside me like this. With trembling hands, I manage to type out a text to him.

ME: Please tell me it's a mistake that I'm being asked to onboard Bella Carmichael as your new assistant . . .

SALLIE MAE: I'll be there in twenty and I promise I can explain.

It's not the reassurance I was looking for. Danny offered me this job on Friday morning, and I accepted that evening. It is now Monday. How could so much go so wrong in two days?

SALLIE MAE: I know how this looks, Kaliya. I am so sorry.

I don't respond.

At this point sweat stains the size of Texas have seeped through my blouse at the pits. I take it off, letting the AC hit my shoulders, bared in my maxi dress. I manage the miracle of one long, deep breath, pushing aside the latest and greatest bout of humiliation to do what I always do—keep working.

In the next twenty minutes, I arrange for Bella's workstation to be set up, place an order for her business cards, print out the employee welcome packet, and put in an IT ticket to get her email account created. And as I complete each task, I swipe away hot tears of anger like Whac-A-Mole.

———

THE ELEVATOR CHIMES. SECONDS LATER, DANNY'S WALKING toward me, eyes hard on mine. Whatever it is that he sees there alters his gait and now he's approaching like I'm a wounded tigress. Before he can speak, I hold up my hand, get up from my seat, and beckon for him to follow. I lead him down the hallway of hits, and it mocks me now as we go. On the way, I tap an intern to cover me at the reception desk. Once we're tucked away in private, I shut the door and face him.

The mail room is a cavernous gray space with mismatched filing cabinets and utility shelving filled with miscellaneous office supplies. Toward the back of the room is a mail sorting system with cubby holes labeled for each WAP employee. Harsh fluorescent lights buzz overhead like a swarm of horseflies, illuminating all the organized clutter. The space is drab and desolate, a postapocalyptic Office Depot—one in which I was looking forward to spending far less time.

Danny stands about five feet away from me now, leaning against one of the utility shelves with his hands in his pockets. I'm perched against a cabinet, clutching the countertop behind me. The space between us is laced heavily with Danny's discomfort and my silence.

He's the first one to breach it. "Kaliya, I've been on the phone for an hour trying to figure out how this could happen without me knowing."

At this admission, my anger is a caged bird set free. The Honorable Lauryn Hill said it best, respect is just a minimum. The very least he owed me was a heads-up. "Don't you think I deserved a phone call before I floated in here on cloud nine this morning and foolishly fired off my letter of resignation? You offered me a job, Danny. Come to find out there wasn't one available."

He reels back as if my words have shot him. "Look. I only found out from Celine this morning," he explains. "Apparently, she bumped into Jim at the Polo Lounge on Saturday, and they got to talking about the production. Jim was there with his niece, Bella. I'd just met her at Friday's screening and asked for her resume—"

At this point I almost leap out of my skin. But Danny lifts his palms in a plea for me to let him finish. "I made her no promises about a job," he says. "I thought at best, she might be a fit for a PA role, but never intended for her to be *my* assistant. Kaliya, please tell me you know I had no part in hiring her for the job I practically begged you to take."

Danny's eyes are a sea storm, rolling waves of contrition that plead with me to believe he'd never hurt me like this. Only thing is, it wouldn't be the first time. But this time, even begrudgingly, I can see he's telling the truth. Still, I'm not ready to let him off the hook—not until he fixes this.

He continues pleading his case. "I was planning to introduce you to the crew as my assistant at our first page turn. I figured you'd want some time to sort things out with your"—he gestures aimlessly—"situation. I called myself being mindful, not jumping out ahead of you. But that hesitation left room for this screwup and I don't know what else to do but apologize as many times as you'll let me."

There's a long pause in which neither of us seems to know what to do or say. I begin to pace, having moved past the initial denial, then the anger, and now on to the bargaining. "But now what? You could pull rank here. Bella can still have a role as a production assistant and I can still be your assistant. I mean, you do realize I *actually* quit my job for you today, right?"

At this Danny rubs his hands over his face. Those tight russet curls on his head tangle between his long fingers. I remember what it once felt like to aimlessly stroke my hands through those curls, his head resting on my chest. Right now, we couldn't be further away from the ease we once had with each other.

Danny lifts his head, a pained expression marring his face. "Celine is my executive producer, and she's in charge of the financing. This morning she let me in on the fact that Bella's family is putting up the completion bonds for the film. Bella's dad is married to Jim Evans's sister, and they inked the deal last night. Demoting her would essentially be the end of this project at WAP."

Then take it somewhere else! I want to shout. But that would be foolish, so I refrain.

I've stopped pacing now. Stopped listening for a moment there, too. When Danny uttered the words *completion bonds,* all remaining hope for me flew out the mail room's nonexistent window. The fact that Bella's family is providing insurance to the film's investors that the production will succeed or they'll get their money back is the nail in my coffin. That private handshake between me and Danny means nothing in comparison. I am shit out of luck.

Before I can blink, seven years of letdowns and rejections become a tidal wave threatening to bring me to my knees. But even worse than the disappointment is the humiliation. Gary's sneering dismissal rings in my ears and try as I might, I can't keep my tears at bay in front of Danny. I slump against the filing cabinet behind me and bring my hands up to hide my ugly-cry face. But nothing can be done to conceal the quiet sobs escaping my chest.

Danny is across the room with his arms around me in seconds. In a flash, the muscle memory of how it felt to have his large body wrapped around mine under *very* different circumstances falls over me like a weighted blanket. And in my diminished state, I don't have the capacity or will to push away the wall of warmth, strength, and security that I find in his embrace.

How could I think that trusting Danny Prescott would get me anything but another broken heart?

I shake free of him to cross the room. We've switched sides now, and under the harshness of the lighting I can see that he, too, looks worse for wear, like he didn't get much sleep at all.

Wiping my tear-streaked face, I let out a shaky breath. "You know the other night when you asked me why I was answering phones, handling pest control?" The question is rhetorical but still, I pause for a beat, leveling him with a stare that challenges him to answer. In his eyes I'm met with only remorseful understanding.

Privilege. Something he's got in spades. But it's done me no good here.

"I've, um . . . I've got to go retract that letter of resignation. If Gary will let me. Good luck with everything." I go to push past him when he places his hands on my upper arms to stop me. I feel chills around the spots where his warm fingers press into my skin.

"Hey," he says softly, dipping down to make eye contact with me. "I still want you with me on this film. It may not be the title or the credit you deserve, but I can hire you on as a production assistant, and we can assign you to the director's unit. The role would be changed in title only. Please, just let me figure out a way to help both of us in this situation." I could kick myself for allowing a spark of hope to flicker inside me in response to his words. "Even if I have to pay for your salary out of my own pocket, I will fix this."

I still can't shake the feeling that there's so much more to this than he's letting on. I need all our cards on the table, but I don't know how. "I just need to think."

"Whatever you want. My offer has no expiration date." Danny steps back and I regret the loss instantly.

Then, like an apparition, a statuesque elephant with glossy hair and bright blue eyes appears in the room, impossible for me to ignore. "Danny, I have to ask—Celine's your girlfriend. Is she on board with the two of us working together?"

At this, Danny's posture goes rigid. He rubs his forehead before stuffing his hands in his pockets. "I haven't told her about us." My eyes bulge and he rushes to explain. "Not yet at least. I will when she's back from London."

A small sense of relief settles over me now that it seems Danny doesn't plan to pretend we don't have a past. Then it occurs to me that this project could be my clean slate, a new beginning. And bringing our sordid history into the picture could seriously muddy the waters, particularly where Celine is concerned.

"Actually, can you not?" I find myself asking, before I can sort out my conflicted feelings. "Look, I know I don't have the right to ask you to lie to her. But can you just leave out the details?" *Details being that I loved you*, I think but don't say.

Danny's silence stretches across the room and his strained expression says I might be asking a little too much.

"It's not like she has anything to worry about with us," I rush to explain. "And this way, we can avoid the weirdness. We can just focus on the work."

"Look, I don't wanna hide what went down between us from her, because that does feel like lying. At the same time, I won't give her a reason to look at you a certain way, either. So for that reason *only, for now,* I won't say anything," he relents.

"Thank you. I appreciate that," I say.

With an agreement to revisit this later if we need to, we make our way to the exit. Upon opening the door, we find Sharon of Xerox fame standing startlingly close to the threshold and wielding a fresh USB.

Caught red-handed, she steps back, straightens, and purses her lips. "Kaliya, I'm in need of your assistance with the copier." Her words to me are sneering. But when she turns to Danny—

"Mr. Prescott, I can't tell you how stunning your last film was. You were simply robbed by the Academy!"

Talk about a code-switch.

After a knowing glance my way, Danny replies to Sharon graciously. "Thank you for saying that. But all things come in due time." He spares me one more look before heading down the hall.

chapter

7

REVERB SURROUNDS ME FROM all sides when I enter our apartment. After taking a few steps into the foyer, it's obvious that Neha is blasting Alanis from her bedroom—a clear cry for help.

Instinct tells me the shit's finally hit the fan with Sam. So, I put down my things and head toward the sound of her sob-singing "You Oughta Know."

When she doesn't answer my determined knocking, I push open Neha's bedroom door. My concern is instantly vindicated at the sight of her sprawled on the bed, waving around a pair of shears like a microphone. I look down and my jaw drops at the sight of loose chunks of dark hair on the floor.

"What have you done?" I shriek.

At the sound of my voice, Neha jumps and reflexively chucks the shears my way. I duck in time to narrowly avoid being maimed.

"Oh my god, Kaliya, it's you!" She gasps in shock, her tear-streaked face and red-rimmed eyes even further signs of the emotional crisis in progress. Still not as clear as the chunks of hair on the floor, though.

"I do happen to live here so yes, it's me," I confirm, flatly.

"W-w-w-why d-didn't you knock?" She stammers, smoothing her hands over her sweats.

I point at the Bluetooth speaker that's booming on her dresser at an ungodly decibel. She tracks the movement. "Oh, my bad, you did knock. I'm so sorry." Her voice tapers off into a wobbly mewl, and I can tell she's bracing for a fresh barrage of tears.

Approaching the bed, I scoop her into my side, and she leans on my shoulder. "Come on, baby girl. Tell me who I'm fighting tonight," I say soothingly, although I've got a pretty good idea.

She hiccups and then sniffles. "I m-m-made bangs," she stammers, avoiding my question.

I finger the blunt, jagged fringe that juts across her forehead. "You sure did."

"I've always wondered"—sniff, sniff—"if I was one of"—sniff—"those girls who could pull off"—loud snort—"baaaaaangs!" Neha's last word comes out on a wail.

I fold my arm across her shoulders and start to rock her back and forth to quiet the sobbing. "Well, if anyone could pull off Tetris bangs, it's you."

She turns to look at me with glassy, pitiful eyes. I'm half expecting her to unleash another wail when instead, she bursts into laughter. Next thing I know, we're both laughing 'til our ribs ache and our guffaws dissipate into calming sighs. My plan is to just wait her out, to see if she's ready to admit what I've already surmised—

"Sam is a cheating scumbag," she finally blurts.

There it is.

"But you knew that already, didn't you?" she asks, her tone matter-of-fact.

"Well, I had no way of actually knowing," I say. "But, yes, I have sensed it for a while. And you knew *that* already, didn't you?"

My distaste for Sam has been an open point of contention for us since back in college when I'd constantly catch him scanning every bar, or club, or dining hall for someone other than his girlfriend to eye-bang. He's also a perpetual flake—hence my private nickname for him: *Dandruff*. I've lost count of the times I'd watch Neha rush home from long nights at the clinic to get dolled up for a date, only for him to call and cancel when he should be on his way over to pick her up. But the worst part has been Neha's tacit acceptance of every red flag.

I should probably thank Sam, though, for getting Neha from New York to LA—but that's all the credit he gets from me. After a gap year backpacking together in South America, she gave up her med-school spot at Stanford to join him at UCLA. Selfishly, I didn't try that hard to talk her out of it, because it meant we wouldn't be long-distance besties. But over the years and on a few tipsy occasions when I was fed up with being a bystander to Sam's continued fuckery, I'd let my true feelings out.

Then Neha and I would bicker and not talk until the next day when I'd apologize, and she'd move on. So, this moment of reckoning has been a long time coming. Still, it's one of those times I find no satisfaction in being right. My best friend has had her heart broken by the man she gave most of her twenties to.

"How cliché is it that I ignored the signs? I've been with the guy a decade. I know we were far from perfect. I noticed the wandering eyes. But I always imagined that somehow, I'd know if he was actually cheating. Like maybe the sex would *feel* different—like what's the opposite of loose vagina? Is there such a thing as loose dick?"

Warren Beatty. Nick Cannon. Others also come to mind, but Neha sputters ahead before I can respond. "And her name is Karen!"

"Well, I guess that tracks," I say dryly.

"Mm-hmm. That loose-dick fucker." Neha's up and pacing now, arms thrashing about. I briefly eye the scissors, flung safely out of reach. "Apparently, she was in his law school cohort, and they've been sneaking around since Torts."

The timeline renders me speechless. I knew Sam was an ass, but I didn't know he was Satan's ass.

"And that's not the worst part." Neha steamrolls on.

"Don't tell me she's pregnant." My heart is in my throat.

"Not that I know of." Her back is to me, forehead pressed against the closet door. "But he's proposing to her next week." It comes out low on a ragged whisper; I almost miss it. But when it fully registers, I'm livid.

"Well. Fuck. Him. Seriously. Throw him *under* the jail. Criminalize *him*, not weed," I shout, though I don't even smoke.

Neha's knocking her head against the closet now, full-on meltdown, and I feel like it's time for a speech. I stand, pad over to her, and switch on my Oprah voice. "Okay, look at the bright side. Today you found out for certain that Sam is not your person."

My *bright side* doesn't land well, and Neha's crying resumes. "Not helpful," she mumbles through tears.

Undeterred, I launch into the rest of the speech I had prepped for the inevitable day that Sam showed his whole Luciferian ass. "Hear me out. All these years you thought Sam was *the one*, but turns out, he was just a stepping stone on the way to finding him. And now, all those special moments with the guy who *will* be your forever—the giddiness you feel after the first date, that electricity from your first kiss, those flirty texts the morning after you spend the night—it's no longer in the past. The good stuff's in front of you waiting to be experienced with the guy who is your *actual* person. Because with the right guy, none of it ends like this." As if by sheer force of optimism and will, Neha perks up a little bit. We are kindred spirits in our hopeless romanticism after all.

"Since when did you become my therapist?" She snorts, looking at me with a tear-streaked face.

"Since the day we met in our dorm room and I took the bed with the good view," I reply.

Her laugh is cut short when she suddenly remembers. "Oh my god! Today was the day you gave your two weeks' notice. How does it feel to be so close to freedom?"

I'd almost forgotten about the hellfire that was my entire day up to the moment I arrived home to find Neha in shambles. I feel as if I've just been pelted with a boulder at the memory of *my* personal crisis. Enough of me being the strong one, we can unravel together. "We're going to need some alcohol and some ice cream," I say.

WE'RE IN HOLLYWOOD AT OUR FAVORITE BURGER SPOT NOW. It's our favorite because they serve spiked milkshakes and hand-cut potatoes fried in duck fat. Basically, this is our crisis control center. The sweet saltiness of duck-fat fries dunked in frosty, bourbon-soaked vanilla is *almost* blissful enough to block out the massive professional wreck I'm in. I just finished catching Neha up on the aftermath of my failed resignation—that after pressing send on my two weeks' notice, I had about two-point-five seconds to bask in my fresh liberation before a lidless blender filled with

horse shit powered on to ruin my day and possibly my life. Neha's
jaw is on the table.

"The worst part is I was foolish enough to believe that Danny
would swoop in and save the day—industry politics be damned!" I
say the last part with a flourish before dunking a fry into my shake
and popping it into my mouth. With each bite seemingly better
than the last, my eyes roll back and a shudder rips through me.

"Did you just have an orgasm?" Neha asks, swirling a straw in
her own shake.

"Mind your business," I reply, pointing a French fry at her
scoldingly. We laugh and commence our feast.

"I guess I can't really be mad at Danny," I continue. "Bella's
family basically went behind his back to buy her that job on the
production, and with the future the movie hanging in the balance, his hands are tied. Obviously, he's got to prioritize the
project."

"Yeah. Okay. Cool. But he did convince you to quit your job
and work for him without making sure he could actually follow
through on the offer. Then it blew up and he's like 'whoopsies'?"
Neha blurts out. "Don't get me wrong, I like Danny—but in the
*he's a ten, but he's also a flake who two-timed you once and is now
dating a woman who'd mispronounce your name and pretend it's
a mistake* kind of way."

Harsh? Yes. But she's not lying. "Okay, fair points have been
made. But you were the one who was all *give-the-man-a-chance*
on Friday," I say.

"I know." Neha sighs. "Why is it that the people we love always
disappoint us the most?" she asks, staring intently into her melting milkshake with Sam clearly weighing heavily on her mind.

I've actually been giving this a lot of thought in light of today's
events. I'm not in love with Danny anymore, but I have yet to fall

as hard for anyone else. And the sting I felt earlier today when I realized that he wasn't going to rescue me is a feeling I know all too well.

"Because he's your mirror," I say. "You see him, and all your wants and desires reflect back at you. Then, when he inevitably falls short of your high expectations, it's not just him you're disappointed in, it's also yourself, for misplacing all that hope." And I'm not sure if at this moment I'm talking about Sam or Danny or some amalgam named Sanny, but I think we both get it.

"Damn. I feel that," Neha admits on a sigh. "So what now? Do you work on the movie, or do you keep the receptionist gig?"

"Well, I honestly don't know," I admit. "If my job at reception sucked before, it's only going to be amplified now that Gary can smell blood in the water. I've basically bungled my escape from Alcatraz and will now be destined for a lifetime of slop duty."

"And what about the movie?" Neha pries again.

I explain Danny's solution of offering me a PA role. How I'd be assigned to the director's unit while working closely with Bella. How messy and tainted it all feels, and how I'm still unsure of Danny's motives.

"Well, and I do mean this with love," she replies, placing a cool hand on my wrist, "what have you got to lose?"

Nothing, apparently. Well, except for my pride, dignity, and the ability to go on pretending I've recovered from what he did to me. *Still* does to me. But before I can answer her, my purse vibrates. I dive in to retrieve my phone.

SALLIE MAE: Can we talk?

Speak of the devil.

"Let me guess, Sallie Mae?" Neha inquires, draining the remains of her milkshake. My eyes must give it away as I read the text several times over.

"Danny wants 'to talk,'" I say with air quotes, replacing my phone in my bag without replying to him. "But this is *our* night. We will drown our misery in Merlot while we binge *The Voice*. The man can wait."

She waves me off. "Nope. Don't avoid Danny on my account. Besides, I've got to join early-morning rounds at the hospital, so sleep will do me good."

In acquiescence, I respond to Danny's text letting him know I'm out and will call him later. We settle our bill and head back home. Once there, Neha grabs a bottle of red from the kitchen and heads to her room. But before she closes her door, I check in one last time. "Are you sure you're okay?"

Neha turns back to face me, leaning on the door frame. "I will be, because you know what?" She takes a swig from the bottle. "Amal Alamuddin didn't find George Clooney until her midthirties and that came after she made a name for herself as a kick-ass human rights attorney. I haven't found my Clooney and that's okay. Because in the meantime, I'm doing alright for myself." She turns and disappears into her room, and I know she'll be just fine.

Moments later, while curled up in my own bed, the faint sounds of "Take a Bow" drift over from the other side of our shared wall. All I want is to melt into my pillows and sleep away the heaviness of the day. But as Madonna's saying goodbye to a love that took her for granted, my phone starts buzzing on my dresser. I plop onto the floor, tiptoe across the room to where it's charging, and answer without looking.

"Hello?"

"Hey, it's me." The sound of his voice sends chills careening from my shoulders down to my toes. "Look, I'm outside your place." My heartbeats kick into overdrive. "I'm not stalking you or anything, but Neha texted me your address about an hour ago."

"You two text?" I don't know why I'm whispering.

"I texted her earlier to see how you were doing with everything that happened today. Didn't think I'd get a straight answer from you so—"

"I'll be down in a minute."

chapter

8

T HE MOMENT I STEP outside I regret it. In part because it's past ten and fifty degrees, which in Los Angeles translates to negative two anywhere else. And in part because Danny's standing just beyond the fence to my and Neha's Los Feliz duplex looking very tall and annoyingly edible in a perfectly tailored hunter green peacoat.

After his latest screwup, I shouldn't want to open the lapels of that jacket and wrap myself up in it with him. But dammit, it's cold.

I scamper across the cobblestone walkway watching the chilly night air spin around him. It rustles the short curls on top of his head as he puffs warm breath into his closed fists.

His eyes are steady on me as I approach the gate. Under his stare, my breathing is shallow and something inside my chest flips over. It's not quite nerves. Those frayed about the time I ripped off my silk bonnet and frantically got dressed to come downstairs. This feeling, like I've been touched by a live wire, has more to do with the clandestine nature of his late-night house call. Doesn't he have someone to go home to?

I latch the gate, stuff my hands in my hoodie's mono-pocket, and join Danny on the sidewalk. "H-i-i-i. What's-s u-up?" The words vibrate across my shivering lips.

His eyes bounce on all the peaks of my face before glancing down at my threadbare NYU sweatshirt, ratty leggings, and fuzzy slippers. The corners of his mouth draw tight, like he's trying to hold back a grin. "I just wanted to talk," he says, shrugging.

I'm not exactly sure what to do with him at this point—or myself for that matter. Our last conversation put me through the ringer. But he's here now, and we're both shivering. Self-preservation tells me that inviting him inside would be a disaster—can't have him in my private space when he's already running amuck in my private thoughts.

Either he senses my indecision or he can hear my chattering teeth, because he's the first to break the ice, asking, "Can we talk in my car?"

I could start a praise dance. Instead, I nod like a bobblehead and dart past him in the direction of a shiny black Range Rover—which could be an unmarked white van and I'd still welcome its warmth.

Danny follows closely behind, confirming I'd guessed his car right. He unlocks the door and hovers his hand over the small of my back, like a consummate gentleman, as I step up and into the car. I let the magnetic feeling of his barely there touch linger longer than I should and then chastise myself when he shuts me in.

Once Danny's settled in the driver's seat, he turns up the heat, and then . . . zzzzooooohmahgod he's got seat warmers. I'm fighting the urge to rub myself all over the warm buttery leather and purr like a spoiled house cat when he interrupts.

"We aim to please." Danny eyes me with a smirk. His soft laugh that follows feels like a caress on the back of my neck, and now I'm shuddering for different reasons.

Embarrassed, I redirect. "I would've invited you in, but Neha's got an early shift and she's sleeping off a pretty rough day."

Danny's forehead creases. "Everything okay with her?"

"Honestly, not really," I say, sinking farther into my seat. "Sam left her for a woman he's been sleeping with behind her back for years. Apparently, he's proposing next week, too."

His eyebrows jump at the reveal. "Wow . . . Fuck *that* dude."

I find Danny's reaction *intriguing* to say the least, given the way things ended with us in college. But perhaps he has changed his ways in the past seven years. Perhaps he's shed the old fuckboy skin and become a dedicated and trustworthy partner. If that's the case, good for him and Celine Michèle. Someone had to be the collateral damage on his journey of self-improvement. And I guess that someone was me.

"So, to what do I owe the pleasure tonight?" I ask, suddenly feeling wary of the unknown purpose for his visit.

Danny smooths his hands down the top of his thighs, a nervous gesture of his that I know well. Sure enough, I look down and one of his knees is bouncing rapidly.

"I did something this afternoon," he says, and by the sheepish look in his eyes, I can't tell if he's about to deliver good news or bad.

He stalls again, so I nudge him along. "Something that has to do with me?"

"Listen," he says, adjusting in his seat to face me. "I know I fucked up big-time. But I'm only trying to do right by you, Kal."

The overfamiliarity of my nickname, one only he's ever used, feels both right and wrong falling from his lips—like coming home from college to your old bedroom only to discover it's been flipped into a luxury guest suite.

"Long story short, I had a call with Jim and Celine, and your boss, Gary, who sucks by the way," he says, and I'll admit it feels good to hear him confirm what I already know. "No idea how you've worked with that guy for so long. But after some back and forth, Jim and Celine approved a new PA position and Gary agreed to grant you a six-month leave of absence from the reception desk to work on the film."

Momentarily distracted by Danny's approval-seeking smile, I'm practically stupefied at this turn of events. And I'm not sure I've grasped the details.

I double back to ask, "So, wait. Why a leave of absence?"

"Because you don't trust me," Danny says. "I get it. *Especially* after today. So this time, before I made the offer, I wanted to make sure you had a safety net."

I cross my arms, protecting myself from the hope that's blossoming at the fragile promise of a fallback plan. "So, what happens then . . . If somewhere in the six months, we decide things aren't working out?"

"Totally up to you," he says, brightly. "I mean, you can go back to the front desk, or you make some connections on the crew and use them for whatever the hell you want."

"Simple as that?" I ask, dubious of the notion that I'd ever have the freedom to do *whatever the hell I want.*

"It can be," Danny says, as if him saying it *makes* it that way.

But he's wrong. Because nothing about this is simple for me. "I want to know something," I say, facing him head-on. "You could have reached out any time in the past seven years. And sure, I had you blocked but there were ways. Not to mention you probably have a line out the door of folks scrambling to work with 'the next Scorsese.'"

I'm rambling now, talking with my hands, too. Danny seems a little alarmed. So I take a deep breath and get to my point. "What I want to know is, why now? Why me?"

To my surprise, a soft smile creeps across his lips, like he's been hit by a happy fragment of the past. "Remember that *Lawrence of Arabia* screening at the Angelika in SoHo—our first date?"

A familiar flutter rises in my chest. "That's not an answer," I protest. "And that wasn't a date."

"I wanted it to be," he confesses casually, distracting me from my initial point. "I was such an idiot for dragging you to a four-hour screening you could barely stay awake for," he says. "Remember how I kept you up?"

A wayward laugh escapes me, and suddenly, I'm walking with him, shoulder to shoulder back down memory lane. "You whispered little factoids about the production—like how all the interiors were filmed in Spain but the exterior shots were done across Jordan and Morocco."

"I guess I was boring you to death?" Danny's eyes light up and I can't help but beam back at him.

It's my turn to confess. "On the contrary, it felt like foreplay." After saying the words, I can't hold his stare for another second. So I retreat to the window. But something pulls me back and our eyes lock like magnets. It's hotter in here now. Like we're playing with fire by openly thinking back on the time when we danced just near the edge of our desire for each other.

"Walking you back to your dorm, the whole time I was trying to find ways to keep myself from touching you, grabbing your hand, anything." Danny shakes his head and smiles down at his lap, giving himself over to the memory.

We're skirting a fine line here. Despite the alarm bells, I let myself bask in this stolen moment, relishing the surprise access I have to him for however long it lasts.

"Why did you hold back?" I ask.

Danny shifts, turning to look out of his own window. "For some reason, I just wanted to be softer with you," he admits. "I was a little older than you and it was like you had all this hopeless romanticism coursing through your veins. Everything with you just felt bigger somehow."

He's right to call me a hopeless romantic. I was a late bloomer, a sheltered eighteen-year-old Southern girl experiencing mutual attraction in the big city for the first time—and with someone like Danny no less, the son of a Hollywood legend. On top of that, he was a walking Armani ad who, based on rumors, wasn't short on NYU girls chasing after him, a few having already caught him, too.

"Believe it or not, I was intimidated by you," he says, and it catches me by surprise. "Before I met you, I was just fumbling my way around the city, making shallow connections, taking classes—going through the motions."

Danny sighs, resting his head back on the seat. "But one conversation with you left me feeling like I'd lived my whole life just sniffing air, not really *breathing* it. Not like you. I wanted to be like that—I wanted to be *with* someone like that. But I didn't know how."

I don't think anyone's ever seen me this way. Learning that, if even for a short while, he was as in awe of me as I was of him, is enough to make me feel light-headed.

Danny continues his story. "But even though I felt like I needed to take things slow with you, when we got back to your dorm, I said fuck it. I leaned in to kiss you and you—"

"I pulled back and ran inside like a scared mouse," I cut in, face-palming at the wretched memory. "I hated myself for that for days," I say. "I thought you'd ghosted me."

The week after our "date," Danny went radio silent and I died a thousand times every day just waiting for him to call or text. I was sure I'd blown my chances entirely. Until I found out with the rest of the world that his dad had passed away suddenly from a tragic fall at home, a fall that happened the night of our date.

"Everything changed for me after that," he says. "Brought me down to earth real quick. Tragedy has a way of doing that, you know? Reminding you that you're human and capable of being gutted."

"And still surviving," I add.

Danny looks at me now, his eyes catching the glow of the streetlights. "A lot of that had to do with you, you know. You and the movie made me feel like I could breathe again after I'd been gasping for air."

"*The Last Song*, by Danny Prescott," I remember aloud. "A renowned pianist whose virtuosic gift is gradually slipping away, crippled by disease. And the talented protégé she discovers in Washington Square Park who plays for her, when she can't anymore."

I pause, a lightbulb moment striking suddenly. "It was for him." I gasp. "You wrote it for him!"

Danny nods, smiling to himself. "He was the pianist, and I was the protégé," he confirms. "That movie was my gift to him, and I wouldn't have made it without you."

At some point, both our hands wound up side by side on the center console. We seem to notice at the same time and pull back like we've been shocked. Scolded by our own consciences, we lean back into our seats, creating distance between us.

Danny exhales sharply. "Truth is, I want you on this project because over seven years ago you showed up for me at my life's lowest point and helped me make something incredible. I don't know what my career would look like right now without that first film. Without *you* helping me make it."

Danny pauses, as if carefully considering his next words. "I want to return the favor in whatever way I can, Kal."

Until now, I'd segmented my life into two parts: *Before Danny* and *After Danny*. A few days ago, Kaliya of year 7 AD had settled into the *after* phase, only thinking of him as often as she thought of peanut brittle, or movie theaters, or fall in New York, or Christmas lights and New Year's Eve. That's what it's like in the *after*—living a whole life without the man you're never too far away from thinking of.

But I have no idea how to exist in the *now* of him, *again*. How to navigate the disturbing feeling that I've been in hibernation for seven years, and now that he's back, I'm awake to new possibilities. Or how to reconcile the fact that walking away from him all those years ago *still* hurts. That what he did to *push* me away hurts even more. And that in the end, none of it matters because he didn't come here for my forgiveness. He came here to make the movie of a lifetime, and he wants to bring me along for the ride.

If I'm honest with myself, holding on to all that *stuff* after all this time feels like a choice. Like in doing so, I'm *choosing* to be weighed down. Now is as good an opportunity as ever to stop being a bag lady. Someone who hoards all her trauma and drama, packing it away in various bags for safekeeping. Carrying them along with her everywhere she goes so she can unfurl them from time to time, if only just to admire all her problems. *It's time to move on.*

"Okay," I relent. "I'll take the job. But on one condition."

"Anything," Danny promises.

"This time, we put it on paper and sign on the dotted line," I say. "No more tightrope walking without a safety net."

"You'll have a contract in your inbox by morning." He takes my proffered hand with his, warm and rough against cold and smooth. It's our second handshake in less than a week. This time, I hope it sticks.

chapter 9

BELLA CARMICHAEL IS EXACTLY who I expected her to be. It's my first day working as a preproduction assistant, my consolation prize, on Danny's film. She and I have shared a tandem cubicle outside his office for all of an hour, and already she's taken it upon herself to set up my TikTok account (I'll never use it) and divulge how she keeps tabs on Travis, her ex—by cross-referencing his Instagram geotags with his public Venmo transactions. At the conclusion of her enlightening and somewhat alarming tutorial, I swivel back to my email, where the latest draft of Danny's script has appeared.

FOR YOUR EYES ONLY blinks up at me from the subject line, and I fight the urge to squeal. In the body, he's written—

A penny for your thoughts? -DP

—and nothing else. No preamble or specific ask. No overview of the script's current problem areas with story beats, and no indication of plot or character elements he wants my critical take on.

He's assumed I don't need the editorial road map he'd likely offer any other person laying second eyes on the script. That means he either wants my unadulterated take on his writing, or he's issuing a challenge—am I as good at this as I used to be? Do I still have that keen editorial eye that took his draft thesis script from good to something really special?

I don't know if I'm flattered or feeling patronized but the excitement settling into my bones can't be denied. Clicking to open the attachment, my bated breath releases like fizz from a just-popped soda can. I'm about to dive into the opening scene when—

"Uggghhhhhh!" A long, strangled groan from Bella's side of the cube penetrates my bubble of focus.

I swivel back around to check on her. "Something the matter?" I ask, venturing cautiously.

My visibly distraught colleague pushes off her desk and, impervious to norms of personal space, rolls across the gap between us until our knees touch. "He just posted *this*!" Bella whispers, in a way that's basically shouting.

I'm sandwiched between my desk and Bella's iPhone screen as two very round, very firm-looking pecs eclipse my field of vision. Pushing her phone back to a safe viewing distance reveals a selfie of a Jason Derulo look-alike posing with a green juice outside what appears to be a SoulCycle. Presumably this is Travis and admittedly, he's quite attractive. I'm irritated—"So the man likes green juice?"—and confused.

Bella glares at the screen. "Look. Closer," she demands, punctuating each word with the stab of a hot-pink-tipped nail. Squinting at the edge of the frame, I can just make out a wavy lock of bleach-blond hair falling along Travis's shoulder. Just beneath it, the bronze curve of an over-tanned arm presses into his side. As these context clues begin to form a clearer picture, I look up at

Bella, who has the expression of a freshly validated conspiracy theorist.

"He just Venmo'd some girl named Shelly"—the name comes out of her on a whimper—"eleven bucks for that Green Goddess shake and now he has the nerve to post her for the world to see." She pauses, lips quivering and shoulders slumped. And then she says, with a wobbly voice, "We only broke up two days ago."

"Bella, can I give you some advice?" I ask flatly. She turns up from her phone to meet my eyes with a look so lost and naïve it muffles my irritation, but just slightly. Without speaking, Bella nods rapidly, eyes wide and upturned like a baby bird awaiting a worm from its mother.

"Compartmentalize." I enunciate the word slowly, dragging out each syllable, hoping it imprints. "Shelly may have Travis's attention for a hot second, but how serious can they be if he's cropped all but a strand of her hair and a fraction of her anatomy out of the picture?" I grab the phone, scroll through his feed, and turn it back to face her. "Look at this." Now I'm the one jabbing the screen. "You're everywhere for him," I say. I'm not even exaggerating as I scroll through shots of her draped across his lap on a yacht, straddling his shoulders at Coachella, holding his hand while leading him on a hike up what looks like Machu Picchu.

"He's likely got it bad enough for you that he'd forget Shelly's name if you texted him so much as a half-assed 'hey,'" I say. "And besides, the Travises will come and go. But assisting a talented director on an Oscar-bait film that's being produced by the industry's top specialty studio is a chance millions would kill for—and it's yours. So put the phone away and deal with Travis later. I repeat, compartmentalize."

At this, Bella tucks in her bottom lip and, dutifully scolded, nods once more before scooting her chair back to the other side of the cube.

Desperate to get to Danny's script, I turn back to my computer.

"I'm sorry, you know," Bella says softly, recapturing my attention. "I heard through the grapevine that my job was originally meant for you."

The intent behind my speech was a reality check, not a guilt trip. I'd rather melt into a pile of green goop on the floor than talk about my professional woes with Bella, the beneficiary of them. And yet, here we are.

"Honestly, don't worry about it," I say dismissively. "I know how these things go. We're on the same team now—no hard feelings." I shrug, smile.

Bella's furrowed brow lets me know I'm not about to get off so easy because she's about to make this *a thing* in three, two, o— "It's just, I've been dreading today because I figured you'd hate me for how it all went down."

At this point, my morning reading has been fully hijacked. So, I close out of Danny's script—leaving it open will just taunt me— and turn my full attention to Bella's catharsis.

"For the sake of my own mental health and our working relationship," she explains, "I just need you to know I was completely in the dark about what my dad had arranged with Jim when I accepted this job." She's got the same excuse as Danny. Fabulous.

"It wasn't even my choice to begin with," she explains, venting to me like I'm her closest confidant. It strikes me now that this might actually be the case.

"I didn't have a stellar performance during my first few years in Chapman's directing program," she admits, lowering her head with shame. "Dad said he wouldn't waste his money for me to just embarrass him in front of his old colleagues there. So, he gave me two choices: I could either take a leave of absence to get some industry work before going back to school, or he'd cancel my tuition payments and cut me off completely."

I'm half appalled that her father is such a controlling hard-ass and half inclined to tell her these are platinum white-girl problems. But I bite my tongue and keep waiting for a sign of a denouement.

"I mean, don't get me wrong," she says. "I'm passionate about creating original content. I'm just not sure directing movies is my path, you know? Of course, my dad is having none of that talk. He doesn't take my podcast or my digital brand seriously at all."

"I'm sorry. Come again? Your what?" I ask.

"My digital brand," she repeats. "I'm an influencer." She whispers it like she's just confessed to being in a cult.

"And what does this *influencing* entail?" I ask. "Diet teas? Face masks? Sketchy vitamin chews?" I'm trying—and failing—not to sound judgmental.

"I promote products, yes," she confirms. "That's the part that pays. But the end goal is to start my own media empire, like the Kardashians. And before you roll your eyes at that," she catches me there, "I'm all about women using whatever it is they admire most about themselves to excel in business, so more power to them—and hopefully to me, too, one day."

"And what is it you admire most about yourself?" I ask reflexively, ignoring the fact that I don't even know the answer for myself. Bella's prompt response prevents me from dwelling on it, though.

"I'm still trying to figure that part out," she admits. "But I know I like to connect with people, to create a space for them to tell their stories. That's why I love podcasting."

In the span of a single conversation, I've gone from being weary of Bella to being mesmerized by her. The way she's bold enough to name her passions and go after them in spite of her dad's lofty expectations. I have to hand it to her.

"That's not a bad elevator pitch," I say.

She's practically giddy. "Thanks! Maybe you can be my guest one day."

"Well let's not get ahead of ourselves," I say, before wheeling back around to my desk. This time, I put on my headphones.

———

BELLA'S OFF TO AN EXTENDED LUNCH, PROBABLY SCOURING Studio City for traces of Travis and Shelly, and I'm on cloud nine. Her absence has afforded me the precious gift of silence and concentration. Except, after reading the first scenes of Danny's script, I have a niggling feeling that we aren't entering the world of the story at the right place.

He opens with a flash-forward. Minnie and Nathan have just boarded a train from Memphis to New York where they plan to elope and forge a life out from under the hot blanket of prejudice they've faced in the South. It's a bittersweet scene with the two of them huddled in a coach car holding hands in public for the first time. In the screenplay Danny describes them as, *so blissfully in love and fleetingly free that they completely miss the scoffs and stares of people passing by, passing judgment.*

Then, he flashes back to six years prior, Nathan and Minnie's first day of seventh grade at Maple Creek Middle School in Memphis, Tennessee.

INTERIOR—LUNCHROOM—ACT 1, SCENE II

A terrified Minnie (12) walks through a crowded lunchroom. Her hands tremble as she clutches

her meal tray. Surrounded by an impenetrable
crowd of her white peers, she walks past their
stares—some vacant, some mean, a few jeering.
Minnie chances a smile at a table of girls,
all with pretty blouses, pleated skirts, and
cold eyes. She's putting out feelers for
kindness and not finding it anywhere. Making
her way to the back of the room, she sits
alone at a table by the window. Minnie battles
back the threat of tears as she nibbles on a
bright red apple. Suddenly a boy (Nathan, 12),
tall and lanky for his age and sharply
dressed, makes his way over.

                    MINNIE:
             (Rising to vacate the table)
        I'm sorry. Have I taken your seat?

                    NATHAN:
        I came over to ask if you wanted to eat
        lunch together.

                    MINNIE:
             (Eyeing him warily)
        You're teasing me.

                    NATHAN:
             (Setting down his tray and pulling
             back a chair)
        Wouldn't do that. I'm Nathan by the way.
        Prescott.

Nathan takes a seat.

> MINNIE:
> (Still standing, increasingly
> cautious)
> Your daddy the mayor?

> NATHAN:
> He is. But I'm not like him if that's
> what's got you so nervous.

> MINNIE:
> (Eyes darting left and right, still
> making no motion to sit back down)
> I'm sorry, I just don't think we can—

> NATHAN:
> Can what? Be friends? I think we could
> try.

> MINNIE:
> Well, how do we do that?

> NATHAN:
> You could start by telling me your name.

> MINNIE:
> Don't you know it from the paper?

> NATHAN:
> I want to know it from you.

```
Minnie takes her seat across from Nathan and
they share a private smile.
```

I'm instantly pulled into the scene. The tentative innocence of Nathan and Minnie's initial interaction—her hesitation, his persistence. But I don't think it's where the real story begins. Not for Minnie at least.

Danny's already given me access to his research archives. So I dive back into the cache of taped interviews he's conducted with his mom, Minnie, on her background. Watching her, I can't help but think of my own mother, who visits me now as only fleeting memories—memories that are saturated at the center but blurred around the edges. Like me running offstage and into her arms in the audience after a dance recital. Or during the years before she left, when I'd tiptoe around the house to avoid the land mines of her temper. This constant navigation of highs and lows with her made the quiet consistency of my grandparents feel safe. Their little redbrick house on the wrong side of town was like my own haven.

But Danny's mother is warmth personified, still soft despite the hardness of life. And of all the hours of recordings I've pored over, one has struck me as a pivotal entry point into Minnie's story. Scrolling through the video files, I click on one titled "The Night Before." It takes a few seconds to buffer, and then she appears, seated at an island in a well-appointed Spanish-style kitchen that's worthy of a Nancy Meyers film. I have to assume the setting is the Prescott family estate in Austin, Texas, where Minnie works as a college history professor.

Within the shot's frame, Danny's adjusted his lens to capture the natural light so expertly that you can tell precisely what time of day it is—early evening, the golden hour. Minnie's delicately aged skin has a bronze-like glow; her hair, deep black, intermixed with strands as silver as spider's silk. The prominent lines around her eyes and mouth give her away as the reason why Danny seems to smile with his entire face. The DNA doesn't lie.

For a brief moment, Danny enters the frame, but we can only see his torso and hands as they adjust the lavalier mic on the collar of his mother's crisp blue blouse. She lovingly cups his forearm with her left hand, where a gold wedding band glimmers in the light. Danny covers her hand tenderly with his for just a moment before he takes his place behind the camera.

Seconds later, we can hear his voice as he begins the interview. *"Okay, Ma. I'm going to start with some questions about your experience at school. Take as much time as you need because it's all just going to be used as background. And we can stop or take a break whenever you want."*

Minnie listens intently then nods before offering a nervous but warm smile and replying.

"Ask away, sweetheart," she says.

Danny clears his throat, then asks, *"What was it like for you, that first day of seventh grade? How did you feel when you went to bed the night before? When you woke up that morning?"*

"Oh, well of course I was a nervous wreck!" Minnie laughs, then looks down at her hands, one cupping a giant mug of tea, the other stirring absentmindedly.

The whirring sound of the metal spoon on porcelain is hypnotic. As steam wafts up toward her face, the clarity of Danny's lens is so pure, it picks up the dancing vapors with precision. He remains silent, allowing his mother to expand her answer. Then a faraway expression penetrates her features as if she's reliving it all in real time.

"Mama, she felt it was important for me to really look the part,"

Minnie explains. *"Back then white people expected us 'colored folks' to be unclean and uncouth, you know, not smart. So Mama and Daddy took me to the consignment store and bought me a new pleated red dress and some Mary Janes. I'd always wanted a pair, and these were just barely scuffed, so shiny you could see your reflection. That night Mama pressed my hair with her hot comb, and then she took her time putting in her rollers. I knew she was serious because my hair only got pressed on Saturday nights for Sunday service. Daddy sat across the room working his crossword puzzle, and the whole time I was bubbling with questions like,* Am I going to have friends? and Will the teachers be nice?"

"And what did Gram and Pop say?" Danny asks.

"Well," she begins. *"Daddy was big on keeping the fear under the surface—'Never let it show.' And he said, 'There's people that won't like you no matter what you do. You just can't give 'em a reason for it.' He told me to walk through those doors with my head held high and that alone would prove to those white people they were all wrong about us."*

Minnie takes a long pause and Danny patiently waits her out.

"I think that's what integration was all about for him," Minnie explains. *"It was about me showing everybody at that school, in that town, that us 'colored folks' weren't what they'd made us up to be in their minds."*

"And Gram?" Danny asks.

"Oh, she just tended to my hair and didn't say a word," Minnie says, waving off the memory. *"But when she put me in bed that night, I could see she'd been crying. She knew all this effort we'd made to make me palatable wasn't going to make a difference. I was going to be well-dressed and well-spoken but still Black. She was scared for her little girl."*

There's another long pause and Minnie looks up from her tea

and directly into the lens. A glossy film of unshed tears has grown thick over her deep brown eyes. She looks up past the camera, directly at her son, before she speaks again.

"I think I'd like to take a break now" are her last words before the picture cuts to black.

WITHOUT HESITATION, I PICK UP MY PHONE AND TAP OUT A text.

> ME: You're starting at the wrong place.

> SALLIE MAE: Afternoon, Kaliya. Can I trouble you for some context?

> ME: I'm reading the draft you sent.

> ME: The first flashback in the cafeteria with Nate and Minnie.

> ME: You're starting at the wrong place.

> SALLIE MAE: I'm listening . . .

> ME: The tension there, it needs to simmer before it boils.

Feeling slightly self-conscious that I've so inelegantly accosted him with a blunt critique, I wait anxiously for his reply. Minutes pass and nothing comes through. Then my phone starts to vibrate. It's Sallie Mae.

"Hey," I say, with caution.

"So you were saying . . . about the simmering and the boiling?" Danny's voice is deep but distant amid a cacophony of city sounds swirling around in the background.

"Um, yeah," I mutter. "Well, I just mean that you do a *beautiful* job of throwing us into that first day at Maple Creek, showing us Minnie and all her quiet strength. But, it's one thing to show us what it took for her to walk through that cafeteria. As a reader though, I want to know what it took for her to even show up that morning."

"Okay. I like this direction," Danny says. "So what did you have in mind?"

"That interview you did with your mom titled 'The Night Before,' the one where she's reliving her mother's anxious primping, her father's expectations. Then she goes to bed after seeing the tears in her mother's eyes. That's it. That's the first flashback." I pause and then demur, "I think."

"Don't do that," he says, somewhat forcefully.

"Don't do what?" I ask, caught off guard.

"Don't back off on how good you are at this by couching a completely perfect note with an *I think*," he explains. "This is your wheelhouse, Kaliya. Own it."

We exchange a few more notes on the opening pages and then hang up the phone. Smiling despite myself at nothing in particular, I have the urge to spin around in my seat. And because no one else is around, I do exactly that.

chapter

10

"S O, SPILL. HOW WAS the date?" I ask, smizing across the table at Neha over the rim of my glass of rosé. She and I are at our favorite oyster bar on Silver Lake Boulevard having a nightcap. It's a tiny, trendy spot at the base of the reservoir below the dog park, situated within an eclectic lineup of charming boutiques and a few neighborhood go-tos like LAMILL Coffee, 7-Eleven, and one excellent Thai restaurant.

Inside, the lights are low and darkness is accented by glowy puffs of amber light cast by tea candles all around. Surrounding us, the sounds of clinked glasses, flatware on china, and flowing conversation create the best kind of mood music for a post-date postmortem. It's the kind of place you take your significant other or your best friend, someone you'd be totally content to sit with in complete silence over a savory meal or to chat with for hours about nothing and everything. And that's precisely why it's our go-to spot for nights like these.

About an hour ago, I was in the middle of making notes on

another draft of Danny's script when I got a *Mayday* text from Neha. She'd been at a wine bar in Los Feliz for her first post-Samuel blind date. One of her fellow fourth years at UCLA set her up with his cousin Colin, a high school history teacher who was *allegedly* a catch. She'd been told Colin was the kind of guy women spent their twenties avoiding but would eventually decide to settle down with once they'd hit thirty-one, all the while kicking themselves for wasting all that time.

Turns out, the allegation was false.

Neha tips back a juicy kumamoto—it's dollar-oyster night. Then, she takes a gulp of her rosé before responding to my request for a recap.

"I'm not sure I have the words," she says, staring blankly ahead as if presently reliving the trauma.

I grimace. "It was that bad?"

"Well for starters," she begins, "he greeted me with a sloppy kiss on my cheek that I had to let air dry because I felt rude just wiping it off. Then we sat down. But before we even ordered drinks, he proceeded to remove his Invisalign trays at the table."

"He did not!" I sort of gasp, sort of choke, and Neha calmly takes another gulp of sparkly blush liquid.

"Oh, we're just getting started," she says. "Brace for a rapid escalation."

"Got it." I mime buckling myself into a seat belt before motioning for her to continue.

"Next, he placed the trays on a napkin near his plate, as one does. Then, he looked me dead in the eyes and said, *It's your job to make sure the waiter doesn't walk off with these.*"

I attempt to find the words to convey my disbelief but only manage to repeat that gasp-choke combo again.

Neha presses on. "At this point, I've decided this is no longer a date. But it is a free meal, and I *can* use the material for my future memoirs. So against my better instincts, I stay put to see where it goes."

"What did you even talk about after that?" I ask, impressed by her fortitude.

"It was a challenge," she admits. "With his glistening dental molds sitting *right there*, staring at me in ways I couldn't ignore. But midway through our appetizer, I was making the best of it and savoring the flaky coconut shrimp when he looked down, yelped, and then started berating me."

"Don't tell me you let the waiter take the teeth?" I am practically on the edge of my seat.

"Well not his actual teeth, but the trays, yes," she admits. "They most likely went missing around the time I let Colin grace me with his impersonation of Morgan Freeman from *The Shawshank Redemption*."

By now, my eyes are tearing up and my stomach hurts from holding in the laughter. "Oh, that must have been riveting," I say, choking back a guffaw.

"It was embarrassing for both of us. But once he noticed they'd disappeared along with the napkin, he demanded to know how I could let this happen on my watch. He got up to find the waiter and that's when I threw some cash down on the table and fled. I texted you while lying down in the back seat of my parked car around the corner. Couldn't run the risk of being spotted by Colin and then invoiced for his dental bill."

"Well, good thing you've got me around to make sure that outfit's not a total waste." Neha looks sassy and stylish in a flirty black halter dress and bright orange heels, ones I'd helped her pick out.

"Seriously, you're the best date I've ever had," she says before knocking back another one-dollar oyster.

"Ditto," I counter. We clink glasses and drain our rosé as a gnawing pit forms in my chest.

What if guys like Colin are as good as it gets for us from here on out? I mean, I haven't been berated by a lunatic on a date, yet. But just about every day my messages on the apps reach a new depth of depravity. There was the one guy who asked if I'd be interested in taking him on as a sex slave. *Let's subvert history!* he'd said.

Another guy, Kyle, seemed promising at first. But when weeks of *Good morning, beautiful*s and *Sweet dreams, love*s by text didn't materialize into anything IRL, my spidey senses went into full effect. It didn't take long for me to discover he was married—to my hairdresser. So I took a double loss on that one, spending the next year looking for a new beautician who was trained in protective hairstyles. Now, by some cruel twist of fate, Neha's in the arena with me, trying to find a lasting connection amid a sea of wacky Colins and wayward Kyles.

We both sit somberly, lost in deep thought as pink bubbles flit about inside the glasses between us. Neha is the first to break the silence. "Why is it that dating in New York seemed so different than it does in LA?" she asks. "I mean, after you finally got over Danny and broke out of your two-year retreat from *all men*, you made it to a place where you'd get so excited to dress up, hop on the train, and meet a new guy at a new bar in a *new-to-you* part of Brooklyn. I used to envy you so much back in those days. And when Sam cheated, part of me was relieved to think now is *my* chance. But all day long, I had this vicious knot in my stomach because it's really all just a crapshoot, isn't it? I'm either going to meet the man of my dreams, a complete disaster, or someone entirely forgettable. And the chances it's the first of the three are only dwindling."

"Okay, so while I did eventually find my sea legs in the city, it's not like I have this *great love* from my college years who still keeps me warm at night. After Danny, everyone else was sort of a blur," I admit, sipping slowly before replacing my glass on the table. "But you're right, we had so much optimism back then. I think the difference must have had something to do with the collective effervescence of our youthful naïveté."

"Come again, please." Neha's sharp reply cuts into my wistful haze. "And in words you haven't stolen from one of those overwrought think pieces."

I roll my eyes at her but have to laugh at myself as well. "We were young and dumb and hopped up on the heady experience of living in a city that promises you everything but grants you nothing in return. We called ourselves the Black and Brown Carrie and Samantha for heaven's sake! We lived our lives based on the false promises of a glitzy TV show that wasn't talking *to* us or *about* us. Now we're just living in a city with a warmer climate where everyone's got dreams but none of it matters if you don't have allies, too."

Because Neha is my best friend and she recognizes that we've veered off into rocky terrain, she latches on to the one part of my rant that matters most in this moment. "I'm your ally," she says, reaching across the table and grabbing my hand with a teary look in her eyes. I want to get up and hug her, but we settle for laughing off our sappiness and ordering another round. This time, martinis.

WE'VE DOWNED ALL THE OYSTERS AND ARE NOW INDULGING in a delightfully jiggly panna cotta dish when the universe decides that this night has not been triggering enough.

I'm in the middle of telling Neha about my disastrous gyno

appointment this morning. With my socked feet in the cold stirrups, Dr. Nealman kept instructing me to scoot farther down the table. But after a few very awkward ass shimmies I nearly fell off and into his lap. Neha's just blown a snot bubble and my sides are aching from laughter when I look up at the party that's just walked into the bar and almost leap out of my own skin.

"Oh my god," I practically scream, before searching the table for something, anything I can use to hide my face.

Neha is understandably alarmed by my sudden outburst. "What is it? What's wrong? Are you looking for a tampon?" She dives into her purse like the dutiful friend she is. But I've barely registered anything she's said because her sounds are muffled by the rush of blood beating against my eardrums.

"Don't. Turn. Around," I beg of her. But the urgent plea is useless because she swivels like an office chair.

Now we're both staring directly at Celine Michèle's back with Danny's palm pressed into the small of it. Sudden death would be a sweet release from being forced to witness the subtle intimacy of that tiny point of contact. It's like a little shard of glass wedged between my ribs and I really can't explain why it's affecting me this much.

When it was just me and Danny at the coffee shop, in the mail room, and in his car parked outside my house, I'd had his undivided attention. I've been working on the production for a month now and while I can't say exactly what I expected our professional relationship to look like, *distant* had not come to mind. To be fair, Danny's been traveling a lot, crewing up in preparation for the first all-hands production meeting that's next week. In the meantime, I've been working closely with Bella and have barely heard from him.

It's not that I'd expect a big-shot director to have a lowly PA on speed dial or anything like that. But I checked, and there's no Tik-Tok explainer for how to handle the complexities of working with your ex *and* his girlfriend. Regardless, seeing them out in the wild together being all sensual and romantic is a hard pass for me.

"Oh shit, she's hot," Neha says, bursting my thought bubble. I glare at her and she rushes to explain. "I mean, in a Victoria's Secret model kind of way. If that's what he's into."

"It's what *everyone's* into," I reply, wondering how we can escape without being noticed.

Neha clarifies her statement by telling me she meant catalog, not runway, while perkily sipping her dirty martini. She's completely unbothered and I couldn't be more so.

"This isn't helping!" I whisper-shout. "Now, focus. How can we leave without them seeing us?"

"What? We can't leave!" Neha proclaims, shocked at the mere suggestion of it. "If you're going to get him back you can't retreat from a little competition," she says primly.

"I'm sorry, what? Get him back?" I ask, more than a little disturbed. "Let's be clear. I didn't take the job for a man, I did it for my career."

"Who says you can't have both?" she asks, blinking innocently.

"You are the absolute *worst* influence," I say.

"Mm-hmm. Now, just replace *worst* with *best* and *influence* with *hype woman* and you'll be onto something," she replies, quite pleased with herself.

"Well," I say, "all that hype got me in a world of heartbreak last time around and I can't do that again."

This garners an expression from Neha that looks a lot like hurt and a little like guilt. I feel instantly horrible and rush to backtrack. "I'm sorry, Nay. I didn't mean it like that, I swear. It's just been *a lot* trying to figure out how to balance getting what I need out of this job, with all the mixed-up emotions and baggage that come with it, you know?"

The look of understanding on her face says *apology accepted* without her having to. "Well, for what it's worth," she says, "I think you make more sense with him than she does. And stop staring, you'll just compel his attention through your eyeballs."

She's right. But just when I cut my eyes away from their fixed spot on Danny's face, without looking I can sense the moment when he's found me from across the room. The gravity of his stare draws me back and there he is, looking at me with an inscrutable expression.

Celine's leaning into his chest with her arm flung across his lap, hand likely resting on his long and lean thigh, which is probably bouncing underneath the table. It eats me alive. The jealousy. The *want*. But most of all, the returned heat I see in his eyes. His Adam's apple bobs up and down along the strong contours of his neck and the muscles bunch along his jaw as he makes a big swallow. He stares at me for long seconds. But he doesn't nod or wave or indicate to his tablemates that he's recognized someone across the room.

Celine speaks with enthusiasm to their dinner companion, who I now notice has a rather attractive profile himself. Danny breaks our eye contact to look down at Celine and the loss of his attention feels like a door closing in my face. She tilts her face up to his, wordlessly asking for a kiss. He answers by gently brushing his lips across hers, not once, but twice. I know I should, but I can't look away.

"Okay, that's it, I've seen enough. We're leaving." Neha motions for the server. "Check, please!"

"But you haven't finished your drink," I say weakly.

"I can make us some at home. Besides, we're not putting you through this again. Not tonight at least," she replies.

I say a silent prayer of thanks when the server returns in under two minutes with our bill. Neha and I both put down our cards to split the cost, and shortly after, she returns with our receipts. We sign and begin to gather our things when I remember that Danny, Celine, and their anonymous friend are seated by the entrance, so there's no way we're getting out of here without having to either interact or look like assholes. Neha's noted this as well, so before we stand, she provides a game plan.

"Here's the deal," she says, with the confidence of a professional team captain. "We're going right up to their table and shooting the shit for no more than thirty seconds. We'll meet their hot friend and compliment Celine's outfit. Then, we're going to prance our fine selves out the door like we can't be bothered."

It goes *almost* just like that. Danny eyes me as we approach their table and I clock his head-to-toe appraisal. For an average height, I'm still leggy enough to give him a show in my low-heeled ankle boots and emerald-green romper.

Once we reach their table, Danny straightens, creating a sliver of distance between himself and Celine. He says my name in greeting and Celine's mouth opens wide as she brings a hand to her face. "That's right!" she exclaims. "You're the production assistant Danny told me about. Who's your friend?"

Danny introduces Neha next, explaining that we're all friends from college to the apparent delight of their tablemate, whose name we learn is Eric Kim. He introduces himself as the assistant director on *What Love Made*. Eric's got the warmest honey-colored eyes I've ever seen, an angular face, and a kind smile. He stands upon introduction, and I'm surprised by his height and strong build—a bit more muscly than Danny but equally appealing.

Eric shakes my hand with his right and cups my elbow with his left. He leans in for a kiss on the cheek, and I find myself sneaking a whiff of his crisp, clean scent. He does the same with Neha and she mouths *He's so fucking hot* at me over his shoulder.

Danny asks us if we'd like to join them, and Neha replies, *"Oh god, no,"* to which I cut in with "She's got morning rounds again and I've got to dive back into notes on your latest revision." I can feel the daggers aimed at me from Celine's pupils, but thankfully, she doesn't take the opportunity to say something petty.

Danny perks up when I mention his script and thanks me for all my hard work on the notes. I respond with an embarrassing "You betcha!" and then we say goodbye, bursting through the door like we've just escaped a time-share recruitment seminar.

chapter

11

T WO WEEKS PASS BEFORE I've fully neutralized the sting of the oyster bar run-in. It helps that in that time, preproduction has kicked into high gear, creating a welcome distraction from the image of Danny and Celine's PDA, which had been seared on the backs of my eyelids.

Now it's a bright and early Monday morning, and thirteen ergonomic chairs, each occupied by important crew and department heads, encircle a large cherry oak table at the center of WAP's main conference room. Today is the official "page turn" meeting for *What Love Made*. It's the first time the department heads on the production team will come together to begin crafting the plan that will turn Danny's vision for the screenplay into a cinematic work of art.

Bright sun rays pierce the conference room's floor-to-ceiling windows, creating an intense glare behind the crew members seated on the other side of the massive table. I lock eyes with Bella, my friendly usurper, who is seated by Danny's empty seat at the head of the table. She mouths the words *I'm sorry* and her doe eyes shine with remorse under furrowed brows. I shrug and offer a wilting smile. It's not her fault that I, lowly production assistant to the director's unit, have been exiled to a standalone chair in the corner of the room.

When I first walked in, Celine was off in a corner holding court with Jim Evans, his assistant, and two other creative execs at the studio. Their boisterous chatter filled the room even though they stood in a circle that was as exclusive and impenetrable as their ranks have always been. On instinct, I quickly scanned the room for a kind face, or at least someone I could make small talk with until the meeting began. When it was clear neither Danny nor Bella had arrived yet, I darted past Celine and Co. to find a seat for myself.

After setting down my notepad and script, I pulled out a chair near the far end of the conference table. I was just about to plop down when out of nowhere—

"Oh, you there!" Celine's crystal-clear voice stopped me in my tracks.

She made an exaggerated show of pointing to a plush accent chair in the corner of the room. "We've got you set up over here," she said with a smile.

Where there had been a light commotion of diffuse conversation taking place around us moments prior, the room now fell completely silent, all eyes on me. Like Tupac.

Fix your face girl flashed across my mind and I wished, not for the first time on the job, that I could disappear. With my expression schooled, I scooped up my things and beelined for a corner that could reasonably be labeled Time-Out if this were a second-grade classroom. I avoided Celine's eyes as she tracked my walk of shame, but still felt the heat from her stare as I went.

Since then, I've been sitting alone stewing as the rest of the crew files in at the main table. I check my watch when the door swings open and Danny finally walks in. He scans the room, and a buzzing sensation dances up my spine when his eyes lock with mine. His brows squish together in confusion, and I can sense a protest to the seating chart on the tip of his tongue when Celine quickly calls the meeting in session.

"Thank you all for joining us today as we embark on this incredible journey," she says, oscillating her megawatt smile over the table like a sprinkler system. "I am honored to serve as executive producer on this project and to be in service to all the immense talent in this room. Speaking of, without further ado, I'll pass the proverbial mic off to our director, Daniel Ellis Prescott."

I might have to wrestle a small army to keep from scoffing at her smarmy introduction. But despite myself, I've got to admit I kind of love having a close-up of Danny the Director again. It's been ages since I've seen him in his element, captaining his own ship. And now it's the big time. Bigger crew, and an even bigger budget. Just like we dreamed up back in film school.

Danny steps front and center and everyone else falls out of focus. Black, thick-rimmed glasses balance on the bridge of his nose where cinnamon-colored freckles disburse across his sand-colored cheeks. A lightweight, pale blue sweater clings to his strong arms and torso. He's pure, potential energy, like a ball set at the top of a hill just before it rolls. Danny doesn't really command everyone's attention so much as he draws it in from every corner of the room.

"Good morning, everyone," he says, absently tapping a pen to his palm. He purses his lips for a moment, looking lost in thought. "Give me just a second," he says before inexplicably darting from the room. He's back in a flash, pushing an office chair through the door and up to the main table. Next, he's motioning for everyone to make space. Celine's mouth twists as the other crew members scoot closer to free up a spot for the chair.

"Kaliya, will you join us please?" Danny asks. I'm stunned at what he's just done. My face heats, but I do what he says, scrambling to collect my things and take my new seat. I look over at Bella who's now beaming from ear to ear. I, on the other hand, want to sink into the floor.

"Okay, before we get started with intros," Danny says, returning his attention to the reason we're all here, "I want to thank you all for joining me on this deeply personal journey. We all know that a movie is never the product of one person's ambition. It is the realization of a collective dream out of a village of artists. So thank you for becoming my village."

The room lights up with applause, like he's just unveiled a mock-up of the latest iPhone. It's corny, but then again, I'm clapping, too.

The commotion dies quickly and Danny proceeds with the rest of his speech. "There's something else I want to say about this movie before we get started. I'm sure we all know by now that *What Love Made* is inspired by the true-life story of two of the most important people in my life. So I'm gonna go ahead and apologize to everybody now for when I get precious about the details as we go. But I can't let us forget that in the time period we're revisiting, my very existence as a biracial Black man would have been proof of a broken law. So I look at *What Love Made* as a tribute to those of us in the past and present who had the courage to love and live freely, even when the law said otherwise."

Danny pauses, and more claps erupt. Scanning the room, Bella is, of course, recording it all on her phone and Celine is wiping at invisible tears of admiration.

"And finally, I have the highest possible expectations and respect for the group of people around this table and am grateful to have each and every one of you along for the ride." Our eyes meet and then linger before he drags his away.

"With that said," Danny continues, "let's do a round of introductions. I'd like everybody to follow my lead. I'm Danny Prescott, director of *What Love Made*, and the best movie I haven't seen is *Citizen Kane*."

He doesn't look in my direction when he says it. Instead, he smiles to himself in a way that feels like it's meant for the two of us. I can't help the chuckle that escapes my throat next and sure enough, about a half dozen glances, including one very icy glare from Celine Michèle, make me want to send myself to actual time-out.

Danny's just lied to a room of people for my sake, and it feels like a secret nudge from him that says *I want you here. You belong.* I stifle a shudder when I can almost feel him whispering those words just an inch from my ear. Instantly, instead of listening to the others make their introductions, I'm lost again to the past.

One random rainy day in October of my freshman year and Danny's final one at NYU, he invited me over to help workshop *The Last Song*'s script. After a third pass over his latest draft, we binged Twizzlers to counteract the dulling effects of the cheap red wine we'd imbibed glass after glass of. And when we were too slaphappy to get any real work done, Danny brought out the copy of *Citizen Kane* he'd purchased from the Criterion Collection.

"It's time to pop your cherry," he said with a boyish gleam in his eye. In a brief lapse of understanding, I could have exploded with my enthusiastic consent had I not caught on to the innuendo a few seconds later.

Danny put the movie in his Blu-ray player, and we settled into the plush sofa in his West Village loft. About an hour in, the novelty of Orson Welles's groundbreaking deep focus cinematography had worn off and I was finding it hard to stay alert. My heavy head fell to Danny's shoulder. For months, we'd danced on the edge of the question: Are we friends or are we more? He moved his hand to cup the inside of my right knee, pulling me slightly closer, and instantly, I was wide-awake.

This from Danny, along with his attempted kiss at the entrance of my dorm after our first not-a-date, was another flashing green light indicator that he did in fact return the attraction that had been burning me up inside from the moment we met. Still, having never been kissed or even outright desired really, I was terrified of what stood on the other end of mutual attraction with a man like Danny.

To that point, romance was purely an ideal to me. Something to covet and ponder and pine for. But experiencing it, that was scary. Because after touching there was kissing, and after that, there was sex. I needed training wheels, and Danny was a space rocket.

But the tentative intimacy of his rhythmic touch on my leg felt too good for me to tell him to stop. It was also too terrifying for me to respond and then have it blow up in my face when he discovered that I, in fact, had no idea what I was doing.

So, I played it safe, feigning sleep for the remaining runtime of the film, lulled into absolute contentment by the repeated motion of his thumb drawing soft circles over the tender skin at the inside of my knee.

"Yoo-hoo! Over there!" Celine's shrill voice snaps me back to the present where of course everyone's looking my way, waiting for my introduction.

I shake away the not-so-distant memory of my first cuddle session with Danny, clear my throat, and speak. "Hi, everyone, I'm

Kaliya Wilson, production assistant on this project, and the best movie I haven't seen is *Funny Face*."

I've also lied to everybody else in the room. But to Danny, I've returned a secret gesture of reassurance. In my own way, I've just told him *I'm in this with you. I'm so proud of you.*

Danny smiles for a moment, again to himself. And surprisingly, he doesn't move right along with the meeting's agenda. He makes an unexpected detour instead.

"Kaliya and I go all the way back to film school in New York. She has a writer and producer credit on the thesis film that got me my agent, so it's a pleasure to be working with her again."

And as my insides commence an Olympic floor routine, First AD Eric Kim—aka hot best friend of oyster bar fame—instructs everyone to open their scripts.

WE ARE DEEP IN THE WEEDS OF NATHAN AND MINNIE'S LOVE story, covering a lot of ground with each passing scene. When we reach their first day at Maple Creek, Sherry Sampaio, our line producer, asks about the number of extras she should anticipate for the cafeteria scenes.

Gail Sussman, our lead costumer, spends a good amount of time discussing the middle school uniforms from that period and whether green or blue will pop best on-screen. That's when Oliver Ferretti, the director of photography, chimes in. He goes on to catalog in great detail his many qualms about shooting with natural light during the early fall.

Danny takes every single question directed his way in stride, giving detailed answers or deferring to the expertise of other members of the crew. It's like watching him conduct a symphony as he listens intently, responds thoughtfully, and even anticipates the wants and needs of his crew. It's such a far cry from the monotony of the reception desk that I could actually weep.

We've just reached the midway point in the script. Nathan and Minnie, now in high school, have shared their first kiss only to be caught by his parents. Mayor Orville Prescott and his wife, Catherine, threaten to have Minnie expelled from school if they find her anywhere near their son again. A pall settles over the room and Eric dismisses us for a break to grab lunch from the ornate crafty setup out on the terrace.

For the first two hours of the morning, I maintained a delicate balance of listening closely while taking copious notes. But it couldn't be helped that my eyes kept finding their way back to Danny. From time to time, he'd match my gaze like he was checking to make sure I was still in the room.

Now everyone's emptying out for the break and Celine's just bounced by, shoulder to shoulder with Jim Evans. This might be my only chance to check in with Danny.

I slowly approach as he's looking at a note over Eric's shoulder, careful of interrupting. Danny's eyes flick up to mine and drink me in. This look is how a girl's heart can so easily get tripped up on the enigmatic landscape of his world.

We speak at the same time, with my "How are you holding up?" crashing into his "I'm really glad you're here."

We laugh while Eric stands there eyeing us shrewdly, like we're at a murder mystery dinner and he's trying to guess which of us is the killer.

"Eric, you remember Kaliya from the other night," Danny says. "She's going to be working with us in the director's unit."

I extend my hand to him with a genuine smile on my face. "It's nice to see you again, Eric. I'm really excited to be working with you."

He takes my hand in both of his and shakes enthusiastically, warmly. I've decided he's good people. "The pleasure is mine, Kaliya. And I'm sorry about how the seating chart started out, by the way." He looks back with pity at my sad corner of the room and gives a slight shake of his head.

I wave a hand to brush it off. "I didn't mind," I say, hoping my cheerful tone will help squash the topic. "It was comfortable while it lasted."

Eric takes the hint, smiles and nods, and then excuses himself to go grab some lunch. Relieved I don't have to talk about it anymore, I turn to Danny, who's eyeing me intently.

"We *are* gonna talk about the elephant in the corner of the room," he says. "What was up with that?"

"First of all, I don't appreciate being called an elephant," I say, half joking, half exasperated. Still, it manages to pull out a soft chuckle from him and break some of the tension. "Second of all, this is a big day for you . . . let's not dwell on the minutiae."

I can tell it's really irking him that there's some clear hateration afoot and that it's at my expense. But sadly, I'm used to being cast aside, literally. He's not. He opens his mouth to press the issue and I raise my palm to stop him. "I'm serious, Danny. We're moving on. Now tell me, how does it feel to have the team together like this?"

Sighing, he accepts that I've changed the subject. "I won't lie, it's bittersweet," he says, scrubbing a hand through his short curls. "I guess I never really thought I'd get studio backing on this type of project. Or that we'd get the budget and marketing I always felt we deserved. But now . . ." He pauses, glancing around the well-appointed conference room. "I'm here with all these bells and whistles and it kinda feels like I gotta sing for my supper."

Hearing this from him catches me somewhat off guard. I guess

I figured with a father like Nathan Prescott, and all the early buzz about Danny's career, he'd be in his element at a place like WAP. But it all goes to show that even though his privilege has shielded him from a lot, at the end of the day, he's still a Black director. And not just any Black director, but one who's asking for big budgets and trying to turn out mainstream audiences.

Inclusion may be everyone's favorite buzzword nowadays, but in my experience, The Powers That Be often prefer the likes of us to be hypervisible while staying quietly content. It's just the sad reality of being a Black creative in Hollywood, I suppose. But if Danny's already feeling the pressure so early in the process, we're in for a long and bumpy ride.

I choose my response carefully. "With this kind of movie, Danny, you probably have to toe that company line a little bit to get what you want in the end. I mean, is WAP already giving you a hard time?"

He glances over his shoulder before leaning in close. I catch his scent and my eyes flutter closed reflexively.

"Mainly with editorial notes and casting," Danny says. "Jim wants final approval before the script gets locked. And that wouldn't be an issue, normally. But he's already tried to bring in a spec writer to 'freshen up' some of the scenes. Says he doesn't want to lean too far on the 'critical race theory' front."

"Danny, that's absurd," I blurt out, shocked more than surprised. Then, to avoid drawing attention I practically whisper, "This is a movie set in the Jim Crow South. What did he expect when he optioned it?"

"I think that man wants to have his cake and eat it, too," Danny whispers back. "He wants brownie points for being his corny version of 'woke' but doesn't want to ruffle any feathers in the process."

"Well, what does Celine have to say about all of this? Surely, she's running interference for you?" I ask. But something I said must have struck the wrong chord, because instead of answering me he deflects.

"Look, I'm sorry. I shouldn't be laying all this on you," he says. "It's fine. It will be fine. I just need to keep my head down and focus on my crew." It's almost like Danny's talking to himself more than me.

And before I can tell him that I understand his frustrations, and that the final film will make all the hoops he has to jump through worth it, Celine reappears. She saunters over to us, curling one spray tanned arm around Danny's waist before resting her other hand on his chest. For some reason, I expect to see him flinch from her touch but . . . no dice.

"Danny, babe, come get some lunch. We can't have you distracted for the second half." She sort of burrows herself into the nook between his arm and chest, looking up at him with pouty lips and fluttered lashes.

If looks could kill, she'd be laid out on the floor pulseless, and I'd be hightailing it out of here. I didn't miss the condescension aimed at Danny, either. He doesn't need to be reminded to eat in order to stay focused.

"I'll be out there soon. We're still catching up." Danny's voice changes when he speaks to her, becoming softer in a way. I hate that it irks me.

"Oh right! Your friend from college, how sweet!" Celine trains a cloying smile my way before extending a flaccid hand to me.

"Celine," she says, introducing herself to me needlessly, because it is in fact the third time we've met.

I venture toward her proffered hand slowly, as if approaching a yippy dog with tiny fangs. Our resulting handshake is like my annual pap exam, shockingly firm and slightly painful, but over in a flash.

"We've met." I smile stiffly as I pull back. "But it's nice to see you again. I love your show on The CW by the way. Primetime soaps are a guilty pleasure of mine." I don't think I meant that as an underhanded compliment, but I can't be too sure. It's true. I wouldn't cop to it on a dating app questionnaire, but I *do* watch the show.

Regardless, she looks like she just downed a gulp of spoiled milk, and I think Danny's stifling a chuckle.

"Well, we're just happy we finally found a place for you on this project. Danny's such a good person, always the first to help a friend in need." She pats his chest to punctuate her point. "It's why I'm around to make sure no one takes advantage of his kindness."

If I'm not nominated for a Nobel Peace Prize for the amount of restraint it takes to keep my eyes from rolling out of their sockets in response to that bs, then I'm calling foul on the whole establishment. And before Danny gets the chance to intervene in my and Celine's embarrassing standoff, I excuse myself to go partake of the craft services. I'm going to need a fortifying burrito if I'll ever get through these next three hours in the same room with this woman.

VIBRATIONS JOSTLE ME OUT of the first fragile moments of sleep. Groggy and disoriented, I shimmy my phone from beneath my pillow and swipe to answer before even checking the caller ID.

"Hey," I say, my voice sounding worse for wear.

"Did I wake you?" Instantly, I'm alert to the unmistakable sound of Danny's voice.

I cough to clear the roughness from my throat and smile despite myself. "A little bit. But that's okay. What's up?" I ask.

"So . . . Bella filled me in on what happened before I got to the production meeting," he says, getting straight to the point. "She's calling it chair-gate."

She would now, wouldn't she? I think but don't say. Bella wasn't in the room when I was banished to the corner by Celine, but I'd given her an earful when we got back to our shared cube. I probably should have known asking her not to say anything to The Boss would be a lost cause.

With Danny out of town for a week and my ego having mostly

snapped back, I thought we'd all moved past it. But if he's calling me this late from the East Coast, it definitely struck a nerve.

When seconds pass and I still haven't spoken, he says, "I wanted to tell you I'm sorry. That never should have happened."

I scoot up until I'm propped against my headboard. "One of these days," I say, "you're going to have to stop apologizing to me, Mr. Prescott."

"How about this," he replies. "I'll stop apologizing when I run out of things to apologize for."

"Well in that case, shouldn't it be your girlfriend who's calling to grovel?" I ask, mainly to tease, but also to pry.

His soft, deep laugh never fails to send shivers up my spine. "We talked and it won't happen again. I promise."

"I appreciate that," I say. "But you don't have to fight my battles, Danny. We're all adults."

"That may be true, but I do need to make sure the members of this crew are good to each other from the outset," he explains. "Petty stuff like that can undermine a production real quick. Besides, I feel like you've had enough of that kind of treatment without this job piling it on."

He's got a point there, which hits at something that's been irking me for a while now. But it's not like I can ask him outright, *What do you see in her anyway?* So, I tread lightly.

"Can I ask you something?"

"Shoot."

"How did you two meet?"

"I'll tell you, but you can't laugh," Danny replies. "It was one of those celebrity fundraiser volleyball tournaments that get put on for charity."

"Oh. My. God," I say, each word punctuated with a barely stifled chuckle. "I had no idea those were still . . . a thing."

Danny laughs to himself, breaking his own rule. "We were on the same team," he explains. "Going after a save when on the way down, she elbow-checked me smack-dab in my eye socket."

"Ouch!"

"Humbled, real quick," Danny says with a sigh.

"And let me guess," I add. "She brought you an ice pack, tended to your wounds, and from that moment on you were smitten."

"Something like that," Danny says, voice tapering off. "No. Actually," he corrects himself, "she kept playing like nothing happened. I didn't see her again until the after-party. That's where she asked me out to make up for the black eye. We saw each other casually off and on for about a year and things between us sort of grew from there."

"Sounds . . . romantic," I say, at a loss for anything else, kicking myself for taking us here. It's quiet for several long seconds as I waffle over whether I should say good night now, press further, or pick a new subject.

Danny chooses for us. "There's something else you want to know, isn't there?" he asks.

"Only if you want to tell me."

Danny sighs deeply and I hear something creak, like he's leaning back in a chair, settling in to explain himself. "Celine has a side that most people don't see," he says. "She's from eastern Kentucky. Family was unhoused off and on growing up. The woman came out here with nothing and had a shit time trying to carve a space for herself in the industry. But she did it, and in a big way. So, I have a lot of respect for the hustle."

"In that case, I can respect it, too," I relent. "I just wish things weren't so icy between us. Under different circumstances I'd like to think we'd have a lot in common."

"I know what I'm about to say is gonna sound trite, but if I were you, I wouldn't take it personally," Danny says. "Just do you, Kal. Don't let her get to you."

"Easy as that?" I ask, rhetorically, feeling the embers of my evergreen frustrations roar to life.

"It can be, if you want it to," he says, with that annoying brand of nonchalance you find attached to people who are far more acquainted with *easy* than I've ever been. I replace the words I'm holding back with a noncommittal *mm-hmm*, and Danny picks up on my irritation. "I'm missing something here," he says. "Tell me."

I roll my head on my shoulders and sit up straighter in bed. "I'm not like you, Danny," I say. "I'm not in a position to not take it personally when I'm repeatedly overlooked and disrespected by the people in positions to either help or hurt my career. It's a privilege to not care about how those in power perceive you and treat you. And as much as I desperately want to just show up and 'do me,' that's a privilege, too—another one I don't have."

After my mini speech I am met with silence. For a minute, I don't know if the connection dropped or if Danny's just quietly considering his response. When I can no longer stand the void I prompt him, "Say something, please."

"Honestly, I don't have anything to add or take away from that," he says softly. "I mean, I get it. I obviously have some blind spots. But I hear you. I see you, too."

I hear you. I see you. I let the words wash over me like rain after a drought. And now it's my turn to fail at finding words.

"But I should let you get back to sleep," he says, cutting into my quiet contemplation.

"Yeah. Right," I murmur. "It's late. I should go."

"Night, Kal."

"Good night, Danny."

I click end on the call and slump down in bed. Then, feeling overheated and overwhelmed, I kick the sheets off my body so the whirring ceiling fan can cool my skin. I'm wearing only an over-long camisole and feeling heightened sensations all over when the distant memory of the first time Danny really touched me takes over, fully eclipsing the more recent memories of his hands on Celine.

Flashbacks of how wild it felt to welcome the soft yet firm press of his lips on mine, the pressure of his strong fingers strok-ing and caressing, first tentative and then demanding. I'd never been touched like that before. It was like a lucid dream.

A pang of secondhand embarrassment for my younger self sends my hands up to cup my hot cheeks as I fight the dueling urge to grin like a schoolgirl and then cringe at how much of a novice I was back then.

But soon, hunger replaces embarrassment as my own hands retrace the path his took all those years ago, from the sides of my face down my neck and to my shoulders, circling around my back. I revel in the muscle memory of his touch roaming my body as he undulated his hips into mine. The sounds of our panting breaths and the reciprocated moans of pleasure and want. How it felt to have his weight pressed on top of me, our legs entwined, after months spent fantasizing about exactly that. The cocktail of emo-tions that overtook me in those moments. The worry there was no way it could feel as good for him as it felt for me. The excitement that it was finally happening. The fear that it would ever stop.

And my last thought before sleep takes over is how that fear eventually came true.

chapter

13

U H, YOU OKAY, BOSS?" Bella breaks the protracted silence that had been companionable, up until a few seconds ago when our driver whipped an inelegant U-turn in the middle of Sepulveda Boulevard.

Danny's still white-knuckling the steering wheel when he clears his throat in reply. "Er-herm. Fine. I'm fine," he insists with a slight wobble in his voice. "Why do you ask?"

"Well, I get that you're the strong silent type. But you haven't uttered a word in"—Bella checks her Apple Watch—"the whole half hour we've been in this car. Also, you're gripping the wheel like it's done something to offend you."

A soft chuckle puffs up from Danny's throat and from the back seat of his Range Rover, I notice a flush across his cheeks in the reflection of the rearview mirror. He relaxes his grip on the wheel, fanning his fingers out one by one before turning onto the residential street where Cowan Avenue Elementary is located on LA's Westside.

"My bad," Danny says. "Didn't mean to scare you. I just missed a turn." His eyes connect with mine in the mirror. "You okay back there?" he asks.

Now it's my turn to awkwardly clear my throat. "Um. Good! I'm great. That's what seat belts are for!"

Why on earth am I shouting?

I refrain from burying my head in my hands as his eyes turn back to the road. I haven't been able to shake the vivid dreams of Danny that plague me each night. And they've only gotten steamier since I finally gave in and let myself release the tension that's been gradually building. Juggling these nighttime fantasies with our daytime dynamic is like walking a tightrope with molten lava coursing below.

Ethically, I know he's not available. Intellectually, I'm not even sure I'd be down to wade through all our baggage if he was. But it's the physical and emotional parts of me, the parts that can't help but wonder *What if?* that I can't seem to coax into formation.

Bella swivels, eyeing me like I've sprouted branches. I ignore her, choosing instead to examine the frayed straps of my tote bag. She gestures between Danny and me before mouthing *What's with you two?*

I simply shrug, hoping she'll read the room and just drop it. Since the page turn a few weeks ago, I've noticed Bella clocking the charged moments between Danny and me, as if she's mentally filing them away until we reach some threshold at which point, she'll stop biting her tongue. Apparently, we haven't made it there yet because she turns back around without a word.

Danny throws the car in park, unbuckles, and breaks free into the early evening breeze. Bella hops out, too, and I hang back a second to collect myself. Something's off with Danny today. If I'm honest, something's been off with him for days.

I'd be a fool to think I still know him on a deep level. But once upon a time, I'd like to think I did. The vulnerabilities we gave each other glimpses of all those years ago now sit behind walls—locked away in a time capsule to the past. Even still, I've held on to those peeks beneath the surface—the things that made him tick and kept him up at night. Like watching him dream up a movie and then throw all he's got at making it. He'd curl in on himself, hiding his truths away so he could pour them into the project. The further along he'd get on the path from page to screen, the more internal he became.

I saw it firsthand during those final weeks leading up to the shoot of *The Last Song*. And these past few days have felt like an intense déjà vu. Today we've ventured out to scout locations for the middle school scenes in *What Love Made* and I'm pretty sure that's why Danny's on edge.

Years ago, on a tipsy midnight stroll across the Brooklyn Bridge—the kind of reckless activity that sounds like an adventure when you're still on your parents' insurance—we had one of those conversations that takes you from knowing someone to really *getting them* on a deeper level. I told him about my high school in Arkansas, how all the Black kids sat on one side of the cafeteria and the white kids sat on the other. How stifling it felt to be in a place where race was something no one openly talked about, but how it magically seemed to dictate absolutely everything: where you lived, who you dated, and even who your friends were.

He'd admitted that outside of school, he'd lived a charmed life. But having a famous director dad and a brilliant mom on Columbia's faculty hadn't saved him from being called an "Oreo" or a "half-breed" by the snobby kids at his Upper West Side prep school. He told me how he struggled to stay focused in class and how he barely passed from one grade to the next. By age twelve, his parents had put him in therapy. Afterward came the diagnoses and prescriptions. When it got really bad, his dad would pick him up from school and bring him to set where he'd get to shadow him and sometimes even share the privilege of calling "Action!"

I fell more in love with him in those moments alone in the cold darkness of that imposing bridge. Not just because he'd let me in on something that felt sacred, like showing a lover your body for the first time. But because it added depth to the picture I'd painted of him in my mind, like an elaborate movie set captured in deep focus. In that instant he was more real, more Danny.

A casual acquaintance may not catch on to how deeply personal the school scenes in Danny's script are to him. But I know they're the ones he's written and rewritten a dozen times, each time obsessing down to the microdetails, hoping to hit all the right notes that capture the emotional stakes for his mom and dad. After all, that first day at Maple Creek was the start of their love story.

By the time I hop out of the car, I find him standing there releasing a slow and measured breath. With his face turned up to the sky, the early evening sun casts streaks of gold across the dips and curves of his closed eyelids. He must sense my attention because he looks at me and I don't have time to glance away and pretend I wasn't staring.

"Lie to me," he says, smirking with his voice low so Bella doesn't hear. "Tell me it wasn't obvious I was freaking out for a minute back there."

Butterflies take flight inside me at this tiny, familiar glimpse of vulnerability. "You're good," I say, mirroring his smile. "Pretty sure Bella thinks you're just a reckless driver."

Speak of the devil, she rounds the front of the car to join us. "George is late. Isn't he supposed to lead this tour?" she asks all huffy.

Bella's referring to Danny's location manager, George Harris, who arranged this site visit with the school's superintendent. He'll be running the show, getting all the particulars from the staff. Danny didn't actually need to be here for this, but he'd insisted after George hit a snag with finance.

Since the night Danny fielded my curiosity about him and Celine, our texts and calls have remained annoyingly professional. The *Hey, can you take a look at this actor's latest project? I'm thinking of him for Nathan* or the *How distracting would it be if we don't film the flashbacks in Tennessee?* kind. The last one came after Jim and Celine balked at the costs of bankrolling a shoot on location in Tennessee. The discussions have been heated for weeks with the studio admonishing George to scout locally and save on travel costs—even though I'm sure the cost of transforming 2022 Westchester into 1966 Maple Creek will probably even things out.

The view from the school's parking lot all but confirms it. Cowan Avenue is flanked by towering palm trees with its central administration building surrounded by a series of mobile classrooms that fan out across a blacktop play yard. With the outdoor cafeteria and the air traffic from LAX buzzing overhead, this certainly feels like a lost cause.

My phone leaps in my tote bag. I reach in and swipe open the screen to a frantic text from George. "Change of plans, guys," I alert. "George's flight was rerouted to Burbank. He won't make it down in time and says we should go on without him."

I glance at Danny. He's scanning our surroundings, probably processing all the visual incongruities with the script. "This isn't Maple Creek," he mutters to himself, then to me and Bella, "Why would George send us here?"

"I think just maybe, he had your back with this one," I say. "Perhaps it's George's way of showing the execs it'll cost just as much to transform a place like this into Maple Creek as it would to aim for authenticity in Tennessee."

This scout is opposition research. I can see the moment it clicks for Danny, even though it clearly bothers him to have to jump through Jim and Celine's hoops.

"Oh, alright, let's get this over with," he relents.

Part of George's text explained that we're supposed to be meeting someone named Kelly inside at five o'clock. So we make our way across the lot. Entering through the main double doors of the school, we are instantly met with a lopsided banner: WELCOME TO CAREER WEEK.

An extremely flustered lady bounds out of a classroom. "Thank god you're here!" she practically shouts. In one hand, she's gripping a megaphone and in the other, she's got a hula hoop. "The Dance Troupe didn't show up. You're the movie crew, right?" she asks, to our utter confusion.

"Um, hello." Danny steps forward, mismatching her urgency by a mile. He extends his hand to the woman. "I'm Danny and my location manager, George Harris, called ahead to arrange our visit. We're just here for the tour."

"Well, I'm here for the health benefits," she says, shaking his proffered hand and steamrolling right over the rest. "Now, follow me and we'll get you all signed in."

Danny, Bella, and I share a three-way glance of bewilderment and then fall into lockstep with Ms.— "I'm sorry, ma'am, what's your name?" Bella asks, helpfully.

"Everyone calls me Ms. Kelly. So you can, too. I'm the director of our after-school program. It's for kids whose parents work late."

By the time she references kids, we've made it to her classroom entrance. Inside it's utter pandemonium. Ms. Kelly asks that we wait in the hallway before shuffling inside. Soon she returns with a clipboard. "Here you go," she says, looking to Danny. "Your friend George said his crew would talk to the kids for our career week programming in exchange for the tour," she explains. "So I need you all to sign in and get in there."

"Ma'am," I chime in. "George never told us that part. So what is it you actually need us to do?" I ask.

"You said you're a film crew, right?" she asks, sizing us up once again. The three of us confirm with a couple of yeses and hesitant nods. "Well, we've already had three groups cancel on the after-school program this week. Those kids in there won't admit it, but their hopes were up. It would mean a lot to them if you could re-gale us all with some cool stories about fake explosions and green screens and all that jazz. We just need you for half an hour, then you can have the tour."

Danny looks at me like I'm a lifeboat and I playfully pat his arm. "Come on. If I can sit through *Lawrence of Arabia* for four hours, you can do this for half of one. How bad can it be?"

Danny shrugs and takes the clipboard from Ms. Kelly. We all sign in before we enter the classroom. By the size of the kids, I'm guessing they're all between the ages of eight and eleven. They quiet down when they see us.

Ms. Kelly addresses the group. "All right, everyone! Let's show our special guests respect by first, listening. And then, asking what?" she prompts the class.

"Appropriate questions!" They all parrot back in their warbly pint-sized voices.

"That's right," Ms. Kelly approves. "Now, today we've got a spe-cial movie crew here to talk to you about filmmaking in Holly-wood," she continues. The room erupts into whoops and applause. I turn to Danny who's trying to fight the smile creeping across his face. Bella's over in the back of the class, no doubt taking pics for the 'gram.

We all make our introductions and then it's time for questions. Danny picks a little boy with carrot-colored hair and a face full of freckles in the front row. Poor dude has nearly dislodged his shoulder, his arm is up so high.

"Let's go with you, little man in the Hulk shirt," Danny says.

The kid stands and adjusts his shorts before asking proudly, "Can you show me how to punch someone in the face like they do in the movies?"

"Good question. But no, I absolutely cannot," Danny says flatly. "Who's next?"

The kid plops back down in his chair with a massive pout and I check my watch. It's only been two minutes.

chapter

14

W E DID OUR TIME. The hyped-up group peppered us with at least a hundred questions. Afterward, Ms. Kelly's teaching aides led the class out to the blacktop for playtime before pickup. Then the lead custodian, Marcus, started our tour as promised. We're almost done now, having reached the outdoor cafeteria that borders the playground.

The early evening sky is a watercolor dance of violent orange, hot pink, and muted lilac. A salted breeze off the not-so-distant ocean wraps its way around dozens of children in various stages of play. The setting might not work for our film, but it's no less cinematic.

We're about to make our goodbyes when a little boy, probably no older than eleven years old, scampers up to Danny with a basketball tucked under one arm. "Hey, mister! Those are some coooooool kicks!" His wide smile frames a set of perfectly bucked teeth.

"Uh, thanks, man," Danny replies. "Yours are pretty sweet, too."

I will not swoon at Danny being nice to a child. It's literally the bare minimum for common decency and we don't give brownie points for that.

"Thanks, but I like yours better. How much will you take for 'em?" The boy has boldly propositioned Danny, who, for a second, appears speechless.

"Dude, you can't afford those," Bella remarks flatly, busying herself with inserting an SD card into her camera.

I nudge an admonishing elbow into her side. "You can't say that to a kid!"

"What? They're a custom edition . . . the kid's dreaming if he thinks Danny's gonna come off those for his lunch money," she lobbies back.

Danny surprises me by kneeling down to address the boy at eye level. "What's your shoe size?" he asks.

"I'm an adult five," the boy mumbles. "But I'm still growing!" He beams up at Danny, and my heart melts a little.

"Okay, well, these probably won't fit you for at least a few more years. But I'll tell you what, I'll ask your teacher to share my contact info with your parents. Have them reach out to me when you're thirteen, and I'll mail them to you." Danny rises up to his full height, looking down at the kid with what I can only describe as affection. In return, the boy lights up like the star on a Christmas tree.

I repeat, *I will not swoon over Danny being kind to a child. It's the literal bare minimum of human decency and yet . . .*

Bella leans over and interrupts my thoughts by whispering, "Danny just promised that kid a pair of Jordans that run an easy fifteen-k."

"Holy shit!" It's out of me before I can reel it back.

"Ooooooooooh, Miss just said a bad word," a little girl with a round face and flopping pigtails pops up out of nowhere, causing me to jump and clasp on to Bella's shoulder to steady myself.

"Jesus," Bella groans, while snapping photos of the play yard, "this is like a haunted house. Little creatures popping up out of nowhere."

I turn to the little girl. "I'm sorry, you're right. I did say a bad word, but you can go back and play now." She eyes me suspiciously. I never said I was a natural with kids.

"We need a jumper!" she declares, undeterred as she eyes me up and down. "You'll do."

"A jumper, for what?" I ask, hackles rising.

"Double Dutch. Duh!" She holds up a set of rainbow-colored jumping ropes and nods back to her friend who stands a few yards away, pinning us with hopeful eyes.

"I'm sure we can find another friend out here who's up for it," I offer.

She looks at her friend, then back at me. "Nah. We want you. We're trying to break a record here and nobody else can do it. We tried."

I hesitate. When I was pint-sized and spunky like her, try as I might, I couldn't master the art of double Dutch. I've rolled my ankle three times trying and the embarrassment lingers. So, there's no way I'm injuring myself again on this blacktop for a child's entertainment. But after getting caught swearing, I need to let them down softly, lest they rat me out to Ms. Kelly. I hem and haw and before I can officially decline—

"Do it. You cussed, so make it up to them," Bella cuts in. I glare at her and she shrugs.

Then Danny, out of the blue, volunteers as tribute. "It's fine, I'll do it," he says flatly.

"You can't be serious, Danny. You were about to upchuck in

the parking lot and now you're like the fairy godfather of the playground." If nothing else can be said for Bella, it's that she keeps him humble.

Danny waves it off. "Recess was always my best subject," he says, winking at us then turning to the little girl and her friend, who's just joined us. "What do you say? Will I do?"

They look at each other and burst into giggles, nodding their heads then grabbing either end of the ropes and getting into position. Then they begin to throw the ropes. The familiar *thwack-thwack*, *thwack-thwack* sound of their circular motion triggers memories of all the times I looked on in jealousy at the kids with the confidence to just jump in and go for it. I'd been them once, and it had ended with a sprained ankle and a bruised tailbone. Never again.

Danny has removed the shoes that cost a year's worth of my share of rent and handed them to Bella to safeguard. Can't put creases in those. Bending his knees, he waits for an opening to lunge between the ropes. The girls start to chant when he successfully jumps in.

"Down down baby down by the rollercoaster . . ."

Danny's feet move with perfect precision, like Riverdance. I should have known that he'd be the Michael B. Jordan of double Dutch. A small crowd of children has gathered now, joining in the chorus and cheering him on.

To my sheer horror, Danny reaches out to me with the goofiest, most ecstatic, face-splitting grin. "Come on, Kal! Get in here!" he calls out to me, eyes lighting up expectantly. Like I'm the only thing missing to make the moment perfect.

". . . shimmy shimmy coco pop shimmy shimmy pow . . ."

"Come on, Miss! Look at him, he's lonely!" A tiny girl with a cherubic face and multicolored beads stacked at the bottom of her flying braids shouts at me. I turn back to Danny who is full-on pouting, laying it on thick. Still, he's not missing a beat with his footwork. The crowd surges around us.

"Mama mama sick in bed called the doctor and the doctor said . . ."

Call it sub-peer pressure, because I'm more than double their age, but suddenly it sinks in that it's now or never for me. And now is as good a time as ever to get rid of the double Dutch albatross around my neck.

I drop my tote bag and step forward trying not to focus on the surge of energy breaking out around us now that it's obvious I'm giving in and doing this. A light sheen of sweat has broken out across Danny's forehead as he continues to bring his knees up toward his chest in concert with the rhythm of the ropes. I blot out the memories of getting tangled up and falling on my face, ignoring the phantom pains where the scars on my knees serve as proof of it.

I've edged up to the side of the ropes now and bent my knees. I look up at Danny once more before taking the leap. "Just close your eyes and go for it," he encourages. "I've got you."

That's exactly what I do. And in a flash, my feet are moving to the beat of the chant.

". . . let's get the rhythm of the head—ding dong . . ."

The thwacking sound of the ropes whipping overhead and around us chart our rhythm. I open my eyes and connect with Danny, who's gazing intensely at me. He raises his hands, palms forward. "Put your hands on mine, we'll stay on beat this way."

I do as he says and the mini shock when our palms touch almost disturbs my footing. Steadying myself, I curl my fingers inward, entwining them with Danny's, and now I'm full-on clinging to him. I look over at Bella who, as expected, is capturing this all on her phone. I can only hope she's not broadcasting it live.

"... let's get the rhythm of the—hot dog . . ."

Around us an ever-expanding group of what must be every child on the play yard vibrates with collective excitement. They switch their little hips and stomp their miniature feet at the direction of the call and response rhyme. My heart, which had been racing in triple time, now beats in syncopation of the ropes. *Tick tack, tick tack.*

"What do you say we try a spin?" Danny suggests, like a maniac.

"Are you insane?" I panic.

"Jury's out on that." He chuckles, glowing now, sweaty and radiant.

His fearlessness. The crowd's merriment. It's all so contagious. For a moment, I feel weightless, like there's absolutely nothing in the way of me saying yes to spinning with him. Next thing I know, I'm grinning from ear to ear, nodding eagerly, surrendering.

Danny counts us down. "Okay, on my count we turn. One. Two. Thr—"

Suddenly we're facing opposite sides, and I can feel his back brushing up against mine as we keep pace with the beat of the ropes. It's exhilarating, triumphant. Until it's not.

"Shit!" My feet get tangled in the ropes. I go down and the crowd goes silent at yet another of my verbal transgressions.

From one moment to the next, my view of the impending pavement flips upside down to a picture of a riot-colored sky. I've been swept up from a downward trajectory. Strong arms bracket my back and legs, cradling me about a foot from the ground.

Danny's kneeling under me, bearing my weight, looking down,

breathing hard. He caught me. "Are you alright? Does anything hurt?"

"No. It's good. Um. I'm good. We're fine," I grind out, scrambling to get out of his hold and onto my own knees, embarrassed beyond words.

Bella rushes over, cell phone aloft. "Don't worry, guys, I ended the live before you went down. Before that, it was cute AF."

"Well, thank goodness for that," Danny mumbles, before hoisting me up until we're both on our feet.

I look down and notice his jeans are ripped, one knee bloodied. "Jesus, Danny. You're bleeding!"

He looks down, too, grimacing at his ripped clothes, and shrugs.

"Ms. Kelly's gonna flip," Bella says flatly.

And then from across the playground she appears, yelling at one of her aides. "I thought I told you to make sure no one got maimed!"

I step forward, hoping to diffuse the situation. "Ms. Kelly, is there a first aid kit nearby so we can get him cleaned up?"

She eyes me up and down, a look of abject disappointment. "Follow me." She turns to Danny. "Please don't sue us for this."

We look back at Bella who waves us off. "You two go on ahead, I'm gonna get some test shots of the exteriors and gym," she says. "Text me when you're cleaned up and I'll just meet you at the car."

⎯⎯⎯

MS. KELLY WALKS ME AND DANNY TO THE NURSE'S OFFICE. WE trail behind her a bit crestfallen, like two scolded kids on our way to see the principal. For a moment there, jumping between the ropes with Danny felt spectacular. Now it feels cautionary, like we've foolishly tried and failed to recapture the fleeting magic of days gone by.

Unlocking the door to the office and turning on the light, Ms. Kelly rummages through the cabinets in search of the first aid kit. "Now I'm going back outside to restore order on the play yard, which means I can't chaperone you two in here. So please behave yourselves." She eyes us knowingly. "Understood?"

"Yes, ma'am," we both answer in unison, nodding our assent.

She hands me the first aid kit and swiftly darts out of the room, leaving the two of us alone with our bruised knees and egos. We linger a moment in silence and then a spontaneous eruption of laughter rolls through us at the same time. Danny's clutching his stomach and I'm holding my chest as our laughs dissipate into sighs.

He looks at me with a bit of remorse. "Sorry, Kal. I shouldn't have egged you on."

"*Pfft*. It's not like you threatened me with bodily harm. Besides, I'm a big girl, I do what I want." I gently press on his shoulders, instructing him to hop up on the nurse's table. "Come on, up you go. Let me tend to your wounds."

He obliges and I pull up the nurse's stool so I can get a better look at his bloodied knee. "This would be easier without—"

"I'm not taking my pants off," Danny cuts in prematurely, his eyes a bit panicked.

"Woah! That's not where I was going with this." I huff, half offended, half shocked he'd think such a thing. "I was just about to suggest I cut away the fabric over the wound."

Instantly, the tension eases from his shoulders. "My bad, go ahead."

"Despite what Ms. Kelly thinks, your virtue is safe in here with me," I assure him.

He demurs, cupping the underside of his leg to give me better access to cut around the torn fabric at his knee. Desperate to dispel the image of a naked Danny on the table, I change the subject. "You were really good with those kids out there."

"You sound surprised," he says as I finish removing the tattered threads.

"I guess I assumed you'd hate being back at a place like this," I say.

"Oh, don't get me wrong. I still harbor a healthy fear of the American school system. Ah!" He hisses at the sting of the antiseptic I've just sprayed on his open wound. Gritting his teeth, he says, "But then, it hit me when that kid asked for my shoes. When you're that age, you have so little control over your circumstances. So much of your entire life is up to the grown-ups all around you."

"Kind of crazy that we're the grown-ups now," I say, while focusing on gently wiping away the debris in his cut with a piece of gauze.

"Exactly." Danny releases the tight hold on his knee, resting it back on the table. "I had a friend in sixth grade who got teased for wearing those same shoes Miles had on out there," he says.

I stop working on his knee for a second and look up at him. "Now in three years, he'll be the proud owner of shoes that cost as much as my car."

Danny playfully rolls his eyes. "My way of showing Miles that it's true what they say, it does get better," he says with a smirk.

"And to think, all I did was expose young impressionable ears to profanity and ruin their chances at a double Dutch record," I muse, pressing a bandage over his knee.

"Hey." Danny extends his hand as if to place it over mine, but pulls it back before making contact. "You made my bad day better."

"Oh, stop." I wheel back the stool and stand to toss the kit in the trash.

Behind me, Danny rises, too. "I'm serious, Kal. It's what you do."

"What? Fall on my face and injure the people around me?"

"Yes, that." He laughs. "But also, you take shitty things like this location scout, and good things, like my script, if I can say that— You take things as they are, and you make them better."

Danny's phone rings before I can formulate a response. He pulls it from his pocket and grimaces at the caller ID. "Can you give me a minute?" he asks. "I can meet you and Bella at the car."

Nodding, I quickly head for the door. Before I'm out of earshot, I recognize the voice on the other end of the line. It's Celine.

chapter

15

"EXCUSE ME, I THINK you dropped this."

The callout pierces through the fog of my loaded thoughts as I'm crossing the parking lot on my way into the office. Turning back, I find Eric, Danny's assistant director, aka the hot friend, walking my way.

Waving like I've just discovered my hand, I wait as he jogs up to me. Eric is taller than I remember, more built. And even though we've already met twice, something about him today just shines.

He approaches and standing close, he gazes down with honey-colored eyes. I get stuck on them a second too long before realizing he's holding my wallet in the palm of his hand. "Um, hi! And thank you," I force out. "Didn't realize I'd dropped something."

I reach for the wallet and his large palm grips mine like a warm blanket, reminiscent of when we first met a few weeks back at the oyster bar. There's a nervous energy sparking between the two of us and I don't know what to make of it. It's not *not* flirtatious and that feels a little like playing with fire.

"I assume we're headed to the same place?" Eric asks, interrupting my overthinking and glancing across the street toward WAP. I smile and nod and we head toward the crosswalk.

"You joining us at noon?" Eric asks, making small talk. He's referring to the casting meeting, which Danny didn't tell me about but Bella did. Two weeks ago, Danny and I had a moment, right after we debased ourselves on an elementary school playground. But I've hardly heard from him since.

"Um," I hesitate, embarrassed I haven't firmly established my place or exact purpose on this production crew yet. "I'm not sure I'm needed."

It's quiet and awkward for a beat or two when Eric speaks again. "You know, I used to be assistant to this big-time director—signed an NDA so I can't name names," he says with a humorous smirk that reveals the deep dimples in his cheeks.

"But let's just say they were an abject nightmare as a boss," he goes on. "Calls at four a.m. demanding I run to CVS for a very specific ballpoint pen that to this day, if I see one, I have the urge to snap it." We've made it to the crosswalk now and Eric presses the pedestrian button. I'm eager to see where this is all going.

"Anyway," Eric continues. "I walked away from that job with a lot of emotional wounds, a few material ones, and one very valuable lesson." He pauses for dramatic effect.

"I'm all ears," I say.

"That director was the kind of person who thought he didn't need *anyone* on his crew to make his masterpieces. But he needed all of us. He needed me to get those pens at four in the morning. Couldn't edit a script without them. And eventually, he needed me to run his sets as first AD."

Eric doesn't have to articulate the moral of the story for me to see it clear as day. Danny and Celine may not have told me about today's casting meeting. They may not even think they need me there. But I can show up and show them that they do.

We still don't have actors for our leads. With countless magazine profiles and scores of public interviews with Nathan Prescott available, finding the right match for him shouldn't be too difficult. But Minnie Prescott is a different story.

Weeks ago, I asked Danny if he'd ever consider sharing the archive of taped interviews of his mom with the production crew. He balked at the suggestion, having only shown them to me at that point. But then Jim started making a series of outlandish casting recommendations for her—kids of friends, people he owed favors. It lit a fire under Danny real quick.

"I've heard a lot of good things about you, Kaliya," Eric says, lifting me out of my heavy thoughts.

"I'm sure it's all been greatly exaggerated," I say.

"Doubtful," he counters. "Danny adores you, told me he wouldn't have gotten through his last year at NYU without you."

"It was a really long time ago," I mutter, hoping he won't pry further into our complicated past.

Eric knowing anything about how tough Danny's last year of college was is my first indication of how close they are now. But the more I think of it, they make sense as good friends. They're both charming in unpretentious ways. Not smarmy like so many of the equally good-looking Hollywood types I've run into. The guys who can hold a full conversation with their eyes glued to either their phones or your boobs. Eric and Danny are a rare breed— successful, attractive, *and* decent.

Eric opens the door to the office building, stepping back for me to enter ahead of him. We're jogging forward to catch a closing elevator when a voice calls out from behind us to hold the doors.

I'd recognize it anywhere.

I turn back and find Danny jogging to catch us while Eric presses firmly on DOOR OPEN. When Danny steps in, he and Eric clasp hands enthusiastically.

"Good to see you, man," Eric says, warmth filling out his voice.

"My guy!" Danny exclaims, leaning in and patting him on the back.

I have to admit, it's kind of cute watching them bro out together. Except now that they've finished, an awkward tension permeates the tight elevator compartment.

"So what? No Celine on your arm today?" Eric asks.

Danny's eyes briefly dart my way before returning to Eric. "Nah, man," he replies. "She came in early. Said something about a meeting with Jim on the budget."

"Ah," Eric says, a knowing look flashing across his face.

Either it's me or it's gotten very stuffy in this metal box and we're moving at the speed of cold molasses. We stop on the sixth floor and a few others join in, causing the three of us to shuffle positions with Eric on the far end, and Danny next to me. His arm is inches from mine and still, it feels like we're touching.

"Hey," he says, eyes forward on the doors.

"Hey," I say back. *Smooth, Kaliya. Real smooth.*

Briefly, I catch Eric's stare from across the crowded elevator with several bodies in the space between us. Next to me, Danny's posture remains rigid, his energy flaking off in waves of anxiety.

"You seem nervous." I state the obvious, trying to cut the tension.

A laugh sputters out of him, and like the end of a storm, I'm grateful for it. He leans over to whisper, "Do I?" There's a spark of recognition in his eyes as if to say, *You see me.*

"It's a big day," I say. "You're about to share your mom with the world and showing the crew your interviews with her is a first step in that."

He nods the slightest bit, gulping back some unknown emotion. My fingers itch to reach out and touch him. But I stifle it.

Once we make it to the eleventh floor and exit the elevator, I forge ahead to my cubicle. Danny and Eric follow behind, having struck up a conversation about the submissions for Minnie's part. But before they pass me by, Danny stops short, taps my desk, and says, "See you in the conference room a little later?"

It takes a second to register that he's inviting me to attend the casting meeting after all. I cough to clear my throat. "Uh. Of course. If you want me." I cough again. "I mean, if you want me *there*, that is?"

"I do," he answers, tightly. And I can see his walls, once again closing in.

"Well, I guess it's settled then," Eric cuts in, cheerily out of sync with the heaviness between Danny and me. "We'll see you in there, Kaliya."

The two of them head to Danny's office, leaving me to my emails.

I'M HEADING DOWN THE LONG HALLWAY TO THE TWELFTH floor conference room to join the casting meeting. The door, once ajar, slowly closes ahead and I pick up my pace. I arrive just in time to lay a hand flat on it to keep it from shutting. Gently, I push forward to signal to whoever's on the other side that someone's trying to come in. But there's resistance.

Celine's head pops through the crack. "We're good in here, Kaliya. Thank you," she says, attempting to once again shut me out.

"It's alright," Danny's voice rings out from behind her. "I asked her to join us for this part."

Replacing my hand on the back of the door to gingerly pry it open, I offer Celine a small shrug as if to say *Take it up with the director* before angling my shoulders through the sliver of space she's allowed between herself and the doorframe.

Inside the meeting room, it's a skeleton crew as expected—just Danny, Eric, Celine, and of course Bella, poised to take notes. Neatly arranged on the conference table is a carousel of actor headshots and resumes. Diego Verga, the casting director, has sent over a slew of stunning actresses, all gorgeously melanated with varying complexions and diverse hair textures—a refreshing sight to see for a lead role in a film of this caliber.

"Good to have you with us, Kaliya," Eric says, giving me a knowing look. "To catch you up, so far we've talked through the casting specs for Minnie Mitchell." He passes me a copy of the spec sheet. "As you can see laid out before us, we have a great pool to draw from. But Danny thought it would benefit our process if we screened some of his personal recordings with his mom before we got further along."

Looking over at Danny, I note his rigid posture. He doesn't speak before he hits play on "The Night Before."

THE SCREEN CUTS TO BLACK AND THE ROOM IS QUIET ENOUGH to hear a million ants march. Bella's discreetly wiping at her wet cheeks. It's my third viewing of Minnie recounting the night she spent preparing to go to school and how she navigated the dueling fear and expectations of her parents. And like each time before, now that it's over, there's a knot in my throat.

All eyes are now on Danny, whose downward gaze is fixed on some unspecified spot on the conference table. If we expected a speech, we're sorely disappointed when Danny clears his throat. "So what's our game plan?"

Eric takes the cue from his friend. "Well, we've narrowed the list down to the seven we have here and I think we should prioritize selecting three to bring in for screen tests. Then, once we have our Minnie, we can focus our search for Nathan and schedule some chemistry rea—"

"Oh, I doubt there will be the need for that, Eric." Celine cuts him off. "Didn't Danny tell you? We already have our Nathan."

At this, Danny's face tightens, but he doesn't object.

"Or at least we *will* have our Nathan whenever Max Crawford can find the time in his tour schedule for a meeting with me and Danny," Celine says, self-assured as ever.

Eric appears to be as confused as I feel. He, Bella, and I each turn toward Danny to get a read on him. "Celine's got her heart set on Max for Nathan," he confirms. But there's no conviction in his words. It's as if it's a battle he's already fought and lost.

It would be one thing if Danny felt strongly that Max was the best choice to play his father. But we're talking about an ex–boy bander turned solo artist who's just recently made the pivot into acting. Max has probably two films to his resume and his performances in each have been panned by critics. Granted, he's filled stadiums of screaming fans and graced the cover of *People* magazine numerous times. Even I added his latest hit, "Hot Like Sugar," to my workout playlist.

But a serious actor, the kid is not. Not yet, at least.

I wait for Danny to put up some sort of a fight here. But again, he gives us nothing. The room is silent for a beat, an undeclared stalemate with only the sound of Bella's wrist bangles clanging as she twists nervously in her chair.

Finally, Eric breaks the tension. "Oh-kay. Well then, looks like we'll need to flip the strategy around and schedule the chemistry reads first. Since we're anchoring our decision on Max."

I'm not so sure being allowed in the room means I'm also welcome to speak but screw it—I'm not here to be a seat filler. I clear my throat. "Might I make a suggestion?" I ask cautiously.

"Let's hear it," Danny says, taking me, and apparently Celine, by complete surprise.

Afraid I'll lose my nerve, I rush through my thought. "Why not consider bringing in three candidates for both roles? Have a sort of 'speed dating' version of a chemistry read?" I offer. "That way you can judge the different pairings side by side, mix and match even. Get a true sense of which pair is the best fit. Finding the right Minnie is just as important as Nathan."

"This isn't some reality TV dating show, Kaliya." Celine's sharp tone sucks the air out of the room. "Max brings the kind of buzz we're looking for, and he's being very selective with his projects. We can't insult him by putting him in a lineup. Let's be real."

"Actually, Celine," Danny chimes in, "I like Kaliya's idea."

Shocked again at his backing, I wonder briefly if I've played the role of a martyr for his cause here. Because if eyes were spears, I'd be impaled by Celine right now.

"Even if Max doesn't want to test for the part," he continues, "we'd be making sure we haven't overlooked anyone who could outperform him. If not, we simply move forward with confidence that Max is our guy and all's well that ends well."

Begrudgingly, Celine agrees. And with a decision made, the

meeting ends, and we disperse. I follow after Danny hoping I'll catch him in the hallway.

"Hey, Danny! Wait a second," I call out.

He stops without turning like he's bracing to face me. "Hey," he says, his voice flat. "What's up?"

"You didn't seem like yourself for a minute back there," I say, trying to read any emotion other than *tired* from him. "Everything okay?"

Danny shrugs. His face is expressionless, like a closed door. "Why wouldn't it be?" he asks with a slight edge.

Losing my nerve, I look away from him. "I don't know, I've just noticed a bit of a shift with you since just before the location scout. All that fire and passion you had for this project when you first pitched me on it—I just feel like it's getting sucked out of you."

Danny screws his eyes shut and exhales sharply. "Look, I appreciate the concern. But it's the last thing I want to talk about right now," he says. "That back there," he says, gesturing toward the conference room. "The tension. The back and forth. It's not helping, either."

Stung a little by what he's implying, I try to salvage this. "I get that bu—"

"No," he cuts me off, and I flinch. "If you really got it, then you'd know I don't have time for *this*," he says, gesturing between us.

Danny could have slapped me just now and somehow it would sting less. I swallow hard past the lump in my throat. He's harsh. But he's also right. I don't get whatever is going on with him right now. And even though I want to, it's clear he's not willing to open up and tell me.

"Noted," I reply, albeit a bit weakly. I gesture behind me with my thumb. "Um, I'm just going to go check in with Eric about coordinating that group casting session."

But before I go, he lightly pulls my arm. "Hey," he says. His energy is still strained, but the hot balloon of his frustration has deflated.

"Look, I know that was . . ." He falters. "Actually, I have no idea what that was. But it wasn't fair of me to take it out on you."

I give him a sharp nod, still feeling chafed by the interaction. "You've got a lot going on," I say. "So how about this, I'll stop prying, and you just let me know if you want to talk."

At my suggestion, he visibly relaxes. He looks as if he's going to say something else, but I turn to go before he can.

"I'll see you later," I say.

Then I walk away.

chapter

16

I T'S BELLA'S TWENTY-FIRST BIRTHDAY and, against my better
judgment, Neha and I are headed to a club in WeHo to help her
celebrate.

It took quite a bit of convincing.

She'd FaceTimed me while I was out running errands and
must have detected my lack of enthusiasm, because before I could
politely decline, she morphed into a lobbyist. *We've got tables in
VIP!* she'd said. *There will be bottle service. A roped-off bathroom.
Snacks! You love snacks!*

She drove a hard bargain. But with the live casting for our
movie happening tomorrow afternoon, and my general aversion
to loud, sweaty, crowded spaces, I still wasn't sold. Not until she
got all stern on me.

"Kaliya." Her mouth went into a hard line as she said my name.
"When's the last time you got tipsy and danced on a table? Let a
stranger with broad shoulders and strong hands grind up on you
on a dance floor?"

I took a minute to think back. Surely, it had been years. Maybe even since college.

"Right. That's what I thought," she cut in. "You are twenty-six, not eighty-five. Now, can I put your name on my list at the door, or should I just sign you up for AARP?"

"Okay, fine." I relented, a little bit mortified. "Can you put my roommate, Neha Thomas, down, too?"

That was three hours ago. Now, buoyed by Bella's shaming, Neha and I have squeezed into our shortest, tightest bandage dresses, and channeling our shenanigans of yore, we're taking shots of Fireball as we wait for an Uber.

"Holy hell, that shit's disgusting. Why did we make this our thing?" Neha asks the ceiling, as she recovers from coughing up a lung.

"*We* did not make this *our* thing. You did. And apparently, I'm a follower," I say, while perfecting the sharp wing tip of my liquid eyeliner.

"It's neither here nor there," Neha says. "Just promise me we'll stick to a one-to-one alcohol-to-water ratio. Otherwise we'll hate ourselves tomorrow."

I look down at my phone to check the notification that just came through before declaring "You got it, doc" with a salute. "Aaand our Uber's here. We've got to go."

I've spent most of the three hours since Bella's invite agonizing over whether or not Danny will show up at the club tonight. It sounds far-fetched, but Bella's not the type who'd give any amount of pause before inviting their boss to a birthday rager.

More than once I stopped short of outright asking her. Was he a complete tool after last week's casting? Sure. Am I attracted to tools? Historically, no. Not unless they vibrate. But for reasons I can't explain, this feeling that Danny and I are on the outs has been killing me. The worst part is that I know he's really struggling, but he won't let me in.

"What are you stewing on over there?" Neha asks, cheerfully cutting into my thoughts. "Tonight's supposed to be fun. Maybe I'll finally get to break the seal after Sam."

"That doesn't mean what I'm sure you think it means," I say.

"And that's fine because *you* know what I mean," she says, wiggling her eyebrows. "But what's got you in a mood?" she asks. "Tell me it's Danny."

"Do me a favor and try not to look so eager for me to be a complete mess over him, 'k?" I say, letting my head rest on the back of the seat.

"Not *a mess*, per se. I just figure, if you're thinking of him this much, it almost guarantees you he's doing the same. Remember, I saw him at the oyster bar." Neha's eyes narrow like she's replaying it in her mind. "Even with Celine draped all across his lap, she might as well have been the napkin on the table. The guy is tethered to you, K. You two are inevitable."

Inevitable. The word jars me, echoing around us like the Voice of God at a Broadway show. I sit with it in silence for a minute, sloshing it around in my head. Like a winter coat, I try it on for size. It would be perfect if not for a few not-so-minor flaws:

A: Danny's already in a relationship, and with his producer no less.

B: He's my ex, who broke my heart.

C: I report to him on a production job that I can't afford to screw up.

And now we have a perfect trifecta of *severely off-limits*. So it's settled, I cannot buy this coat. Even though it *speaks* to me, and I know that if I walk out of this pretend store without it, I'll always think about it. What adventures could we have had together? Would it become a staple in my wardrobe? Keep me warm in December?

We hit traffic on Sunset. Neha's moved on to swiping left on her phone, and I'm stuck on a self-assigned thought experiment that was triggered by the simple word *inevitable*. "I Want to Be Your Man" comes on the driver's playlist, which instantly evokes the iconic high school dance scene from *Love & Basketball*—a film about a love that takes more than a few tries to get right. One that never fails to bring back vivid memories of the night me and Danny shared our first kiss.

IT WAS TWO MONTHS AFTER DANNY HAD TAKEN ME TO SEE *Lawrence of Arabia* on what we'd later determine he'd, in fact, intended to be a date. He'd tried to kiss me that night when he dropped me off at my dorm and I'd shied away. Then he'd ghosted me for a week to deal with what I'd later find out was the death of his dad.

When he did return to the city, I was the first person he called. We spent the next few months in near constant company. On Mondays during our Language of Film class, we passed every midlecture break either workshopping the screenplay for his thesis film or gushing about the favorite movies we had in common and trading barbs about the ones we didn't. This quickly turned into scouting trips for locations where he could shoot his thesis film. Then there were weekend matinees and late-night texts filled with random musings about passing thoughts that reminded one of us of the other.

On a very cold evening in early December, we went to the Union Square Holiday Market in search of hot chocolate and peanut brittle. I had a hankering for the former and he'd never had the latter, which was a holiday staple at my grandparents' house.

I'd convinced him that roasted peanuts baked into narrow bricks of caramelized sugar would change his life, and he brought me there to find out.

DECEMBER 2014 . . .

"Our next movie night choice is yours, Kal," Danny says as we snake our way through the market booths. "I owe you after what I made you suffer through."

Warm puffs of his breath tickle my ear, and instantly, I perk up. For what feels like ages, I've been trying to convince Danny that romance movies are well worth his time. "Tell me you haven't seen *Love & Basketball*," I urge him.

"Nope. But I do like basketball, though," he says, with a sly smirk curving his lips.

I *pffft* so hard it startles an elderly lady shuffling past us with an artisan wreath. "You don't watch *Love & Basketball* for the basketball, Danny. The basketball is entirely secondary," I say, accepting his skepticism like a challenge I'm meant to overcome. "It's just a vehicle *for* the romance. Romance, quite literally, makes the world go 'round."

"If by *makes the world go 'round*, you mean, it's what drives the economy, then I can agree with you," Danny replies with a grin, clearly at peace with his logic.

To my dismay, his point reverberates with the explosion of Christmas around us. We are flanked by red-and-white striped tents, each strung with flocked garland and twinkle lights. Somewhere, a loudspeaker blares "This Christmas" by Donny Hathaway. Children with red cheeks and puffy coats are hoisted above the crowd, sitting high on their parents' shoulders. Smiling couples of all ages mill about with their arms linked. It's festive and, dare I say, *romantic*.

But Danny seems intent on popping my balloon. "Think about it," he goes on. "Holiday romance movies are what bankroll the rest of Hallmark's annual operation. You *think* it's all about the love, when it's really 'bout the Benjamins."

"With that attitude, you don't deserve *Love & Basketball*," I say. Danny laughs, causing my heart to sputter despite my frustration.

Two burly men stalk toward us in tandem carrying a massive fir tree on their shoulders. Danny protectively steps in front of me, drawing me into him with both hands on my arms to make room. We're so close, I can see myself reflected in his eyes.

"Don't let me ruin it for you," he says, staring down at me. He releases his hold when they finally pass. "You're just a little bit more pure than I am, I guess."

Lately, I've tried to dwell a little less on the gap of experience between us. Everything about Danny screams "ladies' man," and not in the sleazy way but in the quietly beautiful, disarmingly sensitive way that makes him so desirable. If I think too hard about all the ways we're different, him experienced and me "pure," I'd be a ball of anxiety whenever we're together. So, I mask how that word stings. But he reads me too well and rushes to smooth it over.

"It's one of my favorite things about you, Kal," he says, eyes going soft. "Besides, I'm all for whatever makes people feel good."

"Ugh! But it's not just a *feeling*," I say, my gloved hands briefly palming my face. "That's the most tired assumption about love." I point a finger at him scoldingly. "That it's just some abstract emotion that makes people be-clown themselves for the sake of returned affection."

Danny grins from ear to ear and at this point, I can't tell if I'm merely entertaining him or actually making sense.

"I'll bite," he says, humoring me. "If love's not a feeling, what is it?"

I am quick with my reply. "Well, for starters, it's a verb. You don't just *feel* love, it's a state of *being*. Like breathing. You don't think about it, you just do it. When you're in love with someone, it *changes* you."

We keep strolling in silence until I can't take it anymore. "What?" I ask, glancing up at him, hoping I haven't scared him off with all my *love* theories.

"Nothing, it's just, you've spent a lot of time thinking about all this," he replies distantly—as if floating away on a cloud of deep thought.

"Sometimes I feel like it's all I think about," I admit. *And other times I feel like you're all I think about,* I think, but don't say.

"Have you been in love?" he asks, surprising me enough to stop me in my tracks.

Suddenly mortified to admit I have practically zero experience with something I clearly feel so strongly about, I settle for the short answer. Because if love isn't what I've been doing, feeling, *being* ever since Danny Prescott walked into my life, then I clearly can't tell up from down.

"Yeah. Once," I say. "How about you?"

Our pace picks up again and Danny takes his time to answer while I wait. "For me, growing up with a front-row view of what my parents had," he starts, "I'd probably spend a lifetime looking and never find it. Don't get me wrong, I know what infatuation feels like, lust even. But Mom and Dad had something else."

He pauses and his mouth draws tight, a somber pall settling over him as he speaks. "But since we lost Dad, whenever I talk to my mom—I just can't imagine giving myself over to someone so completely when one day, I'll be gone or they'll be gone. Either way, one of us is left alone with the loss."

My hand twitches with an overwhelming desire to take his in mine and never let go. Most days, Danny's so good at keeping up the appearance of doing fine after his father's death. But then there are these moments when his quiet grief pierces through the facade like a passing cloud briefly darkening a blue sky.

Cautiously, I say, "Are you talking to someone about all of this?"

"Only you," he replies.

We keep walking through the market, and I get lost in a sea of concern for this boy I've fallen for madly, deeply.

Can he ever love me back?

We stumble upon a charming little booth, overflowing with tiny cellophane and red-ribbon-wrapped novelty candies. Danny grabs my hand and takes off in that direction. When we get there, he doesn't let go. He reaches down for a bag of what is unmistakably peanut brittle. He pays the vendor and hastily unties the ribbon, reaches in the bag, and then brandishes a small square of the brittle bark.

"To romance," he says, eyes sparkling like crystals in the night.

"To romance," I reply.

We both bite into the candy. Danny's eyes flutter shut and his head tips back with an almost primal groan of complete satisfaction.

"Oh my god. So good," he mumbles through chewing lips. Heat pierces through all my freezing layers as I watch him indulge. When Danny tips his face back into view, his eyes dance across mine with delight.

"Did it change your life?" I ask.

"Maybe," he replies, looking at me like I'm the thing he's been searching for all day and finally found underneath his nose.

I know what's coming next like I know my name. He drops the bag of brittle to the ground and buries both gloved hands into my wild curls. He pauses for a second, seeking permission with his eyes. I grant it, and then without further hesitation, he brings his lips to mine. Unsure of what to do with my own hands, I rest them on either side of his hips, bracing myself against him as I first timidly, then hungrily respond to the demand of his mouth on mine. It starts with repeated soft, tentative pecks. And I'm grateful for them because they allow me to adjust to this new sensation of someone else's lips on mine.

We melt into each other, mouths opening slightly, tongues cautiously meeting again and then again. The kiss is a roller coaster, total fear and pure exhilaration laced with the salty caramel and nutty richness of the candy. After endless seconds he pulls back, resting his forehead against mine. Our chests rise and fall, our breaths puffing out into the icy air.

"I told myself this morning I wasn't going another day without kissing you," Danny confesses with a ragged exhale.

I am ruined.

Danny takes my hand, bends down to pick up the dropped bag of candy, and we stride up Broadway toward my dorm, where my copy of *Love & Basketball* awaits us. And later on in the night when we're cuddled together watching Monica and Quincy's love story unfold, we press pause no less than four times to get lost in the intimacy of this new version of us.

NOW, MORE THAN SEVEN YEARS LATER, I SIT IN THIS UBER thinking back on what, at the time, was the most romantic night of my life. I see now what I was too *pure* to see then—what Danny had told me in no uncertain words. Love was pain to him, nothing more, nothing less. So the only thing *inevitable* about us was heartbreak.

chapter

17

OUR DRIVER DEPOSITS ME and Neha on the corner of La Cienega and Melrose. With our names on the VIP list, we quickly get past a line of slicked back, propped up, and bedazzled hopefuls. Once inside, we comb our way through a throng of bodies writhing beneath strobe lights and glittering chandeliers. The pulsing music forms an electric current that bounces off every surface, making them all come alive.

We head toward the back of the club where Bella's table is located in the exclusive VIP section. When we reach her group, bouncers check our wristbands and let us behind the velvet ropes where she and her friends are well on their way into blackout territory.

"Kaliyaaaaaaa!" she sings, lunging over a modular lounge piece to drape her arms around my neck.

"Happy Birthday!" I shout, mildly concerned about her in a way that says I might be too sober for this. I hand her a glittery pink gift bag. Inside it is a sparkling iPhone case with the title of her podcast, *Livin' the Dream*, etched onto it. It's not an extravagant gift, but it's one I felt suited her.

She gasps. "This is for me?" And when she pulls the case out of the bag, a genuine smile lights up her face. "Oh my god, I love it, K!" She moves to hug me again but loses her footing and falls back into the plush sectional where she quickly recovers.

"Okay, let's get her some water," Neha chimes in. Then she hooks her arm in mine. "And let's get us some shots."

With two lemon drops and two water towers down, Neha and I find ourselves shimmying on tables with Bella and the girls. Scantily clad bottle boys and girls cycle through periodically to re-up our stash, sometimes even pouring shots directly into our mouths. I can't imagine how, for a solid two years, we did this every weekend. Tonight alone is enough to send me into indefinite retirement.

Eventually, I start to slow down just as everyone around me, Neha included, begins to ramp up. Not accustomed to this level of alcohol intake, I start to feel fuzzy and loose enough to finally ask Bella what I've been avoiding all night.

"Did you invite Danny to this?" I lean across our table, my words sloshing as much as the drinks I've just disturbed.

Bella's scrolling feverishly through her phone. "Yep. Just got a text from him saying he'll be here in five," she says.

Suddenly, I'm sober again. All night, I have scanned the crowd, vainly hoping I'd find him pushing through toward us. I hadn't thought so far as to what I'd do when he got here, though.

"I knew it!" Bella shouts gleefully over the loud music, only slightly muffled by the drapes around our section. "No wonder you're both always forcing yourselves *not* to look at each other," she slurs with a bemused smirk on her face.

"What are you talking about? I just asked if he's coming. It was an innocent question!" I protest—maybe a little too much.

"The question, sure. But the look on your face when I said he was close? That was the same look I get when I see the waiter burst through the kitchen doors with a hot, steaming platter of my food," Bella says, with a stare that's drenched in accusation.

"Really? It's that obvious?" I ask, deflating.

"Is my hair pink?" she deadpans.

But before I can answer her rhetorical question, a song comes on that must be Bella's favorite because instantly, she's a woman possessed. Second wind unlocked. Bella jumps up, dragging me back toward the dance floor where Neha and the others are giving their best video girl impressions.

There's something freeing about losing yourself to a song on the dance floor of a nightclub. Surrounded by my girlfriends, all of us wearing too much makeup and too little clothing but feeling ourselves no less. I can't tell where the bass starts and my heart-beat stops but at some point they feel like one singular pulsing thing.

Somewhere along in the song I must have closed my eyes because when I open them, he's pushing through the crowd, heading straight toward me from about three bodies away. That heartbeat, the bass, the rhythm of the dance floor, all of it melts away.

"Don't stop on my account." Danny's eyes blaze down my body, taking in my LBD and strappy gold heels before returning to my face.

A bit breathless, both from dancing and from him, I state the obvious. "You're here."

"Against my better judgment," he says with a smirk tilting his mouth.

Someone jostles him from behind, pushing him forward. He steadies himself from falling into me by placing a hand on my hip, splaying it across the bone. The song changes to something slower, more rhythmic by Drake. Surprising me, Danny starts to move. Not out of the way, but with the music, and then with me because, like Simon Says, I start moving, too. We're moving together and against each other, like twin flames in a fire.

"I didn't know you dance," I say.

"There's a lot you don't know." He spins me now, my back to his front.

I *certainly* don't know what to do with this new positioning. I mean, I know *what* to do with it, but I also know I shouldn't. I have no idea what the status is with him and Celine, but I refuse to be the bitch who knowingly gives an attached man an erection on the dance floor. No matter how good it feels to have him pressed close behind me, his body heat sending chills across my skin.

Shutting off the sensory valve, I spin back to face him. It's safer this way. Except for how his eyes bore into me. And maybe it's liquid induced, but I shore up the courage to ask him outright, "What do you want from me, Danny?"

At that he stills, hands falling away from my hips. But he doesn't pull back. His eyes fall to my mouth, and for a second, I'm afraid he's going to kiss me. Not because I don't want him to, but because if he tries, I'll have to find the strength to stop him. But he doesn't kiss me. Doesn't answer my question, either. He just turns, leaving me there alone as he disappears into the crowd.

NEHA AND I LEARNED THE HARD WAY THAT WE MIGHT BE PAST our prime for *da club*. By midnight, she and I were ready to pack it in, but Bella and company convinced us to rally because *YOLO*.

So we stuck it out until about one in the morning when our can't-stop-won't-stop could and did.

Unfortunately, we'd long forgotten to adhere to the one-to-one shot-to-water-tower ratio Neha made me recite no less than five times on the ride over. As such, we severely overestimated the amount of liquid poison a liver in its mid to late twenties could metabolize. So it tracks that we spent the morning and early afternoon in flat recovery. That is, we only got up from bed for Postmates. Then we relocated to the couch, where I remained until one hour ago.

"I want to thank you all for being here today." Casting director Diego Verga addresses a group of actors handpicked to vie for the lead roles in *What Love Made*.

By some miracle, I made it to the casting session. Danny sits off to the side practically incognito with a beanie and a hoodie. I can't help but wonder if he, too, is suffering the aftereffects of last night's debauchery. He's quiet, contemplative, and flanked on either side by Celine and Eric.

Max Crawford didn't show. According to his agent, auditions are a waste of his time. But we have three other lesser-known actors who'll get paired with three up-and-coming actresses for the screen test. They're all seated in director's chairs beneath the bright lights of the stage.

"We're not just looking to see how you as individual artists connect with the material," Diego explains. "Because more than anything, we want to feel Nathan and Minnie Prescott's connection come alive here in this room."

Diego motions to Bella and she runs up a stack of scripts. "I'm handing you each a fresh copy of the sides and you'll have thirty minutes to rehearse the scenes. But before we get started, let's do a round of introductions."

We're in a black box theater in Diego's casting office and apart from the stage, it's dark in the room. Bella returns to join me in the back row where I'm nursing a piping-hot cup of coffee and a pounding migraine to boot.

"How are you feeling?" she whispers, sounding a little guilty for her part in my current distress.

"Like a doggy bag that was left in the back seat of a car," I answer. "But no one remembers because of olfactory fatigue."

I reach inside my purse and pop another Advil before chasing it with a swig of black coffee, not my typical sugary milky blend because I don't think even I could stomach that today. "I should be asking how *you're* feeling? Better yet, how are you standing?"

"I got up and hiked Runyon this morning," Bella brags, looking at me with what can only be described as pity. "But don't you worry, you're just out of practice. We'll get you there."

I suppress a shudder and return to my coffee. Bella and I have forged an alliance of sorts since that first day when she forced me onto TikTok. Together with Danny, we're like a dynamic little trio. She keeps him humble while I talk him off proverbial ledges when the studio tries to overstep his creative boundaries. I wonder if she saw us on the dance floor last night, and if she did, would she remember?

Bella leans over to whisper. "You should probably take off your sunglasses, though. Someone's going to think you're hiding a black eye."

I roll my eyes and regret it when a surge of pain instantly smacks me in the middle of my forehead. "*Pfft!* Who would punch a face like mine?" I ask, rubbing at my temples.

"Celine, obviously," Bella says, with way too much ease for my liking. I feel like I've been splashed with cold water. Did Bella see me and Danny after all? Was Celine there, too? Have I wrecked a home?

"Tell me what you're not telling me," I demand of Bella. Then, in a panicked whisper, I ask, "Was Celine at the club last night?"

"No," Bella confirms. "But now I have a lot of questions." She eyes me suspiciously.

When I freeze without a follow-up, Bella adds more. "I considered inviting Celine but seeing as she and Danny broke up that would have just been weird. And obviously my loyalty is with him—"

She stops abruptly when my coffee goes down the wrong pipe and a hacking cough rises from my chest. Bella starts whacking me between my shoulder blades like I'm a rug on fire.

"Everything alright back there?" Eric calls from the front of the room. I've drawn the attention of everyone now and since I still can't catch a breath, I just give a big thumbs-up as if to say *Don't mind me! As you were!*

When I can breathe again, I straighten and put down the coffee. At what must look like two eight balls protruding from my eye sockets, Bella whisper-shouts, "Oh my gosh. You didn't know?"

Guilt washes over me like a deluge. It's settled, I've wrecked a home.

"Apparently it happened a month ago," she reveals. "I assumed you knew by now."

So . . . I *haven't* wrecked a home? "A month ago?" I ask.

If true, this means they broke up *before* the casting meeting that went up in flames and before the school visit even. No wonder they'd been so tense together at the casting meeting. But why on earth am I hearing about this from Bella and not Danny?

"Why didn't you say something at your party?" I whisper-shout right back.

"You can't really expect me to remember anything from last night," Bella mutters flatly.

"And since you're on the long list of reasons *why* they broke up," she continues, "I assumed you maybe already knew. Besides, you and Eric have been getting kind of flirty lately, so I figured it's all probably moot for you at this point."

If I could repeatedly bang my head against the wall without attracting stares of grave concern right now I would.

"Moot?" I ask in disbelief. "Nothing about what you've just said could *ever* be moot. And wait, how exactly do you know all of this?"

"I'm Danny's assistant," she says, tossing her long pink-blond hair behind her shoulder. "It's my job to be all up in his business."

The shades have now come off. I place a hand on my hip and cock my head to the side, looking at her expectantly. She gets the hint that now it's time to *spill*.

"Okay, so I've eavesdropped on a few of their lovers' spats, and surprisingly, they talk about you like . . . a lot," she casually admits.

I won't pretend that hearing this news doesn't make my belly flip over on itself with a whole lot of surprise and a tad bit of guilt. Despite Neha's best efforts, I never took her up on the offer to plot a romantic reconciliation between me and Danny. And despite my occasional indulgence of the *What if?* question, it was never my intention to actually break them up. But this new intel changes everything.

As my wheels are spinning, Bella shows mercy by launching into a full download. "So look," she whispers. "I think we all can observe that Celine and Danny are on opposite ends of the creative spectrum. Actors, locations, equipment, budgets . . . you name it, it's been an argument.

"To make matters worse, Celine always sides with Jim. But the nail in the coffin was when she confronted Danny about you and he admitted that the two of you don't just have a history, you have a *history*," Bella says, bracketing that last word with air quotes.

I fight the urge to face-palm. I asked Danny to keep the sordid details of our *history* under wraps from Celine. I knew it was no small thing to basically request that he lie by omission to his creative partner and girlfriend. But I wanted her to respect me—which, clearly, was never in the cards. Still, Danny honored my wishes, even if he did so begrudgingly. Now, it's backfired on both of us. Celine has hated me since day one. And with them broken up, their creative stalemate can only get worse.

"What happened after that?" I ask.

"Celine gave Danny an ultimatum—he could have you on his crew or her in his bed, but not both," Bella reveals. "And I gotta hand it to her, it was a good line."

Chills break out on my neck, then flames chase down my arms. How could I be so oblivious to all this drama? No wonder Danny's been so all over the place with me. "And what did he decide?"

"Well, you're here, aren't you?" Bella looks me up and down. "Anyway, there were a lot of expletives from Celine. She stormed out of his office. And that was basically it. At least the parts I heard. Things have seemed relatively calm ever since." She finishes with a shrug, as if she's just checked the weather app and informed me it's going to be hazy until noon. "Oh! And one more thing," she remembers. "Celine had a moving company come get her stuff from his house last week."

I'm floored. As in, my soul has disembarked my fleshly shell that now lays prostrate on the cold hard ground. It's entirely too much to process right now so I tell Bella I'll have more questions for her later. We return our focus to the front of the room.

chapter

18

DIEGO HAS FINISHED PREPPING the actors and the first two are on their marks. We have Naomi Ibe reading for the part of Minnie. She's stunning but in an understated, unassuming way—no makeup, natural hair, and glowy skin. I would seriously like to know her routine. Like the rest of the actors here today, Naomi has that look that says she's not like the rest of us—she belongs on a supersized screen.

Glancing down, I see her résumé reveals that she's played several guest parts on a few hit streaming series and has two indie features under her belt. She'll start by reading opposite David Pierce, whom I recognize from a supporting role in Chris Nolan's last war movie. Diego signals to the actors that he's ready for them to start, and moments later we're all transported.

```
INTERIOR—NEW YORK CITY, 1970

It's eight in the evening and Minnie's busy
preparing dinner in the kitchen of her and
```

Nathan's cramped apartment on the Lower East
Side of Manhattan. Nathan walks through the
door, home late from work on set in Midtown.
He's disheveled, face bruised, shirt ripped.
But he doesn't want Minnie to notice.

NATHAN:
Hey, baby. Smells good, whatever you've
got on the stove. Let me go wash up, and
I'll be right over in a second.

Minnie, having already received a phone call
from Nathan's boss, stops him before he can
head down the hall to the bathroom.

MINNIE:
Nathan! What on earth happened to your
shirt, your face?

NATHAN:
Nothing, just someone on set whose bark
was worse than his bite.

Nathan attempts to laugh it off, throw Minnie
off the scent of any trouble.

MINNIE:
Nathan, tell me you didn't get into a
fight at work today. I got a call from Mr.
Levy saying you're on probation, but he
wouldn't give me any details.

NATHAN:
(Slightly agitated)
Seems you already know the answer to
that question you just asked, honey.

MINNIE:
Was it that man that scowled at us when I
carried your lunch up there the other day?

Nathan doesn't reply; he releases a heavy
exhale, looks down.

MINNIE:
Nathan, you've got to stop this! You're
gonna get yourself hurt or worse!

NATHAN:
Dammit, Minnie, I can't just stand by and
let people talk about you like that.
Callin' us all kinds of names. It's
enough we have to deal with the stares
left and right every time I so much as
deign to take my wife out on a walk or
to the movies. If they're gonna be bold
enough to say that word to my face, then
I can be bold enough to make 'em wish
they hadn't.

MINNIE:
(Minnie turning away from Nathan,
shaking her head, balling her fists in

distress. More to herself she
says . . .)
You just don't get it!

NATHAN:
(Nathan lightly pulling at her elbow,
turning her around until they're
grasping hands, faces close.)
Don't get what, baby?

MINNIE:
Don't you think I see it, too? I spent
all my life judging every interaction
based on whether or not the other person
hated me 'cause of my skin color. I had
to learn early to read the cues, even the
subtle ones. And no matter the response
I'd keep my head down and press forward.
Not because I'm so strong and brave, but
because my life depends on me lettin'
things be. A reaction only gives 'em what
they want anyway. This is the life I led
'fore I even met you. But you, baby, when
you're not with me, you get to walk
around proud, own every room you enter.
It's not 'til I'm on your arm that
anybody looks at you like anything less
than a king. And yeah, every now and
then somebody's gonna be bold enough,
hateful enough, to say something to you.
Call you a "nigger lover" or sneer at me

like I'm trash. But your reaction's only
gonna give 'em a rise. Make 'em do
something stupid or dangerous. And then
where does that leave me?

Nathan's grown emotional now. He burrows his
head into Minnie's chest. She brings his face
up to meet her eyes. Tears well in his.

        MINNIE:
It leaves me without you.

        NATHAN:
   (Voice cracking)
But, baby, I'm your husband. I'm supposed
to defend you, to defend us.

        MINNIE:
But where does that leave us if I don't
have you?

END SCENE

WATCHING DANNY'S SCREENPLAY PERFORMED FOR THE FIRST
time breathes a whole new life into Minnie and Nathan. After living with these characters day and night for three months, they've
finally begun to feel like people to me. Especially in this scene,
which shows how Nathan and Minnie were just two kids fumbling their way through life the best they knew how, desperately
clinging to each other for some semblance of stability when every-

thing around them seemed like a threat. Barely eighteen and far away from home, it's a miracle they were able to make anything of themselves, let alone the beautiful life they had together.

For the next three hours, Diego auditions each actor pairing, swapping out different combos from time to time. They read through several scenes each, and by the end, it's apparent who the strongest of the bunch are. Naomi and David blew everyone out of the water, their chemistry and connection so vibrant and compelling, it's a wonder they never met before today.

When Diego wraps up the casting session, Bella heads to the front of the room to go grab all the lavalier mics and scripts from the actors, leaving me alone in the rear to finish up my notes. Before the actors clear out, Danny addresses them directly for the first time, thanking each one for their hard work. Diego informs everyone that he'll be in touch with their agents in the coming weeks.

The day has dragged. Even without the hangover, I'd feel worn down by the weight of the material. Not to mention the bomb that Bella dropped on me before we started. So, I head to the kitchen to make a cup of coffee for the short drive back to Los Feliz.

I FIND DANNY HUNCHED OVER THE TEA KETTLE IN THE CASTing office's tight galley kitchen. He looks up just as I'm about to turn and leave, stopping me in my tracks.

"Hey," I say softly, wishing I'd had more time to prepare for this.

Danny sets down the kettle and turns toward me. "Hey," he replies, arms crossed and his gaze landing anywhere but my face—like he, too, isn't ready to address the elephant in the room.

Vivid images of Saturday night play across my mind's eye—the two of us pressed close on the dance floor, creating friction against each other as the bass of the music pulsed between us. His hands, firm on my hips, pushing me away as much as pulling me closer, like he couldn't decide which part of himself to listen to. I have the sneaking suspicion he's since made his choice.

Without a plan in sight, given what I've learned today, I end up blurting out, "You disappeared last night. Just before I thought you were going to kiss me."

His eyes shut for a beat. "If I ever kissed you in a nightclub, you better believe I wouldn't be the only one sober."

His point is fair but still, I roll my eyes. He's really not one to judge right now. "Well, I wouldn't be the only one who's single," I shoot back. And it looks like the dart landed because Danny's posture goes slack.

He releases a ragged breath before admitting, "I should have told you we broke up, before I—"

"Before you came on to me on the dance floor?" I blurt out. "Yeah. You should have." We're standing a few feet apart in the tiny kitchen, the energy sparking between us now that we're no longer avoiding the obvious—that we're attracted to each other.

"I have been feeling *awful* about what I was so close to letting happen with you when I thought you were still with her," I admit. "Why wouldn't you tell me? Why did I have to find out from Bella? I mean, you could have at leas—"

"Because it was my shield," he blurts out, cutting me off. He begins to pace, his honey-and-lemon scent clutching me from all sides.

Confused, I press him further. "What does that mean?"

"It means I'm attracted to you, Kaliya. Of course I am. *That* never changed." He stops short with an agonized sigh that strips away any chance I'd be flattered by what he's just admitted.

"But just because I'm free to act on it now doesn't mean that I can. Or that I should," he goes on. "Saturday night I let my guard down with you and that was a mistake."

"A mistake?" I repeat, my voice rendered weak by the sting of the word. Perhaps I've been in total denial. All this time, it was easy to deny my feelings for Danny were anything more than nostalgia and attraction because he was taken, off-limits. So how is it possible that I'm feeling so gutted right now?

He must see the hurt in my eyes because his melt instantly, like two bright green stones turned into pools of regret—for which part of it, I'm not sure. He shakes his head. "I don't mean it like that. It's not *you* that's the mistake," he relents, and I feel a surge of ill-fated relief until he adds, "It's us and it's now."

Ouch. Surprising myself by how open I've left my heart to being crushed by this man, after everything and all this time, I can only let him finish.

"We've been down this road, you and me. And it didn't end well," he says. "Losing you back then at one of the lowest points of my life . . ." He falters for a second, eyes falling to the floor. "It took a long time to bounce back from that," he says.

His words are laced with pain and regret so deep, it catches me off guard. *I'm* supposed to be the injured party. The hurt one. The one who's had to find a way past the heartache. Meanwhile, he's out here thriving. The flashy director with his star on the rise, while I'm "the front desk girl" who can't catch a break.

"It may have taken you a long time, Danny. But—"

"Kaliya, can I have a minute?" I'm cut off from telling Danny that I have yet to bounce back from the way things ended with us, because Eric walks into the kitchen. And if it felt tiny before, it's a matchbox now.

"Hey, man," Danny says absently, having gone back to futzing with his tea mug.

Eric returns the greeting, but I don't register their small talk. I've kept my focus on Danny, searching for a sign that we're not done here yet. After a few long awkward seconds, when he still doesn't meet my eyes, it's obvious that the window of opportunity for a heart-to-heart is closed for now. He's basically just professionally distanced me, much like he did Celine. And if that's what he wants right now, I'm prepared to give it to him. So, I count my losses and stalk off to join Eric in the hallway.

"Everything okay back there?" he asks as we walk toward an empty office, both of us knowing the obvious answer is *Not really*. But pretending Danny and I were just debriefing about the casting feels safer than acknowledging the fact that we just blew the top off the capsule to our past.

"Yeah," I say, my voice hoarse. "I was just getting clarity on something."

Eric and I walk the rest of the way to his office in silence. Once inside, he closes the door just as I realize I have no idea why he's called me in.

"So, I'm sure you're wondering why I've asked you here," he says with a nervous smile.

"Please tell me Jim Evans or Gary Anders haven't sent you to fire me?" I ask.

Eric laughs and the funniest part is that he thinks I'm joking. "No, never!" he answers. "Actually, I've been wanting to ask you this for a while now."

I've never seen this nervous energy from him before, and immediately, I want to put him at ease. "Well, unless you're a cupcake, chances are I won't bite. So, shoot."

"Have dinner with me," he says before a heavy exhale.

"Dinner as in a *date*?" I ask, stunned.

"Yes, I'm asking you on a dinner *date* with me," Eric confirms, grinning wide, his teeth sparkling like a Crest ad.

I feel like I need to sit. If I googled the words *too much* I'm certain today's date would pop up. Maybe it's the headache from my hangover, or my exhaustion from the day, but before I can think too hard about Eric's offer, I find myself answering him. "Yes. I'd love to."

The moment the words are out of me, a surge of panic heats my face. But with the way Eric beams at me from across the room, I can't quite bring myself to regret this, yet.

IT'S SETTLED. I AM IN FOR ANOTHER NIGHT OF RUINED SLEEP as I lay awake in bed turning my talk with Danny over in my mind. Examining it from all angles, I fixate on the things he said and even more so, the things I didn't.

We've been down this road, you and me. It didn't end well.

To put it lightly is what I could have, *should have*, said in response. Because how could he say those words to me? As if I could forget. As if I wasn't there, in love for the first time and crushed by the sight of him with someone else.

I'm ashamed now to admit that for a fleeting moment, after Bella's download, I saw an opening for Danny and me to try again. Maybe not now, with the production underway and his breakup so fresh. But I didn't imagine that *almost* kiss on the dance floor. Or the look in his eyes when I found him in the kitchen today— like he couldn't trust himself to be alone with me. Just like I haven't imagined the way we still gravitate toward each other in a crowded room. Or the way I can practically hear his smile anytime we're on the phone.

But I have pushed everything beneath the surface. I have followed *his* lead, deferred to *his* avoidance. He accepted our past. So did I. He was unbothered. I tried to my best at that, too. But like always, the ball has been in his court. And he picked today, of all days, to finally talk about *us*. And not at all like our previous trips down memory lane where we stayed in the safe zones, just on the border of the hard stuff. This time he went right for the epicenter of our broken past.

Losing you back then at one of the lowest points of my life. It took a long time to bounce back from that.

You didn't just lose me, Danny, you pushed me away. If I could find a way to turn back time and scream the words, I would. But the truth is, that's only the tip of the iceberg.

If I told him the truth, if I really let it out, I'd tell him all the things I've rehearsed through inner dialogues with shower walls and bathroom mirrors. The things I've bored Neha to tears with on those drunken nights after terrible first dates, when the dullness of past hurts grew sharp around the edges.

That once I was in love with a boy who utterly and completely shattered my rose-colored glasses, and I came to terms with never having closure, never getting the chance to tell him how ruined I've been for other loves ever since. That I can accept I may have hurt him, too, but the simple truth is he hurt me first.

chapter

19

OUCH!" I YELP, JUMPING out of Neha's torturous clutches. As if my nerves weren't bad enough, at this rate I'll be calling Eric to cancel our date from the inside of a burn unit.

"Okay, for this to work you *really* cannot move," Neha warns.

I'm applying the final touches of my makeup while Neha's on her knees pressing the wrinkles out of the hem of my dress . . . with her flat iron. As in the tool she uses to straighten her hair. She's just burned my outer thigh for the third time in the past five minutes after insisting that this little life hack would be *quick and painless*—a lie on both accounts. With one fresh pass over the front of my skirt, she veers a centimeter too close to my tender parts. Since I refuse to waddle into the restaurant with a burnt vagina, I reach down to pull her up from the floor.

"Okay, I love you, but can you please get away from me with that thing?" I beg.

She breathes out her exasperation. "Alright fine, just take the whole dress off and I'll go over it with the steamer."

Relieved, I reach down to the hem of my slip dress and shimmy it up over myself before tossing it to Neha.

"How did you ever make it through this life without me?" She poses the question with a self-satisfied grin before disappearing down the hallway and singing along to "Drunk in Love" as it blasts from the Bluetooth speaker in her room.

"I ponder it daily," I deadpan after her, then turn back to the mirror and smile to myself.

I know how lucky I am to have someone like Neha around to help me primp before seeing me off on a date. I was so young when my mom left, and my grandmother was of the generation that was more likely to make sure I'd eaten *before* I went out than to help me with my makeup. *Can't be wolfish on a date and scare the man off, Kaliya*, she'd say.

I've heard so many horror stories about people who have to lock up their belongings from kleptos they found on Craigslist's roommate search and tales of so-called friends you can't trust around the person you're dating. But Neha and I struck gold early on with each other in college. I know she'll be here when I get back from my date, glass of wine in hand, ready for a download.

And even though going out with Eric throws a wrench in her plan to get me back with Danny—she really got her hopes up when I told her he was *technically* back on the market—she's being a good sport about it.

Neha returns with the steamer but lingers at the door to our bathroom, eyeing me suspiciously. And though I've long recovered from the body insecurities that wreaked havoc on my formative years, my mind still goes there, wondering what it is she could be gawking at. "What? Have I sprouted a third butt cheek only you can see?" I ask her, craning my neck to look at my backside.

"No," she answers. "But your choice of underwear is scream-ing: *If found, return to nearest convent.*"

I scoff because it's not like I'm wearing high-waisted period panties that could turn the perkiest apple bottom to a sagging flapjack. I've opted for a pair of modest but still cheeky black boy shorts. I twist a bit to look back at myself and see that my ass is more plum than peach but still, *not bad*. Since I'm pairing the panties with a solid black strapless bra that gives my B to C boobs just a smidge of that coveted lift and split I see all over TikTok, I'm rather pleased with myself. Because on the off chance Eric and I do end up venturing beneath each other's clothes tonight, I certainly don't want him to think I planned for sex.

"I'm going for the effortlessly sexy look. Can't lay all my cards out there this soon. Plus, I'm still not even sure what I want out of all this." I trail off as I rub a dollop of curl gel between my palms and muss it through my hair.

"You mean you haven't decided if you're doing this to make Danny jealous or because Eric is fine as hell and you want a glimpse at what becoming the future Mrs. Kim would be like?" Neha asks.

My face floods with heat. If only the answer were as simple as one or the other. But Neha's not asking for simple. She's asking for *honest*. So, I give her that.

"For years I have walked into that office practically begging someone to see me, to value *me*," I say to her reflection in the mir-ror. "And I know Eric is no one's participation trophy. That's not what I'm saying here. It's just . . . the man is a catch, and he looks at me like I'm one, too. So maybe I owe it to myself to see if there's something there?"

"Look, K," she says, stepping closer to me so that our arms

touch. "That question wasn't meant to stress you out. I just wanted to make sure you're thinking through the possibilities here, because some doors lock when they close."

She's talking about Danny, and how tonight's date with Eric could be a bell that can't be un-rung. And to what end? Am I attracted to Eric? Yes, after all, I have *seen* the man with my own two eyes. Is he charming, funny, talented? Yes. Have I also thought about what it might feel like to be felt up by him? Yes, again. Would I have agreed to a date with him if Danny *had* kissed me on the dance floor? The answer makes my stomach flip. Suddenly, I have the urge to call Eric and cancel. But when my phone jolts to life on the bathroom countertop, it's a text from him.

ERIC: I've been looking forward to seeing you all day.

"What can I say?" Neha peers over my shoulder at my phone. "The man has game."

Our eyes meet in the mirror, and she must sense the distress in mine when she quickly changes gears. "Look, scratch everything I've just said. You still have options here, K. You'll go out, have a nice meal, get to know the guy. If you're not head over heels for him by dessert, cut your losses and bounce. No harm. No foul."

This brings me in from the ledge. Releasing a slow breath, I turn to face her. "You're right. I can do this. It's dinner, not a mating ceremony."

She winks at me. "You're on fire by the way. If you both manage to keep it in your pants tonight, I'll volunteer to drop you off at the convent together."

She's not lying. I've done *the most* with tonight's look—tastefully so. My slinky purple dress stops midthigh, hanging off each shoulder and perfectly offsetting my rich brown complexion.

Exfoliated to the gods and slathered in cocoa butter, I even went to the trouble of booking a last-minute wax appointment. Which is to say I bought a tub of that microwavable goo at a nearby Rite Aid and went to town on my pits and parts. For final touches, I slick on some hot pink lipstick and pop in a pair of gold dangling earrings. Then, I slip on a pair of strappy heels, grab my mini trench and my clutch, and head for the door.

By now, Neha's sprawled on the sofa under a weighted blanket resting a bowl of buttery popcorn on her chest, gearing up to binge some TLC show on overpriced wedding dresses. For a hot second, the sharp urge to blow off this date, toss my heels, and stay in this safe haven we've created together almost wins.

She notices me idling at the door and calls out from her cocoon. "Don't worry, whenever you get back, I'll still be here with Randy and the bridezillas. Now go, go, don't keep the man waiting!"

"I'm counting on it. Save me some red." We air-five and I'm out the door.

THE UBER PULLS UP TO THE CURB ON CAHUENGA RIGHT IN front of Hollywood's Beauty & Essex restaurant—one of those trendy places where it helps to know someone to get the best table. Eric texted a minute ago to let me know he'd be waiting near the alley entrance. Lo and behold, when I exit the car, he's there looking like a six-foot Armani ad in a crisp black button-up with dark jeans and leather boots.

Sleeves rolled up a third of the way reveal corded forearms and a flashy watch. If I'm not mistaken, he's gotten a haircut, too. It's short on the sides and a bit floppy up top. Edgy, with a side of dreamy, it begs to be tugged. Even if I didn't know this from the conversations we've had at work, I could guess by his sun-kissed skin that he spends his mornings catching waves at Manhattan Beach.

We lock eyes and his face breaks into a wide smile. That any woman would be lucky to call this man hers crosses my mind as I walk toward him with open arms.

"You're beautiful," he says warmly, smiling down at me. It feels nice.

"You look amazing yourself" is my reply. It's true. He's gorgeous.

Eric leads me toward the entrance with his hand at my back before politely greeting the host who confirms our reservation. We're taken through the main dining room and seated at a cozy table on the upper terrace. The semiprivate, charming space is illumined by ivory candles with twinkle lights strung overhead. It's a cozy, sexy vibe, like what you'd find on a Google Images search for "perfect date night."

I slip out of my jacket before taking the seat that Eric has pulled out for me and his face gives away how affected he is by my dress. I won't pretend I'm not internally high-fiving myself at his reaction, either. The first-date jitters have now morphed into a simmering curiosity and an expectation that, if nothing else, we'll have a nice time.

"So, I have to admit," Eric starts off timidly. "Gosh, I can't believe I'm opening with this, but . . . I was so nervous to ask you out." The confession makes him blush.

"Really?" I ask. "You find me . . . intimidating?" I waggle my eyebrows, teasing him.

"No, it wasn't that," he says, laughing. "I mean, not that you aren't intimidating . . ." He trails off, as if curating his next words.

I lean in. "Please. I am all ears."

"I guess I'll just say it." He shakes his head with a self-deprecating smile, and now I'm back to being nervous. "I wasn't sure what to think of your history with Danny," he admits. When his friend's name passes his lips, it contorts them into part grimace, part smile.

A pit forms in my belly. My breathing shallows, and I feel sweat break out along my spine. I didn't realize we'd arrive *here* so quickly. If at all.

The server arrives at our table to gingerly place two tall glasses of ice water between us. I welcome the momentary distraction like an open window in a stuffy room. When she takes our drink order, Eric opts for vodka on the rocks with a twist of lime. I ask for a glass of pinot gris and instantly regret not saying *tequila, straight up*.

The server floats away leaving us alone to pick back up where we just awkwardly left things.

"So yeah, that part," I start rather ineloquently. "I'm guessing you spoke with Danny about this?" I gesture between the two of us.

"I did," he confirms, taking a gulp of water.

"And?"

Eric exhales sharply. "And he told me you were amazing, and he thought we'd be good together," he says in a very matter-of-fact way. And he lets it linger between us like an unmarked envelope—like it's up to me to decide what to do with it. A test of sorts, and one I can't imagine I'm going to pass.

"Oh." It's all I can manage in response. Then we sit in silence for a minute that feels more like an hour. This is going great.

"I'm sorry," he says. "I just made this really awkward, didn't I?" he asks, his cheeks deeply flushed.

"No. It's just, I didn't expect Danny to stake a claim or anything like that. I mean, college was forever ago, and he's made it clear he has no intention of—" I stop short, for fear I've already said too much. Because if I'm honest, I had hoped, clearly in vain, that Danny would feel even a tinge of jealousy at the prospect of me being pursued by someone else. The same way it ate at me to see him with Celine.

Eric sits, still and quiet as a statue, save for the deep line forming between his brows. Things have progressed from stilted to awkward and thankfully, the server returns with the alcohol. I take a small sip of my wine and let the tangy liquid cool my tongue, hoping it'll calm my nerves, too.

I'm about to change the subject, ask Eric about his morning surf session, where he's from, if he's an only child, anything *not* Danny related when he takes me by complete surprise, yet again. "You loved him," he says, out of the blue.

I almost spit out the wine.

It's not a question, and it freezes my swimming thoughts. Suddenly, when spoken so plainly, *love* feels too inadequate a term to describe the feelings I once harbored for Danny. But now that I've been made to think about it, I realize I didn't just love him, in the same way that I don't just love movies. Like movies, Danny was my passion. So, in that sense, I suspect I'll always feel *something* for him.

In the moments it takes me to form a response to Eric's emotional blitz, he seems to have already made up his mind as clarity dawns across his handsome features.

"You *love* him," he says. This time there's no *d*. And again, he's not asking.

"I mean, I wouldn't exactly use the term *love* in the present tense," I say, stumbling over my words and taking another sip of my wine. "But yes. I was in love with him once." It feels like a lie. Like saying I had a heartbeat once.

Eric remains quietly calm and eerily attentive, like a therapist whose talkative patient is on the cusp of discovering for herself what he's already diagnosed. Something about his patient presence lowers my guard, though. And apparently, it loosens my tongue, too.

"If I'm honest, I don't think I fully understand how I feel about Danny anymore," I tell Eric. *It crosses my mind now that I'll likely be a lost cause to anyone who pursues me until I do.*

"If you ask *him*, we'd be a mistake," I say. "To me that says we have a history, but definitely not a fut—" I pause, determined to stop oversharing. "I'm sorry. Let's change the subject. How's your drink?"

More beads of sweat have formed and this time they're at my temples. I wish I could blink and somehow disappear to a calm, quiet place where I happen to have my shit together.

Eric stares at his drink, untouched and covered in condensation as he finally responds. "I shouldn't have asked you on this date," he says. It's a whisper, directed at the table but loud enough for me to hear and admittedly, it stings. He looks up at me now and I can see in his eyes that there's no salvaging tonight.

"No, don't get me wrong, Kaliya," he says, surprisingly smiling. "I've only known you a few months and can see that you're an amazing woman, seriously smart, and freakishly insightful. Not to mention so beautiful it's hard to think straight when you're in the room."

Okay, stinging a little less now, but still.

"And I don't blame you at all for any lingering feelings you might have for Danny. First loves are hard to kick. It's just that what felt like a question to me before doesn't anymore," he says. "You and Danny are unfinished business. It's written all over your face right now. And if I'm honest, I've seen it in him, too. He just does his damnedest to push it below the surface. He's one of my closest friends and I never would have pursued you without his blessing. But still, I had a feeling, and maybe that's why I sprung that question on you like that. Which now feels like it was some sort of cruel trap. And for that I'm sorry, but . . . I never should have asked you out on this date. God, I feel like an idiot doing this to you."

I can't help the flicker of relief I feel at Eric's confession. I came into tonight thinking I was the only one questioning myself when it turns out, he was, too.

"Well, can we at least have a nice meal?" I ask. "I was really looking forward to the meatballs. We can go half. Or better yet, it's on me."

"Don't be silly." Eric waves off my suggestion. "Yes. Let's have dinner *on me*. I'm sorry I was so blunt. It's something I'm working on." He laughs at himself. "I am sure I'll kick myself tomorrow for torpedoing this so fast. I actually really wanted to impress you. But then we sat down and you look so beautiful . . . I just couldn't shake the feeling that maybe I was cutting in where I shouldn't be. I hope you'll forgive me?"

While I might have reason to be embarrassed with how this all turned out, or even offended by Eric's emotional pop quiz, I can recognize that he's in a precarious position, guarding his friendship as well as his feelings. I can also admit that had we both gone through the motions tonight and somehow ended up in bed together, we'd absolutely regret it in the morning. So I'm actually grateful for how this turned out.

Even if I'm still confused as hell.

"Yes," I say. "But only on two conditions."

Eric's kind smile seeps up to his eyes. "Anything."

"After dinner, we order dessert."

Eric nods with a laugh.

"And from here on out no more talk of Danny."

"I think we can manage that," he agrees.

We clink glasses and proceed to have a lovely dinner. And all the while, I'm patting myself on the back for choosing the boy shorts over the G-string.

chapter

20

NEHA WAS *THIS CLOSE* to crashing our dinner. Her repeated *are you alive* texts went unanswered, because apparently, I committed the cardinal sin of not charging my phone before heading out for a date.

You could have been in a ditch! she'd said when I walked through the door, and only a fully detailed recap of my tragic dinner could distract her. Now it's midnight, and instead of staying up to agonize about how awkward things are about to be at work with both Eric *and* Danny, I choose sleep.

Because sometimes, unconsciousness is the only remedy for a hot mess day like today.

In my room, I fish my charger out of my work bag and connect the device on the dresser. Then I collapse into bed, emotionally exhausted and raw. The sweet nothing of sleep begins to drag me under from the moment my head hits the pillow.

Ping!

The sound jolts me out of the lull. For some reason, instead of putting off until morning what's probably just another email from Celine about her displeasure with craft services, I climb out of bed and pad over to the dresser to check. I tap the screen and my heart leaps in my chest—an email from Danny Prescott with the subject "Confession . . ." pops up. Without thinking twice, I do what I always do for this man. I give him my full attention.

Date: Thursday, July 7, 2022
From: dprescott@me.com
To: KaliforniaDreamin@gmail.com
Subject: Confession . . .

Kal,

I owe you an explanation for a lot of things. But not kissing you on that dance floor and making you think we'd be a mistake are at the top of the list. Just after promising you a job and then not following through.

Clearly, I haven't been at my best when it comes to you, Kal. But when Eric called me tonight and told me he thought you might still feel something for me, even after everything I've put you through, it meant to me that I had one more shot to do right by you.

So, my confession . . . You know that feeling when a song comes on the radio that you haven't heard in years, and instantly, it's your favorite song all over again? That's you. You have been my favorite song all over again since the

moment I walked into WAP and saw you at that
reception desk.

I heard your voice before we locked eyes and, in that
moment, the seven years I'd spent wondering how you
were and what you were doing crashed down on me in
one fell swoop. It didn't help that you were so fucking
gorgeous, you made it hard to breathe.

I thought I could do this—get you back in my life and
keep all these feelings I have for you locked up in a box
that I could hide away in a corner. It worked for a while. I
made distance, set boundaries—stopped myself from
calling you at night. Took midday meetings on the other
side of town. I made peace with myself by deciding if
we couldn't work things out in the past, we'd be fools to
try again now.

But when I said as much to you after the casting, it felt
like the biggest lie I've ever told myself. Because when
all is said and done, you are perfect to me. And I am
ready to stop pretending that getting along fine will
suffice in the place of perfect. And that means I'd be a
fool not to try again with you. If you'll let me.

I know it's not fair that I'm dropping all this on you after
you've already gone out with Eric. But it would be even
worse, I think, if I kept holding back.

There are so many things that have to factor into you
even considering me, I know. But I'm asking you to

consider me anyway. Because on the dance floor when you asked me what I wanted from you, I wasn't ready to say it out loud. But I am now. My answer is everything.

Yours,
Danny

———

I SCROLL BACK UP TO READ IT AGAIN, AND AGAIN, UNTIL I'VE memorized every word. I imagine that somewhere some fourteen-year-old version of me is lying in bed staring wistfully up at the ceiling. All the "cool kids" are probably out necking in the parking lot after a football game. But she's at home dreaming of the day her own version of a Danny Prescott sends her a love letter like the one that's just appeared out of the ether and into my inbox.

She'll spend too many years pining after the boy to whom she feels invisible. She'll fall asleep at night with fantasies of being wanted and desired by him, and in the daytime watch him walk on by with his arm around someone else. And one day in the distant future but at precisely the right time, she'll find herself completely breathless at the words spilled out of him for her, embossed in electronic blue light . . . *you are perfect to me*.

And because she waited so long to see her own desire reflected back, she won't rush to satiate his thirst. She'll bask in the glow of his affection in private, keeping it to herself if only for a little while. Because when you've finally found what you've always wanted, that's when things get scary.

So, she'll go to sleep, and figure out the rest tomorrow.

chapter

21

I DIDN'T INTEND TO MAKE Danny sweat by leaving his email unanswered. But assessing how I felt about his confession with the fresh clarity afforded by a good night's sleep seemed like a good idea.

Last night, I dozed off to fantasies of the two of us, barely awake and barely dressed, alone in his kitchen at the break of dawn after a night of passionate fucking. I pictured us delirious, giddy, and famished. So as one does, we decided to make breakfast. I sat perched on the kitchen counter wearing only his old NYU T-shirt. He stood next to me facing the stove, clad only in gray sweats that hung low on his hips, barely clinging on beneath the taut, rippling expanse of his tanned torso.

As he whisked away at the golden yolks, the flex and release of his strong forearms became too much for me to resist. So naturally, I bent down from my elevated spot on the counter and playfully bit his shoulder. Then, I sucked his collarbone before pressing my open mouth into the curve of his neck. Eggs be damned, he turned off the burner, faced me, and stepped between my legs.

Then, he gripped the backs of my thighs and carried me over to the kitchen island where he proceeded to have me for breakfast instead.

So, it had been a *very* good night's sleep. It's morning now and I have checked my email a dozen times to make sure I didn't dream that up, too. And knowing it's all real makes me unsteady as each breath I take gets tripped up on my own frantic heartbeats. Today is another inflection point in the seemingly endless saga of me and Danny, and this time, I hope I know what I'm in for.

THE OFFICE IS A GHOST TOWN AS I WALK PAST EMPTY CUBIcles, listening for movement or voices across the open floor plan. It's a relief to be greeted by silence given my low aptitude for casual conversation at the moment.

I reach my desk and take a minute to settle in before fishing my phone out of my bag. Danny should arrive within the hour, and I think I've made him wait long enough for a response. So, I type out a text.

ME: I guess it's my turn to confess that I don't want to pretend I don't want you anymore, either.

The ping of his response comes mere seconds after I hit send.

SCHOOL DAZE: Come in here. Please.

My head snaps toward Danny's office where I find him standing in the doorway. He eyes me with an intensity that makes me feel like I'm already undressed. I hadn't considered the possibility he'd get here first, and it makes me wonder if he slept at all last night. Or, if he lay awake anxiously looking for a response that never came.

I get up and pass through empty aisles to meet him. Entering the private office, I close the door behind me. He's perched on the edge of his desk and I'm just inside the threshold. Tension crackles in the space between us as we stand apart, silently taking each other in. Danny's wearing a forest-green cashmere sweater that hangs elegantly from his strong arms and torso. The five-o'clock shadow from the weekend's casting session has grown into a low-profile beard. Without his hat I notice his hair is longer, too, with soft brushstrokes of cinnamon curls that tease the corners of his face.

For my part, I knew what I was doing this morning when I put on a slinky slip dress. The satiny golden yellow material perfectly accentuates my shape, hinting at the curves that mark the underside of my breasts and taper off at my waist, then veer wide at the angled slope of my hips. It's a sexy, dinner-date frock and I've dressed it down by throwing a cropped denim jacket on top. The thirst in Danny's eyes says the outfit is doing what I'd intended it to.

"Lock it," he says. Voice deep and thick, without pleasantries.

I do as he says and he's across the room and flush against me in seconds. Like canned heat, he's barely holding back the attraction we've both kept in check all these months since our surprise reunion.

But before this goes any further, I have to ask, "Were you drunk when you wrote it?"

"No. But two hours later when you still hadn't gotten back to me? Tipsy. Maybe." He shrugs and he's so close I can smell the icy mint of his breath.

"Do you regret any of it?" Another question I need answered before I show any more of my cards.

"Only the delivery," he says, his eyes intensely searching mine. "That it was an email and not in person. I needed you to know I was done fighting this and I hoped you could understand why I ever did."

I have rehearsed his reasons, memorized them even. Still, I deserve to look in his eyes and hear the words directly from him. "Tell me again," I practically beg.

Danny sucks in a breath and releases it slowly. He's so close our bodies touch, but maddeningly, he keeps his hands to himself.

"Basically, I'm an ass," he admits. "I didn't know where to put my feelings for you after all these years, and what that would mean now with an ex in the picture. When Celine and I broke up, I thought I had time to figure all my shit out. Then we almost kissed and I panicked at how fast it felt. But when it was clear you had other options . . ."

"When you're in the frame I don't see other options, Danny," I cut in. Impatient with waiting for him to touch me first, I wrap my arms around his waist, fitting us together like the pieces of a puzzle. His breath hitches and he cups my face. I get lost in his seafoam eyes, forgetting my next question, forgiving him without words.

Danny gently brings his forehead down to mine, and I still sense his restraint. "Tell me what you want, Kal. I'm ready to give you anything. Everything. Say the word and I—"

"I want this," I cut in, covering his heart with my hand. I tilt my head up to match his downward gaze. I slide my hand from the center of his chest down his abdomen and over his belt buckle. Brazenly, I graze my palm over the hard impression of his arousal, which pushes against the front of his jeans.

"And I want this, too." It's a declaration and a request.

A flare of relief heats his stare. "Jesus, Kal," he mutters, bringing his hands up from where they've been bracketing my hips to cup my jawline. His long fingers splay into the curls at the back of my neck and entangle there. I'm aching to kiss him when he opens his mouth to speak. "I've wanted to touch you like this for months, to see if your hair is still as soft as I remember."

For the briefest moment, I feel a pang in my chest and fight the urge to screw my eyes shut—to will away the hurt conjured by his mention of the past. Those months of falling for each other, and then how quickly we fell apart. Truth is, I didn't free-fall into love with Danny Prescott. I jumped headfirst and tumbled my way here. And even after all those cuts and bruises, I'm still falling, wondering if maybe this time we can land together.

Finally, Danny brings his soft, full mouth to mine. I open up to him willingly, welcoming the intrusion of his tongue with mine in a sensual embrace. We begin a tangled dance of frantic breathing and wet licks, my soft sighs and his guttural hums of satisfaction becoming an intimate score for our first kiss in seven years. Already, it feels like we're making love—something we've never truly done before.

Danny pins me to the door of his office firmly pressing his hips into mine. The delicious contrast of his hard, wild need pressed against my softness drives me wild. I lift one knee, hooking my ankle around the back of his leg, and his sense of control seems to snap. He brings his hands down to my ass and lifts me up, fusing his core to mine. Without hesitation, I wrap my legs around his waist, and he makes his way across the office to the sofa without breaking our connection.

Danny manages to ease us down to a sitting position with me straddling his lap and my body weight pressing him into the soft cushions of the couch. Now that we've found ourselves in this very suggestive position, with only thin layers of clothing between us,

I consider where we are and what we're doing. But only for a moment, because in the next one, I decide that I don't care. He said he'd give me everything and I'm prepared to take it.

"There are no boundaries with me, Danny," I manage to pant out in the brief seconds when our lips aren't locked. "You can touch me anywhere, everywhere. I want everything I can get from you."

That's when his final thread of restraint unravels and we're writhing rhythmically together. The friction of his hips thrusting up into the soft wet place where seemingly all my nerve endings culminate obliterates my inhibitions. I respond in kind by rolling my hips and the movement elicits what can only be described as a primal growl from deep within Danny's chest. Sexiest sound ever.

But then, he does the unthinkable.

He brings his hands up to my shoulders and gently pulls me back before saying, "Kaliya, baby, we have to stop."

"What? Why? What's wrong?" I feel like I've lost all ability to think. We were quite literally riding our way to ecstasy, and he just pulled the plug.

Danny's head falls back on the wall behind the sofa with a thud. Pinching the bridge of his nose, he lets out a heavy sigh. "Absolutely nothing is wrong," he says. "There's not a language in existence that can describe how badly I want you right now. But I'm not fucking you for the first time on a tiny sofa in this ridiculous place."

Realization dawns on me even if I can feel myself pouting. Between my legs I'm literally throbbing for release so badly it's painful. But I understand where he's coming from. Better we stop ourselves now than to give off the impression to our colleagues that something indecent happened here. Even though it very much did.

I pull up the sleeves on my denim jacket, which had slid down my shoulders, and the light brush of the fabric across my taut nipples almost sends me over the edge and into oblivion. I have to shake away thoughts of him sucking on the tips of my breasts through the thin fabric of my dress to keep from climaxing on his lap.

"Come to my house tonight," Danny says. "We can have dinner and you can stay the night." His smile counters my pout as his fingers draw soft circles on the small of my back. I take the briefest moment to say goodbye to images of Danny taking me on his desk, but then perk up at the thought of an intimate night together at his home.

"So, you're going to cook for me?" I bounce a little in his lap and he winces, no doubt relishing *and* cursing the sensation. With firm hands he grasps my hips and gently deposits me next to him on the sofa.

He brings my legs across his lap and while rubbing his calloused hands across my calves he turns to look directly at me. "I'm not just going to cook for you." He kisses my collarbone. "I'm going to pour you some wine." He kisses my neck and I whimper involuntarily as he continues his tantalizing assault on all my senses. "I'm going to make you dessert." He sucks briefly on my earlobe. "And then I'm going to taste you between your legs and everywhere else before taking you to my bed, where we'll fuck until we fall asleep."

I think I might have just squealed. But I can't be too sure, because he silences the sound by indulging me in one more openmouthed kiss. I don't know how long we spend making out before abruptly coming up for air when someone knocks loudly on the door. We scramble to our feet and quickly straighten out our clothes. Danny kisses me softly one more time before he crosses the room to open the door. I busy myself by shuffling papers on the desk.

And when he opens the door, of course Celine is on the other side of it. "What's going on here?" she asks, accusingly.

Danny's whole posture deflates. "How can I help you, Celine?" he asks. And I can't help but hope he's no longer sporting that erection.

"I have to hand it to you two," she says. "You held out for almost a whole month. Talk about self-control." She crosses her arms and leans against the doorframe, like she's relishing watching us squirm.

I have no intention of sticking around for whatever's about to go down between the exes. "I was actually just leaving," I say, brushing past Danny and out the door. I glance back briefly to meet his eyes, which burn with endless promises for tonight. I watch as he lets Celine in and I know it's going to be a long day at the office.

chapter

22

MY HEART THUDS AND stutters in my chest on the way back to my cubicle. For a moment, briefly suspended in time, I forgot people existed in the world outside Danny's office and the little bubble of intimacy we created inside it. Then entered Celine, literally, like a gut punch—a reminder that Danny and I are a far way off from sailing into the sunset.

A brief glance at the reflection on my desktop monitor reveals I am in no shape to just go on about my day as if I hadn't been writhing astride Danny on a love seat merely five minutes ago. To say I look a tad indecent right now would be an understatement. And how I feel can only be described with words like *radioactive* or *electrified*—given the way my nerve endings seem to singe with the residual sparks of a denied release.

If anything is certain right now, it's that productivity is currently out of the question. First, I'll need the discrete confines of a bathroom stall, where I can fall apart and collect myself in that order. Then, I'll need a mirror.

On weak legs, I take my waddle of shame all the way down the hall toward the restroom. On the way, it occurs to me that I am more turned on by what *didn't* happen with Danny than by all the other sexual *happenings* of my life. At twenty-six, I can count the number of satisfying experiences with an intimate partner on the fingers of one hand. I tend to get by on my own—with the help of some strong batteries and thoughts of how it once felt to be completely undone by my desire for another person.

Who knew Danny had all that in him? Don't get me wrong, he is fine with a capital F. But dirty talk? Didn't know he had it like that. His vibe had always leaned more toward *whispers sweet nothings while caressing you softly* than *rips off your panties and fucks you from behind against the wall*. But now I'm thinking maybe he's a little bit of both, which is the best kind of combo there is. Even though I'm not the timid virgin I was when we first hooked up, after twenty minutes of no-holds-barred passion with this man, I'm ready for life-altering, splitting-of-the-universe sex tonight.

At least I think I am.

Finally in the stall now, I breathe deeply and lean against the cool steel door. I want to laugh, jump, dance, scream, and cry all at once—like that scene from *Unfaithful* where Diane Lane falls apart on a public train after finally giving in to an illicit affair. But I stand still, breathing in and out through a rush of relief and anticipation, mixed with a few tiny stabbings of doubt.

Danny's email was a revelation of sorts. It's colored my whole memory of the time since we've reunited in a new shade. But it also raises more questions. Last night I may have been on too much of a high to analyze Danny's words, but now, after relearning what it feels like to be touched by him, it's all scarier somehow. More real. Danny Prescott wants me again. And he spoke as if he never stopped. If that's the case, why did I *feel* so unwanted?

Then there's the Celine of it all. If the state-of-play between the

two of us before could be described as tense, I wouldn't be surprised if she's packing a flamethrower the next time we cross
paths. But even on a most basic level, I get it. For months, she's
thought of me as a threat, not a teammate. And that was finally
confirmed today. Never to be outdone, she's probably working on
a plan to knock me down a few more pegs.

And she's not alone in this sea of hard feelings, either. She's
had full access to Danny's mind and body in ways I have yet to
claim. A pang of white-hot jealousy slices through me at the
thought. To picture them together in that way or imagine that up
until a few weeks ago, she was *his* . . .

Maybe this is why I've found it so hard to manifest, in the real
world, the kind of romance I've built up in my mind. It's the spec-
ter of the inevitable *ending*, the idea that I'd ever become the
dreaded ex-girlfriend that sends me back behind my walls.

There's something so desolate about the notion of fully inter-
twining your life with someone else's only to one day find out he's
moved on to the next. I think that all this time, the part of me
that's still broken from the dissolution of my and Danny's college
relationship has been afraid to let go and open back up to another
potential loss. Yet here I am, on the precipice of diving back in,
risking it all for the chance that maybe this time, it doesn't have to
end. After all, an HEA might be guaranteed in a romance novel,
but it's a crapshoot in the streets.

An abrupt *click* from the latch of the restroom door before it
whooshes open snaps me out of my existential crisis. Instantly, I'm
reminded that I'm at work and have actual things to accomplish
aside from pondering my romantic future. So, I spring into action
and get myself together in the stall.

I quickly exit then head to the sink to wash my hands and
check my reflection. And what I see is less glow and more glare:

my eyes are as wild as my hair and my already-full lips are notice-ably swollen from Danny's purposeful mouth. I wet a hand towel and run it under my eyes to catch the smudged liner. Then I finger through my mane of curls to add some intention to their shape, take one last glance and one deep breath, and venture back out into the open.

BACK AT MY CUBE, I FIND A TEXT FROM DANNY. MY CHEEKS hurt from smiling at seeing his new caller ID pop up on my screen. I changed it from *Sallie Mae* this morning after waking up to im-ages of the two of us in compromising positions emblazoned in my mind.

SCHOOL DAZE: I'm sorry we got interrupted . . .

SCHOOL DAZE: But we need to talk

I would wager a month's pay that when used in a sentence, in that order, the words *we*, *need*, *to*, and *talk* have never inspired any-thing but cyclical thoughts of dread. *The thing* to be talked about is hardly ever "good" news. If it were, they'd just tell you then, rather than leave you suspended in limbo, wondering what *the thing* is. Even so, I fight the urge to assume the worst, as I am wont to do. It's fine. Everything is fine. Still unconvinced, I tap out a reply.

ME: Can't wait to pick up where we left off tonight ;). You know where to find me xx.

Like canned heat, I sit anxiously staring at the three-dot bub-ble near the bottom of the screen. It bounces around for several seconds. Then, to my utter deflation, it disappears. Danny's left me on read and instead of being levelheaded and assuming he's just been tied up with work, true to form, I begin to catastrophize. Thoughts like *Maybe he's off somewhere with Celine hashing out their differences* flood in. *Or worse, they've already reconciled and are having make-up sex in his car. What if I was just the fluffer?*

I smack myself, figuratively, power up my desktop, and decide to get to work. Dozens of unread emails sit stacked in my inbox—a true sign that production is underway. I am fully at the halfway mark of my six-month stint as part of this production. The script is officially locked as of this week and that means all cylinders are firing on *What Love Made*. Eric is prepping the shooting schedule. Department heads are finishing crewing up their teams. Locations are being scouted. And casting for supporting roles, bit parts, and extras is underway.

Danny has set principal photography to begin in Tennessee in only six weeks. We'll shoot the rest in New York and do pickups and reshoots here on the back lot. In two weeks, Danny and Eric will travel down South to meet with George and his team who've scouted the big-ticket locales, like Maple Creek Middle School and our leads' family homes. That means Bella and I have a ton of work to do with prep and research.

I've just opened up Tennessee's location database for what feels like the one-millionth time when I *feel* more than hear someone approach me from behind. When a throat clears, the hairs on the back of my neck stand on end.

I turn slowly and find Celine with her sharp, pale shoulder leaning against the frosted glass wall of my cubicle. Her long legs are crossed at the ankle, toned arms folded across her chest. She's wearing a sneering smile—a *smeer*, I'd call it—on her face. It's unsettling enough to straighten my back as I brace for another unpleasant exchange.

"Need something, Celine?" I ask. My words are even, cautious, *knowing*.

Hers come fast and jagged as if they're meant to leave marks. "I'm not sure what it was that I walked in on earlier in Danny's office," she spits out. "But despite what I recently learned about your history, I'd *hoped* you would respect yourself enough to stay out of our relationship."

A chill goes through me when she refers to their *relationship* as if it isn't over.

"Danny's under a lot of stress," she continues. "The last thing he needs right now is an opportunistic rebound whose only purpose is to dist—"

"Enough," I say, raising a hand to stop her vitriol. "Look, Celine, my private life doesn't concern you. And neither does Danny's. Not anymore. Now, is there something *work related* I can do for you?"

Celine has pulled up to her full height now, looming over me as I remain seated at my desk. "Well, that's where you're mistaken, Kaliya." She tosses out my name like spoiled leftovers. "I've got one million dollars, of my own money mind you, invested in Danny's vision. And as his producer, anything that threatens the project is *literally* my business."

Unfortunately, she's not entirely off base. If I were in charge of a multimillion-dollar production, I'd be worried about drama on set with the director, too. But I'm not foolish enough to think she's merely confronting me in a professional capacity.

"Look, Celine, I'm not trying to mess up—"

"Oh, don't flatter yourself," she scoffs. "Danny will be fine at the end of this. So will I. But you?" She sucks her teeth and shrugs one shoulder dismissively. "Be careful is all I'll say."

It's not exactly a threat. But it kinda feels like one.

"Anyways," Celine pivots on a dime, "the real reason I came over is because Max Crawford got a break in his tour, so I need you to book two red-eyes to New York. First class. Make sense?"

Reeling from the whiplash of her gear switch, and with a monastic level of self-control, I manage to reply calmly. "It does," I say, with my voice barely above whisper.

She has the nerve to clap once sharply. "Great! I'll email you the other details shortly."

Then she spins around and glides away.

I HAVE STRESS EATEN TWO COMFORT MUFFINS IN THE TIME IT has taken to shake off the ick from Celine's drive-by scolding. To make matters worse, Bella is off with Danny at meetings on the Westside all day. So, I'm left to stew alone without a sounding board. My computer pings, interrupting my downward spiral. I peel my face from the desk to find an email from Celine—her travel requests. I click it open and wince at the length.

Date: Friday, July 8, 2022
From: celine@helloworld.com
To: Kaliya.Wilson@wideangle.com
Subject: Travel

Kaliya,

As mentioned, you're booking a last-minute trip to New York for me and a companion (see passenger names within). Everything I've outlined below is a must-have so please exercise attention to detail when booking. I trust you'll manage to forward all confirmations within the hour. Time is of the essence. Thx.

I might need another comfort muffin.

After summoning my eyeballs from the back of my head, I scroll and scroll and scroll down what looks to be a full-on dossier. It's possible Celine requires a higher level of maintenance than a public toilet. At least the busywork will be a proper distraction from all my overthinking. Booking her flights is first up on the to-do list.

2 tickets, first class, JetBlue. Lay flat seats. Red-eye. LAX -> JFK. LaGuardia is not an option. Other special considerations below . . .

- In-flight meals: vegan/gluten free options are critical and choice beverages are Perrier, brut champagne, and barrel aged scotch.
- By all means necessary, find a way to avoid a deplane at the gate. We simply won't have time to taxi with the other passengers.

At this point, I wonder why she didn't just charter a jet. But of course not, that would have actually *made sense.* Nevertheless, I'm on it. That'll be one Presidential tarmac deplaning upon arrival at JFK with a motor escort to the airport VIP lounge, coming right up!

I skim the next few bullets of fluff to find instructions for the car service.

- An SUV (with partition) is ideal but a luxury sedan (with partition) will do—as backup—and only after you've exhausted all other vendors for the SUV.

I briefly consider just calling in a favor from my college friend, Tina, who dropped out to tour as a backing vocalist for Katy Perry. Last I checked, her dad still drove a livery cab in Queens. I'd commit a petty crime to see Celine's face if he showed up. Maybe he'd even snap a pic. I wouldn't dare, but a girl can dream. Lodging is next.

- Premium suite at the Waldorf Astoria with freestanding tub and steam shower. Minibar well stocked with herbal teas and tonic. Room service on arrival. I'll send you our breakfast selections before we land.

I scroll past a few more paragraphs of personalized requests to find the passenger information she promised would be at the bottom. I can muddle my way through her laundry list of preferences later, but there will be no trip at all if I don't snag these flights.

I need to confirm each passenger's official name since I learned the hard way that in Hollywood, almost nobody goes by what's on their government ID. That's why it's no surprise when I see *Passenger 1* listed as—ASHLEY CELESTE MICHAELS. Naturally, her real name doesn't quite roll off the tongue like *Celine Michèle*. I'd revel a little more in the fakery if the next line didn't flood my veins with ice. Right beside *Passenger 2* and in a font that might as well be called "tragic sans" are the words: DANIEL ELLIS PRESCOTT.

Instantly, my skin weighs a thousand pounds. Danny and Celine are jetting off together. Tonight. To New York City. *Our* city.

Well fuck me. Except, that's apparently what's *not* happening tonight. I feel like I've been shot. This email might as well have been their wedding invitation, with the sign-off elegantly calligraphed in gold leaf: *In lieu of gifts, please kindly go fuck yourself.*

I have got to hand it to Celine. The girl is savage.

I scroll back up through the email to confirm, yep, she's requesting ONE suite at the Waldorf with a king bed no less. She's asked that I make sure there's a freestanding tub, which of course there is, it's a five-star hotel. Now, her intentions are crystal clear. She's warned me off Danny while offering a preview of how she plans to win him back. But in this case, I'm not just standing by to watch. I'm *assisting* her.

With shaky hands, I check my phone to see if I missed something, anything, from Danny. But it's in vain because aside from his last cryptic message, I have zilch. Not a smoke signal, not a carrier pigeon, not a veiled warning typed out in binary code. Just a vague, somewhat foreboding text followed by a disappearing thought bubble. A tragedy.

My chest draws tight as the air in the office seems to thin. I feel a horrifying urge to cry. Not only because Danny's being whisked away by his ex on the same day I *sort of* got him back, but because there's nothing I could do about it anyway. This is a work trip—appropriate, innocuous, and some might even say . . . necessary, given how soon we're set to go into production.

Despite the logic, my panic has no chill. But instead of melting down completely as Celine no doubt expects, I promptly book every aspect of the trip down to the finest detail. It takes me about just under an hour to execute each specific request and collect the confirmations. Once I've saved all the documents into a shared folder, I copy the link and paste it into an email with the note ENJOY YOUR TRIP! I hit send to both Celine *and* Danny, whom I cc'd on a whim because I am a chaos demon unfit to walk the streets.

Within five minutes, Danny's thought bubble reappears and then disappears. Then reappears again.

SCHOOL DAZE: Shit Kal, I was hoping we could speak about this. I need to head straight to LAX from my next meeting.

SCHOOL DAZE: I will call you later. Please answer.

At first, I come up blank for a response. Then I am momentarily blinded by a mental picture of the two of them tangled in those buttery Waldorf sheets, and my fingers start to fly.

ME: Don't bother, you jerk!

I delete it, smacking a palm to my forehead before trying a different approach.

ME: It's fine! Gonna be a scorcher though. Stay hydrated!

Nope. That won't do, either. But when I go to delete it, my finger slips and hits send. I'm thankful no one's around to hear me squeak in horror. Figuring it's time to put the phone down, I do just that and turn back to my computer. But when it starts vibrating across my desk, I jump.

Danny is calling.

I let it ring until it stops. When it does, I sit staring at the rectangular piece of glass and tin lying motionless on my desk—like a freshly defeated corpse, liable at any time to resurrect. Seconds later, it does.

But I want off this ride for the day. And I've got work to do. So I turn it off.

I spend the next hour battling myself, struggling to force the defeatist thoughts to the outer edges of my mind. To *compartmentalize*. Like I told Bella on our first day working together. It's the only way I'll get through the day's task list without becoming a blubbering mess.

I've just finished logging all the top takes from the chemistry read when, again, I sense someone behind me. I know it's him before I even turn around. And when I do, his face is set with deep lines, his eyes searching mine. My instinct is to be cold and hard, impenetrable in the face of yet another blindside. But Danny's gaze bores into me and my armor crumbles.

"Your flight?" I say. It's part question, part urging. I booked the thing, and checking my watch, he's cutting it close. He doesn't seem to care.

"Can we talk?" he asks, voice low but insistent. Reflexively, I look around to check for prying eyes. But our colleagues are all in various states of preoccupation, so I rise without speaking and follow Danny into his office.

Once inside, he closes the door behind us and for a second, I flash back several hours to him pressing me up against it as his rough hands traced up my thighs. I shake the image away. "Look, Danny, I know this trip with Celine is for work, but if what happened in here earlier today was just some kind of blip, you can spare me the expla—"

"No. Don't do that, Kaliya." His interruption catches me off guard. "Don't question what we did this morning, or what I said last night. Because I'm not. I meant every word. I want this," he says, gesturing between the two of us. "*Of course* I'm going to explain."

I'd come in here braced for another blow, expecting this to go a lot like our conversation in the mail room on the day of my botched resignation—with me in shambles and Danny coming up empty. But apparently, we've made progress. Because when Danny sits on the edge of his desk, raises his arms, and motions for me to fill them, I go willingly. I've spent too many years missing him not to. I walk forward, stepping between his legs and he circles my waist, resting his hands just above the curve of my butt.

"Okay," I say. "Tell me what's going on."

Danny exhales heavily, his cool breath tickling my face. "So, Max Crawford submitted an audition tape after all and turns out, he's not half bad. There's a gap in his schedule before the European leg of his tour and we've got this tiny window to meet him in New York."

Sighing, I sink farther into his embrace, absently worrying the collar of his sweater between my thumb and forefinger. "I'm guessing this is what she stopped by to tell you about this morning?"

He nods, then nestles into my neck.

Instantly, I'm electrified with want. But when I remember the Waldorf I pull back. "Okay. I get it. I do. It's just . . . you're staying at her hotel?"

He tips my chin up so I can read the sincerity in his eyes. "I already booked a separate room. And a separate flight for that matter. Celine and I were done long before either of us admitted it. Now, we're just business partners. I want this second chance for you and me, Kal. Can you trust me enough to try?"

Maybe it's because it feels so good, letting myself try *us* on for size. But I nod and then smile. He smiles, too. Then our smiles meet in a searing kiss that almost makes me forget that under all this relief, there's more than just a little fear there, too.

chapter
23

Y OU SHOULD HAVE BANGED him when you had the chance," Neha declares.

Since I've come clean about my tryst with Danny in his office—and everything that followed—my best friend has made it crystal clear where her priorities lie.

"Like in that one movie," Neha muses. "You know the one with the secretary who lets her baby-faced boss spank her and do all these naughty things after hours."

"You mean *Secretary*?" I ask.

She blinks at me. "That's what I said."

"No, I mean that's what the movie's called," I clarify. "You know, the one with Maggie Gyllenhaal and James Spader."

I search for a spark of recognition on Neha's face and then wonder if maybe she's referring to an actual porno. I shake my head. "Never mind that," I say. "And besides, with my luck, Celine would have snapped pics of us with our pants down and sold them to the highest bidder."

Neha's head dangles upside down, framed by the fluorescent V of her bright pink spandex-wrapped legs. We're in the backyard of our duplex, folded over like tortillas on yoga mats, trying to find a state of zen.

It's been a week since Danny flew across the country in the lap of luxury with his ex. He has yet to return. What was supposed to be an overnight work trip has turned into more of an open-ended absence. Of course Celine found ways to keep him sequestered on the East Coast with multiple "business" meetings and, more importantly, far away from me.

So far, it's working because we've barely had time to talk. He's not playing hard to get so much as he's been busier than a mall-Santa in December. Aside from a few texts each day of the *Good morning* and *Thinking of you* variety, there's barely been much to decode or obsess over.

"Trust me," I say to Neha, who is dismounting from a headstand. "If it were up to me, I'd have spread myself across Danny's desk and begged him to rock my world. But timing, place, The Universe: all of it conspired against us."

I rise up from child's pose on my mat to find Neha engrossed in something on her phone. "What's that look on your face? Another 'take me back please' text from Sam?" I ask.

"God no," she says, shuddering. "I blocked the motherfucker. Uh, uh, this . . . this is something you'll need to brace for." Neha grimaces, turning her phone counterclockwise as if looking from a different angle might change what's there.

"But maybe, you don't want to see it all," she says, worrying her lip between her teeth. "Ugh! I can't decide if this is one of those times where I should shield you from something potentially upsetting or show you because we don't keep secrets." She looks up at me, her eyes a swirl of indecision, any ounce of peace we'd achieved with our early evening yoga session dissipating into thin air.

"Well, let me help you out with that," I say, lunging for her phone. It's in my grasp before she can wrestle it back. She looks on with bated breath while I see what all the fuss is about.

At first, it takes a second to register what I'm looking at. Partly due to the glare from the sun and partly because the images are hard to compute. It was one thing to book Danny and Celine's trip, detail by explicit detail. But it's an entirely different thing to *see* it all in vivid color, captured by the paparazzi.

On autopilot, I thumb through a carousel of images of the two of them out and about in New York City looking very much like the Hollywood power couple the public still thinks they are.

"How did you get this?" I ask absently, fixated on their body language in the photos—how they seem to exist near and around each other with such familiarity and ease.

"I might have a Google alert set for Danny Prescott," Neha admits. I stare at her in blank disbelief. "You knew I was this way when you asked me to move in," she reminds me, and I can't refute it because it's true.

I dive back into the photos.

In the first set of images, clearly taken the day of their arrival, Danny and Celine are exiting the sleek black SUV I booked. They stroll into the Waldorf Astoria, with matching luggage no less. In another image, Danny's hand hovers at the small of Celine's back as they breeze through the hotel lobby. My chest tightens at the sight, and a vivid memory of the night at the oyster bar reappears. I know the feeling of his hand at my back—like a strong magnet hovering an inch away from its counterpart.

I've only made it to photo eight of twenty-seven and I know no good will come of me going further. But after teetering on the edge of indecision for a few seconds, I jump feetfirst down the rabbit hole.

I thumb through several more technically harmless, but still annoying, pap shots of the two of them out to dinner with boy-bander-turned-thespian Max Crawford. They're an impressive trio. Celine is effortlessly chic in her "clean girl" makeup and taut ponytail. She's in one of those shift dresses that looks expensive in the way that simple yet perfectly tailored garments tend to. Both Danny and Max are deliciously tall and full of sharp angles and planes. Together, they are The Pretty People—the ones who turn heads whenever they grace the outdoors.

Like a woman possessed, I keep swiping through each passing still frame of them sipping wine, fiddling with their salads, engrossed in conversation. I try to envision myself sitting in Celine's place at that table. After all the ways this industry has forced me to the margins, could I be so bubbly and seemingly carefree at a "business dinner" with industry heavyweights? Could I suppress the urge to rail against *the system* and simply play along as they talk shop from their respective perches of privilege? Could I fit into Danny's world now? Could I ever?

My swiping continues, as if I'll find the answer to all these questions somewhere in the gallery. Images of the dinner reveal what looks to be an intense conversation over a sumptuous meal. Danny speaks animatedly, hands waving. Celine beams across the candlelit table at him. Max appears to hang on to every word.

In the next series of images, they're all smiling broadly and clinking their glasses. I guess that means Celine got her way and Max got the part.

I reach the end of the gallery, photos twenty-five and -six. They show Danny and Celine idling at the curb outside the restaurant. Assuming they're waiting for their car service back to the Waldorf, I'm flooded with relief that nothing egregious appears to have happened. I promised Danny I'd work at trusting him before he left. But I'd be lying if I said I wasn't still waiting for the other shoe to drop.

I swipe once more to the final photo and a pit forms in my stomach. Danny and Celine are still on the curb, but now she's wearing his jacket. She looks up at him adoringly while he stares off into the distance, his expression unreadable on the grainy photo.

I feel like something that's been dropped and stepped on. It's not a kiss. They aren't holding hands. She's not straddling him with her tongue down his throat. But still, it feels wrong—like their breakup was just a figment of my silly imagination. On top of that, I can't reconcile this version of Celine who's having cozy dinners with Danny and wearing his jacket with the one who'd stop at nothing to make me feel small for the hell of it.

"I take it you got to the end?" Neha's cautious question cuts through the fog of my thoughts. Perhaps she registered my sharp intake of breath or the chills that have broken out across my skin. Meeting her eyes, I simply shrug as a single tear falls down my cheek.

"Oh, honey. It's just a jacket," she says. "It could be absolutely nothing."

I drop the phone and scrub my balmy hands down my face while shaking my head. "I know. It's fine," I insist, swatting at my ridiculous tears. "I just . . . I really hate it here," I say, referring to this all too familiar place of deep insecurity.

"Look, K. Why don't you just call the man and talk to him? You know, the part you skipped over last time," Neha says, invoking the faraway past. But before I can answer, her phone chimes from where I dropped it in the grass.

"Hold that thought. It's a delivery," she says, with a raised finger.

She hops up from the mat and races through the back door of

our apartment. Alone now with my thoughts, and with the evening sun setting the yard aglow, I fall onto my back and into savasana, close my eyes, and try to clear out all the mess in my head.

Minutes later, the soft crunch of Neha's feet disturbs the grass. Reluctantly, I peel myself off my mat and sit up with crossed legs. It's impossible to miss the enormous bouquet of pink peonies and peach tulips blocking her face.

"Tell me those aren't from who I think they're from." A chill climbs up my back as I wait for her to confirm.

"See for yourself!" She plops down in front of me and thrusts the vase into my hands.

I can only admire the fact that even though she's been burned, perhaps worse than I have, Neha's managed to hold on to that hopeless romanticism that brought us together back in college. In the end she just wants me to be happy, the same thing I want for her.

I reach down and pluck out the crisp white envelope wedged inside the bouquet. I open it and see words from my favorite Prince song.

Kal,

How can I get through days when I can't get through hours?

Yours, Danny

I don't know whether to swoon or to cry. I settle for thrusting the card toward Neha and burying my head in my hands.

She whistles after reading. "Well, if that doesn't inspire involuntary Kegels I don't know what will," she practically hoots.

"What am I supposed to *do* with this?" I groan.

"Um, well, you could start by picking up the phone and saying, I don't know, *Thanks for the flowers. I've finished spiraling in self-doubt, now let's bang*? Ooh! Maybe send him a picture with you holding the bouquet but strategically frame it so he can see your ass in the mirror behind you?"

"You really don't seem all that concerned about the fact that the man is out gallivanting with his ex in public," I say, flatly.

"Okay, that's a bit much. But hey," she says, jostling my knee. "It feels shitty, I get it. Just do yourself a favor and talk to him this time, please?"

"What's with you these last few months?" I ask, my confusion peaking at Neha's change of heart for the questionably reformed cheater. "Whatever happened to the Neha from college who offered to sneak into Danny's loft and glitter glue all his Jordans?"

"Meh." She shrugs. "I still hate that he's hurt you. But I'll never forget the look on his face the night you skipped his wrap party, and he came to our dorm looking for you. I turned him away because I knew it's what you wanted. But I saw that spark die in his eyes when it hit him that he wouldn't get the chance to make things right with you. And I don't know . . . it made me hope that maybe one day he would."

chapter

24

THE FLOWERS STARE AT me as I pace in my bedroom. My phone burns a hole in my hand, too, as my thumb hovers over his contact. When I press down and it starts to ring, he picks up too fast for me to duck and hide.

"Hi, you," he says, and I can hear his smile.

You'd think we hadn't spoken in a decade, not a week, by the way my heart sputters at the sound of his voice. "Hi," I say back. "I love the flowers. And the card."

"I didn't know if it was smooth or corny as hell." His timid laugh tugs on my heartstrings, making me wish we could both fully relax into whatever it is we're doing—without all the complicating factors closing in around us.

"Hate to break it to you but it's a little of both," I tease, trying my best to sound steadier than I feel.

He laughs again, and it's slightly less cautious this time, which helps to crack through the tension in my shoulders. "But mostly, I'm impressed you remembered my obsession with Prince," I say.

"What will it take for you to believe me when I say I remember everything about you, Kal?" he asks, and it turns me to jelly.

I sink back into my pillows and slam my eyes shut. Danny's doing it again, disarming me with his signature brand of unvarnished vulnerability. He's all the way on the other side of the country but he might as well be in this bed wrapped around me.

"Besides," he says, breaking the weighted silence, "how could I forget that night you dragged me out to karaoke with Neha? The way you tried matching Prince's falsetto. And then you dipped low with those sorry little pitchy bass notes. If I wanted to forget it—which I very much do not—I don't think I ever could."

I haven't forgotten, either. The night in question had been our first one out as an official *us.* We'd gone to dinner with Neha and Sam but he'd abruptly cut out early to head back up to Columbia to *study*, on a Friday night.

Understandably, Neha was a little tipsy and a lot upset. I figured karaoke would lift her spirits and Danny was game for whatever. Prince was only a small portion of my set list that evening. Neha and I performed an overly enthusiastic rendition of "Single Ladies," and I convinced Danny to join me for a rousing duet to "Un-Break My Heart."

It's probably the best night out I've ever had—back when a hangover didn't put me out of commission for a full twenty-four hours. It also didn't hurt that the night ended with my first non-self-induced orgasm, courtesy of Danny's hands and hips alone.

"That was a really good night," I say. But the words fall flat as I struggle to revel in sweet memories from our past when our present feels so complicated.

He calls me out on it, too. "What are you *not* saying right now?"

I wrestle the urge to deflect. Then, remembering Neha's advice to *just talk to him*, I decide to take the plunge. "I saw these photos online of you and Celine in New York and—"

"I can explain those," he says.

"They are self-explanatory," I cut in. "And that's the hard part for me. Because when *I* look at these pictures, I see you out at a pitch dinner with your producer . . . and maybe a moment or two of wayward chivalry with the jacket. But when anyone else looks at these photos, *they* see a Hollywood power couple being cute out in public. And I guess I'm just gonna have to figure out how to handle that . . . unless you two plan on releasing a statement on your 'conscious uncoupling' sometime soon?"

"I had my publicist draft one weeks ago," Danny says. "But Celine's team put it on ice and got the studio's PR people involved. They unanimously decided that making a statement now would not be in the best interest of the project—their words, not mine. They said it would direct the 'wrong kind of attention' to us."

"You would think Celine would kill for the press," I say flatly.

"You're not wrong. But she cares more about control. Take last night for example," he says. "I sure as hell wouldn't have been out on a curb with her wearing my jacket if I knew she called the paps on us."

My languishing hope begins to evaporate now that my darkest suspicion is all but confirmed—it's not the right time for us. "Do you think maybe we should press pause on whatever it is we're doing until the production is over?" I ask, chewing on my lip.

Danny makes a sharp intake of breath and silence stretches between us for a few long seconds. "We've been on pause for seven years," he says, finally.

"But what does this look like for us if we don't wait?" I ask, avoiding the pang in my chest at what he's just said. "Never going out in public because we might trigger a media firestorm? Going rogue of PR to expose what's basically an on-set love triangle? Then what? We become the next *Don't Worry Darling*?"

I don't even know what I'm suggesting we do instead. Like Danny, I don't want to deny what's between us any longer. But Nathan and Minnie's love story deserves a fair shot with the press, not the morbid attention of a five-car pileup. Or worse, to be dismissed as the product of a dumpster fire production.

Danny doesn't answer, a sign that the reality of our situation is sinking in with him, too.

"I think we both know you were right before when you said we shouldn't put our feelings above the project," I say. "Maybe it would be best if we kept our distance for now, at least with the personal stuff. And when the production's finished we can see where we are?"

"I feel like all I ever do is lose out on you." Danny's words are drenched in resignation.

I breathe in deeply and sink farther into my pillows, comforted only by the fact that this isn't letting go of a dream, just deferring it for a little while. "I'm not going anywhere, Danny," I tell him.

"Then neither am I," he says back.

We spend the next twenty minutes catching each other up on what's going on from our respective coasts. Danny confirms that Max Crawford will, in fact, be taking on the lead role of Nathan Prescott, even though David Pierce's audition at the chemistry read was objectively stronger. Half of me just wants to tell him to say *fuck it*, rip up his contract with Jim Evans and Celine, and go indie with his production. After all, why put your heart and soul into making something so deeply personal if you have to defer all the big decisions to the people holding the purse? I think he senses my misgivings when he says, "I know what you're probably thinking."

"What am I probably thinking?"

"He's rich. Why doesn't he just make the movie on his own terms then sell it at a festival?"

"You're right. That is what I'm thinking," I confirm. "So, why don't you?"

"I thought you'd never ask." He sighs. "Well, for starters, I'm not as rich as you might think. My dad set it up so that I can't touch the bulk of my inheritance until I'm thirty-five. And while I'm far from a *struggling artist*, I am nowhere near having enough to bankroll an entire feature-film production of this size while paying for union crews. I could take meetings all over, plead my case, and try to piece together the funding from multiple sources. But then I'd just have even more bosses telling me what to do. And since this is my first time directing a full-length film with my own original screenplay, I don't know, I guess I felt like I needed the weight of a respected studio behind me to give my parents' story the budget and exposure it deserves."

The argument makes more sense given the newer intel about his inheritance. But it still sounds more like a good problem to have than an actual hardship. "You know, I think your dad might have been onto something."

"How do you mean?" he asks.

"I think, while it might feel like some sort of arbitrary test right now, in his own way, your dad was setting you up to have a more fulfilling kind of success," I say. "Maybe he wanted you to see what it's like to have to weather the natural elements of the industry without a safety net like so many of us do. That way, once you *can* access the funds from your trust, you won't take the creative freedom that comes along with all that money and power for granted. Besides, look at what you've already accomplished *without* those resources. You're an Oscar-nominated director before thirty!

You've got a career that every film school kid would kill for. You're already making Nathan Prescott proud."

The line is quiet for several seconds, and if not for the sound of Danny's measured breathing, I'd think our signal dropped. "I've missed you so much, Kaliya," he says.

"I know, Danny. Me too."

chapter

25

"HEY, GUYS! WELCOME TO another episode of *Livin' the Dream*. I'm your girl Bella, and today we have some juicy topics to dive into."

I'm sitting, or lounging I should say, on a beanbag chair eating only "soft snacks," per Bella's orders. When she invited me to observe a recording of her now viral podcast *Livin' the Dream*, I expected her setup to be a bona fide audio production studio. Come to find out, she's house-sitting and conveniently, you can record a podcast anywhere—even a trippy penthouse in Century City.

After pressing pause on my and Danny's affair, I needed a distraction from doom scrolling to see if there were any more pap shots of him out with Celine. So, for a mental health break, I figured I'd come see how the podcast sausage gets made and keep Bella company while Danny's on a location scout in Tennessee.

Bella's guest for the day is Rue Michelson, a former high fashion model who turned to acting after delivering a breakout performance in last year's Best Picture Oscar winner. Rue is what you'd refer to as an It Girl, such a hot commodity that Jim asked Danny to consider her for the role of Minnie. Never mind the fact that Rue is one part South Asian, one part Scandinavian, and no parts Black. Still, she's joined Bella today to talk about, and I kid you not, *the pitfalls of being young and gorgeous in Hollywood.*

Bella leans into her mic and channels James Lipton by balancing the tip of her eyewear on her lower lip. "So, Rue, you recently tweeted that you'd quit modeling for good. What was the catalyst?"

"Honestly . . ." Rue takes a long drag of her herbal tea. "After my first brush with acting I just couldn't go back," she gravely declares.

"Tell me more," Bella asks, jotting down a note.

Rue is pensive before answering. "Well, I always looked at actors and models like artists but also like vessels. You know?"

"Oooh!" Bella practically squeals into the mic, making me flinch. "We love a metaphor! Expound. Please."

As if thrilled to have someone interested in her *vessel theory,* Rue's whole energy brightens. Setting down her tea, she speaks with her hands. "So like, with modeling, I was just a vessel for other people to project their notions onto. What's attractive right now? Who's hot right now?"

"What's in? Thick or thin?" Bella throws out.

"Exactly that! Eventually I just felt empty every time I strutted down the runway like a robot," Rue says. "Did you know that in couture fashion they coach you to be expressionless? Nothing on your face can move. Not even your eyes."

"No way!" Bella's jaw is on the table in a show of feigned astonishment . . . at least I think it's feigned. She recovers in time to ask a follow-up. "But with acting, your experience was different?"

"Oh. It was night and day. As an actor, I get to fill my vessel with everything I've researched for the part. I get to bring a different piece of myself to each character."

"Like you're pouring yourself into the role?" Bella asks.

And they go on this way for another half an hour. I try my best to follow the meandering conversation—every now and then gleaning some deep insight into their young-er minds. In the end, I've learned a lot about shady brand deals and exclusive influencer circles. I've also had it shockingly reaffirmed just how pervasive sexual harassment is in the industry.

Now that Rue is all packed up and on her way, it's just Bella, me, and the beanbag chairs. I'm also now allowed to eat the loud snacks.

"So that was . . . interesting," I say, munching on a tortilla chip smothered in guacamole.

"Wasn't it?" she asks, cheerfully. "Takes them a second to warm up, but I always manage to find that conversational spark. I was *shocked* when Rue revealed that she was the unnamed plaintiff in the SH suit against her former agent."

So was I. "Good for her for stepping forward. I know it couldn't have been easy given who she was up against."

Bella stiffens at this, and instantly, I worry I've struck a nerve. "Did I say something?"

She attempts to shift in her beanbag chair, but it's like quicksand. "No. It's fine, it's just— Well, never mind."

"Bella, at this point I hope you know we can talk about anything," I assure her.

Biting her lip, she folds in on herself, crossing her arms. "So you know that lot courier, Tommy?" she asks.

Instantly, my hackles are up. Tommy comes by our office several times a day to deliver mail and what he calls "friendly flirting" often crosses the line. After a year of his unwanted advances, I finally lied and told him I was engaged. That's when he stopped. It never occurred to me that Bella's been dealing with the same unwanted attention.

"Well, the other day," she explains, "I told him to just leave me alone. Up to that point he ignored all my excuses for not wanting a date. But when I put my foot down he sort of flipped, said I should have told him weeks ago if I didn't like the attention. So I started to think, maybe he's right. How's he supposed to know if I don't say anything? But then again, I didn't want to be *that person*."

"Bella, no," I protest. "Don't let him flip it around on you. He's the one that's out of line. You're at WAP to work, not to be propositioned and catcalled." I rock forward in my beanbag to sit up straighter, but again, it's in vain. Still, I persist. "He's a fully functioning adult, he knew what he was doing. Ugh!" I sigh. "I should have reported him ages ago."

It's the catch-22 of being *that person*. No one wants the burden. But if I'd said something back then, maybe Tommy would have been stopped by now and Bella wouldn't be feeling this way.

Bella shakes her head, waving her hands in surrender. "Oh no. I don't want to make it *a thing* you know? I just wanted him to stop," she says. "But now, when he sees me, he just gives me this look. Like *I'm* the one who offended him."

"Bella, if you want, we *can* report this," I say. She visibly bristles. "It would be anonymous," I assure her. "The couriers on the lot are represented under a union and they have strict sexual harassment policies that cover intimidation and retaliation. They could put him through training or reassign his route. There are options."

The look on her face is one of awe. "How do you know all of this?" she asks.

Shrugging, I explain, "When you're a receptionist for as long as I've been, you eventually become a repository of information. I feel like I know this industry like the back of my hand."

"You should do something with all of that," she gestures vaguely in my direction and it's like a light has just switched on. But I don't have time to explore the room of possibilities that light reveals because Bella's phone rings and she checks the screen. "It's Danny," she shares.

Instantly, my heart is a kick drum.

Bella answers on the second ring and puts it on speaker. "Hey, boss! How's that Tennessee heat? Run over any armadillos yet?"

"My god we've got to get you out of LA." Danny chuckles, and his voice is like slipping into a spa.

"Oh, and you're on speaker by the way," Bella informs him. "It's me and Kaliya." She winks at me and shimmies. I roll my eyes but say nothing.

"Hey, Kal," he says. Two words and it's like he's just run his hand up my spine. "I was actually hoping I'd catch you two together," he says.

"Well today's your lucky day!" I say it so loudly, I sound like a game announcer. Bella's looking at me like I've just sprouted a third tit, and I would very much like to disappear. So I dial it back a little. "I mean, what can we do for you?"

These days I'm aiming for calm and casual with Danny—toeing the line between wanting to do a good job with the production and wanting to finish what we started in his office. At the same time, I'm avoiding all interactions with Celine like the plague.

Danny very generously ignores how awkward I am and rolls ahead. "So, I need one of you to meet me in Austin this Friday if you can swing it. I know it's last-minute but there's a trove of old photos and letters in my parents' attic that I could use some help cataloging. Obviously, expenses will be paid, and my mom's got a killer guest house."

"Oh, that's all Kaliya," Bella shoots out. I throw her a withering glance, but she's not deterred. "Plus, I have that thing this weekend . . ."

"Oh, that thing?" I ask, before making an L on my forehead with my fingers and mouthing the word *LIAR*.

"Kaliya," Danny cuts in, his voice clear and resonant as a bell. "My mom would love to meet you," he says. "If you're up for it, I mean."

Bella's smile, full of mischief, stretches from ear to ear. If her beanbag had wheels she'd be spinning right now. Can I really do this? Travel back home with Danny without succumbing completely to the pull between us? Realizing it's my turn to answer him, I slam my eyes shut and say the simple truth: "I'd love to meet your mom."

It's settled. I'm going to Texas.

chapter 26

MY EYES BURN FROM staring blankly out of a small oval that frames a sheet of fluffy white clouds. In my ears, Amy Winehouse croons about falling in love and being laughed at by the gods in her signature, tragic alto. We've begun our descent toward Austin's airport and the inner ear pressure from the change in altitude is a welcome distraction from the cyclical thoughts that have plagued me since takeoff.

I'm simply not emotionally prepared for what this trip could do to me. Then again, I haven't been prepared for anything that's transpired in the months since Danny waltzed back into my life. Taking little trips down memory lane with my ex when he was unavailable, my boss, and therefore entirely off-limits, felt like playing with fire. What happened after that ex-slash-boss became single and confessed his feelings for me over email was like jumping into the fire and rolling around. But as I, quite literally, barrel toward Danny and the emotional gray area we've found ourselves in, I am no longer just playing with fire. I have become the flames.

Because no matter how I choose to play it, I am likely to do some major damage to my heart, my career, or both—and as Celine has already astutely pointed out, I'm the most at risk here.

It was easy enough to straddle the fence when I was back in Los Angeles and he was off traveling with Eric, George, and their crews. But *easy enough* ends here on this plane, because Danny and I are about to be alone together in a place where we've never been that way before.

Home.

It happens every time, whenever I drag my world-weary bones back to Arkansas to see my grandparents. The hard shell that protects me from the sharpness of the world I've chosen to inhabit crumbles. Simply being under their roof, sleeping in a room down the hall from theirs, eating at their table—it breaks down my defenses and makes the rush and hustle of my fast life feel miles away. If being at home with Danny and his mom is anything like that, this trip could be my undoing.

AFTER THE HASSLE OF DEBOARDING, I MAKE A PIT STOP AT THE restroom to change out of my flight clothes. I'm not one to care about traveling in style, but I can't meet Minnie Prescott for the first time in a hoodie, tank top, and cut-off shorts. So, I scurry into the stall with my carry-on roller case and shrug out of my grubby clothes. After applying a fresh coat of deodorant, I slip into a flowery sundress from Neha's closet.

At the sink, I splash some water on my face and spread a thin sheen of peachy gloss across my lips. I squirt a dime-sized amount of curl gel into my palm and start to fluff my hair.

"You got a *boyfriend* picking you up?" The gravelly voice

startles me. I swivel to find the lady who'd been emptying the garbage receptacles in each stall glancing at me over her shoulder.

I'd noticed her when I first rushed in and thought instantly of my grandmother. Same silver hair. Same slope in her back. Realizing I haven't answered her, I blush, embarrassed I've been caught primping in the airport bathroom. "No, ma'am. Just a friend."

"Must be a *good* friend." She winks at me with a knowing smirk then returns to her task.

Turning back toward the mirror now, I see a woman who presents well enough on the outside. But inside she's a mess with a wave of mixed emotions pinning her in place.

On one hand, the months I've spent working on Danny's production have given me the freedom to stretch unused muscles, reigniting a flickering, dormant passion. I've made relationships that could actually open doors for me down the line. The hallway of hits at WAP doesn't mock me anymore now that the elusive *produced by* credit seems within reach in ways it hasn't been in a really long time.

Against all odds, the thrill is back again—in large part, thanks to Danny.

On the other hand, when it comes to the prospect of love with him *again*, all that optimism stalls out. I can't keep pretending it's just his recent past with Celine, or the potential fallout for the film, or even the ethical question of dating my boss that's holding me back. I can't even pretend it has to do with doubting I'd ever fit into his world of privilege and power. Like his email said, there are plenty of reasons for me to second-guess a relationship with Danny. But chief of all is the lingering question mark of our past. My grandmother's favorite advice has always been: *Don't confuse history with mere memories of the way things made you feel.* I guess I never fully understood it until now. All this time, the painful memories of me and Danny have just been fodder for more questions—questions I've been too afraid to ask.

But as I stare at my reflection, the truth that was once a small flicker is now a flashing red light—I can't let myself fall for Danny again until I understand why he didn't catch me the first time.

chapter
27

One week into the new year and the magic of New York City during the holidays has all but disappeared, along with the glittering snow. In its place are heaps of gray slush flanking the sidewalks and a bone-chilling cold that has a special way of making your ears freeze and burn at the same time.

In the movies, a New York winter is all about gawking at the windows at Saks Fifth Avenue or riding in carriages in Central Park while sipping hot cocoa under a cozy blanket. But in reality, it's trying not to crack your skull or bust a kneecap after making contact with the invisible yet omnipresent black ice. And as the wonderment of wintertime in the city has worn off, so have all the hopeful expectations I harbored for my freshman year internship with Donald Esposito, agent to the stars.

"Kalifa!"

I startle at what sounds like a strangled improvisation of something close, but not quite, my name. Since it came from the direction of Donald's office, I drop everything and head his way. While en route, I mentally prep for whatever by proxy verbal lashing he's got locked and loaded. With the way my luck is set up, it tracks that his assistant, Regina, is out of the office the day before Donald's big trip west for the Golden Globes.

I've been working at the illustrious Creative Artist Partners for three months now but have yet to read one script. It's not because I haven't done my prerequisites. I have mastered the phones, the daily press clippings, the soda-to-water ratio in Donald's mini fridge, and any number of countless and sometimes sketchy errands throughout the five boroughs.

For three months, I have spent every waking moment outside of class at either Donald's or Regina's beck and call. Even today, it's past seven p.m. and I'm still here, scrambling to get him prepped for travel. But I'm told this is what *paying your dues* looks like, so I keep my head down and do the work. Besides, I'd rather be in the arena than on the sidelines.

I arrive at the threshold to Donald's office with my invisible shield in place, ready to do his bidding. "Hi, Donald. Need something?"

He startles, as if I'm an unexpected interruption. "What? Oh. Yes, you. Come in," he says with a clipped tone.

I step just inside the doorframe, careful not to encroach on his sacred space, and wait for him to finish typing. I look on in amazement as his pudgy fingers flit across the keyboard like dancing sausages. When he stabs the send key, I'm drawn out of a momentary daze.

He speaks without looking up. "Regina's *allegedly* come down with a bout of the flu and is taking advantage of the situation at the worst possible time." He groans, removing his thick black frames to rub his eyes. Briefly, I wonder if he's just called me in here to vent.

"She's cashed in on PTO to 'recover,'" he continues, adding air quotes.

"That being said, as you know, I'm off to LA for the Globes in the morning and I'm going to need you to run point for me back here while Regina's being availed of her benefits package."

A bit taken aback by the request, and the amount of responsibility now being placed on my amateur shoulders, I stammer in reply, "S-sure. I'm ready. Whatever you need."

Donald regards me shrewdly, as if this is the first time he's looked *at* me, really *seen* me. He drops his gaze, extending the pause, then abruptly turns to reach into the file cabinet behind his desk. When he swivels back around, he's brandishing a thickly bound stack of paper—a screenplay. My heart thuds in my chest.

"Columbia sent over a new project they'd like Charles Wesley to consider. When it comes to my clients, I make sure everything's vetted before putting it in front of them." He slides the script across his desk and points at it. Then it occurs to me that he's probably just going to ask me to scan it over to Regina to read while she's on her sickbed.

"Usually, I'd ask this of Regina but since she's out of commission . . . prove yourself for the next few days and *if* you do right by me, when I get back from LA, I'll be interested in hearing your thoughts on it."

The blood rushes from my face. "It would be an honor, sir. I promise you won't be disappointed." I'm having an out-of-body experience as I speak, and if I'm not mistaken, the corners of Donald's mouth turn up in something resembling a smile.

"Now go," he says, his words clipped. "That's all for the evening. I've got packing to do."

You would think he's just handed me my first Oscar by the way I levitate out of Donald's office, clutching the script like it's my most

prized possession. Turning it over in my hands, I read the cover . . .
Working Title: See Me Yesterday. Instantly, I recognize it from *The
Black List*—a yearly roundup that, according to top creative execu-
tives, represents the best unproduced screenplays in Hollywood.

Writers dream of making the list because it guarantees eyes on
their work. And for those lucky enough to have their projects optioned by a studio, it can be their ticket out of obscurity.

Packing up my desk for the night, there's one person I want to
share the news with. I grab my phone and open the Messages app.

ME: I have news! You free tonight?

A response comes when I'm at the elevator bank.

DANNY: Tonight's not good. Maybe tomorrow?

I almost miss the elevator doors for how long I've stood here
staring at this text. Lately, talking with Danny has felt like squeezing water from a rock. I last saw him a week ago on New Year's. Ever
since, his texts and calls have been unusually flat and scarce. The
first few days of his cold shoulder treatment, I tried to dismiss it,
knowing he'd be busy at the start of his final semester of college and
that things were ramping up with his thesis film shoot happening
next week. But now I'm starting to panic.

I clamber onto the crowded elevator, mentally sifting through
every detail of that night, examining all the moments that culmi-
nated in the one that somehow flipped us upside-down. I remember
it all in scenes, as if from a film I've replayed over and over. The
night had started off blissful and stayed that way for a while. Then
things turned awkward and finally, downright confusing.

I watch the elevator's indicator panel flash and ding above me. As we descend the floors one by one, I'm drawn back to New Year's Eve in a way that feels like reliving more than remembering.

TEN, NINE, EIGHT . . .

The dance floor was full of bodies, but I was hyperaware of the one pressed firmly against me from behind. Danny's strong arms snaked around my waist, and I could feel the music vibrate between us as we counted down to the ball drop with the revelers all around.

SEVEN, SIX, FIVE . . .

Danny spun me to face him and maybe I was light-headed from the champagne or dizzy from the dancing, but I felt weightless and wild. Like the tethers to all my insecurities had snapped. Like I couldn't possibly let the ball drop on 2014 without him knowing.

FOUR, THREE, TWO . . .

"Danny, I'm in love with you!" I shouted into the chaos.

The words were out there, irrevocably so. Danny's eyes flashed with something like shock in response to my confession. What was once a privately held truth was now a known thing in the world. The room erupted like a ball of chaos as gold and silver confetti descended all around us. Through the sheets of tumbling debris, for a split second, I saw shades of mirrored affection in Danny's eyes. But before I could linger on what that meant, he was kissing me utterly senseless. Everything surrounding us, the bustling bodies, the shouts and cheers, the blaring crescendo of "Auld Lang Syne" over the sound system, it all faded away.

WE BURST THROUGH THE DOOR OF HIS LOFT WITH OUR mouths pressed and wanting, hands tugging at coats, legs stumbling toward a surface, any surface, that could brace our clutching bodies. He reached down to lift and press me flush against him. My legs had nowhere to go but around his waist as he walked us back toward his low platform bed. He let me down to stand in front of him and looked at me like I was the only girl in the world. It was almost enough to make me forget that he hadn't said it back.

He shrugged off his coat and reached for the buttons on mine. "Is this okay?" he asked.

I nodded in reply, my eyes never leaving his. We helped each other peel off our layers until we were down to our underwear. That part, we'd done before. But I wanted more and felt like it was the night to have it.

Looking down, I tried to mask my tiny gasp at the sight of his erection, straining against his boxers. It wasn't the first time I'd seen and felt his arousal pressed against me as we touched and kissed, but there were always thin layers of fabric between us.

He reached for the clasp on my bra. "Can I?" he asked. His words a whispered plea. I said *yes*.

He released the clasp and eased the straps down my shoulders, freeing my breasts to fall under his gaze. His hands glided up my sides to gently cup them and I felt his arousal jump between us. The next moments were a blur of our tangled bodies on his bed. His hand grazed down my stomach toward the apex of my thighs, resting over the lace fabric of my underwear.

"Can I take these off?" His words softly ghosted across my collarbone.

"Yes, please," I practically begged in response. I couldn't imagine wanting anything more than for him to touch me *there*. Soon, I got my wish. His strong fingers played and prodded and I writhed beneath him.

"Can I taste you?" he asked next, his eyes wild with desire and fixed on mine.

We hadn't done that yet. The idea has always thrilled and

terrified me, but also, it was something I'd been wanting to experience with him. I've wanted *everything* with him. So I gulped down all the insecure, bashful parts of me and said *yes* again.

He wasted no time, kissing his way down my neck and chest, then farther and farther again.

"God, Kaliya, you're perfect," he said, before sinking down between my open thighs. He was up close and personal with the most private part of my body, and it took every ounce of sheer will for me to choose pleasure over insecurity. His ministrations drew warring emotions from me and I felt like I was short-circuiting. The overwhelming emotion was pure desire, but underneath it was a pervading sense of doubt. *Am I doing this right? Is this how it's supposed to feel? Is he enjoying it, too?*

I couldn't get out of my head and into my body enough to really savor what we were doing in the moment.

He stopped kissing me, lifting himself up on his forearms. "Is this okay?"

I screwed my eyes shut and made what I was hoping were sounds of affirmation. But Danny saw past my crumbling facade to everything I'd been hiding. He came up to lay beside me. He knew.

"Have you . . . done this before, Kal?" he asked, his voice kind but cautious.

"No," I replied, swallowing thickly, trying to hold back tears. I was embarrassed by my lack of experience, yes, but also by my lack of transparency. It was foolish to think he'd never notice.

"Which part?" he wanted to know.

"All of it," I confessed. I hadn't done any of it with anyone but him.

Several seconds ticked by before I realized he hadn't replied. "What's wrong?" I asked, my voice hardly above a raw whisper. He insisted it was nothing and suggested we get some sleep. So we curled around each other in bed beneath the covers and lay there in silence. It took the better part of an hour before I felt his body relax.

The next morning I woke up reaching for him on his side of the bed, which had long gone cold. Then, I found the note.

> Kal,
>
> I'm off to Queens to help Shawn shoot some locations. I won't be back until later this evening so you don't need to wait for me. And I'm sorry for last night.
>
> —Danny

Of all the things about the note that I found troubling, namely that it was there in bed with me in Danny's place, it was the "you don't need to wait for me" that crushed me most. And because I'd promised Neha I'd spend New Year's Day with her, I didn't.

BY SOME MIRACLE, I'VE MADE IT BACK TO MY DORM ROOM with my skull and kneecaps intact. I pop a Cup Noodles in the microwave and settle in to stay up until the wee hours of the night reading *See Me Yesterday*.

By the time I'm finished with my first pass, I'm riveted. The script is daring, visceral, shocking—the perfect vehicle for this point in Charles's career. For these reasons, I type "strong consider" at the bottom of my script coverage document. But I can't stop here. To really make the case to Donald that I am worthy of a promotion, I need to fully flesh out my analysis.

My fingers itch, once again, with the urge to call Danny so I can bounce my thoughts off him. But the chances he'd answer are slim and I need to focus. So I silence my phone and get back to the pages.

The next morning, I wake up to a persistent vibration somewhere in my sheets. When the buzzing continues, I groan, forcing my eyes open. Something's off. It's too bright in the room. An uneasy feeling settles in my bones as I roll over to my nightstand. With blurred vision I barely make out the ten a.m. glow on my alarm clock. I overslept.

The buzzing continues.

I grope beneath the covers for my phone, answering before checking the caller ID. I cough to clear the sleep from my throat before speaking. "Hello?"

"Are you in the hospital?" The voice creeps, eerily calm, like a snake in the grass. "Have you been kidnapped? Held against your will? Sold into a trafficking ring?" The questions come in fast succession as my mental fog clears. Then the realization of who is on the other end of the line hits me like a freight train.

Frantically, I pop open my laptop to check for any missed emails. At first glance, I almost faint. Fifteen messages from Donald Esposito have gone unanswered as I slept through the alerts.

"I'm sorry, Donald," I rush to explain. "I was up all night working on notes for Charles Wesley's script."

"Notes? Notes! She was up late working on her notes!" He shouts, mocking me in third person. Then he really unleashes. "Burn them. And your employee badge, too."

Next, Donald provides a complete rundown of what I've missed. Regina is on a flight to LA with an iPad containing confidential client records. If I'd been responsive, I'd have known that he'd left it at the airport before boarding. The potential for irrevocable harm to his clients if the iPad had fallen into the wrong hands would be catastrophic. But there I was, off in la-la land, too busy making notes on a script to pick up the damn phone.

"I can't even express to you how pathetic an excuse that is," he says. "And to think I'd begun to have even the slightest expectations of you. Clearly this opportunity has been wasted on your incompetence, Kaliya."

And now would be the time he'd pick to get my name right.

I sink farther into my lumpy dorm-room mattress. With my self-worth at the bottom of a pit of despair, I somehow manage to find the strength to plead my case. I've come too far, withstood too many verbal lashings to wilt so easily under this one. "Donald, please," I beg. "This is one mistake I know I will NEVER make again. If you could just—"

"Oh, honey you'll make more mistakes," he cuts in. "Plenty! But not with me. And don't ever call me for a reference."

Click!

The line goes dead—along with my fledgling career. My first real industry opportunity is circling the drain with a great heaping scoop of dramatic irony. I glance down at the stack of pages lying near the foot of my bed—the script, chock-full of my notes scribbled in the margins. How could something so precious to me mere hours before so quickly become my downfall? Even I can see the tragic error of my ways. Like Icarus, I've been so blinded by my first shot at *more* that I completely lost sight of the task at hand. Instead of being the reliable, responsive Kaliya that I've always been, I have flown too close to the sun, and now, my ass is toast.

I am lucky enough to have a short list of people who'd take my call and listen to me dissect the shock and shame of this moment. I could call my grandparents and sob at the mere sound of their voices. Or, I could interrupt Neha's biochem lab and convince her to go get day drunk with me.

But there's only one person who could fully register the gravity of this moment for me. And because recent experience says he probably won't even answer my call, I decide to pay Danny a house visit. Worst-case scenario, he'll blow me off. But if that's truly what he wants, this time he'll have to do it in person.

Now showered, dressed, and slightly frozen by the wind chill wafting off the Hudson River, I have made my way down Christopher Street toward Danny's loft.

On the train ride down here, I had second thoughts about not calling or sending a warning text, but I decided again that catching him off guard is the best move. After all, he did say *maybe tomorrow* when I asked him if he was free last night. And *tomorrow* is *today*, so technically, I'm not far off the mark. Besides, he already knows I love him. We've already been intimate in ways I've never been with anyone else. We are past formalities.

I keep a fast pace down the avenue toward his block clutching my scarf to my neck to blunt the frigid air. Just as I am about to cross Greenwich Street, I stop dead in my tracks. Danny is walking toward me a block up ahead. He's not alone.

Next to him, nestled into his side with her arm wrapped around his waist, is a girl I recognize from frequent sightings on campus. I'd even heard rumblings that she and Danny used to date. Hannah. She has fire-engine red hair that billows out from under her fur-lined winter hat. The pale skin of her face is rosy from the cold. She's leggy and gorgeous. Danny's arm lays protectively over her shoulders as they walk and talk and laugh. They look like lovers out for a casual stroll after a lazy morning in bed.

I can't breathe.

A million thoughts swim in my mind. How I spent last week wallowing in self-doubt, racking my brain for what I could have done to make him flip the switch so quickly on us. How I reached out to him last night, bursting with excitement about my first script coverage assignment after waiting so long, and how he so quickly shut me down. How I stayed awake all night, obsessing over the chance to prove, for once, that I was good enough, all the while willing myself not to call him so he could tell me I was. How this morning was the single most humiliating experience of my life, apart from right now, and how Danny is the only person I wanted to help me through it.

But now I know he wasn't with me because he's been with her.

All my firsts, I've given to Danny Prescott. My first date, first kiss, first *I love you,* and tragically, my first brush with real intimacy. With everything in me, I wish I could take them all back, especially the first that's piercing a hole straight through me right now.

My first heartbreak.

chapter

28

I SEE HIM FIRST. SLEEK aviators block his eyes, but I can tell he's scanning the bustling crowd of new arrivals, looking for me. Ignoring every cell in my body that silently urges me to run to him, I walk steadily, enjoying the view.

Danny stills with his gaze fixed on my path, and I know he's found me. Suddenly, the distance between us feels like miles. But once those miles become a few feet, he springs forward to capture me in a steady, strong embrace that smells like lemon and honey, and a little bit of sweat from the Texas heat.

"I finally got you here," he says. And spoken so close, his words vibrate against my eardrums, scattering chills everywhere.

There's a lightness and an ease to him that, try as I might, I can't match. Colleagues. *Right now, we are only colleagues*, I remind myself before gently pulling out of his arms. "How was the

Tennessee scout?" I ask, stepping back and adjusting the strap of my duffle.

"Good. We locked in some great locations. Eric and George are pleased," he says brightly. Then he straightens and takes a step back as well. He removes his shades, revealing eyes that reflect the same cautious uncertainty I've been feeling since getting on the plane.

Danny leads me through the airport exit into what can only be described as an atmospheric oven. I reach into my duffle for a sun hat I'd packed last minute. In the parking lot, intuition tells me before he does when we've arrived at his car. It's a classic red Jeep still in pristine condition. He opens my door and extends his hand to help me into the passenger seat.

"Her name is Carmen," he announces proudly, after shutting my door and placing my luggage in the back.

I turn the name over in my mind for the few seconds it takes him to find his place behind the wheel. "After Dorothy Dandridge in *Carmen Jones*?" I ask, cheeks tight from smiling so wide.

I look to Danny and he's doing the same. "I knew you'd know it," he says, craning his neck around as he backs out of the parking space.

The Jeep is a bit rugged, a bit sexy, a lot like how Danny looks right now. He's wearing a vintage T-shirt, leather sandals, and cargo shorts. I've never seen it before, but I could get used to his version of casual. What he's giving isn't his usual *swaggy Hollywood hotshot* or *sensitive artist*. Right now, he's giving *ease*—the kind you feel when you're at home visiting the woman who raised you.

Silence stretches the forty-five-minute drive from the airport to the Prescott's wealthy enclave amid heavy tension that's as quiet as it is loud. We haven't seen each other since our moments of confession and passion in the confines of his office. We've talked it out a few times over the phone—for now and until further notice, we are friends and colleagues with the film as our top priority. But I have no idea how to play by those rules in person. And this trip is the first test in finding out if we actually can.

WE TAKE THE HIGHWAY OFF-RAMP. THE HOT WIND THAT HAD been whipping around us on the highway calms to a soft breeze as Sade's "Love Is Stronger Than Pride" plays on the radio. We pull to a red light and everything, save the music, stills.

"My mom can't wait to meet you," Danny says, seemingly out of the blue.

I snatch my eyes away from his sun-drenched forearms as they grip the wheel. "Really? I'm just the PA."

He shakes his head. "She knows you're a lot more to me than that, Kal."

For a second, it looks like he means to go on, but he stops himself and the silence returns.

A few minutes later, we pull down a quiet road lined with stately homes with glittery Lake Austin in the distance. We creep slowly past the tucked-back mansions with their imposing Tudor- and colonial-style roofs peeking out above opulent hedges and gates. Danny pulls up to a cul-de-sac and what appears to be a series of three matching Spanish revival homes. But upon closer inspection, I realize it's all just one. The Prescott family home literally *is* the cul-de-sac.

Danny's Jeep moves along the circular path toward a gate that's sandwiched between thick verdant hedges. He punches a code into the security box, and it slowly swings open, revealing even more of the front elevation. The driveway is lined with several mature olive trees, a tableau so picturesque, I'd think I was staring at an impressionist painting if not for the tiny leaves flickering in the breeze, catching the light of the early evening sun.

Standing just outside the entrance, I spot a petite woman nearly eclipsed by a floral sun hat. She is dressed in a matching linen blouse and culottes, her long salt-and-pepper curls dancing on the wind as she enthusiastically waves us in.

"That's my ma," Danny says quietly, lovingly.

I can't help the wobbly smile that spreads across my face, or the threat of tears stinging my eyes as I prepare to meet the woman who raised the man of my dreams.

Danny talked about her almost as much as he talked about his father back at NYU. But after watching her describe her experience integrating into an all-white school at only twelve, I've sprung my own well of admiration for a woman I don't even know.

Danny hops out of the Jeep and grabs my roller case and duffle before helping me down from my seat. His mom bounds toward us with a face-splitting smile that's clearly the prototype for Danny's. Surprisingly, she swats him out of the way to wrap her trim but strong arms around my shoulders in a snug embrace. She, too, smells like lemons and honey.

"I'm so happy you're here, sweetheart," Minnie says, her genuine, comforting energy and faint Southern accent tugging hard on my heartstrings.

"Thank you for having me, Mrs. Prescott." My voice feels small in my throat, as if limited by the emotion behind it.

"Oh my goodness, so formal! Call me Minnie now. You hear?" She winks and clasps her small, smooth hand in mine. Before turning to the house, she takes Danny's hand in her free one and kisses the back of it.

I glance from their loving gesture up to Danny and our eyes

lock. A vague intensity settles between the two of us as we walk hand in hand with his mom through the home's massive double doors—my earlier suspicions about this trip being my undoing all but officially confirmed.

The moment we step inside, I'm drawn to a breathtaking Bisa Butler piece that hangs prominently in the grand foyer. It stops me in my tracks, drawing out a small gasp.

"It's called *Southside Sunday Morning*, based on a photo by Russell Lee," Minnie says of the elaborate quilt by an artist whose work I've only seen on television and in magazines. In person, it reads like a painting made with stitches and textiles rather than brushstrokes and oils. In it, five Black boys are dressed in vibrant suits and ties with fedoras perched proudly on their heads or dangling from pointy knees. "Ms. Butler says it made her think of how we tend to dress our children up in our love," Minnie explains.

"It's stunning," I say—the understatement of a century.

"Well, how about we get you situated before dinner?" she asks, cupping her hands together beneath her chin. I nod and she turns to Danny who's been standing off to the side watching us interact with the art and each other.

Minnie asks Danny to carry my bags to the guest house and he winks at me before taking off with them. Now, it's just the two of us.

"Your house is beautiful," I tell her. Even though the term *house* feels entirely reductive at this point. What I'm standing in is nothing short of an *estate* worthy of a spread in the pages of *Architectural Digest*.

"I just hope you'll feel at home while you're here," she says. "Let me give you the lay of the land." Minnie leads me farther inside where an expansive wall of windows separates the great room from the garden. Through sliding doors, she walks me past aisles of colorful rose bushes and, just beyond, to a crystal-blue pool. The whole backyard feels majestic, set against the backdrop of the rippling lake.

Back inside, Minnie shows me a study lined with books and her sitting room, where I spot the *What Love Made* screenplay resting on a coffee table next to a pair of reading glasses. Despite the clean lines and modern furniture, like the Butler piece, Minnie's home is full of color and texture, making it feel like a lot of life happens here.

With each passing room, the home becomes less intimidating. Not because it isn't expertly designed and spotless, but because every detail reflects the warm elegance of Danny's mom. We enter the very same kitchen where she sat for her background interviews, and I am suddenly famished. The smells that greet us elicit a grumble from my stomach that's so loud it feels like betrayal.

"Lucky for us, dinner is in the works," Minnie announces with a smirk, having clearly heard my biological intrusion. "I've got my base for chicken and dumplings simmering in the crockpot. Danny told me you didn't have any diet restrictions. So I hope you like it."

"He's right. I'll eat anything," I blurt out.

"A girl after my own heart," Minnie says, laughing on her way over to the fridge where she pulls out a baking sheet lined with cut dough. "You just wait 'til I get the cobbler in the oven."

My taste buds dance at the promise of dessert as Minnie ties on her apron. Feeling a little useless, I offer my middling skills. "Can I help with any of the prep?"

Minnie perks up. "Of course you can. See those peaches over there in the bowl?" she asks. "Think you could slice them up and add the zest and sugar?"

I nod and we both get to work. Minnie puts on an Aretha record and we both hum the lyrics as we tend to our respective dishes. Danny's still not back from handling my luggage and I have the sneaking suspicion that he's idling on purpose to give us time to bond.

Fifteen minutes have passed, and the chicken and dumplings are simmering in a large pot on the stove. I've just zested and sugared the juiciest peaches I've ever seen and Minnie's moved on to the cobbler crust. As if summoned by the intoxicating aromas, Danny walks in and I am flooded with the familiar feeling of heightened awareness. Every part of me takes notice of him. My face heats. The tiny hairs down my arms and on the back of my neck stand on end.

"I could get used to this," he says before straddling a kitchen stool. He reaches for a peach and takes a massive bite, licking its juices from his lips. My eyes slowly track upward from his mouth, and I'm busted for staring. Because so is he.

"Boy, I had plans for those peaches," Minnie scolds, and it snaps the tether between our gazes.

I look over at her barely suppressed smile then back at Danny who, duly chided, looks like he has no idea what to do with the fruit anymore. Perhaps sensing his inner conflict, Minnie gives him an out. "Go on finish it now, Daniel Ellis. Just don't ruin your dinner."

Danny takes a sheepish bite and I smile to myself as I focus on disbursing strategically placed scoops of Minnie's batter over the seasoned peaches.

chapter
29

AFTER POPPING THE COBBLER into the oven and programming the timer, Minnie banishes me and Danny from the kitchen with instructions to set the table and to *make it nice.*

I follow Danny into the dining room through the butler's pantry, where we pick up plates and flatware.

"You holding up okay?" he asks, pulling candles from the hutch.

"Danny, you've practically brought me to a palace, not a trap house," I say. "I'm . . . amazing. Honestly, everything is . . . the house, your mom, the peaches. I couldn't find a complaint if it were lodged in my contact lenses."

I join him by the hutch to pick up water and wineglasses to place at our table settings. Noting his silence I look at Danny, who's lighting candles with a smirk on his face. "What is it?" I ask.

"Nothing, it's just . . . I've noticed that whenever you're either really anxious or really excited about something you tend to get really expressive in the way you speak. It's cute," he says, shrugging.

My mouth hangs open in stunned confusion at this micro-observation. "And?" I ask, setting down a crystal glass a little too assertively.

"Well, which is it? Are you anxious, or excited?" Danny asks as he straightens, crosses his arms, and levels me with an expectant stare.

Anxious is my answer. One hundred percent so. But I don't have time to tell him before Minnie floats in with a dinner cart that looks and smells like it just dropped out of heaven.

"Hope you're hungry!" she chirps, as she comes bearing a Dutch oven full of simmering chicken and dumplings, a bowl of tossed salad, a bread basket, and a few bottles of vintage cabernet.

Soon, we're gathered 'round the candlelit table enjoying the sumptuous meal. As the wine flows, Minnie quickly becomes a welcome buffer for the crackling tension that's coursing between me and Danny. Throughout the meal, I catch him aiming expectant glances my way, like he's still waiting for my answer and hoping it's *excited*.

But I avoid eye contact with him at all costs as Minnie entertains us with tale after tale of her and Nathan's early days in New York—how they'd had a tiny matchbox apartment in Alphabet City. And how she balanced classes at Columbia with shifts in the ticket booth at Radio City Music Hall while Nathan apprenticed on set at 30 Rockefeller Plaza.

I've just savored the last drop of my first glass of wine when . . . *Ding!*

The kitchen timer goes off, signaling the cobbler has finished baking. Danny hops up to get it, likely to avoid the round of embarrassing stories his mom just dipped into.

Minnie's pouring herself, and me, another glass of red and telling me about the time a three-year-old Danny walked right into a scene with Meryl Streep and Ed Harris and promptly shouted that he needed to potty. Nathan had been behind the camera and Danny's on-set nanny had accidentally locked herself in their trailer.

I'm laughing so hard, I have to gulp back the wine to avoid a spit take. "What happened next?" I ask when I finally compose myself.

As if perfectly timed, Danny returns with the cobbler and flushed cheeks. "Dad called *Cut!* and ran onto the set," he says flatly, as if he's been made to recount this story a million times. "But Meryl shooed him off and took me to the restroom instead. I remember none of this, mind you." He aims a pointed look my way.

"It was one of Nathan's favorite days on set," Minnie adds, with tears of laughter and perhaps nostalgia in her eyes. "Turns out, she was missing her own children while she'd been shooting on location—still sends Danny a birthday card every year."

Danny sets the baking dish down on a mat and Minnie begins ladling heaping scoops of cobbler into our dainty dessert bowls. She tops us all off with a dollop of Blue Bell ice cream. I sink my spoon into the golden crust, take the first bite, and suppress a gratuitous groan. I may have helped prep this, but I somehow missed whatever practical magic Minnie sprinkled in the batter to make it so delectably flaky.

We indulge in companionable silence, save for the clanking of our spoons and a few errant moans of satisfaction when . . .

Ping! Ping! Ping!

Danny's phone lights up with a flurry of notifications—an abrupt reminder that a director is never truly off the clock. It's also the first time in hours that I've even thought about the production.

"Sorry, ladies, it's Jim Evans. I'll try to make it quick," Danny says, before excusing himself from the table.

Minnie's eyes linger on Danny's retreat and a maternal sense of concern weighs down her expression. "Not to pry," she says, turning back to me. "But I get the sense he's having a rough go of it this time around."

Absently, I trace the scalloped edges of my charger as I carefully weigh my response. "I really only have one other instance to compare this to," I say, referring to Danny's senior thesis project. "But yeah, it looks like WAP is putting him through the paces."

Minnie lowers her voice, as if she's about to let me in on a secret. "I shouldn't have been listening, but earlier today I heard him on the phone talking about the script. It seemed tense, like maybe the studio isn't on board."

I think back to the copy I saw in her study during my tour of the house. Then curiosity gets the best of me. "Have you read it? What did you think?"

Minnie's smile is warm. "You know, I've spent thirty years grading my students' writing. But now that it's my son, and he's writing about me and his father . . . suddenly, this professor doesn't know where to begin with giving notes."

"I just know your opinion matters to him more than Jim Evans's or anyone else's ever could," I say.

Minnie nods, taking another sip. "If that's true then yours would be a close second," she says, and it catches me off guard.

Then I remember what Danny had said in his Jeep, how his mom knew I was more to him than just a production assistant. I'm still not quite sure what to do with that. But I am genuinely curious to hear what she thinks. So, I press again. "I think the script is brilliant. But it's also not *my* life."

Minnie hesitates, pursing her lips. And then her eyes flick up to mine. "My only note is I think Danny's still writing from a place of deep sadness, like mine and Nathan's love was this heavy burden." She gingerly sets down her wine. "And I'll admit, at times because of our circumstances, it was. But now, when I look back on our life together, it's just the joy that stays with me. So, it's hard for me to go back to the dark places."

"Do you think—" I stop myself, afraid to pry too far.

"It's alright, honey," Minnie says, raising her glass. "I've had wine and I'm feeling a little chatty. So shoot."

"Do you think Danny's come to terms with losing his dad?" I ask, tentatively. "I feel like he carries this guilt for not being there with you when the accident happened."

She pauses for a beat, her eyebrows knitting together in deep thought. "There's this funny thing about the past," she says. "It's all about perspective."

"How do you mean?"

"Well, I've been trying to work through *my* guilt all these years and never really considered this project was his way of doing the same," Minnie admits.

Surprised by her answer, I ask, "What would you have to be guilty for?"

She takes a long sip of wine, and glances out to the courtyard where Danny can be seen pacing on the phone. "Can I share something with you I don't think Danny's ever told a soul?"

"Of course," I answer, and it's barely above a whisper.

"The first night Danny was with me in the hospital after his father's fall was the first time he told me about you," she says. The admission makes my hands shake and I have to set down my glass for fear I'll drop it.

"Nathan was hooked up to all these machines," Minnie continues. "I'd told the doctors I wanted to wait to make the final call until Danny could be there. So we could all be together one last time."

Her eyes grow watery and her voice turns thick, but she continues undeterred. "When Danny arrived that next morning, I was sick with guilt. If only I'd taken less time at the store, I could have found Nathan before it was too late. I don't think I could speak for hours and when I finally did, I asked Danny to distract me. To tell me something good, anything that made him happy.

"He told me about you," she says, looking me in the eye. "This girl he'd met who'd dropped her suitcase in the street and then popped up in one of his classes. She had this sweet Southern drawl. He said that reminded him of me." Minnie laughs and wipes at tears as they fall. "He was excited about this girl because she loved the same movies he did, movies no one else in his class gave the time of day."

She looks out the window at her boy, and a small smile brightens her face. "I asked him if he was planning on asking her out and he said he was working on it."

We laugh together, and for a moment, it eases the ache in my chest.

"It was a long few days at the hospital before we said goodbye to Nathan. Me and Danny . . . we were both just two shells pacing the halls, clinging to each other. I'd never seen him look so scared." She looks back out the window. "It didn't occur to me until later that he was scared for me."

I sit glued to my seat, speechless from the tonal shift of our conversation. Memories of all the time I'd spent with Danny in the months after his father died flood my mind as I try to keep up with Minnie's revelations. Even now, I'm amazed at how strong Danny was through the loss. As I've learned more about Minnie's story, I figured he got that way by simply taking after her. But I'm beginning to see that sometimes the strongest people became that way simply by leading heavy lives.

"We had Nathan's service a week later," Minnie continues. "It was a nightmare. The lead-up felt like it would never end and then after, everything happened so fast—too fast. Everyone who'd flown in disappeared almost overnight. Danny went back to school and I was totally alone for the first time since that day walking into Maple Creek Middle School. When there were no more affairs to handle or boxes to pack up, grieving Nathan consumed me. I felt like my heart could hardly beat without his."

She pauses, looking up to me. "I'm sorry, I don't mean to dump all this heaviness on our nice dinner, I just—"

"No. No. You can share whatever you're comfortable with," I say, and I really mean it. After all, it was my probing question that brought us here.

She adjusts in her seat and takes a deep breath. "I'm not proud to admit this. But in those first months after Nathan died, I barely had it in me to be a mother to Danny," she confesses. "He was the one calling *me* from New York every day to make sure I got out of bed, or that I'd eaten, or to encourage me to go outside for fresh air and sun." She stops for a beat, reaching up to rub her neck. "It should have been the other way around."

Her tears are now flowing steadily. She twists her hands into tight fists on the table. I don't know what to say, so I reach out and she takes my hand.

"There's a reason I'm telling you this," she says. "On all those calls, whenever I'd ask Danny to tell me about his life in the city, the conversation always found its way back to you—what you thought of the script he was working on for his thesis. Or a funny story you'd told him about your grandfather, or a debate the two of you were having about nineties rom-coms. And that's when I realized, while he had been taking care of me, *you* were taking care of him.

"You should never have had to do that," she says, tearfully. "God, you both were so young, but especially you, Kaliya. I'll always be grateful for the way you loved him."

And when she says it so plainly like that, I know it's still true. I loved him and I *love* him. I have since the day I met him.

Minnie releases my hand and grabs a napkin, delicately dabbing at her eyes, getting her emotions back in check. "At some point I realized he'd stopped mentioning you altogether," she recalls. "I'm ashamed I never asked him what happened between the two of you. I assumed things hadn't ended well. But I dropped the ball in so many areas where Danny's happiness was concerned and I never asked. I just hope you know he was in a world of pain. So whatever it is he might have done, with some exceptions of course, I hope he finds a way to make things right with you now. Because I haven't seen him *this* far gone over anyone since."

Minnie excuses herself to the powder room while I sit, silently processing everything she's laid out for me. But with Danny still outside on his call, I feel restless sitting alone. So, I get up and wander into the study. I approach a shelf that's filled with photographs of what appear to be various Prescott family members and friends. Mixed among them all sits a picture I've never seen of a memory that's been locked in a sacred corner of my mind for years.

It's a photo of me and Danny dancing at Bethesda Fountain in Central Park. It was a few days after we first kissed at the Christmas market. We were in that bubble of intimacy that seems to radiate off freshly infatuated couples. A saxophonist played Stevie Wonder's "My Cherie Amour" under the bright afternoon sun. As we walked toward the fountain, Danny took my hand, spun me around, and pulled me against him. The musician came to kneel beside us and suddenly, his performance became a serenade. Then a petite woman, likely in her seventies, came up to insist that Danny hand over his Canon 5D so she could capture the memory.

"For your grandkids," she'd said. He handed her the camera, then we laughed and kept dancing.

"Something the matter?" Minnie asks, joining me in the sitting room. Startled, I turn to face her as she notices the frame in my hands.

"Always figured that was you," she says, gesturing toward the photo. "I found it in his room a while ago." Minnie smiles down at me and Danny and something inside me breaks loose.

"How long ago?" I ask.

She shrugs. "Oh, it had to be about two years now. He came home to do some early research when he first started working on the script. He rummaged through a bunch of old photos and put most of them away. But this one . . ." She taps the frame's sharp wooden edge. "He left it on the desk in his old room. When I turned it over and saw what he'd written . . . I'd never seen you, but I put it all together from just the look on his face. Next thing I knew I was putting the picture in a frame."

I turn it over in my hands. "Would you mind if I—"

"Sure. Sure." Minnie nods, granting permission for me to open the clasps on the back. And when I do, I'm met with Danny's slightly smudged but perfectly legible handwriting.

December 20, 2014 - A perfect day.

I cup a hand to my mouth to stop the rolling surge of emotions from spilling out. I came here with a burning need for answers. But the events of the past hour have been complete information overload. With a shaky hand I replace the frame on the shelf just as Danny's walking back in.

"Am I interrupting something?" he asks.

"Oh no, sweetie. I was just about to clear the table," Minnie says.

"Don't you dare," he insists. Then he turns to me. "We can take care of it, right?"

***

MAYBE IT'S A FOOD COMA, OR PERHAPS AN EMOTIONAL HANG-over from *gestures broadly all around*, but I am in a state. Still, I push through to help Danny clean up after sending Minnie off to relax with a book. We clear the table and then head to the kitchen to take care of the dishes.

I mask my inner turmoil by asking him about the call with Jim Evans. He insists it was just the slick exec hemming and hawing over *budget stuff*. And given Danny's intentional lack of detail, I lay off from prying. It helps, as well, that I am overwhelmed for entirely different reasons.

Whenever Danny hands me a new dish, I evade his searching stare, convinced the moment we lock eyes he'll somehow know that my conversation with Minnie after dinner was like an earthquake—it's shifted everything. So we continue cleaning in ill-choreographed silence—that is, until the first track from Stevie Wonder's "Songs in the Key of Life" begins to play from the direction of the study.

By the time I have rinsed off the last dish, the opening harp strings of "If It's Magic" waft into the kitchen like a soft summer breeze. I've closed the dishwasher door and programmed the wash cycle when I feel him step close behind me. Figuring we've got two days left here and I've avoided him long enough, I turn and find him looking down at me with quiet intensity. He looms large, blocking my view of anything but his chest and shoulders.

"Dance with me?" he asks, as I stand frozen and apparently mute. When I make eye contact it's clearly a mistake. Because the plea in his eyes pounds any resistance I have left into submission.

"I understand why you asked for space," he says. "But, it's killing me having you here, away from everything that's keeping us apart back in LA and still, I can't touch you the way I want to."

My second mistake is nodding my head *yes* and letting Danny clasp our hands together. He places his free hand at the small of my back and gently pulls my body flush against his. It's been weeks since that day in his office—the last time we were this close—and years before that. I've been so deprived of the feeling of him that I can't help but sink into it.

Danny rests our hands on his chest, and I lay my cheek just beside them. He nestles into the crown of my head, tracing lazy circles at the base of my spine with his thumb. Then, we sway in silence—a more solemn rendition of the pas de deux we performed in Central Park all those years ago. Once again, I am disarmed by this man.

When Stevie asks *if it's magic, why can't we make it everlasting* for the last time, Danny lets go of my hand to wrap his arms around my waist. I burrow into his chest and cry. I cry because I'm in love with a man who apparently loved me, too, but hurt me, and I still don't know why. And maybe now isn't the time for the answer because we can't *really* be together anyway. Can we?

Danny tightens his grip and I can't remember when we stopped swaying, but we stand still holding each other as one song fades into another.

"Talk to me, Kal. Tell me where your head's at."

At this, I straighten and pull back. "I . . . I think I just need to go and get some sleep."

I break away, leaving Danny alone in the kitchen. I head to the

chapter

30

THE DOORBELL RINGS THE moment I shut off the water. Stepping out of the shower, I hastily dry off and wrap myself in a towel before padding through the bedroom to the front of the guest house.

When I open the door, Danny's standing on the other side. His hair and gray sweats are nearly soaked through, a sign he'd opted for some outdoor cardio after my abrupt departure from the study. His breathing is heavy and his eyes bore into me, like he's just run a marathon and I'm the finish line.

"Can I come in?" he asks.

I nod and step back, making space for him to follow. We're alone now and I am freshly aware that I'm naked underneath this towel. Given the way Danny's eyes crawl over every inch of my exposed skin, it's clear he is, too. We go no farther than the entryway, stopping to face each other with our backs to opposite walls.

"I'm sorry for leaving like that, Danny," I say, figuring I owe him at least an explanation. "I've had a lot on my mind since before I even got on the plane. Then I talked with your mom and—"

"We need to talk about what happened seven years ago," he cuts in.

Stunned, I step back flush against the wall and tighten the knot on my towel. Since the moment he picked me up from the airport there's been a tense undercurrent running between us, like he's been seeking something from me. What it was, I wasn't sure. Not until now.

"That's why you asked me here," I say.

"If you're wondering if I lied about this being a work trip, the answer is no," Danny says. "But we both know I could have had my parents' records shipped to LA. So yes. I wanted to steal time for us to just . . . be. To talk."

"So, let's talk," I say, as a reckless sense of this being one of those *now or never* moments sets in bone deep. "When you and I ended back in college . . . there was never really an actual *end*. We just faded away like we'd been nothing. How was it so easy for you to let go?"

"It wasn't," Danny says, with a hardness that cements his words. "When you didn't show at the wrap party, and I saw you'd blocked my texts, I left everyone at the bar to come see you. Then at your dorm, when Neha told me I was too late, I felt the ground fall out from under me. I had to let go then because I knew I'd already lost you."

He's halfway right. I stopped trying with Danny after that day on Christopher Street, when I saw him out with Hannah after blowing me off for a week. I'd wanted to obliterate every connective thread between us then and there. Block him in that moment so I wouldn't be tempted to beg for answers. But we had a film to shoot. So, for the next week on set for his thesis project, I played the consummate professional. And worst of all, he mirrored me. Only weeks prior, we'd spent our afternoons in bed together, wrapped around each other with our fingers intertwined. But for those seven days of principal photography, we were casual colleagues.

Whenever he'd approach me on set to earnestly ask about scheduling or locations, I'd answer competently, all the while internally begging him to throw me a bone—something, *anything* to help me believe that everything from before had been real. And even though I could see a storm of uncertainty, perhaps even remorse, churning in his eyes, he gave away nothing. Every day I played it cool was pure masochism. But I persisted until the final take. Then I was done.

So he's halfway right to say he'd already lost me by then. But the part he hasn't owned is that he'd pushed me away long before.

"Let's back up a bit," I say. "I need to know why you went cold on me after New Year's. After I told you I loved you, and that I'd never been kissed or touched by anyone but you?" I've needed this answer for seven years and now that it's within reach, my heart is racing.

Danny's expression crumbles. "I shouldn't have done that. I've regretted it every day since. I should have—"

"That's not what I'm asking," I cut in, desperate to keep us on track. "I need to know the why. *Why* did you do it?"

Danny rubs his hands down his face, like the answer is something painful and inconvenient. We're both quiet for a beat while he gathers his thoughts. "It was too much," he says, finally. "Everything about you, everything I felt for you. All of it was too much." He shifts now to lean back against the wall. To my surprise, a small smile curves his mouth. "I gravitated to you instantly. You were beautiful and open and different, and I wanted every part of you. And it wasn't long before I could see that I mattered to you in a big way, too. But wanting you quickly turned into needing you. Everything for me changed after that."

I can only assume that he's referring to the turning point of our relationship—the night of our first not-a-date date, which was the night his father died. Something about that night, and the weeks that followed, deeply altered the fabric of who we were to each other—who we'd always be.

"We don't really learn about grief until we're in it," Danny says, staring vacantly at some point past my shoulder. "We can read a million pamphlets and watch a hundred talk shows on the topic, but nothing prepares you for what it *feels* like. It's gaping and persistent and cold. I felt like the best I could do at the time was grab on to the brightest spot in my life just to feel a little warmth."

"That was our December," I say, knowingly. That first winter in New York was a whirlwind. I fell fast and hard and it felt like Danny was falling with me, like maybe we were at the beginning of *us*.

"Yeah," he replies. Then his eyes lock with mine. "The first time we kissed I felt weightless. Like I was spacewalking. I was so damn happy. But then came the guilt. The constant questioning of how I could be happy when my dad was gone and my mom was in agony."

I rub the center of my chest in a vain attempt to ease the pang that's settled there. "I wish you'd told me this. I wish I could have helped you."

Danny laughs without humor. "I mean, let's be honest, I couldn't have put words to it back then even if I'd tried. I just felt like too much of a mess to deserve you. Even now, I only understand what was going on with me after years of talking to a grief counselor."

Danny pauses at my sharp intake of breath. "After graduation, Mom and I . . . we ended up going together," he explains.

Despite the circumstances, this admission warms me. I'm glad he finally talked to someone, and that he did it with Minnie.

"Anyway, I can't deny that I was petrified on New Year's when you said you were in love with me. I'd sensed as much, but hearing you say the words triggered something in me that said *retreat*. Then later that night at my apartment when you wanted me to be your first, I'd already taken so much from you, I knew I had to pull back before you gave me that, too."

All of this, I can understand. Even forgive. But there's still the part I can't wrap my head around. "But I saw you with *her*," I say, and he flinches.

"A week after New Year's," I continue. "You'd left me alone in your loft after that night and then you barely took my calls or answered my texts. It was a shitty Saturday morning." To say the least. "I'd just lost my job and you'd blown me off all week. So, I decided to just show up on your doorstep and make you talk to me. I was walking down your block when I saw you with her. Hannah was her name. You had your arm over her shoulders and—"

"I think I saw you," he cuts in, like he's only now realizing it. "I didn't know it was you then. But I think I saw you running the other way."

He's right. I did run from them. I ran and didn't stop until I'd reached the underground subway platform. And when I got back to my dorm, I cried for hours and spent the next seven years trying to forget him altogether.

"On set that next week, I felt like I was on autopilot—like I could see you slipping away from me but I couldn't make myself act on it," he says. "If I'd known what you'd seen and what you'd been feeling, I want to believe I would have tried harder to snap out of what probably looked a lot like indifference. But I don't even know if I was capable," he admits, stepping off the wall and coming closer to me. "You'd offered me everything and I was so overwhelmed I couldn't accept it."

I swallow past a lump in my throat. "I can see that now. We had bad timing."

Danny shakes his head. "I know it doesn't make it okay, but I need you to hear this," he says, with his voice dropping low. "I didn't sleep with Hannah. We hung out a few times that week working on some scenes together. She maybe wanted more from me, but *nothing* happened. I never even kissed her. I was a fool, but I was still in love with you."

He's right, it doesn't make how he treated me okay. It sure as hell doesn't erase how low I felt when I saw him with her that morning. But hearing his explanation makes everything click, like we've just slid the last piece of a puzzle into place and can finally see the full picture. And even though it isn't pretty, what matters most is that we're both standing here looking at it together with the kind of clarity that maybe only time allows.

"You loved me?" Shamefully, it's all I can come up with to ask.

Danny stalks forward, crowding me in so close I have to tilt my neck to meet his eyes. "Love," he says, lightly grazing his fingertips up my arms from my wrists to my shoulders, leaving chills in their tracks. "I love you, Kaliya. I never stopped."

I close my eyes and fat tears roll free. Danny catches them with his thumbs, bringing his face a few inches from mine. "I swear to you, I don't ever want to hurt you like that again. And maybe these two days are all we can have right now, but—"

"It's enough," I cut in. "For now, this is enough."

chapter

31

H IS MOUTH CRASHES DOWN on mine.

And this, *this* is our reunion. This time, we know there will be no doubts, no stoppages, no interruptions. This time, with all our cards finally on the table, we are choosing to dive in head-first, to fully surrender to each other's gravity.

Danny slowly pulls away from the kiss, placing his forehead on mine. "We don't have to do this tonight, Kal. If you want to wait 'til after we wrap up the production . . . it might kill me but I'll make do," he says with a wry laugh. "The ball is in your court."

In response, I take Danny's hand and lead him through the living room and bedroom, toward the primary bath. Once inside, he grasps me from behind with his hands on my hips, peppering hot kisses along my neck and shoulder. We stumble forward as I go to turn on the shower, still steamy from the one I took just before he knocked on my door. I turn around to meet his stare.

We stand across from each other in front of the vanity, eyes locked and chests pounding. He said the ball was in my court. The old me would cower beneath that challenge but the *now* me is bolder, freer, and ready to act on her desires.

I loosen the knot on my towel, letting it fall to the floor, leaving me totally bare in front of Danny's deliberate gaze. His eyes leave my face for an indulgent perusal of everything I'm offering him. The muscles of his neck tense as he swallows thickly.

"God, Kaliya, you're perfect," he says. It's almost a whimper. If it's even possible for me to blush, I'm sure I'm doing it right now.

Then, with one hand, Danny reaches behind his neck and pulls his white T-shirt over his head in a single swift movement. Now it's my turn to behold perfection—long and lean and etched with precision, hard in all the best places. His broad chest tapers down to a washboard torso and then to narrow hips, where his gray sweats barely cling and a pronounced V-cut juts inward just above the waistband.

Danny toes off his shoes and hitches his thumbs behind the elastic, inching his sweats lower. I almost pass out at the sight of his straining erection, now freed. Everything about him is as expected and somehow . . . more.

We've stripped ourselves of our clothes and inhibitions, allowing our gazes to wander lazily as we present our naked bodies to each other. Somehow, we both know when the remnants of whatever emotional barrier that previously existed snap and fall to the floor between us, along with our discarded clothing. Because, without another word, we fuse together like magnets. His mouth on mine is searing, robbing me of my balance just as his hands reach down to my ass to press me closer against the place where his body reaches for me. We stumble sideways into the expansive rain shower kissing and groping, feeding on each other's air.

Danny closes the shower door, and instantly, we're enshrouded in a cloud of steam. His strong hands traverse my body roving for all the places he's left untouched for far too long. When he finds the tender aching spot between my legs, we both heave a sigh of relief.

I reach for him, too, firmly stroking along the length of his arousal, relishing the novelty of this new access he's granted me to his body. He groans into my mouth— *"Shit, Kaliya, yes, just like that."* His thick fingers slide firmly between my folds in search of their entry point. When they finally breach it, my head falls back and my vision blurs. Danny takes the opportunity to lavish attention on the sensitive skin of my neck and across my collarbone with his mouth.

Before I can stop myself, I'm begging to feel him inside me. But instead of answering my shameless plea, his hand abruptly stops and his forehead falls to my shoulder. I lean back, searching for his eyes.

"What's wrong?" I ask, slightly embarrassed by the panic I feel at the notion that anything could be wrong when everything feels so, so right.

"Nothing at all. It's just," he sighs. "We don't have protection. Unless you have something?" He's gone from distressed to hopeful in such an unvarnished way I'd find humor in this moment if only I, too, wasn't equally ill-prepared. Instantly a sinking feeling forms in the pit of my stomach. I was so wrapped up in desire I didn't even think of a condom. Danny brings both hands to either side of my face. We're so close. It's still not enough.

"I know I recently ended a relationship. But I took every precaution to make sure I was in the clear before I made the choice to act on my feelings for you, Kal. I wouldn't risk you like that. But I get it if we can't go beyond this point. I didn't ask you to fly down here expecting sex."

"No, it's okay," I say with a reassuring smile. "I'm covered with the pill. And it's been—let's just say, it's been a long time since I've been with anyone. And hey"—I touch his face to underscore what I say next—"I trust you, Danny."

He looks at me like giving him my trust means I've just handed him the world—a sign that tonight we're tending to the places we've both made sore. And there's nothing left to apologize for or explain, only to be together.

He kisses me now, long, slow, and deep—and the kiss eats at every second guess, doubt, and reason why we shouldn't be doing this. Done with waiting, I break our connection and push lightly on his shoulders, letting him know that I want him to sit on the bench that's affixed to the back wall of the shower. As he slowly lowers himself, his eyes slide from my face to my breasts and stomach, down to the small patch of dark curls above my pubic bone and back up again.

I step forward between his open legs and our knees graze past each other. Placing my hands on his shoulders as he grasps my hips firmly, I slowly ease myself down onto him, fitting us together like a lock to a key. He groans, I gasp, as if to say *in unison, at last*.

The feeling is overwhelming, finally *being* with Danny, naked and alone with him inside, beneath, and around me, I'm all-consumed. He smooths his large hands up my sides, stopping briefly to cup my breasts. "*So perfect*," he says to himself before bringing his hands to either side of my face and tilting my forehead down to meet his.

"Come on, baby, ride me." His words are strangled but clear and they spur me on to undulate my hips, releasing a sharp jolt of pleasure that sends both our heads careening back.

Then, we start to really move, a singular being with two racing hearts. We alternate between blissfully slow and languid and feverishly fast and deep. Our lovemaking is chiaroscuro, a perfect juxtaposition of opposites—more powerful together than ever apart.

"Fuck, yes, Kaliya," he rasps out. I'm almost at my tipping point and apparently Danny is, too, with his teeth grazing my shoulder and his hands pressed firmly into my hips. I arch my back, thrusting my breasts forward a bit, my not-so-subtle way of telling him where I want his mouth. He catches on quickly, hungrily feasting on the tips of them. It ratchets up the intense sensations sparking along my spine and down to my toes.

Danny stands, lifting me, taking me with him. I brace my legs securely around his hips as he walks me backward to press me against the shower wall. He clasps our hands, stretching our arms up along the wet tile. In full control now, he deepens the angle of himself inside me.

"Tell me if it's too much," he says through gritted teeth as he grinds his hips into me. I shake my head frantically.

"Never too much," I manage to pant out.

"That's my girl," he groans. His smile is dazzling, mirroring mine, and then it twists into a strained look of ecstasy as he picks up his pace in earnest. I wish I could watch us right now. Him mainly—to see the long lean muscles of his back and legs and ass as he thrusts himself into me. But then I think better of it, because seeing him might somehow diminish what it's like to *feel* him. With that thought, everything else intensifies, from the wild sounds of our bodies slamming against the shower wall to his *"Holy shit, Kaliya"* and my *"Yes, yes, god, yes."*

Suddenly I am completely coming apart in a protracted release of electric tension that causes my whole body to shake. Danny follows shortly after as the peak of his climax crashes into mine. Together, we form a tidal wave of pulsating bliss that washes away the regret of seven years spent apart.

Once we've come down from our orgasmic highs, we take our time lathering each other in soap, gently massaging away any residual tensions not released by our previous act. It's tender and playful and . . . effortless, like we're new to it and old pros all at once.

"Who knew showering could be this fun?" I muse, while absentmindedly tracing the soap suds on his shoulder.

"Literally anyone who's ever had sex in a shower before," he deadpans, his deep voice coming out like a rumble against the side of my neck where his open mouth is currently pressed.

I roll my eyes and playfully swat at his chest. "That was a rhetorical question, sir!"

He chuckles and as always, it's like a soft thunder. Then he pulls back to look me dead in the eye as a sudden seriousness settles in across his face. "From now on, just me and you. How does that sound?"

"Like everything I've ever wanted," I say, almost breathless.

Who knows how long we spend making out under the rainfall showerhead. But once fatigue sets in and our fingers turn to prunes, Danny suggests we consider a change of venues. So after lazily toweling each other off, we stumble into the bedroom and fall into a heap of tangled limbs on top of the king-size sleigh bed.

Sprawled on his back, Danny pulls me to lay directly on top of him so that now we're face-to-face, the length of my body taking up only a fraction of his. I fold my arms across his broad chest as he traces the curve of my back with his deliciously calloused hands. It's pure intimacy, pure contentment.

"Remind me why it took us so long to do this." He sounds foolishly happy, just the way I like him. I playfully bite his nose and then replace it with a quick kiss. And before I pull back, he catches my lips with his and we get lost in each other again for an undetermined amount of time.

"Pride, youthful idiocy, stuff like that," I offer as an answer when we come up for air. I mean to be playful but listing off the things that threatened Danny and me becoming an *us* in the past just conjures a whole new set of concerns about our immediate future.

"Hey, where'd you go just now?" He reaches up with his fingers to smooth the furrow in my brow.

"I'm just . . . trying not to think about the mess that's waiting for us back in LA," I admit. I have no idea how we're going to spend the next three months denying ourselves what we've just experienced.

But before I can dwell any more on it, Danny abruptly flips me onto my back and braces his forearms on either side of my head, bringing himself between my open legs. He nips at my lips and then my earlobe and shoulder, working his way downward. Chills scatter across my skin and I shudder in response.

"What are you doing?" I ask on a gasp. He takes turns sucking each of my breasts into his mouth, grazing his teeth across the plump tips, sending shock waves down each of my limbs.

"Clearly I haven't put my best foot forward if you're thinking about all of that right now," he says, his face looking quite determined.

Next, he kisses a wet trail down the center of my chest to my stomach and across the space between both my hip bones. Then, he sinks beneath the covers and gently pries apart my thighs. He takes several moments to admire the most private part of my body, and with any other partner, I'd feel mortified, but not with Danny. Then, he proceeds to make it impossible for me to think about anything but his mouth on me. And this time, we get it *just* right.

chapter
32

T HE SMELL OF BACON and sexy neo soul melodies lure me out
of a bone-deep sleep. I reach up to stretch my arms and then
groan at pangs of overuse that extend to nearly every muscle in
my body.

I savor the ache as a not-so-subtle reminder that last night,
Danny and I finally made love. As cringey as that phrase always
seemed to me before, now . . . I get it. *Making love* comes with the
added understanding that on top of this undeniable chemistry
and attraction, our hearts are in on it, too. We didn't stop there,
though. We didn't *just* make love. We also *fucked*. With our
bodies, we expressed and then released all the hurt, anger, regret,
and longing that had been pent-up inside us for seven years. It was
vigorous and ecstatic. It was freeing.

I could stay here, luxuriating in the feel of this cloudlike mattress and these buttery smooth sheets, *or* I could pry myself from
bed and go get my man, and that bacon.

The choice is easy.

I scoot to the edge of the giant bed and then tiptoe over to the bathroom where Danny's T-shirt lies strewn across the marble floor. A shiver runs through me at the memory of him peeling off that very shirt last night, right before he took me into the shower and changed my life. So, it's only right that I pick it up and pull it over my naked body, then savor the smell of Danny's intoxicating sweet citrus mixed with rain.

Can I be so bold as to walk out there in *only* this? I turn around in the mirror and see the shirt just barely covers my ass. Remembering that Minnie is only a stone's throw away and liable to come knocking at her guest house anytime, last-minute, I decide to grab my thin cotton robe from the hook on the back of the door and throw it around me.

The primary bedroom of the guest house opens directly into the kitchen. I pry open the door to peek through, cautiously confirming Danny's alone. The sight that greets me through the crack in the door is enough to propel me forward. It's Danny's naked back. The long, lean muscles flex and contract as he cracks eggs into a frying pan and begins to whisk. Involuntarily, my eyes drift from his shoulders down to the sexy indents of his lower back. Instantly, my mouth waters. Then my eyes fall a few more inches to his perfectly firm—

"Hi, you." His voice makes me jump. Without turning around, he knew I was standing here, ogling him. Perhaps he felt the intensity of my eyes, like little horny laser beams trained on his ass.

"Hi, you," I parrot back. Sauntering forward, I wrap my arms around his waist from behind and melt against his backside. I look down at the counter and notice a basket packed with fresh fruit and several mini mason jars. I pick one up and turn it over in my hand. "What's all this?"

"Peach preserves. Mom dropped them off this morning with a note that said, 'Enjoy breakfast.' So . . . I figured we should do as we're told."

"Good boy." I chuckle before setting down the jar and re-plastering myself against him. Next, I'm mindlessly humming into his shoulder blade.

"Pretty sure I've had dreams about exactly this," he rasps and then I feel his deep, sexy laugh rumble through his chest.

"I'm pretty sure that whenever I dream, it's about exactly this." I've fully leaned in to the idea of us now, like maybe we *can* have it all. Even if we have to wait a while. Sheryl Sandberg would be proud.

Finally, Danny turns, enveloping me in his arms, before walking us a few steps away from the stove toward the center island.

"I dream about this, too." He swoops down to catch my lips in a slow, sultry kiss that lasts longer than it should with bacon on the stove. "And also, this." He snakes his hands down the small of my back and then lower to firmly squeeze *my* peach.

Giggling, I pry him off me and shoo him to the side so I can check on the burner. "Okay, before we get ourselves carried away, we need to turn these off. I can't be the reason the Prescott palace gets burned to the ground."

"Hope you like your bacon crispy," he says, reaching past me for the skillet so that he can transfer the semiburnt bacon over to a waiting platter. Once he's done that, he turns to the basket with a spark of mischief in his eye. He picks up one of the jars and slowly twists off the lid. He steps closer until he's flush against me, pressing me into the countertop.

"Here, try this." He dips the tip of his finger into the jar of peach preserves before bringing a dollop of the glistening nectar to my lips. Without breaking our eye contact, I open my mouth just slightly, welcoming a taste. When the tangy sweetness of the preserves touches my tongue, I wrap my lips around his finger and suck. Hard. My eyes fall closed at the same moment I register his sharp intake of breath followed by a deep groan. It spurs me on and before I think twice, I bite the tip of his finger.

"Fuck!" He hisses.

My eyes shoot open. "Did I hurt you?"

"Not even close." Chuckling, he moves my hand between us to graze over the crotch of his gray sweats. "Quite the opposite actually," he says with a megawatt smile. My heart flutters and heat pools between my legs. But something changes in the way he's looking at me, briefly quieting our lust.

"What's wrong?" I ask, uncertain of the sudden shift.

"I want you to know that I understand why you had doubts about me. I know it wasn't just the shit from our past," he says as his hands wind around the small of my back to bring us closer. Our foreheads touch and I close my eyes.

"This business hasn't been kind to you, Kal," he says. "But I wasn't kidding last night. I never stopped loving you. That means, whatever happens next, I got you."

His words are tender and fierce, like a vow. I've never felt more seen, and it means more than he could ever know. I lift my hands to cup the sides of his face, and then I kiss him to stop myself from crying. "I love you, Daniel Ellis Prescott."

I've said it again, for the first time since my badly timed New Year's confession. But this time, without fear that I'll be left hanging.

"And I love you," he says as his stare is overrun by flames and a smirk tips the corner of his mouth. "I love you in nothing but my shirt." He starts pulling off my robe. "I love you more in nothing at all."

I reach into the waistband of his sweats and slide them down revealing his straining length. He lifts me onto the island and I wrap my legs around his waist just as he enters me. Both our heads fall back at the blinding sensation of being joined together again in this way.

Breakfast can wait. We've got more love to make.

THE MIDMORNING SUN SHINES THROUGH ORNATE BAY WIN-dows, bathing us in warm light as we sit in the cozy breakfast nook of the guest house. After getting lost in each other on the island, we dressed ourselves and settled in for breakfast. We ate our scrambled eggs, crispy bacon, and toasted biscuits with peach jam in companionable silence while exchanging heated glances, with our legs and feet tangled below.

Danny reaches across the table, lacing our fingers together. Looking down at our hands, I remember aloud, "Copper and sand." Our eyes meet and I know he remembers, too.

It was that same crisp October night just two months after we first met. We strolled down Broadway toward the Angelika for a screening of *Lawrence of Arabia*. Only friends at this point, and new ones at that, neither of us had let on to our mutual attraction. We were freshly getting to know each other, sharing random facts about ourselves when Danny casually let it slip that he was color-blind.

Astonished, I spoke before I could think. "So then, what do I look like to you?" I asked. Then instantly, I flushed with embar-rassment at my bold question. But to my surprise, he didn't laugh it off or roll his eyes.

Instead, he took my hand. "When I look at us," he said, turning my palm over in his. "My skin looks like sand and yours—" With his free hand, he traced across the thin, smooth skin that covered my knuckles, leaving behind what felt like tiny electric pulses. "Yours has a bit of a glow. Like copper."

I don't know if he meant for it to be sensual at the time, but the place where he'd touched me felt like a live wire. Like I'd shed my outer layer and opened myself up to the elements. We kept eye contact without words as I tried to picture what it might look like for copper and sand to kiss.

All these years later, Danny laughs deeply at the memory. "You know, that conversation was when I knew you'd be trouble for me."

"I had you beat, then," I say, resting my chin on my free hand. "I knew I was in trouble the moment I got out of the cab with that big old suitcase and saw you crossing Broadway."

His smile falters just slightly and his eyebrows lift. "Wait, you saw me first?"

I laugh, surprised I never told him this part. "You might be the reason I didn't see the cyclist coming," I say, as heat floods my face.

The smile Danny aims at me in response is so broad and bright, it nearly knocks the wind out of me. He leans forward, bringing his hand to the back of my neck to gently pull me in for a kiss. We tangle there for a long moment until Danny's phone rings, cutting into our reverie. For a second it seems he intends to ignore it.

"It's probably important," I say.

He squeezes my hand before letting go to check the caller ID. "It's Eric," he says. "I probably should get this."

I nod and take a sip of my lukewarm coffee as Danny answers the call. "My man!" he says, heading out to the courtyard. His voice fades as the door closes behind him.

I busy myself by spreading peach jam on another biscuit and basking in its sweetness. Content to the point of distraction, it's not long before I'm savoring the last bite and Danny's coming back inside. Within seconds, I can sense the call was bad news. The strained look on his face and his rigid posture give it away. He rejoins me at the booth and I venture cautiously, "I take it all isn't well back in LA?"

"Afraid not," he says, settling back in and re-tangling his legs with mine under the table. "Apparently my executive producer decided the script that was locked a month ago needed an over-haul with a brand-new writer," he says flatly.

Danny passes his phone to me and on it, there's an email from Celine to Max Crawford's agent.

> We're working on an overhaul of the current script that focuses less on the romance. We aren't trying to make a new *Loving* after all. And Minnie's arc is just less compelling. Now that Max is on board, I want the script to focus on Nathan Prescott's rise to fame out of obscurity. Trust me, this new direction will make it a role that breaks Max out of the mold.

My blood runs cold when I've finished reading. "How did you get this?" I ask.

Danny scrubs his hands down his face in frustration. "Max's agent is good friends with Eric and thought he needed to know," Danny explains, and he's practically vibrating. His leg bobs rapidly under the table and thick veins burst from his temples.

"Okay, so let's think," I say, trying to project a sense of calm into the atmosphere. "What are our options?"

"First, we gotta get back to LA," he says, before downing his coffee and grabbing my hand to lead me out of our nook of bliss.

chapter

33

WE TAPED UP THE boxes from Minnie's attic and shipped them to her second home in Malibu. Needless to say, we'll be cataloging the family photos and records later. We said our goodbyes and boarded an overnight flight back to Los Angeles, where we arrived early Sunday morning.

With Neha out of town, Danny invited me to stay with him at his home in the Hollywood Hills for the week. Despite this fresh wave of drama with Celine and the production, we're still basking in the afterglow of Friday night. So, it was an easy offer to accept. We banked only a few hours of sleep after landing. Then, I saw Danny off to go talk strategy with Eric.

It's Monday now and we're at the office for a day of damage control. So far, Danny's plan is to take a discreet lunch meeting with Max's agent to reinforce *his* vision for the film. If Danny can get Max's team on board with the original script, it'll be even more convincing when he meets with Jim to issue an ultimatum—the script stays as is, or he'll walk with the talent.

It's a gamble. Jim could always opt to enforce the operating agreement and replace Danny with a new director. But Danny's in possession of his father's archives *and* holds the rights to his life story. Plus he's counting on the powerful studio head being decent enough to let him tell it.

So with this plan underway, Danny's currently across the studio lot having lunch with the agent. I, on the other hand, have spent the morning dusting off my old headset and covering the reception desk.

At six a.m. this morning, I lay awake tangled up in Danny and his million-thread-count sheets, looking cross-eyed at an SOS text from Gary. Apparently, his front desk temp had called out sick and I *owed him* for abandoning my post and leaving him in the lurch. Figuring it best for me to steer clear of the impending "above the line" drama on the eleventh floor, I agreed, albeit very reluctantly.

By now, it's late afternoon and I regret the decision exactly as much as I thought I would.

". . . As I was saying, in the opening scene of the film, a very rare and quite endangered Cuban Black Hawk is pierced through with a spear—"

"A computer-generated spear," I interject, cutting off what feels like the ninetieth caller of the day. She's an animal activist with a bone to pick about Wide Angle's latest action release, *A Hunter's Game*. I've been at it with her for nearly ten minutes, attention fading in and out and my patience wearing thin.

"So you claim," she adds. "But as I said before, without the disclaimer, how am I, as a viewer, to know for certain that the animal was not harmed?"

"Look, Nancy, was it?" I ask sharply, my irritation spiking up a notch or two. "The scene was filmed in front of a green screen on the Galaxy Films back lot, not in the wild as it appeared. The hawk itself was not real. Neither was the spear. The 'no animals were harmed' label only applies to productions that involve *actual* live animals and that have been monitored by American Humane's film and TV unit. I'm sure you can see now that this is a nonissue."

"Well, they make it look so *real* these days! Again, how was I supposed to know this?" Nancy exclaims.

Instead of firing off with, *Well, Nancy, here's the thing, now you DO know*, I lie, politely. "Oh, look! I have someone on the other line. I hope this has been helpful."

Click!

Just before I'm about to drop my head onto the keyboard in despair, out of the corner of my eye, I notice good old Sharon-from-Accounting moseying up to my desk. With my cubicle several floors up, I haven't seen her in months. Can't say I've missed her.

"Oh, there you are!" she exclaims. It's nice to see she hasn't changed, still pitch-perfect with her special brand of phony enthusiasm. "I was wondering how long that little experiment with you working upstairs was going to last," she muses.

There are *things* I want to say to this woman. Things she deserves to hear. But the sad truth is I won't get away unscathed when she no doubt reports me to HR for saying them. So, per usual, I swallow the words whole, fix my face, and bury it all beneath the facade of professionalism.

"Need something?" I ask coolly.

In reply, she drops a thick stack of paper on my desk—collated budgets that, by the looks of it, need stapling. "The staple function on the Xerox is broken," she alleges. "But I saw you here and figured, you know what to do."

Sharon expects me to manually staple this enormous stack of budgets by hand—a task that she, no doubt, is wholly capable of completing herself. And a task that would have been par for the course for me months ago. But not anymore. I may be sitting *at* the reception desk right now, but I am no longer *of* the reception desk. Without answering her, I open the drawer and brandish a good old-fashioned hand stapler before plunking it on top of her stack.

"I think this is what you're looking for, Sharon," I say, before getting up to leave her there, mouth open wide. I am heading toward the kitchen to re-up my coffee when my pocket starts to vibrate. It's a text from Bella.

BELLZ: Are you in today?

ME: Been covering at reception. Why? What's up?

BELLZ: Meet me in Danny's office STAT.

Bella is being cryptic, and it puts me on edge. Whatever the cause of this Mayday text, it can't be good news. Immediately, I think of Danny's plan and wonder if it's already up in flames. But he's still at lunch with the agent and his meeting with Jim is not 'til morning.

My pocket buzzes again with a new text from Bella.

BELLZ: Be sneaky. But fast.

Hackles up, I abandon my coffee at the reception desk and head up the elevator. When it deposits me on the eleventh floor, I check behind each shoulder before padding softly down the hall to Danny's office.

When I'm just outside his door, I hear voices. Turning the knob, I pry it open ever so slightly and just enough for me to see

Bella alone at Danny's desk. She squints over his laptop as a pit of unease lodges in my stomach.

Bella looks up. "Close. The. Door!" She whisper-shouts as she beckons me to come inside.

When I enter and shut the door, the formerly faint voices from Danny's laptop are now loud and clear. Bella's been eavesdropping.

I have half a mind to tell her to shut the screen when I hear—*"But Hollywood loves a 'race movie.' I mean, people eat this shit up!"* followed by a guffaw.

Only now do I recognize that the voices and laughter belong to Celine *and* Jim. My heart drops to my stomach. I scurry over to join Bella behind Danny's desk. Once there, I quickly surmise that Danny's laptop is dialed into the office video conference system in the main meeting room. A camera and mic that have been mounted in the corner of the room give us eyes and ears on Celine and Jim's not-so-private meeting.

"But you see, here's the part no one wants to say out loud." Jim's voice rings out with its customary air of self-importance as he sits reclined in a chair. His leathery hands gesture broadly, punctuating his words. Celine is seated next to him, leaning in, hanging on to every phrase.

"People are growing weary of all this race business and the cancel-culture hoopla. If it's not slavery, it's Jim Crow, and if not that, it's all those marches and sit-ins and freedom rides. Don't get me started with this BLM business," Jim spews.

I lock eyes with Bella and the shock on her face mirrors my own. This *is* her uncle speaking after all. She motions to the corner of the laptop display where there's a red light showing she's screen-recording it all. My face heats. This just became a real-life install-ment of Charlie's Angels. I turn my attention back to Jim's tirade.

"You know, I've been around this town longer than you've been

alive," he says to Celine and his words are dripping in condescension. *"And I remember the days when it brought the studios prestige to navel-gaze about social justice issues. We made all these bleeding-heart flicks about 'civil* rights.' *It's this stuff that gave folks like Denzel a career, mind you. But the shit never ends. And my generation is so tired of all the guilt and the self-flagellation. We're artists, not activists,"* he whines. *"And what's it all for now anyways, if not just overcompensation? How is this stuff even relevant anymore?"*

My feet are nailed to the floor and blood retreats from my limbs. It's one thing to *suspect* an older rich guy with an obscene amount of power and privilege might harbor some backward notions about race. But to *witness* it all in play is something else entirely. And this is the type of person who gets to decide which stories get told in this town?

A new realization washes over me like cold water. Jim might be a Hollywood dinosaur with questionable ethics, but he was our lifeboat—the only vote that mattered for Danny to get his film back. Now that plan's evaporated.

"You have a point there." Celine chimes in and at this stage, I can't be surprised at the levels to which she'd stoop.

"Look," Jim says. *"The long and the short of it is, we've all seen a version of dear old Danny boy's movie before. The race trope is tired. If he thinks he'll win by getting* his *version of the script locked, he has another thing coming. I mean, it's a sob story about his parents for fuck's sake. Talk about a vanity project! So get this. I've spoken with business affairs, and looks like there's some wiggle room in the distribution clause."*

Celine leans in so far, she's practically in his lap.

". . . I'm gonna cut the theatrical release here. Sell the rights to one of the streamers—they'll give it a nice push in February, capi-

*talize on Black History Month and all that jazz. Then we'll get him
a middling ancillary deal with foreign rights and call it a day."*

"*But what about Max?*" Celine asks, concern suddenly furrow-
ing her brow. "*He would have never signed on if he knew the studio
wasn't fully backing the picture. Plus, there's no way Danny's going
to take this lying down.*"

"*I'll handle Max,*" Jim assures her. "*As for Danny, he's not going
to know until I get my ducks aligned and there's no turning back
contractually. I don't want to risk him finding a loophole in one of
the clauses and then running off to Focus or Searchlight and turning this into an awards darling like his dad did with that last
film—the fucker screwed me out of an Oscar with that one. And not
to mention how the headlines would bury me as some 'used-up
has-been who can't recognize a hit' if it ever happens again.*"

"*But where does this leave me?*" Celine asks. Any hope I had for
her having a moral breakthrough has just jumped out the window
and died on the pavement. "*I have skin in the game on this project,
too, you know.*"

"*Trust me, sweetheart. You sit tight on this one, and I'll get you
a first-look deal with the studio. Do right by me and I'll do right by
you, too.*" Jim extends his hand and they both shake on it, cement-
ing this unholy alliance.

Then, almost absentmindedly, Celine glances up in the direction of the camera and all the color drains from her face. She must
recognize the small green light indicating the camera's been on
throughout this entire conversation.

What follows is like a sad comedy of sorts with Celine grasping Jim's arm to silently direct his attention toward the camera, as
if the damage hasn't been done already. Then, like a white-collar
criminal who's just answered a midnight knock from the FBI, Jim's

face goes bright with shock. He grabs the Polycom remote and the screen on Danny's computer goes dark.

Bella and I silently stare at the black square for several long seconds, each of us processing what it is we've just witnessed—a treacherous plot to cut Danny's theatrical release and ruin his chances at Oscar eligibility.

"Holy shit, Kaliya," Bella exclaims. "I swear I had no idea he was like this. I mean the guy's an asshole, sure. A bit handsy with women who aren't my aunt, even. But a racist? That was nowhere on my bingo card for Uncle Jim."

Bella's shock, while still dripping with naïveté, strikes me as entirely sincere. She's a young woman of immeasurable privilege but she's never showcased denial of that fact, or worse, apathy. But in all fairness, we've got bigger fish to fry.

Jim and Celine are plotting to sabotage Danny's film. And right now, Danny's counting on Jim to take his side against Celine's wayward creative direction—only he has no idea that Jim is already in bed with her, figuratively.

Next, I grab my phone, open our texts, and tap out the only message that makes sense for a time like this . . . WE NEED TO TALK.

My head swims with thoughts of ways to help Danny out of this situation. I turn to Bella. "I know Jim is your family and that might mean you can't help me out here," I say. "I promise I'll understand if that's the case. I'm still going to—"

"Stop. Say no more." Her words are intentional, decisive. She leans over Danny's laptop and quickly opens up her email. She attaches the video file to a message and sends it to herself.

"Everything we need to warn Danny should be captured in the recording," she says, with a wobbly smile and glassy eyes. Then she shrugs. "Here's to being on the right side of history."

The weight of her decision to go against her family is not lost on me, so I pull her in for a tight hug. "Okay. You should run before someone realizes we're in here. I'll stay and shut down his laptop so there's no evidence in case Celine comes around to snoop."

Bella winks at me as she rushes from the room. I lean over Danny's desk, figure it'd be smart to erase his conference call log while I'm at it. I right click on the call log and select DELETE. I'm closing out of Danny's open projects, ensuring everything's saved, when I hear a familiar voice slither across the room.

"What are *you* doing in here?" Celine's words ring with heavy accusation, as if *I'm* the one attempting the coup.

But I can't let on to what I know if I'm going to warn Danny in enough time for him to strategize a way out of all this. And if Celine knows that I know what she and Jim are plotting, everything could blow up prematurely. So, I regulate my voice and shrug casually. "Just popped in a second ago to grab some info Danny requested off his laptop."

Quickly, I rise and make a path past Celine and straight for the door.

She catches my arm and squeezes, forcing me to stop in my tracks.

"Whatever you think you heard just now, forget it," she says. "Because if you breathe a word of this to Danny, I will personally see to it that you never work on another film. Not even the phones. One call to the right people about how you whored your way into my relationship and onto this production, and you'll never find another person in this industry who's willing to give you a shot."

I bristle at the venom in her words. But she's deluded if she thinks her threats hold any sway with me at this point.

I shake my arm free of her clutches, square my shoulders, and look her straight in the eye. "Celine, I am genuinely sorry for anything I may have done to hurt you personally. But nothing happened between me and Danny while the two of you were together. I am not your enemy, but I'm also not your doormat, either."

I pause to look her up and down. "And you don't scare me," I say. Then, I shake free of her grasp and walk away.

chapter
34

Oh, thank god. It's been two hours since I texted Danny from his office and, with no response from him, my workday had ground to almost a complete halt. It was all I could do not to sit staring blankly at my phone just willing it to ping. Now my fingers can't text back fast enough.

ME: What took you so long?

SCHOOL DAZE: The meeting went over. Everything okay?

ME: We need to talk.

SCHOOL DAZE: Gathered that. You gonna tell me what we need to talk about?

ME: Not here. Meet back at your place?

SCHOOL DAZE: OMW now.

SCHOOL DAZE: We'll cook dinner and then we can have dessert. [peach emoji]

He's entirely too calm about this. Granted, he doesn't know what *this* is yet. But I'd had a feeling Eric's call about Celine's plans to torpedo the script was only the tip of the iceberg. And it never let up for a second. Now that there's proof, I'm not in the mood for *dessert*. And I'm sure after Danny hears what I have to say, he won't be, either. But before I can respond, another text comes through.

SCHOOL DAZE: Hey. Whatever it is, we'll be okay. Remember, I got you . . .

My heart swells, because now, we get to communicate like lovers do. And despite all the mess we've returned to, this feeling of being an *us* is heady and wonderful and finally, it's ours. But if history has taught me anything, it's that it's fragile, too.

———

I PULL UP A STEEP DRIVEWAY THAT'S EDGED WITH TOWERING cypress trees that bend and sway in the breeze. At the top is Danny's house in the Hills, an understated ranch-style home that sits overlooking Hollywood.

Made up of sharp angles and painted mossy green, the minimalist exterior camouflages what makes it so unique. Danny's home was gifted to him in his father's will and designed by legendary LA architect Paul Revere Williams. With walls of sliding glass that blend the outside with the in, it's considered a midcentury masterpiece.

I let myself in through the white oak front door with the key Danny had given me shortly after we landed. Sounds from Herbie Hancock bounce on every surface as I walk through the foyer and into the open plan living room. I find Danny in the kitchen opening a bottle of wine.

The pit that formed in my stomach hours ago is now a valley. When Danny sees me, he reaches for a tiny remote to lower the music and rounds the kitchen island to sweep me up in his arms.

"Hi," I manage to squeak out, taking a moment to savor this calm before the storm.

"Hi," he says before dipping down for a soft kiss hello. He goes back to the stove where now I see he's already started prepping dinner.

"My lunch with Max's agent was *interesting* . . . but good," he says, preparing to chop garlic. "But you go first."

"Can you put down the knife?" I ask. His brow furrows in confusion but he sets it down.

"I don't know how else to do this," I begin. "So, I'm just going to come out and say it."

"Okay, well sounds like we're gonna need these," he says before passing me a fresh glass of wine. I take a sip for liquid courage, then let it all out.

"Jim is no longer a reliable ally for getting back control of the film," I say. "It's not just Celine who's working behind your back to undermine the project; they're working together against you."

Danny sets down his wineglass. "And we know this, how?" His words are calm and measured, like water before it simmers.

I take one full deep breath and let the rest spill out like a bag of marbles. "I overheard a private conversation between Jim and Celine today while you were out. They were together in the main meeting room but didn't know your laptop was dialed into the teleconference system. Basically, Jim's had it out for this project from the beginning. He says Hollywood is tired of 'race films' and never intended to make this movie a success. Now he's found some loophole in the distribution clause of your contract." I pause to gauge Danny's reaction. His face is expressionless, his posture like stone. I sigh. "Danny, if you can't find a way to breach your contract with Wide Angle fast, *What Love Made* isn't going to get a theatrical release."

Danny remains silent, but he grips the edge of the island, staring blankly at a spot between us.

"There's one more thing," I add. "Jim promised Celine a first-look deal if she keeps quiet. He didn't want her warning you so you could find a way out of the contract."

"And you're sure about this?" Finally, he speaks and it's not at all what I expected to hear.

I could easily call Bella and ask her to forward me the recording, but I decided on my way over here that I didn't want to involve her in this if I didn't have to. And I *shouldn't* have to for him to believe me. "Of course I'm sure," I say, trying to soothe the sting of his doubt. "I wouldn't be telling you if I wasn't."

Danny's eyes flick up to mine under a creased forehead. His wheels are turning, and try as I might, I can't get a read on him. "Look. I know this is a lot to process," I say.

His grip tightens on the edge of the island as his head hangs low between his shoulders. "That's not it," he says. "I just . . . I need to talk to Celine."

Another sting. But I ignore it. He's reeling right now, not thinking clearly. "Wait. You're going to call her?" I ask, cautiously. "You really think that's a good idea?"

He straightens from the countertop with an inscrutable look on his face. It's emotionless, like he's on autopilot. "She's still my business partner," he says. "We've both invested in this project. It's one thing for her to wrestle me for creative control, but what you're describing is total self-sabotage."

It's on the tip of my tongue to tell him about Celine's threat to damage me if I came to him with the truth, in hopes it might hammer the point home. But I stop short of doing so. I've given him all the details that matter as far as his production is concerned. And when it comes to finally seeing the truth about the person he's been so intimately involved with, it's clear to me now that he's just going to have to get there on his own.

I can hardly find words, so I simply nod and say "Good luck" in quiet resignation.

Danny circles the island and presses a kiss on the top of my head before disappearing into his office. I'm left alone to wonder what the hell happens next.

FOR TWO HOURS, DANNY'S BEEN ON THE PHONE IN HIS OF-fice with the door shut as I've paced the living room, anxiously sipping wine and trying not to eavesdrop. I gave in to hunger pangs and ordered us Thai food, figuring that dinner he'd planned to prepare would have to wait for another night.

By nine o'clock, exhaustion from the events of the past two days has me dozing on the sofa. But when Danny's office door clicks open, I sit up straight.

"Hey," he says, joining me on the couch. He sits close enough for our bodies to touch, and then he melts into the cushions.

"Hey. How'd it go?" I ask, reaching for him.

He laces our fingers together and rubs his temple with his free hand. "It took her an hour, but she finally fessed up."

I'm relieved as much as I'm surprised to hear it. I reach up to rub his neck and ease some of the tension there.

"I'm sorry about before," he says, leaning into my touch. "I knew it was true the moment you said it. I think I just needed to have that last conversation with her, and to let her know that I won't let them win."

I slide my hand around to cup his face. His eyes fall closed, and for a moment, he looks as peaceful as he did in the sun-drenched kitchen of the guest house in Austin. It's hard to imagine that was only two days ago.

"What happens now?" I ask.

Danny sits up, bringing our clasped hands to rest in his lap. "I spent another hour on the phone with my agent and lawyer," he says. "He'll go to bat and try to get the operating agreement dissolved so the film rights can revert back to me. But it'll take time. So, for now, the production is shuttered."

I should have anticipated this being a possibility but hearing him confirm it makes my stomach drop. "Oh."

"I knew things were bad. I just don't see how we got *here*," he says, angry with himself. "The fact Jim is doing this to get back at my dad, who won him an Oscar, by the way. It's just wild."

"You had no reason to assume they'd stoop *this* low," I tell him.

Danny moves closer to me now, resting his head on my shoulder. I wrap my arms around him, holding him close, attempting to siphon off some of the stress.

"I love you. I'm sorry," I whisper into the crown of his head. "One day things will be easier." I feel the tension slowly ease from his shoulders. For a long while I stay there, wrapped up in him, wondering if what I've said is true.

NAYNAY: I'm going to send you a link to something but promise me you're sitting down before you open it.

NAYNAY: And remember you are loved by the people who matter.

Neha's message bubble pops up as I'm steeping tea. It's been two days since Danny shuttered the production and he's been in a constant state of triage with his lawyers ever since. With my roommate out of town, I've been holing up at Danny's place. Much to Gary's astonishment, rather than reprise my role as "the front desk girl," I opted for relying on my savings account to float me while I apply for temp jobs elsewhere.

I add a spoon of sugar to my Earl Grey before typing a reply.

ME: You're scaring me. Has someone died? Tell me it's not Stevie.

NAYNAY: Stevie Wonder is alive and well last I checked.

NAYNAY: But seriously. Kal, promise me you're sitting down.

ME: Phew! Someone put that man on Life Alert. We can't
lose another legend.

ME: And okay, I'm sitting.

The three dots dance and then a link comes through in a message from Neha. When I click it, I'm directed to Glitter 'n' Dirt, a
notorious web blog that's run by former entertainment reporter
turned salacious gossipmonger, Rick Fenway. Lately, he's Hollywood's preeminent "source" for the kind of celebrity reporting
that any publicist worth their paycheck would *never* sanction. But
because his scruples are loose to nonexistent, nothing is off-limits
with Rick—which is precisely why everyone's so afraid of him.

If your name or face shows up on the G&D website or worse,
his daily carousel of Instagram stories, it most likely means you're
either the victim or the perpetrator of something criminal or crim-
inally shameful. Ever the strategist, Rick's MO is to blend a swirl of
circumstantial facts into a concoction of salacious speculation—a
formula he's generated for content that aims to be *believable* rather
than true. And in this town of make-believe, nothing else really
matters.

His site is an eyesore. Obtrusive pop-ups and a barrage of jarring weight loss ads test my patience while the home page slowly
loads. I pray I haven't infected my laptop by venturing to the
nether regions of the internet where the likes of G&D reside. But
as the junk clears, a grainy photo comes into view. To my sheer
horror, it is unmistakably a pap shot of me and Danny.

Snapped only days ago, the photo depicts the two of us at the Hollywood Farmers' Market. We'd stopped there on our way home from the airport. It was a peaceful Sunday, the calm before the storm. So we'd ventured to the market to stock up for a week of dinners for two at his place. I stare at the photo, heart tugging at this view of us from someone else's vantage point. It would be totally innocuous if it weren't taken for the purpose of lining Rick Fenway's pockets. Danny leans down to kiss the top of my head while I laugh at a joke I can't recall.

Admittedly, the outing was unwise, given the public's ongoing impression of his relationship with Celine. But we were still lost in the bliss of our time in Austin and had foolishly let our guards down. We never even registered the flash.

A shudder runs up my spine when my eyes snap to the headline:

WHEN HOLLYWOOD ROYALTY FALLS FOR "THE HELP"

I spot the caption on the photo and my insides twist.

[pictured above, Tinseltown legacy Danny Prescott, director and son of deceased mogul Nathan Prescott, peruses the Sunday farmers' market with "the other woman"]

It is an out-of-body experience, witnessing the secure anonymity I've enjoyed for more than a quarter of a century slip away. Against my better judgment, I scroll down to read the whole thing.

Some Hollywood hopefuls pay their dues to get to the top. Others, like Danny Prescott, son of four-time Oscar winning

director Nathan Prescott, are born with a silver spoon in their mouth. Then there are those who just sleep their way up the ladder, like Prescott's new girlfriend, Kaliya Wilson. G&D has learned that Wilson makes copies and answers phones for a living at a glitzy Hollywood studio—the one distributing Prescott's next flick. But it appears the twenty-six-year-old receptionist has found her true calling as "the other woman."

Unless you've been under a rock since May, you've seen my coverage of the rumors spinning around long-time lovers and sometimes collaborators, Danny Prescott, the big-shot director, and Celine Michèle, the multihyphenate actress, producer, and entrepreneur. Several sources had implied that an unconfirmed split in late spring may have been due to irreconcilable differences around his latest production, *What Love Made* (which I'm told will be going straight to streamers). Today, I can put all those missives to rest because a source very close to the situation has confirmed the split, and the real reason behind it. Turns out, after two years together, Prescott shamelessly stepped out on Michèle with his college ex, the previously unknown Wilson.

Those sources confirmed the two attended film school together the better part of a decade ago. But after several years of no contact, Wilson, the jilted dreamer, reappeared asking Prescott for a job. As the film's executive producer, Michèle agreed to offer Wilson a coveted role on the crew. But Wilson had other motives.

"It's a shame really. I guess the saying's true that no good deed . . . well, you know the rest," remarked the source, who requested to remain anonymous.

To say the movie's up in flames hotter than the ones in Prescott's bedroom would be an understatement. He'll be lucky if this hot-mess flick ever makes it to the can, let alone a theater.

Per usual, I never end a report without offering sage advice to all parties involved:

Danny Prescott—In the post-#MeToo world we live in, no one likes a womanizer on a set. Sir, you've got some explaining to do.

Celine Michèle—We hear you recently struck a first-look deal with Wide Angle Pictures. So we have a feeling you'll be just fine.

Kaliya Wilson—Honey, you may have gotten the guy, for now. But good luck finding another job in this town!

Rick Fenway, over and out!

They say the internet is forever. All those photos of me as a homely eighth grader with braces, sporting my school's quiz-bowl polo, will likely follow me to my grave. Along with the questionable outfits centered on my collection of cinch belts in college. Those, I can deal with—chalk them up to a life full of *choices*. But this is not that. Now, my name will be inextricably linked with the words *home-wrecker* and *opportunist* for anyone I encounter on my journey toward being taken seriously in this industry. RIP to my reputation.

But before I've even processed any of this, I hear the subtle hum of Danny's car pulling into the driveway. Feeling numb and sluggish, I sag on my stool at Danny's kitchen counter. If Neha had not demanded I sit down, I'd surely be a heap on the floor. Fat tears roll off the tips of my lower lashes and splash onto my hands that lay loosely on my lap.

The front door swings open and in comes Danny, at one with the sunshine, completely oblivious to the storm brewing inside me. He's spent the last few days in varying stages of tense determination. With the production on pause, we've been cooped up together in a war room of sorts as we figure out next steps in wresting back the rights to the film. Each morning, he's awakened to calls from his agent and each night, he spends hours in consultation with his lawyers.

But this morning was the fifth in a row that I got to wake up with his body pressed against mine, lulled into a fragile sense of peace by the rhythmic movement of his breathing. Amid the turmoil in our careers, this closeness with him has been like a balm. I have never felt so deeply connected to another person and yet so terrified that at any moment, the connection could snap.

Danny pads across the living room and into the kitchen while balancing several takeout bags from his favorite breakfast spot and what appears to be a bottle of champagne. "You're going to love what I picked up for dessert—" His booming voice goes quiet at the same time his face falls flat. Worry wrinkles his brow, presumably when he sees the tears I can't stop from falling.

"Baby . . ." The word leaves his lips steeped in concern.

Without speaking, I turn my laptop around to face him as he sets the bottle and bags down on the island. Then, I watch him read as first shock and confusion, then unbridled anger distorts his beautiful face. I know he's finished when he slams the laptop shut. He takes several measured breaths before meeting my eyes with an intensity that would knock me down if I didn't already feel so low.

"I can fix this," he says. "I can call Darryl and—"

"No! No. Your lawyer can't fix this, Danny." I'm standing up, as if somehow getting on my feet will make him understand that this is a bell that can't be unrung. "It's out there. It's forever. Even if on the off-chance G&D retracts it, this can't be erased. It's always going to be there. It's going to follow me. Everywhere."

"Baby, no," he says, stepping forward as I step back. "I'll handle it. I'll find this 'source' and we can take it from there." His words are cautious and deliberate, as if he's trying to pacify an unbroken horse. I'd admire his composure in this situation if I weren't on the verge of my own panic attack.

Taking a deep breath, I try to mirror his calm. "I already know who the source is. It's Celine," I say flatly.

"Well yeah, probably someone in her camp but—"

"No," I cut in. "You don't get it. The source *is* Celine." The final threads of logic and rationality in my mind are quickly unspooling while I desperately grasp for them. *How does he still not get it?* I think but don't say. And then I remember, he doesn't know the full story.

Because I haven't told him.

"I didn't believe her when she threatened me," I explain. "And I didn't want it to affect your decisions. I wanted you to save the project first. But when Celine found out that I overheard her plotting with Jim to sabotage your movie, she threatened that if I revealed their plan to you, she'd find a way to ruin me. I thought it was an empty threat, but clearly, I was wrong."

Danny's eyes are green orbs of fire. They dart erratically from my face to the laptop on the counter, as if it's some sort of ticking time bomb. He's processing all this information in one fell swoop and, like me, he's coming undone. "Say something. Please," I beg, unable to stand the silence.

"What did I say to you in Texas the morning after we made

love?" he asks. "I said *I got you*, and I meant it. I wish you'd told me. I could have found a way to take care of the movie *and* you. I could have—"

"What? You could have what?" I spew back at him with a sharp anger that makes both of us flinch. "This production has been spinning out of our control since day one, Danny. And each time, *I* end up the casualty. How was it going to be different this time?"

My words deplete him and instantly, I wish I could take them back. But they're another bell that can't be unrung.

He rebounds quickly, stepping toward me again. "Baby, I'm sorry—"

"Please do not say sorry to me, Danny. Not again," I cut him off. My emotions are now a runaway train barreling down a track. "It's not even your faul—"

"But it is." He takes a turn at cutting me off. "You're in this position because of me. This whole time I've had you out on a limb with me, trying and failing to be your safety net. But I want to fix this *with* you, and you won't even let me near you right now."

I have barely registered his attempts to come closer. But he's right, I've moved away from him on instinct. My back is now up against the kitchen cabinets.

"I don't think I can do this anymore, Danny." The words are out of me before I even know what I'm saying.

"Can't do what?" he asks, dipping down, searching for eye contact. "Look at me, please," he demands.

I do as he asks, and my own tears distort the view. "I can't do . . . us," I say over the heavy lump in my throat.

"Don't say that." His voice cracks and with it, so do I. But I failed to stop that unspooling thread of logic and reason and now, all that's left is defeat.

"What do you want from me, Danny?" I ask. "This whole saga of us has been an endless stream of heartache with a few fleeting bright spots of bliss. All for it to come crashing down over and over and over. And somehow, I'm always left in the rubble, picking up all my broken pieces."

"What do I want?" he asks, nostrils flared. "I want what I've always wanted, Kaliya. I want you in my life. I want to share *all* of it with you, every single day. The good and the bad. Just like my parents, we get through it together. I want you forever. And yes, this bullshit on the internet about us, about you, it's forever, too. But it's also not *real*. You know what's real, Kal?"

He grabs my hand, interlacing our fingers, and I'm too weak to pull free. "This," he says with fire in his eyes. "You and me, Kal. *We* are real. Always have been. But if you can look at our whole story and see only *a few fleeting bright spots of bliss*, then that's not really worth holding on to anymore, is it?" He lets go of my hand but holds his stare.

As much as I want to conjure the same hope he has for us, I can't. My tank is empty. I've weathered too many blows, and this one feels fatal.

"I—I just think maybe if we take some time to let things settle down . . . I can step away and you can focus on saving the movie," I offer weakly. "I'll find another job and—"

"I really thought this time you'd stay," he says with a humorless laugh and a shake of his head that loosens the tears at the corners of his eyes.

We cry together. Because having your heart broken hurts like hell but breaking the heart of the person you love most in the world is a special kind of agony.

"I thought you were in love with me," he declares.

It's an accusation that I have no rebuttal for because it's true. But it doesn't change the fact that loving him hurts. "I *am* in love with—"

"No." He cuts me off. "Don't say those words if you're gonna say them and still walk out that door." He jabs his finger to the front of the house.

I don't know what to say for myself. Because when I look at this man, all grown-up with the faintest lines of time and experience etched into his beautiful face, every version of the Danny I've known reflects back at me through the broken look in his eyes. The boy I projected all my silly notions of love and desire onto while he was carrying a world of hurt around inside of him. The boy I'd foolishly entrusted with my heart without realizing that he was busy tending to his own. And now we're both broken.

I feel now, with every fiber of my being, that for us to ever have a chance at being good together, first we have to heal. But I can't let him think I don't love him. I feel like I've loved him longer than I've truly even loved myself—and that's part of the problem.

"Loving you is like breathing for me, Danny," I tell him, explaining it in the simplest way I know how to. "It's undeniable and it'll never stop. But right now—" I pause for a beat, wiping my tears. "It's getting hard for me to breathe. And that's why I have to go."

He drops his chin to his chest and we both stand in his kitchen, leaning into each other but still not touching. We wait there silently, letting the moments pass slowly, savoring these remnants of closeness. Suddenly, he steps back and it's a loss that makes me cold.

"Do you think," he speaks with a raw voice, "that maybe not now, but someday you could find a way to love me *and* stay?"

The answer comes to me as steady as a heartbeat. I nod my head with an enthusiastic *yes* and the hope that springs from acknowledging the possibility of an easy-breathing kind of love with Danny sends a fresh wave of tears coursing down my cheeks.

"When?" he asks, with a flicker of hope in his sad eyes.

"When I don't feel so lost in your world," I say. "And when you're not the center of mine."

His eyes shutter closed as more tears fall, and the smallest smile of acceptance turns up the corners of his mouth. I place my hand at the center of his chest and go up on my toes to kiss his forehead.

I brush past him to collect my things and head straight out the door.

chapter

36

THE INTERNET QUICKLY BECAME a sinkhole. Rick Fenway's post was re-blogged and re-shared throughout every gossip outlet known to man—and under the unfortunate hashtag of #TheHelp no less.

I'd always hoped the first time I made headlines would be because I'd finally broken up Hollywood's impenetrable glass ceiling, not its favorite It Couple. Suddenly, after working for years to gain some form of recognition behind the scenes in my job, I was now a trending topic on TikTok where to some, I was a cautionary tale, to others, an all-out villain, and to a small but very insistent few, I was a victim of systemic misogynoir.

Truth is, I feel like I am a mix of all three. After all, I *did* get the job on the production because of my history with Danny. He *did* leave a long-term relationship, in part, to be with me. We *did* sleep together while I was still a member of his crew. So as the days slipped by and the chatter grew louder, it became increasingly difficult for me to identify solely as an injured party in all of it. I had to admit that I, too, played a role in this convoluted mess. And maybe, just maybe, I could have seen at least *some* of this coming if I hadn't been blinded by love.

But even though I could admit it to myself, confronting it every day, on top of the gaping wound of missing Danny, became too much to bear.

I needed to disassociate.

So, I put my head down, got a temp job at a studio across town, and avoided social media apps on my phone and laptop at all costs.

Two months have gone by and I'm starting to adjust to this new, gray normal. It has its ups and downs. Two weeks ago, I was stewing in regret while working as a temporary assistant to a marketing exec at Marvel when Bella FaceTimed asking me to be a guest on her podcast. Apparently, it was time for me to tell my side of the story instead of *cowering in a heaping vat of useless shame.* Her words, not mine.

My initial answer was *Hell to the no.* But the headlines kept coming.

Coby the Cobalt and I barely escaped being chased by the paparazzi on one scary occasion. And I've had other close calls—camera clicks and jarring flashes when I'm filling up my tank or worse, exiting CVS carrying tampons and zit cream.

Besides Bella, Neha is the only person I've seen outside of my new coworkers, who all treat me like I have the plague. So, upon further reflection, I figured, *fuck this,* it's time to address all who'll listen.

"Hi guuuuuys, it's your girl Bella and for today's episode of *Livin' the Dream* I want to introduce you all to someone I've come to know pretty well over the past several months."

Bella sits across from me now in the rather posh studio she finally rented out for her podcast. We've got glasses of sparkling rosé—to lubricate the flow of conversation, she claimed. But I think it's mainly meant to take the edge off my nerves.

"Maybe you've seen her name in recent headlines," she continues with her guest introduction as I sit on pins and needles just praying for it all to be over. "Maybe you've heard the chatter around a faux scandal that's got Hollywood abuzz with gossip. Well folks, I can tell you with certainty that none of what you've read is as it seems. And my guest is here to finally speak her truth.

"But first, a disclaimer. If you've read my blog, follow me on TikTok or Insta, or know me at all, you'll know things tend to come pretty easy for me. Now, that's not to say I haven't had my challenges, but let's be real, I was born with a platinum spoon in my mouth. And while that won't guarantee my success in this business, it certainly offers me a leg up. So, I'm happy to finally be able to recognize and check my own privilege. And I have this woman to thank in many ways. So, to do just that, today I'm offering her my platform. Without further ado, meet my guest, Kaliya Wilson."

"You know I have to issue a correction to something you said up at the top in your introduction," I say into the mic. "You said that nothing written about me in the tabloids is as it seems, and I beg to differ."

Bella practically squeals. "Oh, we LOVE a correction!" Her energy is bubbly and contagious, and like the rosé, it's helping to settle my nerves.

I adjust my headphones and lean closer to the mic. "It's true that I fell in love with the director of the movie I was working on," I admit. "It's also true that we met eight years ago in film school and that he offered me a job on his latest production, *What Love*

Made. A movie, by the way, that deserves . . . no, that *needs* to be made and distributed as he envisioned it. It's also true that I spent years languishing as a receptionist, hoping for an opportunity to show my worth and prove myself."

"Okay . . . so what's the part that's not true?" Bella prods.

I take a deep breath and my coworker-turned-true-friend shoots me two thumbs-up from across the recording studio.

Then, I come out with it. The truth. "Danny Prescott and I never had an affair. I also didn't sleep my way into a job," I say, and it feels so damn good to get the words out. "That timeline is all wrong and quite frankly, it's beyond insulting to women like me who've struggled to be taken seriously in this town since the dawn of cinema. It's especially insulting to me as a woman of color, a Black woman, who has to work three times harder than everyone else to even be *seen*. Not to mention to be listened to, valued, paid, and promoted."

Bella nods passionately as I speak. Her enthusiastic support is transformational, like the wind machine at Beychella. "Well, thank you for clearing that up definitively," she says.

"Now, I want to know more about the real Kaliya. Not the one we've read about in the *blog we won't be naming on this podcast*. You've been in the trenches for a while now. What brought you to Hollywood, and what's kept you here despite all the roadblocks in your way?"

This question is an easy one. But as I open my mouth to speak, a certain face flashes across my mind's eye. Green eyes, russet-hued, curly hair, and a smile that makes my heart beat faster, stronger. I push away the image along with the emotions it conjures and power through.

"Movies," I say. "The dream of making movies is what brought me here. Well, if I'm honest, New York City is where I fell in love with making movies. And there was a time when I thought I'd found my rock bottom there, but LA certainly proved me wrong."

Despite myself I have to laugh here. "But my love for storytelling, for a medium that lets me walk around in someone else's shoes, if only for two hours—that's what's kept me here despite everything I've been through. That, and the dream that one day I could be a part of the magic that moviemaking is. It's what drives so many people like you and me to put up with all the abuses that Hollywood has crystalized and sold to us as 'paying our dues.' We're led to believe that being perpetually overworked, underappreciated, and, even worse, underpaid is some sort of rite of passage or ticket to entry. When the worst-kept secret is that so much of the key to success in this town is based on who you know, what you look like, or what you own."

Bella poses the million-dollar question. "Okay, but what do we do with all this truth you're dropping?"

"Well, look," I say, laughing at how full-circle this moment is for us. "I'm not here to torch an entire industry to the ground. I'm just here to (A) point out that Hollywood has a serious equity problem and (B)—" I pause. I hadn't really planned to share this part.

"Don't leave us in suspense," Bella demands. "What's B?"

My plans are premature, nowhere near ready for public scrutiny. But there's no time like the present to manifest what I've already begun to dream up in my head. "B is that I am going to do something about it," I declare.

"Ooooh! We love a self-starting woman here on *Livin' the Dream*," Bella says. "Care to share any deets?"

"When I have them, you'll be the first to hear," I say.

"Yes! We love a cliff-hanger, too!" Bella cheers. "Alright folks, well there you have it. You'll have to keep tuning in to find out how Kaliya Wilson plans to dismantle the system of oppression that is Holly—"

"Okay, not so fast," I chime in. "I'm not a miracle worker but I'm hoping I can move the needle, if even just a nudge."

"Knowing you, I have no doubt that you will," she says, before signing us off.

"SOOOOO . . . DON'T YOU WANT TO KNOW HOW DANNY'S DO-ing? The production may be on pause but he's still my boss." Bella's words are muffled as she speaks over a mouthful of onion rings.

We finished recording the podcast and decided to grab lunch at a nearby burger joint in Studio City. I'm midslurp on a choco-chunk milkshake when Bella says his name and I nearly choke, inducing a brain freeze. I'm relieved despite the pain because *of course* I want to know about Danny. I've just been too much of a coward to ask for myself—or to pick up the phone and call him.

"Of course I do," I admit. "You know my feelings for him are like glitter. You think you've swept it all up, but when you look in the mirror it's in your hair and all over your face."

She goes quiet, peering at me over the top of her burger before taking a huge bite and chewing slowly. I throw a fry her way and it bounces off her nose. "You're stalling! Stop it. I'm dying over here!" I say.

"Okay, okay," she relents. "He's still in gridlock with Jim and WAP's lawyers. Turns out the fucker, ahem, I mean, my dear uncle is actually looking to replace Danny. And he plans to put the new script in production as soon as he finds someone."

Ice runs cold in my veins at this news. This is a nightmare.

Instantly, I'm scrambling to think of ways to get him out of this dumpster fire.

"But wait! There's more," Bella says, quieting my frantic thoughts. "On my podcast just now, when you talked about wanting to do even just one little *something* to right the wrongs in this industry?"

I nod, anxious to see where she's going with this.

"Well, I think I have an idea," she says as a smirk curves on her lips.

chapter

37

MOVIE MOGUL & SILVER-SCREEN STARLET CAUGHT ON TAPE IN RACIST PLOT TO SABOTAGE PRESCOTT'S PICTURE

We at Glitter 'n' Dirt don't like to eat crow, but we wouldn't be the world's most credible source on Hollywood if we didn't admit when we got things wrong. And boy oh boy did we get it wrong this time. The story of the Prescott/Michèle split took a major turn this morning when we received a recording of a (supposedly) secret meeting between Celine Michèle and Jim Evans, top production executive at Wide Angle Pictures, revealing their plot to downgrade the release plan for Danny Prescott's flick on the grounds of it being a "race movie." For those unaware, *What Love Made* is set in the Jim Crow South and chronicles the forbidden love story of Prescott's parents, Nathan and Minnie Prescott.

A source close to the situation has revealed to G&D that Michèle and Prescott brought the film to Evans and

WAP with hopes of turning it into a major Oscar contender. To do so would require, at minimum, a limited theatrical release. And if you heard the recording at the top of this page, which was provided exclusively to G&D, then you know that Jim Evans never intended to give Prescott's film what he'd promised. And, for Michèle's part, she was playing both sides of the fence the entire time.

I'm told that since the leak, Evans won't take Michèle's calls, which means she can kiss that first-look deal at WAP goodbye.

This comes as a significant blow to WAP, whose parent company, Galaxy Films, is already conducting major damage control after an open letter was published in *THR* and signed by over one hundred and fifty of its most marginalized employees who've claimed rampant discrimination and vast pay gaps company wide.

We expect heads to roll soon.

As always, we can't sign off without a final word to all parties. So . . .

To Jim Evans—We at G&D can't wait for the day when it's finally Time's Up for dinosaurs like you in this town.

To Celine Michèle—You can't be an ally and a perpetrator at the same time.

To Danny Prescott—Word on the street is you couldn't salvage your second-chance romance with Kaliya Wilson. But we're hoping you can still salvage the movie.

And finally, to Kaliya Wilson—G&D extends its deepest regret for the anguish our column has caused you. We encourage our followers to listen to Season 2, Episode 12 of Bella Carmichael's *Livin' the Dream* podcast to hear Kaliya

Wilson's side of the story and about her plans to change
Hollywood for the better.

Rick Fenway, over and out.

It's now been three weeks since the recording broke the
internet. Bella's *idea* at our post-podcast lunch involved the two of
us potentially breaking a law by leaking the secret recording of Jim
and Celine's not so private meeting. But we covered our bases and
consulted a top entertainment lawyer, who happened to be
someone on Jim's personal shit list. He'd confirmed that technically, Jim and Celine had no claim to a presumption of privacy
given the fact *they* were the ones who initiated the call to Danny's
office. Whether they meant to or not was immaterial.

The moment the suggestion left Bella's lips, I knew it was the
right thing to do. Possibly the *only* thing that could move the
needle for Danny in the fight to get back the rights to his project.
But her insistence that we leak the tape to Rick Fenway was where
our mission hit a snag.

It took me a week to wrap my head around the fact that by doing this with him, we'd be directing more eyeballs, and therefore
ad dollars, to his detestable site. But he was the top destination for
updates on the fallout from Danny and Celine's and, subsequently,
Danny's and my breakup. Which meant if we wanted this tape to
have the impact we'd intended, Rick was our guy. So we negoti-
ated. We'd give him the recording if he published a retraction, an
apology, and a plug for Bella's podcast.

He did all three.

The fallout has been nothing short of biblical. Weeping.
Gnashing of teeth. The works. First came Jim Evans's departure.
The chairman of the film group at Galaxy Films promptly invited

him to resign of his own volition. Last I heard, he'd been offered an eight-figure contract buyout and took off to hang out his own shingle with plans to revive Westerns.

Then came Celine's apology tour. It started with a Notes app post on Instagram in which she vowed to "listen and learn" and "do the work" to recognize and check her privilege. That eventually escalated to a Facebook live session with the newest member of her damage control team, a certified "accountability coach."

Glitter 'n' Dirt has created a front-page widget for daily updates on what they've now coined #WAPgate, which to my significant relief, has replaced #TheHelp on TikTok's trending topics.

Then came the most surprising development of all—the sick-outs.

Those employees Rick referred to, the ones who'd signed the open letter that exposed the hostile environment and discriminatory practices that were endemic to Galaxy's studio lot—they all called in sick on the same day. All one hundred and fifty of them. Inspired to take a stand against the gross unchecked power and prejudice displayed in Jim Evans's recorded rant, they issued a warning—they'd continue to coordinate sick days on a rolling basis. They'd strategically schedule those sick days to be particularly disruptive for the company's bottom line—TV upfronts, box office debuts, red carpet premieres, etc. And they would do this until a series of demands were met.

As it turns out, being a service employee of a major studio has its upside, because rounding out that list of demands was a call for Galaxy Films to do right by Danny Prescott and revert the rights of *What Love Made* back to him. The years I spent as *the face* of WAP came in handy when the aggrieved workers reached out to me to review their list of demands.

Anything missing? they wanted to know. And even though I'd already risked life and limb to leak the tape, news from Bella about the contract negotiations was that WAP wasn't budging, and Danny's film was still in limbo. So, I decided to give them a nudge.

"IT WORKED," BELLA SQUEALS AT ME FROM ACROSS OUR BISTRO table, looking up from her phone. It's a hazy Saturday afternoon, and she asked me to meet her for lunch at a Los Feliz café. We sit together, cozy, in a corner by a large, frosted-glass window, sipping espressos in tiny little mugs.

"Danny just texted to confirm," she explains. "WAP caved to the pressure and voided the contract. The movie is his to make however he wants!"

Try as I might, I can't stop myself from bursting into tears at the news. Bella immediately jumps up to come around the table and hug me. "Oh my god, honey! It's okay!"

"No! No. It's alright, these are happy tears," I assure her, swiping aggressively at the wetness on my cheeks. "That's everything I ever wanted for him and more. It's the whole reason we did what we did. I just—"

"You wish you could be there to bask in this win with him, don't you?" she asks. "You know, it's not even clear to me why you two aren't together right now. I mean, you're clearly downtrodden and he asks about you. All. The. Time. It's kind of pathetic at this point."

"Sometimes, the reasons why I left are crystal clear, you know?" I say, blowing the tears from my nose into a napkin. "But then there are times when I can't find it in me to care how valid those reasons are. I just want to be next to him. But that solves nothing. Because knowing me and knowing *us,* if we don't get our shit together, we'll just keep finding new ways to hurt each other."

"So let me get this straight," Bella says. "You basically broke his heart, and yours for that matter, so you could go figure out how to *stop* breaking his heart, and yours for that matter?"

"Yyyyes," I say, while realizing how ridiculous it sounds when put that way.

"Huh." Bella sits back in her chair. "Well, *that* sounds exhausting."

"Look," I say. "Clearly I'm a deeply troubled individual who runs at the first sign of abandonm—" I cut myself off with a gasp. Just like that, I've discovered my fatal flaw. I cling to consistency, and when faced with unexpected sharp turns, I bail before I can be bailed on. It's why I chose to stay in a dead-end job three years too long. And it's why I turned away from Danny when things got so murky I couldn't see a way out.

"I feel like you're having an internal therapy session before my eyes," Bella deadpans while she reaches across the table to grab a biscotti.

Dabbing my tears on a napkin, I manage to collect myself. "I am," I say with a sad laugh. "Look, it would be so easy to just call Danny and apologize for walking out on him." I grimace at the memory. "But nothing's changed. He got the film back but there's still a mountain of damage to sort through before the production is on track. Also, let's face it, I *just* got the press off my back. Imagine the firestorm *me* jumping back in the picture would create? He doesn't need that kind of stress right now."

"He may not need the stress, but what if he needs you?" Bella says, pursing her lips with self-satisfaction when I do a double take. "But seriously, fuck the press," she adds. "A good friend once asked me a great question: Do you want to be liked? Or do you want to be happy? Answer that and damn the rest."

"I hate it when you out-wisdom me," I mutter, taking another sip of my espresso. "But it doesn't change the fact that I need to go after a dream that isn't Danny for the first time in a long time—no matter how much it hurts to keep my distance for now."

"Yes, *that* part I can support," Bella practically cheers. "Be the boss you're meant to be. *Then*, go get the guy."

I have to admit, I like the sound of that.

DESPITE MY FRESH CONFIDENCE AFTER BRUNCH WITH BELLA, my first instinct is to call him, ask if he's okay, tell him I love him, and take everything else back. Granted, that's my first instinct at the start of any day. By the day's end, like always, logic and reason and *growth* kick in, reminding me that my reasons for walking away are still real and important . . . even if at times, they seem like tiny specks of dust.

So that conviction keeps me from calling him. But it's fear that keeps me from answering when he calls me. Fear that despite the good news, I'll sense the hurt in his voice. Hurt that I've caused. Or worse, that he'll sound perfectly fine. Like he's done what I can't even bear to imagine, that he's moved on.

Weeks pass, and eventually, he stops calling. And now the *real* sadness kicks in, along with a punishing sense of finality that fully marks my transition from living in the *now* of us, to living in our *after*—again.

chapter
38

N EHA'S BACK FROM A baecation in Costa Rica with her new bae, Alejandro. We're curled up on our couch with popcorn and Bravo. I'm about to head to the kitchen to refill our wineglasses when my butt starts to vibrate.

Reaching between the cushions, I fish out my phone to find a text from Bella. It's been two months since we leaked the tape and aside from one happy hour and the occasional FaceTime check-in, we haven't seen a whole lot of each other.

BELLZ: I'm not supposed to say this but the love of your life is going on Colbert in five.

Dryness seizes my throat, and my adrenaline kicks in at the mere mention of him.

ME: He's already doing press? You guys haven't even finished shooting!

The three-dot bubble pops up to taunt me.

Neha's laughing at some nonsense and debauchery from one of the yacht crewmembers on the screen. "Oh my god, he is *so* getting docked for that sloppy-ass towel duck! It looks as drunk as he is."

I block her out when Bella's text finally appears.

BELLZ: His PR wanted buzz for anything BUT #WAPgate.
Colbert is under a strict 'don't-even-mention-it' clause

ME: I guess I'm relieved

BELLZ: Look, I'm texting you for a reason. He just went out there. Turn. on. Colbert.

I do as she says. Without thinking to warn Neha, I grab the remote and flip over to Colbert.

"Dude! They were just about to fight over tips—" Neha protests. "Oh look, it's Danny! I didn't know he—"

"Shhhh!" The interview's already begun and I don't want to miss another second.

Danny's seated in a plush chair next to Stephen Colbert's bulky hosting desk. He looks—tired, if I'm honest, but still so good my chest hurts. Like it's taken a beating from the wild rhythm of my heart. He's cut his hair into a low fade. Goodbye luscious curls.

"My god, you must have done a number on him. He's gone and cut all his hair off!" Neha yelps, like she's not still struggling to rebound from her own do-it-yourself bangs.

I ignore her and finish my assessment of Danny. He's grown out his beard. Dressed casually, in a designer sweatshirt and jeans, he's also wearing his signature flashy Jordans. My skin burns, every part of me itching to be with him—in the wings, waiting to wrap my arms around him when he's finished, then to smell his honey-lemon scent and feel his arms squeeze me back.

"So this film of yours has been the talk of the town for months now, for better or worse—" Colbert's question snaps me out of the daze. "But at its heart it is a love story about your mom and dad." He pauses for the audience reaction, a chorus of *ooh*s and *ahh*s, before continuing his question. "The whole world knows your dad, of course, the legendary director Nathan Prescott. We grew up on his movies. We cried at that Oscar speech. But you've said this movie isn't about his work. It's about his love. What inspired the choice to show us the man behind the movies?"

As expected, Danny isn't at all at ease in the hot seat. His left knee is bouncing a hundred miles an hour. His hands are clasped tightly on his lap, clinging on for dear life. Still, a small smile creeps across his lips.

"My mom, really," he says. "She was such an incredible part of the story that's never been told. It's funny because to me, they were always two halves of a whole, my mom and dad. In my eyes there's no Nathan Prescott without Minnie." He pauses, a soft chuckle escaping him as he looks down at his hands. "Someone once told me that after everything my parents endured to be together, they deserved a happy ending."

At that, my heart lurches in my chest. Neha grips my arm. "It's you! He's talking about you, K!" I *shhh* her again even as my heart leaps into my throat.

"So that inspired a new direction for how I was looking at telling this story," Danny explains.

"It's not news to us, either, that your father passed away tragically when you were still in college. And you and I talked a little about this backstage," Colbert cuts in. "About how we've both coped with grief from the loss of loved ones. I'm curious about whether this production, making this film about the both of them, has helped you process the grief of losing your dad?"

"We've both lost our fathers, Steve, so I'm sure you can relate when I say that my dad's death rocked me to my core," Danny says, and instantly, my eyes sting with the threat of tears. "But it was watching my mom take on the weight of it all that really broke my heart. When he died so suddenly, it was like she had to carry all the love they'd built together on her own. But then—" He pauses again, clearing the knot of emotion in his throat.

"At some point I realized that she'd turned a corner," he says. "It was like her grief wasn't a burden anymore. It wasn't just a re-minder that she had lost the love of her life. But it was proof their love existed. For sixty-three years he was here and he was hers. That doesn't just go away now because he's gone."

With the studio uncharacteristically quiet, likely moved to si-lence by the subject matter, Colbert pivots. "Would you say that's why you're making this movie?" he asks. "To prove that this kind of love can exist?"

"I don't think I need to prove it," Danny answers. "I think, in a way, we all know it does. If you don't, it's because you just haven't found it yet."

"I mean, I don't want to pry, Danny, but a lot of people would be disappointed if I didn't ask . . . Have *you* found that kind of love?" Colbert's gaze flits knowingly to the studio audience as his mouth tips into a tiny smirk. Once again, a clamor of *ooh*s rings out from the crowd.

Danny stills. For several seconds he doesn't answer. From my ratty couch, I'm silently at battle with myself. Part of me longs for a sign that there's hope for us. The other part still wonders if we're safest on our separate paths.

As if he's heard me, he finally answers. "I did, yeah."

My heart leaps. The audience erupts into applause. But Danny raises his palms to calm them down. "I found love, and it's the best thing in the world," he explains. "But I've lost it, too—which feels like a metaphor for life. How it's just an endless cycle of things lost and found."

Colbert reaches out to pat Danny on the arm. "Well, Danny, if you've found a love that's anything like the one your parents had together, I have no doubt that by the time the story's written, you'll find your way back to it."

Danny smiles a sheepish smile as more *awww*s play out from the audience. Colbert turns back to his guest. "So tell us when and where we can see *What Love Made*."

"I have to finish shooting it first," he says, laughing softly. "But, if all goes well, we should be in theaters soon."

The audience cheers again as Colbert throws to a commercial. Neha and I sit in silence for long seconds.

"You know," she breaks the tension, "when I was falling apart over Sam and you told me that he was my mirror, but like, in a bad way?"

"Yes," I say, tentatively, not sure where she's taking it.

"Well, I think Danny's your mirror, but in the best way," she says. "Think about it, you reflect each other. There was a time when he was closed off and emotionally unavailable and you blew in with your special way of feeling everything for everybody, and without knowing it, you helped him through a really hard time. And years later, isn't that what he did for you?"

I stare blankly at Neha, stunned by the clarity of her assessment. "Costa Rica really did a number on you, didn't it?" I joke.

She laughs and pelts a pillow at me. "Alejandro did a number on me; Costa Rica was just a bystander." She wiggles her eyebrows suggestively. "So, are you going to call him?"

For the millionth time I consider it. Perhaps he *was* speaking directly to me tonight, putting out a signal that he's still waiting. But I know I'm not ready yet. I've still got things I need to see through for myself. Besides, something in his words has settled the restlessness in me. It quieted that warring urgency I've felt to rush to him and the guilt for even wanting to.

It's like he's granting me permission to take this time and space to figure it out, assuring me that he's not going anywhere while I do. Loving me from a distance. Like he said to me all those months ago in the mail room: *All things come in due time.*

I turn to Neha, with peaceful tears in my eyes. "No. I'm going to go to bed."

chapter
39

A S AN UNDERGRADUATE CINEMA studies major, I was only required to complete one semester of classes on TV history. And while I remember learning about the medium's origins in radio and vaudeville and the contributions of David Sarnoff, "the pioneer of television," what always stuck with me was how the production modes for TV differ from film. It's all in the pacing. On a movie set, you might spend an hour setting up a single shot and then additional hours running take after take, just to capture mere seconds of perfection. But with live TV, everything is immediate. Fast. Ephemeral.

"Kaliya Wilson! Do we have Kaliya Wilson on her mark?"

A loud whisper permeates the darkness backstage at Times Square Studios. I wasn't nervous before, but hearing my cue sends a shock wave of anxiety through my body. With a firm hand at my back, my segment producer Deena ushers me forward to the edge of the set.

"Okay, Kaliya, you're on in fifteen," she whispers into my ear. "Remember the talking points we discussed and you're golden."

Her instructions are encouraging but also scream *Don't fuck up my segment!* Then comes the countdown.

Five, four, three, two . . .

"Joining us now to talk about her work to make the entertainment industry more inclusive is a woman whose name you've probably heard of by now. We're thrilled to welcome Kaliya Wilson—"

"Go, go! You're up!" With one final push, Deena thrusts me into the blinding light of the set. At the last second, I remember I was told to smile. On wobbly legs, I beeline to my designated director's chair opposite Robin Roberts.

Once seated, Robin beams at me like we're old friends at happy hour. "Kaliya." Her voice is like velvet. "Welcome to *Good Morning America.*"

"Thank you so much for having me," I stammer, still not warmed up to this.

"Just last year," Robin says, "you found yourself at the center of a true Hollywood scandal when you were accused of sleeping your way into a job on a film production and breaking up a Hollywood power couple." *Oohs* and *ahhs* sound out from the studio audience and Robin pauses to give them their moment.

I try not to grimace. On the bright side, if this is where we're starting, it can only get better. I suppose.

Robin forges on. "But you've managed to turn things around in your favor by raising over half a million dollars that'll go toward supporting people, like you, who've struggled to make their way in the cutthroat film industry. The obvious question here is: Where did you find the courage to fight back after hitting rock bottom?"

"Uh, well, you know—" Who knew my first nationally televised words would be so eloquent? "I don't really think of it as courage. I think of it more as a necessity," I say.

Robin's eyebrows knit and she leans forward. "Tell me what you mean by that."

"I mean that in life, we all have tools to work with," I explain, picking up some steam, finally. "Some of those tools we're born with, others we're given. And others we cultivate." I pause, and Robin narrows her eyes, daring me to land the plane.

I take a deep breath. "I suppose I've always felt like I was never given a true chance to put my best tools to use. I mean, I spent four years answering phones and delivering packages when my dream was to produce movies. But after all that time waiting for someone to give me that chance, I finally got it."

"By that you're referring to your production assistant role on Danny Prescott's film, *What Love Made*," Robin cuts in.

"Yes, exactly," I confirm. "And as you mentioned, it all kind of blew up in my face."

"To put it lightly, yes," she says flatly. The audience laughs.

Oddly enough, I find strength in their reaction, like they're somehow invested in my journey. "So through that experience," I say, "I learned a valuable lesson: it's really not my business what other people think of me."

At that, the audience bursts into applause. I hear a few *you go girls* and *speak on its* and suddenly, I'm flying. "What matters most is if at the end of the day, I can say that I took everything I had, all the tools at my disposal, and focused them toward an end goal I could be proud of. But for so long, I wasn't doing anything close to that."

"Well, by the looks of it now, that's exactly what you're doing," Robin preps her segue. "Can you tell us more about your nonprofit, OpenHollywood?"

"I was a guest on my good friend Bella Carmichael's *Livin' the Dream* podcast." I turn to Camera A now. "You should all give her a listen."

Robin shifts in her seat and gives me a pointed look that says *Stick to the script.* "Anyway," I pivot, "after telling the truth about my experience on Bella's podcast, I started getting messages from people from every corner of the industry who identified with my struggle to be seen and heard in Hollywood. I always knew I wasn't alone, but there was never a way for me to connect with people who lived my same experience. So, I was inspired to create a platform for people to come together and speak openly and publicly about the inequities they've faced, whether it's harassment based on power or sex, unfair pay, or discrimination of any kind, OpenHollywood brings these issues, well, out into the open."

"And it doesn't stop there, does it?" Robin asks, beaming at me.

"No. We don't stop there," I confirm. "We aren't just about shining a light on these issues. At OpenHollywood we partner with progressive legal minds, industry veterans, and others who are in positions of power and privilege, so they can share resources with people like me. Sometimes we get stuck admiring our problems, but nothing changes if we don't actually confront them. That's what OpenHollywood is all about."

"Wow! Well as one of those industry veterans myself, tell me where I can sign up." Robin winks at me and then turns to face Camera A before tossing us to a commercial break.

And just like that, my five minutes of TV fame are over. I've never been more relieved.

DEENA ESCORTS ME BACK TO AN EMPTY GREENROOM, THANKS me for my time, and gives me her business card. We air hug and then she shuffles off to see to her next segment.

Depleted now after the rush of adrenaline from being on-air, it takes me a second to notice the bouquet of pink peonies and peach tulips perched atop the vanity on the far side of the room. For a protracted moment, I just stare at it. Like if I move an inch, I'll wake myself out of a dream. A dream where Danny's still out there somewhere thinking of me.

Of their own mind, my feet carry me toward the flowers. Then my hands reach forward to lift and open the clean white envelope revealing a handwritten note.

> Kal,
>
> And now the world can see what I've always been in awe of. Congratulations on the accomplishment.
>
> P.S. In the end, you had me.
>
> Forever indebted,
Danny P.

A strangled sound bursts from my throat. It's part lungs gasping for air, part heart leaping from chest. An entire year passed as I stared at my finger hovering over his contact in my phone, frozen, incapable of touching the screen. I'd often convinced myself that too much time had passed, that surely he'd moved on, despite the hope he wouldn't. That maybe I was right when I left him, that love wasn't supposed to be this hard in the first place.

But, now I know definitively that I can do hard things. Launching a nonprofit at a time when the world is calling you a Jezebel is hard. Being Black and a woman in Hollywood, in general, is hard. Loving Danny has been hard. But like the others it's also a constant, sure, and beautiful fact of my life. So in that case, who wants easy?

After all the chaos surrounding *What Love Made*, I needed

time and I took it. But who says we have to be apart to heal ourselves? Maybe that was the problem to begin with. Back in college, I made the mistake of deciding that Danny was perfect. Then, when the cracks of his humanity started to show, I couldn't reconcile the real Danny with the perfect image I'd drawn in my mind. Not to mention that it was my crippling inability to cope with my own imperfections that really doomed us in the end. Again and again, I ran from him when life and circumstances and misunderstandings made it all too clear that we were both flawed. I decided if Danny and I couldn't have it all together, then we'd have to find it apart.

With any luck, that ends today.

———

I DIDN'T CALL DANNY. DIDN'T TEXT HIM, EITHER. INSTEAD, I scooped up my flowers, hailed a cab, and sped to my next appointment for lunch with an old NYU writing professor in Chelsea. Then I dropped everything off at the hotel before racing back up to Midtown for a meeting with my literary agent, because that is now a thing that I have—a literal literary agent! Turns out, all those tear-stained pages of my journal chronicling the many lows of life as a Hollywood receptionist and sprinkled with a few cringeworthy retellings of doomed Tinder dates, might one day become an actual memoir titled *Black Girl, Thwarted*.

But how I've been able to stay on task and project anything close to normalcy all afternoon and early evening is nothing short of a miracle. I am a tightly wound ball of anxiety, liable to burst at any time—whether into celebratory dance moves or tears of panic remains to be seen.

On the one hand, *it's all happening*. And just like I'd intended, too. I was *supposed* to make this past year for and about me, lean into what I want out of life. Soul-search for who I want to become—other than the girl who dreamed big but lived small. But the whole time, while I was out there finding myself, I knew this day was coming. The day when I'd know beyond a glimpse of doubt that it was time to make my grand gesture.

To my utter delight and simultaneous annoyance, Danny wasn't going to leave it up to fate and let me come to him on my own accord. No, he had to nudge me with my favorite flowers, a sweet handwritten note, and tickets to his premiere on the opening night of the New York Film Festival—as if I wasn't already planning on crashing it, sneaking my way into his greenroom with flowers of my own, and confessing that I was finally ready to stop running.

I've read the script, probably a hundred times. I know it by heart. I've followed all the production updates in the trades. But seeing it on the big screen in vivid detail, with every scene carefully coaxed to life by Danny and his talented crew, felt spiritual in a way. Like even though I was seated alone in the back of the theater, I could feel him beside me, fidgeting, emanating sparks that warmed me from mere inches away.

I started crying with the opening scene as A FILM BY DANNY PRESCOTT flashed on the screen.

And by the final scene, I could hardly catch my breath.

DECEMBER 1995 appeared over an establishing shot of Central Park. Oliver Ferretti and his specialty lens had done masterful work capturing the early evening sun as it cut sharp shadows and golden highlights across Bethesda fountain. A little boy, the age of a toddler, ran clumsily through the park with his mother chasing after him. His father hung back a few dozen feet, snapping photographs of his two loves.

Suddenly, rich satiny melodies lifted up beneath the sounds of their laughter and took flight, filling the theater—a saxophone, played by a stoop-shouldered man who looked strikingly familiar. His song was unmistakable.

"As" by Stevie Wonder.

The mother spun round and round, lifting the boy in the air while singing how she'd be loving him always. Then a petite woman, likely in her seventies, approached the father, gesturing for him to hand her the camera. Of course he did as she asked.

The man joined his wife and son and they spun to the music as a montage of memories danced in and out of frame—a boy and a girl sharing a smile across a crowded cafeteria, running through the rain chased by angry classmates, holding hands and locking eyes on a train to New York City, clinging to each other on the stoop of their first apartment, cradling a rounded belly under a fuzzy robe, walking the red carpet at a movie premiere.

As the memories accumulated, gradually the screen faded to black, leaving one thing abundantly clear.

Theirs was a life that love made beautiful.

The credits rolled and I sat for every name, wiping tears from my face when I saw my own. I cried some more after all was said and done, and Danny brought Minnie on stage. They hugged and I joined the standing ovation.

Now here I am in an old dusty office at the back of the Angelika, waiting for him to finish his post-screening Q and A. It's no coincidence that this is where Danny and I had our first not-a-date nine years ago. Where I sat frozen for four hours of *Lawrence of Arabia*, obsessing about how, when, and where he might place his hand in mine.

I decided to go classic with a bouquet of two dozen red roses.

It would have been too obvious for me to carry them down the step and repeat. I can see the headlines now: *Hollywood Home-wrecker Crashes Premiere, Gets Body-slammed by Security.*

To avoid that, Bella did me a solid and arranged to have the flowers delivered, on my dime, just as Danny made his curtain call. Then, she came and grabbed me from the audience and led me backstage where she left me to stew, and cry.

I did not take into account the fact that I'd be doing all this "grand gesture" stuff *after* seeing the movie for the first time.

The tears haven't stopped.

The city is crying, too. Looking out the window of this back office, outside is dark and slick with rain, an enchanting night set aglow with puffs of light reflecting off the surfaces of wet streets and tall buildings. I'm nearly lost in the pitter-patter on the windowpane when the door unlatches and swings open, letting in a clamor of voices from the hall.

Wiping my face, I turn to find Danny standing frozen in the doorway, his agent yammering on about something in his ear. Our eyes meet and time slips because suddenly we're alone in the room with Danny having nudged his team back into the hallway before shutting the door.

The office is tiny, so I could probably reach him in a few paces. But his presence stills me. His hair is still short and his beard full. And his eyes, so clear and intense, seem to cut across the space between us right to the center of my chest. Like Patti LaBelle, I'd memorized my lines, rehearsed them a thousand times. But it's all but left me now.

"I thought you wouldn't show." He breaks the silence, the sound of his voice enveloping me like a warm blanket. I shut my eyes for a second to savor it. "The seat I held for you," he continues. "It was empty the whole time. I—"

"I sat in the back," I cut in, my words thick with tears.

"I'm glad you came," he says, placing a hand on a nearby chair, like he needs the support to stand.

I close my eyes tight, as if the action might hold back my perpetual tears. "I was going to return the favor," I say, figuring if I just keep talking, eventually what I'd planned to say will come out right. "I thought about just leaving the flowers and then disappearing into the night like some secret admirer," I tease.

"I'm glad you stayed," he says, no smile or laugh. "Why did you?"

I take the plunge. "Because I was hoping that now might be the right time for us to start over?"

"Oh?" he asks, his chin tipping to the side.

"I thought maybe I'd reintroduce myself." I step closer and for a second, confusion mars his face.

I forge ahead. "I'm Kaliya Wilson and my *favorite* movie is the one where a girl meets a boy on a sidewalk in New York, and even though they're from different worlds, he becomes the best friend she's ever had."

Confusion gone, he steps forward, too. And for the first time since entering the room, he's smiling down at me. Suddenly, I'm seeing him again for the first time on the sidewalk at 10th and Broadway. I laugh in spite of myself and drop my face to my hands. I can't believe we're back here and that it feels this good.

"The *best* movie I've seen," I say, "is the one where that boy becomes this breathtakingly brilliant artist whose father would be so"—my voice breaks on a swell of emotion but I recover quickly—"He'd be so proud of his son. Because he's now a man whose love for him is so strong, it made a masterpiece—" I stop, chest heaving. Because my next words are a bonfire on the brink of combustion.

"The best movie I *haven't* seen," I continue, "is the one where that man tells that girl, who's a woman now, that she's not the only one who's still in love, that they've wasted enough time apart. That he forgives her for the times she's walked away. But that he understands why she had to. That despite it all he's still going to be hers, as she has *always* been his. And that, together, they can figure out how to stay in love forever—like Nathan and Minnie."

I've finished my speech. And I swear I hear crickets. His smile dissipates as his features set into hard, serious lines. "That movie you haven't seen, Kaliya," he says. "It doesn't exist."

My heart stops. The thought of walking out of this room without his hand in mine is wholly unbearable. But maybe I am too late. Maybe the flowers in my greenroom were just a kind gesture from an old friend. Maybe he is genuinely happy for me, but no longer in love with me. How utterly anticlimactic and emotionally desolate would that be? Crestfallen, I turn back to the window to grab my bag and coat that rests on its sill.

"Yet," he rasps, his voice just above a whisper.

Still it's loud enough that it stops me in my tracks. I turn from the window, drop my coat and bag, and nearly melt into the floor.

"This morning, when I woke up, I felt like today would be different," he says. "And not for the reasons you might assume with the movie opening and the festival and whatnot. I felt it would be different because I like to think that when you love someone fiercely, and with all your heart, the way that I love you—you don't let days like this one pass without making sure they can feel it. And when I woke up, I felt it."

Danny's standing less than a foot from me now. "So that movie you haven't seen, it doesn't exist yet. But if you want, we can make it. We can start tonight," he says.

Then he smiles, a real Danny Prescott smile. And as always, it's like the sun breaking through the clouds after a torrential downpour. He lifts his arms in a plea for me to fill them, and I close the distance in a flash, touching his face, his neck, his shoulders and waist. My hands find purchase anywhere they can land to make sure he's really here. He does the same, as if checking that I'm here, too, ready and willing to accept and return everything he's given to me.

I bring my hands up to his face, softly wiping away the tears that have escaped from the tips of his lashes. We lock eyes, exchanging wordless promises that we'll get it right this time around.

"I'm so sorry I made us wait for this, Danny. I'm sorry for every second I spent running away from you," I murmur through my own tears while taking in the smell and feel of the most perfectly beautiful man I've ever known.

He chuckles, his tears falling between us like rain drops. "Does this mean I'm no longer the center of your world?" He places his hand in the middle of my chest, just over my heart.

"I was wrong. You were never the center," I say. "You were the gravity."

Then, he kisses me, and time stops. We open up to each other, angling our bodies in contrasting unison to deepen the connection. His mouth is soft yet insistent on mine, his hands are pressed against my back and tangled in my hair. We whisper into the kiss all the ways we intend to love each other tonight and every night after. The whole world falls away and yet, I have never felt more grounded.

epilogue

ONCE UPON A TIME I thought I was born to make movies. And when that crashed and burned in extravagant fashion, I pivoted, channeling all that unrequited ambition into making the moviemaking business more accessible to people like me. And for the past year, it has felt like *that* is what I was born to do. But once again, it seems I've been proven wrong. Because as I stand here looking at myself in this floor-length mirror, it's becoming clearer with each passing second that what I was *actually* born to do is wear this dress.

It's a couture Maison Valentino gown and it feels like a second skin. More luxurious than any other inanimate object that's ever been this close to my body. Yards of bloodred silk, soft as butter and weightless as a cloud, billow out from my shoulders and waist. A deep-dive neckline reveals an expanse of skin that's been kissed by the French Riviera's sun while still hiding the boob tape that's got me lifted and separated to perfection. The flowing sleeves serve to counterbalance how much skin I'm exposing. But the pièce de résistance has to be the sumptuous layers that flow down from the cinched waist, seemingly endless, like the Red Sea. With a deep crimson lip, a smoky eye, and my shoulder length curls loosely pinned up, Greek goddess style, I *almost* don't recognize myself.

The color of love looks good on you, girlfriend.

I know he's here without turning around to see him enter. It's a chemical thing, maybe molecular. But since that first day of film school all those years ago, I've always been able to sense when Danny Prescott was in the room. And now that I can hear his footsteps, my spidey sense is confirmed. Within seconds, I see him step into view behind me in the reflection of the mirror. The sight of him takes my breath away. He, like me, is dripping in Valentino from head to toe. He dons a bespoke black tux made to hug every inch of his long, lean, powerful frame.

"How does it feel to be the most beautiful girl in the world, Ms. Wilson?" He purrs against my neck, making all the tiny hairs there stand on end. There's no one else on the planet who could elicit the same reaction from me. Not even Idris Elba.

"Oh, I don't know. Tell me, Mr. Prescott, how does it feel to be nominated for your second Oscar? You know, they're saying you're a favorite this year to win Best Director," I tease him in response, leaning back against his rigid torso. I let him absorb my weight as I delight in how flawless we look together and how perfect we feel when we're this close.

"I don't know, I suppose it could be better," he says with a look of mischief on his face.

"Is that so?" I ask on a soft chuckle as he snakes his hands around me, bringing them to rest at the front and center of my waist. And then, all the air seeps out from my lungs when I notice his pinky finger holds an enormous emerald on a yellow-gold band, set between two hefty diamond baguettes. My jaw hits the floor.

"What is that?" It's a miracle that I still have words.

"What? This?" He casually lifts his pinky, and the ring sparkles radiantly in the mirror. My breaths are shallow. "That depends entirely on you."

I turn around to face him and he drops to one knee. I'm about to lose it when he finally speaks.

"I used to think that falling in love meant risking losing more than I could ever gain. Well, I've lost you more than once in my life and still, I wouldn't change a thing. Because finding you, again and again, makes everything else worth it." He swallows thickly as tears stream down both our faces. "Kaliya Elise Wilson, my love for you is far too great for me alone. Will you do me the honor of helping me carry it for the rest of my life? Will you marry me?"

And just like loving Danny Prescott, saying *yes* is as easy as taking my next breath.

Acknowledgments

I F THIS WERE A movie, now would be the part where the silver screen fades to black and *A film by Myah Ariel* would appear. Next, the sparkly opening chords of Janet Jackson's *When I Think of You* would flood the theater. Heads would be bobbing and shoulders shimmying, and I'd be in my seat sporting a face-splitting smile, overwhelmed with gratitude for those who've helped me on the journey toward realizing this dream. Finally, the end credits would begin to roll and without a doubt—in this imagined scenario—the happy tears would start to fall.

CAST

In order of appearance:

- Grammy and Grandaddy, as my Soft Place to Land. Thank you for creating a haven for me in that little redbrick house on the wrong side of town. Thank you for sending me off to film school and telling me if things didn't work out in Hollywood, I could always come back to Arkansas and work in radio or local news or at the art museum—the message being if the world Out There ever got too hard, I could always come home.

- My mother, as my Inspiration. Minnie Prescott's school-age bravery is an extension of your experience. She's a reflection of our best memories and a thank-you for being my mom. I would have loved for you to have been here to see this.

- Dillon and Henry, as my Great Loves. Without the two of you cheering me on with your frequent pep talks *and* interruptions, I am absolutely certain this debut novel wouldn't exist. And to our extended family who've supported and lifted us up along the way, my gratitude is endless.

- Faith, as my Sister. Through all of its ups and downs, you've been my life's most constant companion.

- Kelsey, Allison, Amy, and Nicole, as my Forever Friends. Let's face it, you stuck by me through my mom jeans phase in middle school—that's true friendship!

- Pris Benson, Carol Ann McAdams, and Ellen Jones, as the Teachers Who Encouraged Me. In a time and place where it was difficult for me to feel like I belonged, you made me feel seen.

- *In memory of* Jonathan Kahana, who was my First Film Professor. Thank you for prompting us all on that first day of Intro to Cinema Studies to name our favorite movie, the best movie we'd seen, and the best movie we *hadn't* seen. It's true. I've never watched a film the same way again.

- Jeannie De Vita, as my First Reader. You told me, in no uncertain terms, that I was a writer and that those early drafts would be a book one day. I'm so glad I believed you and kept going.

- Rachel, Rebecca, Naz, Carol, Sarah, Regine, and Lauren, as my Early Readers. I'm so glad I connected with such brilliant, kind, and talented authors on this journey.

- Sami Ellis, as my DV Mentor. You fell for Kaliya and Danny's love story in a way that made me believe again when I was just about tapped out. I'm so glad I met you.

- Lane, Ashyle, and Faith, as my PitBLK co-conspirators. Thank you for coming along for the ride. It's an honor to do this "authoring" thing with you.

- Kim Lionetti, as my Agent. You gave me a second look and told me this book was "powerful." They say "Don't have a dream agent" . . . Well, it's a good thing I'm bad at following rules. I'm grateful as well to everyone at Bookends for their endless support.

- Esi Sogah, as my Editor. From the first call, I wanted it to be you. Thank you for helping me find the story that was waiting in the wings.

- Sareer Khader, as my Assistant Editor. You're *so* good at what you do. You took this book to new heights with your thoughtful notes and I am ever grateful.

- Oboh Moses and Katie Anderson, as my Cover Artist and Art Director. You brought to life a version of Kaliya and Danny that, until now, only existed in my wildest dreams.

- Tina Joell and Anika Bates, as my Publicity and Marketing Team. Thank you for helping me present Kaliya and Danny's story to the world in a way that honors the passion and inspiration that went into it . . . and also to Hope Ellis, my copy editor, as well as the one-hundred-plus talented book people at Berkley—without whom this novel would not exist.

- And last, but certainly not least . . . All of you, as My Readers. This book, which has been so deeply mine for the past three years, is now very much yours. Thank you for spending time with her.

When I Think of You

MYAH ARIEL

Behind the Book

THE WORKING TITLE OF this novel was *Cinema of Attraction*. I was in love with this title. Married to it, you might say. On its surface, it simply screamed *romance* to me. But dig a little deeper, and it was like catnip to the former cinema studies major in me—the girl who sat in basement screening rooms at NYU with her fellow Tischies, watching obscure films and scribbling down my illegible observations in the dark as the subway rumbled below me.

I would learn in those freshman intro courses that "cinema of attractions" was a term coined by film scholar Tom Gunning.

So upon starting this manuscript, roughly a decade after earning that degree and six years after abandoning my moviemaking dreams, it gave me a little thrill to imagine some unassuming film critic or cinephile stumbling upon my book, based on the title alone, and being surprised by what they found inside.

Rather than an analysis of spectacle-driven early 1900s cinema, they'd discover a story about a Black woman searching for and finding a forever kind of love and respect—not just with a man, but with herself. They'd find a story set against a backdrop of a post-#MeToo and -#HollywoodSoWhite film and television industry that's still struggling to practice what it has only very recently begun to preach.

More than likely, these readers wouldn't make it past the book's *stunning* cover before realizing the contents would likely not be what they had in mind. But the notion that I could achieve an almost dual address with a title like that excited me.

I keep *Cinema of Attraction* near and dear to my heart, because in the simplest of terms, I've always been attracted to the cinema. Perhaps more precisely, I've always been attracted to the *romance* of cinema.

The pull was so strong for me as a kid growing up in Arkansas that I was determined to get to New York to study "the movies" by the time I turned eighteen. Of course there were naysayers. According to one of my high school teachers, no one got a scholarship to go out of state with college entrance scores like mine. But miraculously, I did! I remember my grandfather's airport send-off vividly. With tears in his eyes, he kissed my hand and said, "Take care of yourself."

I landed in New York with big plans and leaned into them wholeheartedly. I hoped, at the time, I might even find love in The Big City in the ways I'd seen it happen on The Big Screen. Films like *You've Got Mail* and *Brown Sugar* made New York seem like it possessed a sort of magic that imbued all the millions of people milling about its avenues with Main Character Energy. Everyone was a Kathleen Kelly or a Sidney Shaw. After eighteen years of what felt like rehearsal mode, this would finally be my opening act.

I imagined that, like Kaliya, I'd stumble out of a cab on 10th and Broadway and instantly meet a tall, handsome stranger who'd sweep me off my feet. There would be first dates and first kisses.

There would probably be heartache, too. Most of all there would be *romance*. How could there not? It was New York!

Clearly, this working title did not survive the harrowing gauntlet that has been getting a debut novel from point A to point B, with point A being a blinking cursor on a blank page and point B being held in the hearts and minds of my first-ever readers. And when it came time to name the book for real, my fabulous editor allowed me to indulge my obsession with '90s pop and R&B music, and we found our way to *When I Think of You*.

It felt fitting for a second chance romance that's predominantly set in the present but has moments of potent nostalgia placed throughout—the way my memories of New York City dance in and out of time for me still.

And in the same way various working titles have marked past versions of this book, there are titles that mark past versions of me.

Like Kaliya Wilson, I once answered phones, made coffee, sorted mail, and yes, even checked mouse traps, for far longer than anyone with dreams of actually touching the moviemaking process should have. And when I decided it was time for the book idea that had been brewing in me for years to finally come to life on the page, I knew I'd be drawing from the years I spent working as a "front desk girl" to write it.

Finding Kaliya's voice and zeroing in on her wants and wounds was as simple as remembering my own when I was in her shoes. I went back to the headspace of sitting at the front desk of a movie studio, just out of reach of my dreams, feeling constantly utilized but never truly valued. I retraced the scars from absorbing the constant blows of rejection borne while "paying my dues."

I wanted Kaliya to be sincere, guarded, and a little earnest. I wanted her witty, damaged, but still very warm. And most of all, I wanted her to feel *real*.

It was important to me that hers wasn't a story where the heroine perseveres through hardship and ultimately reaches the goal she'd set out to achieve from the start. I wanted Kaliya's payoff to come, not from being validated by an industry she'd fought to feel *seen* in for so long, but from truly seeing *herself* for the intensely capable and impressive woman she always was—whether others saw it or not.

Because sometimes dreams look a little different when they become reality.

So when I think of that "front desk girl" from all those years ago, I'm not sorry for her anymore. She didn't get to make a movie. But she made a pretty cool book. What a dream!

Discussion Questions

1. Is it important to you that your career and your passions align? What are some of the reasons you feel this way?

2. For years, Kaliya has been denied promotions after being told that she's not equipped for work beyond the reception desk due to lack of experience, despite her passion and talent. What to you is more important, experience or grit?

3. The term *nepo-baby* has contributed to hot debates in popular culture. In what ways does Bella Carmichael break away from that stereotype? In what ways is she a perfect fit?

4. Privilege is a recurring theme in this book. What forms of active or even passive privilege did you see at play throughout the story, and what were some of their most egregious displays?

5. In what ways can concepts like "paying your dues" be used by those within the entertainment industry, and other professional industries like it, to take advantage of eager hopefuls who want to break in?

6. Eric Kim plays the role of a sounding board for Kaliya on more than one occasion in the story. Who are some of the best sounding boards in your life and what qualities make them so?

7. In Danny's interview with his mom, Minnie, she describes the shiny Mary Janes and new-to-her red plaid dress her parents purchased for her first day at Maple Creek. She talks about the care her mother took with pressing her hair the night before. What do you think the significance is of present-day Minnie choosing to hang Bisa Butler's *Southside Sunday Morning*, which depicts well-dressed Black boys, in her foyer?

8. In the leaked recording that exposes Jim Evans and Celine Michèle at the end of the book, Jim claims that Hollywood has overdone it with "race movies." Why are movies that depict racism from a historic lens still meaningful, important, and timely?

9. When Danny visits the fictional Colbert Show, he talks about the moment when his mom "turned a corner" in her grieving period for his father. Earlier, he reveals to Kaliya that he and his mom went to grief counseling together. What are some of the things that you think can help the most with coping after the loss of a loved one?

10. In their "third-act breakup," Kaliya decides she must leave Danny because she's become lost in his world and realizes that hers has become centered on him. What do you think makes a person ready to find "forever love" with someone else?

11. Neha shares a lovely moment with Kaliya at the oyster bar, after discussing their dual postgrad disillusionment, in which she vows to be her "ally." What makes a good ally in a friend, partner, or family member?

Recommended Readings & Viewings

- Read *Reel* by Kennedy Ryan—Watch *Love Jones* (Film, 1997)

- Read *7 Days in June* by Tia Williams—Watch *Love & Basketball* (Film, 2000)

- Read *Queen Move* by Kennedy Ryan—Watch *Brown Sugar* (Film, 2002)

- Read *The Princess Trap* by Talia Hibbert—Watch *Something New* (Film, 2006)

- Read *The Art of Scandal* by Regina Black—Watch *Beyond the Lights* (Film, 2014)

Photography by Dawan M. Brown

Myah Ariel's early love of movies led her from Arkansas to New York City where she studied film at New York University's Tisch School of the Arts. She went on to earn an MA in specialized journalism for the arts from the University of Southern California. As a medical mom and a hopeless romantic, Myah is passionate about inclusive love stories. She lives in Los Angeles with her family, where she works in academia.

VISIT MYAH ARIEL ONLINE

MyahAriel.com

Ready to find
your next great read?

Let us help.

Visit prh.com/nextread

Penguin
Random
House